W9-BTL-923

LYONES

DARKSOLSTICE

ALSO BY SAM LLEWELLYN:

LYONESSE

THE WELL BETWEEN THE WORLDS

LYONESSE

DARKSOLSTICE

BOOK II

SAM LLEWELLYN

ORCHARD BOOKS
NEW YORK
·

An Imprint of
SCHOLASTIC INC.

Library of Congress Cataloging-in-Publication Data

Llewellyn, Sam, 1948–
Darksolstice / Sam Llewellyn. — 1st ed.
p. cm. — (Lyonesse; [bk. 2])
Summary: While Idris Limpet, Rightful King of the Land of Lyonesse, is making the treacherous journey to the distant land of Aegypt to rescue his dear friend and sister, Morgan, he meets a company of friends who shall become his Knights of the Round Table and lead armies to battle the evil regent, Fisheagle.
ISBN 978-0-439-93471-8
[1. Fantasy.] I. Title.
PZ7.L7723Dar 2010
[Fic] — dc22
2009006283

10 9 8 7 6 5 4 3 2 1   10 11 12 13 14

Printed in the U.S.A.   23
Reinforced Binding for Library Use
First edition, February 2010
Book design by Christopher Stengel
Maps by Kayley LeFaiver

*For Innis, my mother
and Teona and Alexandra,
my cousins*

·PART ONE·

Lyonesse lay ironbound, waiting for spring. But in the darkgardens they did not care. There was no spring in the darkgardens, only bitter water, and the huge, awful drift of the Helpers, and the waiting. She waited with them. What a drowning it would be, with so much blood! And when it was finished, where now the hills stood granite-topped and the tree buds stood waiting for warm breeze and bee-buzz, there would be dark and chill and quiet.

The Helpers drifted steadily toward the pillars of light that came down the Wells, readying themselves to conquer, and to call her their Queen....

A pain, piercing, like the prick of a thorn. Something was happening. Her cold drift became a shudder of rage. She grew wings of scale and slime and flew through the bitter water, up, up, through the wide hole in the living rock until the rock became built stone, up through the passages into her palace of the Mount, and entered the body that lay on the hard black bed in the Kyd Tower.

The body still, the blood a gluey seep. Suddenly a pulse in the neck. A gasp. Lips pulled back from pointed teeth. Pure-black eyes opened to darkness. Ears hearing.

Hearing the shriek of her lovely son at play in his blood-red apartments. Hearing the murmur of the people's thoughts. Hearing the creak of the land's bones, sinking from above, pressed up from below, ready to burst.

This was usual.

The thing that had disturbed her was not usual.

She sat up. The joints of the body crackled with disuse. She walked to the window. The sharp-nailed hands went to the catches of the shutters. The bronze flaps wheezed open.

Light smashed in like arrows, and she screamed, the deathly shriek of a fisheagle. Then she loosed her mind to roar over the land in a freezing beam, scorching into every cranny from the Marshes of the Broken Wall to the dragon-melted crags of the Sundeeps.

But the thorn-prick was gone.

The eyes closed. The body lay back on the bed.

There was not long to wait.

ONE

At dawn on the fifteenth day after he had been washed up on the shore of Ar Mor, Idris Limpet started dreaming again. A thing with leather wings had been flying after him through bitter water. He woke, shouting.

Idris recognized the white-limed ceiling over his head, the wreckwood beams, and the voice of his foster mother, Harpoon of the Fishers, laughing in the cookroom. He lay a moment revelling in the soft old linen sheets. Outside his door, feet were hammering on the stairs and the Precious Stones, his foster sisters, were twittering like marsh birds. He would lie here for another four breaths. Then he would roll out of bed and go down and eat a brekfuss of seal cheese and spelter bread, and drink weedwater thickened with honey, and start a normal day in the normal life of a boy in Ys, capital city of Ar Mor.

Idris pulled the sealblankets over his face. But as his face was covered, his feet turned cold. They were his old blankets, woven by Harpoon from the inner fur of ocean seals. He had had them all his life. They were too short.

But he knew it was not that the blankets were too short. It was that his legs had grown too long.

He did not like the thought. Idris threw off the blankets, pulled on his trousers, and ran downstairs.

Bright sun streamed into the kitchen. Harpoon looked around from the firepit, the smile crinkling the cat-whisker Fisher tattoos on her heat-pink cheeks. "Bread's on the table," she said. "I'm going fishing. Want to come?"

The sea flooded into his thoughts, cold and salty. He wanted nothing to do with the sea. He wanted to be a child again, warm in the house of his foster family, whom he had lost and found again by a miracle.

He opened his mouth to say, "Fishing? No."

And was surprised to hear himself say, "Yes."

"Bait's in the barrel," said Harpoon, taking her blue woolen boat-cloak from its peg. "Don't get it on your clothes or you'll stink for a moon."

Idris followed her out of the low granite door and into the town of Ys. Kek, his gull, flapped into the air from his perch at the rooftree and glided overhead.

Idris had been brought up in the Westgate of Lyonesse, where the seaward side of the world was bordered by a wall the height of nine tall men standing on one another's shoulders. There was no wall around Ys. The gray granite town ran down to the quays of a harbor facing a quiet gray winter sea. Walking there gave him the uneasy feeling that the land was too high and the sea was too low and that he might at any minute roll down the hill and off the quay.

Harpoon's boat was moored among others in the crook of a stone jetty. It was a long, stout rowing boat with oars carved from wreckwood. "You row," she said, sitting down in the stern. Idris stepped in, dumping the stinking bait barrel in the boat's bottom. Kek soared overhead, watching it hungrily. Idris untied the boat and rowed in silence, enjoying the pull of the oars in his shoulders, the cold, still winter air on the nape of his neck. He was glad he had come. But he still did not understand why he had said yes instead of no.

The sea thoughts returned. Thirty leagues to the north was the land of Lyonesse, of which he was the rightful King. Sixteen days ago, he had fled his kingdom on the ship *Swallow*, pursued by the malice of the monstrous Regent Fisheagle and her cruel son. The *Swallow* had been sunk by Aegypt corsairs. In the wreck Idris had lost allies, including Penmarch, the *Swallow*'s Captain; his sword, Cutwater; and cruellest of all, he had lost his sister, Morgan, and she would never return.

Idris hauled the oars fiercely through the water, blinking away tears. Best not think about Morgan.

In a couple of glasses the land had dropped under the horizon and buoys were bobbing alongside. "Here we are, my love," said Harpoon. "Clap on and haul."

Idris got his hands to the slimy buoy rope and hauled the traps up from the black deep and drew forth three brick-colored crabs the size of dinner plates and a midnight-blue lobster with claws as big as his hands. Then he baited the traps, and heaved them over the side to sit alongside the weed-waving rocks far below, and scrubbed the bait slime off his fingers with seawater.

The boat rocked on the faint swell. There was the slosh of the waves on the hull, and the creak of the oars, and the Fisher tune Harpoon was singing under her breath to welcome the lobster up from the deep, and the great empty sea-silence—

Someone was calling in his mind. It was a weak voice, but sharp. *Here*, it said.

Automatically Idris put his mind up to Kek, his gull.

And suddenly he was a double bowshot above the gray sea, looking down at the leaf shape of the boat, the early winter dusk creeping in from the east.

Here, said the voice, thin and tiny.

Kek banked steeply on the chill air, sea and sky streaming past his eyes. Something was floating on the water in front and below. Something square-shaped. And on it, something that had two arms and two legs and a head.

Something that had once been a man.

As Idris saw the face turned down under the arm, his heart kicked in his chest. He shoved out the oars and began to row.

"What is it?" said Harpoon.

"Get out your medicines," he said.

Harpoon pulled out the medicine chest and sat in the stern sheets watching the gray horizon. A couple of glasses passed.

8

Suddenly a white dot was rising and falling over the rim of the world.

"How far?" said Idris. His shoulders were on fire, and sweat was pouring down his face.

"Half a league. It's going to blow."

"Let it," said Idris, and saved his breath for rowing.

The white dot became a gull. The gull became Kek. The thing in the water became a floating hatch cover.

Idris brought the boat alongside it. "Captain Penmarch," he said.

A cold green wave sloshed up the hatch cover and into the sprawled man's face. The man coughed. It was a tiny cough, feeble as a baby's, but it sent the blood racing around Idris's body. He cut the ropes with which Penmarch had lashed himself to the raft. Then he and Harpoon grabbed the Captain by the sodden shoulders of his jersey and hauled him into the boat. "Bones broken," said Harpoon, pulling out a long filleting knife. "Give me your clothes. Then row."

By the time Idris had struggled out of his jersey and his breeches, Harpoon had cut Penmarch's clothes from his body. There were terrible blue marks on it, dents where there should have been no dents, a gaping wound under the ribs, pale and bloodless. Strong Harpoon wrapped him in Idris's clothes and took him under her great wool cloak as if he had been a baby, and Idris rowed, thinking, This is the way she took me in, dear Harpoon.

The sea's gray darkened. White beards of water spilled down the wave fronts. Night came down and the wind got up, cold and sharp and wicked. Then there was the boom of the sea on the jetty, and yellow lights wavering in sheltered black water, and Idris scrambling up the quay steps and running naked through the cold streets of Ys shouting for help. People appeared. Four men lifted Penmarch gently from the boat onto a stretcher piled with silver sealblankets and bore him away.

Idris went home and pulled on dry clothes. The Precious Stones were back from school, and the Boys from their apprenticeships, and Ector, his foster father, back from his work as a carpenter. They fell silent as Idris left his room carrying the scabbard Holdwater. Ector bowed, his eyes on the scabbard, which had magical properties. And Idris saw with a sinking of the heart that they thought of him not as one of the family but as a King in hiding.

He said, "Don't wait with zupper," and walked out to the road.

Idris loved his family and he knew they knew him better than anyone. He had caught monsters in the dreadful Wells of Lyonesse, and lived in the magnificent Goldfinch Chambers of the Great Ambrose, and defied Fisheagle. They were right. The house in Ys was a place to hide, not a place to live. Captain Penmarch had called to him from the cold sea as a King's man calls his King, and Idris had brought him ashore. It was time to stop avoiding the truth.

He walked up to the low white House of Healing, built in the healthy breezes at the top of the town. Torchlight from the doorway fell on the standing stone set before the house to draw healing energies down from the stars. It brought to Idris's mind his friend and teacher Ambrose, wise in the magic of star and stone, now buried with dragons. Comforted by the memory, or perhaps by the power of the stone, he walked inside.

A healer looked up from a table and said, "Yes?"

"The man who was brought in from the sea," said Idris. "His name is Penmarch. He is to be treated with honor."

The healer's mouth turned down at the corners, and he prepared to ask Idris who he thought he was, cheeky little brute. Then he went white, and Idris realized he had put his mind out to touch him. "Sire," said the healer, bowing deeply. He scuttled around the desk and led Idris down a long corridor lit with seal-oil lamps.

Penmarch's room was warmed with a barrow of granite pebbles heated in the courtyard fire. Penmarch lay on a bed, eyes closed. Two more healers were bending over him. They had splinted the arm and the leg. Now they were looking at the dents in his ribs and the wound. "Well?" said Idris.

They turned upon him, ready to tell him to go away. Then the thing happened in their faces, and one of them said, "You cannot set ribs. He is hurt within. His blood is almost gone."

"And chilled," said the other. "Goodness knows how long he was in the water."

"Fifteen days and nights."

"Fifteen?" The healer shook his white-capped head. "Impossible. It is over for him."

Idris gripped the scabbard Holdwater and stepped forward. "Good healers," he said. "Might I try this?"

"Try what you like."

The colors in the scabbard shifted as Idris laid it on the body. Not long ago, this same scabbard had healed his sister, Morgan, of a deadly spear thrust, spreading fresh pink life through her in the space of three breaths.

Not now.

Penmarch lay with the scabbard upon him and his face blue-white. The suggestion of a smile touched the corners of his lips; that was all.

"His time has come," said the healer gently.

"No," said Idris angrily. "Holdwater will not fail. We watch."

They watched for the space of a glass. The injured man lay motionless, the lamp flame flickering on his hollow cheeks.

"It has failed," said a voice in the doorway.

The healers had cast themselves on the ground. Idris turned, ready to argue. Then he saw that the speaker was a small, dark man in a crimson robe with bits of gold wire twisted into his beard and an explosion of curly black hair. And he bowed. For he was in the presence of King Mark of Ar Mor, whose palace lay deep in the heathery hillside behind the city of Ys.

King Mark made a faint inclination of the head. He said, "What is this scabbard?"

"It is the scabbard Holdwater, which is the home of the too high sword Cutwater. I drew Cutwater from the Old Well in Lyonesse, to claim it as the Land's King. And I was given Holdwater in the Sundeeps, to hold Cutwater and to cure all wounds. But now," said Idris, with a deep feeling of loss and emptiness, "Cutwater is on the bottom of the sea, and Holdwater has lost its power, and I am King no more."

There was a silence. Then King Mark said, "Come," and led him to a little room with a bright fire. "Sit," he said and gave him a glass of seal's milk, thick and warm. "Now," he said. "Tell me what is in your mind."

Idris bowed. His thoughts were disordered with grief, and he felt in no state to talk to a King. "The monsters and their men must be stopped in Lyonesse," he said. "I came to beg your help. For they will sink the whole world, if they can. Or so said my teacher Ambrose. But I have lost my sword, and my sister, and without them I can be no King—"

"Ambrose?" said Mark sharply.

"Of the Sundeeps, mage," said Idris.

"He was your teacher? Did he tell you what he had done here?"

"He said he had built the powerfields of Carnac."

"Indeed he did," said Mark. "Well, well. Ambrose." He considered, frowning. Idris got the impression of a restless good nature behind the fierce black eyes. "Swords and scabbards do not make Kings," he said. "It is the other way around." He bowed, deeply. "Idris of Lyonesse," he said, "I welcome you to my kingdom as friend. As you say, the monsters threaten us all. Ar Mor is higher than Lyonesse, but if men start being friends with monsters it may still not be high enough. So I will consider how I can help you." He frowned. "As to your friend, I fear he will die, but he rests easy. Tomorrow we will take him into the powerfields, to try what the stones can do to ease him. Now go and rest."

Idris bowed, slung the useless scabbard around him, and left the healers to their work.

Zupper was quiet. Idris was busy with his thoughts, and the family left him to them. Next morning he walked out of the town up a green slope bristling with the lines of standing stones that made the powerfields. He could feel the tingle of their energy in his body and the new clarity they brought his mind. A man was striding toward him down an avenue of the stones: a tall man, old, in a hooded robe of grubby white wool, muttering to himself. Idris recognized him. "Stonekeeper," he said.

The ancient looked up, cross at the interruption of his thoughts. "What?" Then his face cleared, and he smiled, showing dirty teeth in his white-and-yellow beard. "You!" he said. "How very fortunate!"

"For me also," said Idris, in the Manner, but meaning it, too, for the Stonekeeper was a kind man and had been the first to find him after he had been washed up on the shores of Ar Mor.

The Stonekeeper made an impatient noise. "I wasn't just being polite," he said. "I mean it truly is lucky because I was coming to look for you, and I am so old that really the power-fields are all that keep me alive, and when I walk beyond the stones the whole of me hurts like the toothache." The old fingers sank deep into Idris's arm, surprisingly strong for all his complaining, and dragged him through a long flicker of stone shadows. "We put him on the altar stone," said the Stonekeeper.

They arrived at a block of granite half the height of a man and a man's height square. On its flat top, Penmarch lay covered with sealblankets in the winter sunshine.

When Idris's shadow fell on him the eyelids lifted. The eyes focused. The face tried to smile, but smiling seemed to hurt, so it stopped.

"Thank you for taking us out of Lyonesse," said Idris. "I will always be grateful."

"Duty," murmured the Captain. The effort seemed to tire him. The lids came down. "My King."

Idris bowed his head, abashed by this loyalty.

Come, said Penmarch's voice in his mind. *In. See.*

Idris turned cold with fear. He did not want to go into Penmarch's mind, for he would be looking at death.

The Stonekeeper said, "It would be kind, my lord."

Idris took a deep breath. Penmarch had laid down his life

15

for him, after all. This was not the time for childish fears. He put out his mind.

Far away he heard someone gasp, and realized it was him. But by then he had flown through agony and darkness, and beyond the darkness, into ... *joy*?

Yes, joy. And peace, and happiness. Captain Penmarch had thought his King drowned, but now saw him alive with his own eyes. His life had not been lived in vain.

The picture was shrinking. It was no more than a dot in a huge darkness. At the last moment it changed. Idris suddenly knew he was being given a message.

There were waves like moving mountains. There were two ships among the waves, side by side. One of them had lost her masts—Idris recognized her as Penmarch's *Swallow*. The other was red and rakish, with the bronze-skull ram of an Aegypt corsair. Returning boarders were swarming onto her from the *Swallow*. Two of the men, huge and brown with red turbans and blackened teeth, were holding a red-haired girl. They held her firmly but delicately, as if she were a valuable jewel that must not be let fall. Idris saw her lifted and taken onto the red ship....

The picture shrank and slid over an edge into darkness. Idris's heart was pounding. He tried to follow, but he felt himself pushed back, and he knew this was a place where he must not go. Far away, a voice was saying something. Idris returned to himself. He found his face was wet with tears. "What?" he said.

"He is dead," said the Stonekeeper. "It is amazing that he lived this long, stones or no."

"He was a loyal subject," said Idris, full of kingly pride. "He had something he must tell me."

The Stonekeeper bowed, a deep bow. "His pyre will be here at sunset. What was it that he told you?"

"It was my sister, whom I thought dead," said Idris. "Apparently she is alive." And he walked back to the town, weeping for Penmarch but full of joy. Morgan lived.

But as a slave. In wicked Aegypt, far away.

He felt the despair settle again. He was only a boy. What could he do about it?

Nothing.

Harpoon had made crab stew with wild garlics, Idris's favorite. The house was quiet because the rest of the family was at school or at work. Afterward, he helped Harpoon load her nets into the boat and watched her row out of the busy harbor into the bright sea. Around him, fish curers split their catch for drying, and stevedores hauled cargo out of trade boats and craned it onto aurochs carts bound for the mountains of the interior. It was all extremely interesting.

But he scarcely saw it. For high in his mind was the picture of the girl with red hair being carried aboard the red ship, and the joy he had felt in Captain Penmarch even as that noble seafarer died. Joy that his King lived and would fight for his sister and his kingdom.

As the shadows lengthened, he walked back to the power-fields. Ahead, the people were collecting around Penmarch's pyre, built at the end of a long avenue of stones that led from the altar. The crowd parted before him. At the end of the alley, beside a brazier of sea-timber burning before the dark bulk of the pyre, stood King Mark.

"Welcome, Idris of Lyonesse," said Mark, looming against the pinkening sky. "It is our custom that the pyres of great men are lit by the King's hand. Captain Penmarch was such a man. We will send him skysailing together, we Kings of Ar Mor and Lyonesse."

Idris turned to look at the crowd. The setting sun shone full on their faces, so he saw each one in sharp detail. Among them he saw Harpoon of the Fishers and Ector Limpet. He saw them join in the crowd's chest-deep roar. He saw the low sun glitter in the tears of pride that ran from Harpoon's eyes.

"You are his King," said Mark. "For you he died. Send him to sail among the stars."

Idris bowed to Mark, but to his destiny as well. He took the brand from the brazier and held it sputtering above his head. The sun sank into the sea, lower and lower until only a fiery chip of it remained above the rim of the world. As the sunset bell boomed in the belfries of Ys, the orange chip of sun turned a true, piercing green. The crowd sighed long and deep with wonder, and Idris plunged the brand into the pyre. Darkness rushed in from the east. The orange flames roared upward from the oil-drenched logs, and the essence of Captain Penmarch flowed skyward to sail with his friends till time should end.

And on the ground, the flames winked in something bright and polished that stood at the far end of another avenue, on the altar stone of the powerfields of Ys.

Idris stepped away from the pyre and walked toward the spark. The crowd followed him without knowing why. The sky was deep blue, and the stars of the Oar winked in the north. A planet hung red as a blood-drop above the altar at the end of the avenue of stones.

Idris felt his heart beat in his chest, not hard and excited now, but with a slow, confident pulse, for he had been given a sign, and his way was clear. He could feel the curiosity of King Mark at his shoulder. He had no curiosity himself. He knew what he would see.

The crowd surged up to the altar stone in a wave. Then they fell back, eddying, whispering among themselves.

In the granite of the altar stone stood a sword, a sword plain but beautiful, driven to half its blade-length into the rock.

"What is this?" said Mark sharply.

"It is the sword Cutwater, of which I told you," said Idris. "My sword, which leaped from my hand in the sea fight, so I thought it was gone forever and that I was meant to go back to be a child with my family. But it has returned, and my destiny with it."

"I have heard of it," said King Mark, frowning. "In legends."

A boy was standing in the front of the crowd, perhaps a year older than Idris. Idris beckoned to him. "Help me," he said. "Pull that sword out of that stone."

The boy shrugged, walked up to the altar, grasped the hilt, and pulled. "It's stuck," he said.

"Pull harder."

The boy jumped onto the altar stone, put both hands on the sword's hilt, and heaved. The dark silhouette of his head turned left, then right. "Won't budge."

Idris leaned over, closed his fingers around the familiar hilt, and drew the sword from the stone as easily as he might have lifted a spoon from a cup. "Behold," he said, raising the blade so it caught the light of the blood-drop star. "This is the sword Cutwater. With it I shall avenge my friend Captain Penmarch and destroy the enemies of Lyonesse. And," he said, remembering his duty in the Manner, "I offer its service to King Mark and Ar Mor, for your enemies are mine." He sheathed the sword in the scabbard Holdwater.

King Mark bowed to him, respectfully, as an equal. "I thank you," he said. "You are very young. The monsters of Lyonesse are powerful. With respect, Idris, how can I be sure that if I bring my armies across the land bridge to Albion and into Lyonesse, we will not be swept away, nor will my soldiers' families be left fatherless, nor will my kingdom fall?"

Idris felt disappointment rise. Then he saw Ector in the crowd, straight and proud. Ector would see the sense in what

Mark had said. Idris put his hand on Cutwater's hilt and felt strength flow from it. A thought came to him.

"I have made a vow," he said. "I have sworn to find my sister, who was captured by Aegypt corsairs in the wreck that cast me ashore in your kingdom. So I shall find her and save her. And in nine moons I shall give you proof of this rescue, and then we will plan to destroy the false rulers of my lands."

King Mark stood for a moment, frowning. "I know little of Aegypt," he said. "Except that it is ancient and wicked, and ringed with walls bigger and smoother than the Walls of Lyonesse, and does its work with slaves instead of monsters, and is ruled by creatures that are not monsters, but worse and more powerful." He frowned. "Five years ago a Knight of mine, Wrax, a powerful man, was away from his hall when the corsairs raided and took his family. Wrax called together a band of his fellows and left for Aegypt. We know they got there, for I saw them in a dream, and Wrax was a dreamspeaker who could send messages to me when I slept. But we also know that they never came back. And I know I dreamed a terrible dream, that showed Wrax and his people...torn to pieces...by huge mad creatures in a city without windows." The hot, dark eyes rested on Idris as if they could see into his mind. "Wrax was a strong man, and those who were with him were the flower of my army, and the Aegypt creatures tore them bone from bone. You are a mere child. What makes you think you will succeed where the best of Ar Mor have failed?"

Idris fixed his own eyes on Mark's, saw grief and loss, and felt the power of destiny gather under him like a wave. "The same belief that makes me certain I can destroy the usurpers of Lyonesse," he said.

Mark's eyes hooded, as if he was considering. "Very well," he said at last. "If you can do the one, you deserve help with the other. If you rescue your sister from Aegypt, I swear I will help you take back your kingdom from Fisheagle. And I will give you letters to the Duke of Kaldholm and the Overlord, telling them what we have agreed and asking that they help on the same terms." He turned to the scribe at his side, a wizened man with a skin frame and a seal-oil lamp strapped to his brow. "Record the bargain," he said. "And write the letters." He turned back to Idris. "Idris of Lyonesse, this is a terrible undertaking, and I shall be astonished if you do not fail. But I admire your courage and hope I am wrong. Good luck." There was warmth in the eyes under the heavy brows. Idris of Lyonesse could see that King Mark meant what he said.

Which was all very well, thought Idris Limpet later that night under his too-short blankets, after a family zupper of lobster and eggs and winter greens and a hilarious game of Whales. But he had no idea whether what he had felt had been destiny or mere pride. Certainly he had gotten carried away. If the greatest warrior in Ar Mor had failed, how would he get to Aegypt and rescue Morgan?

Well, he would just have to find out for himself. Idris bashed his pillow into shape and went to sleep.

Next day was busy with preparations for the journey. At zupper, Harpoon started fussing. "You must take a new sealblanket," she said. "I've baked you some hard biscuit and packed up some dried ling—"

"Ugh!" said the Precious Stones, making faces of disgust.

"Hush," said Ector, frowning. Idris saw that his foster father would have been fussing, too, if he had not been on his best behavior in the presence of the King of Lyonesse. "Look, sire, er, Idris, I'll come with you."

"I must go alone," said Idris.

"There are bad people where you're going," said Ector darkly.

"I'm pretty bad myself," said Idris. He saw the Boys slide admiring eyes to Cutwater in Holdwater, hanging on the nail behind the door, and felt their longing to come, too, and the warmth of their affection. But he said, "You be here and do your work, and I'll go and do mine. And when I come back you can help me throw the Dolphin off the Mount."

He tried to sound confident, and the Precious Stones cheered, and the Boys started fencing with lobster claws. But he could see that Ector was not fooled, and that any minute Harpoon was going to cry, which would be most unlike her.

At that moment hooves ground the cobbles outside the door, and a fist banged on the panels. A servitor stood outside, holding a little mare by her reins and bowing deeply. "His

Majesty sends you letters and a horse. I am Loick Farwalker, a traveler by trade, so he has asked me to tell you what I know of the journey you plan."

Idris closed his mouth, which had fallen open with delight, for the horse was small and sturdy and altogether beautiful, with a soft, intelligent eye and a proud flare to her nostrils. Ector led the horse to the stables, and the servitor came in.

He was brisk and businesslike and not at all humble. "The land of Aegypt, now. I have not traveled it myself; I know none who have. But I have heard that it is a three-moons' road, and a hard one. Start on the South Road. When the road ends, follow the sun halfway between dawn and noon. A day, and you are in the forest. Seven days more, and you will come into the hills. Fourteen more, and there will be a great river, Lugh, and the castle of Eytgard. You have a letter to the Duke of Kaldholm, who lives there. Then you must travel up the River Lugh until the mountains and cross them. The Overlord lives on one of their high peaks in his Wooden Palace. For him also you have a letter. Beyond the mountains you will find a great plain they call the Lowland. Travel south until the grass turns to sand, and you will find the salt fires of the Lower Sea." He frowned. "Which they say is not a sea but a great river that runs out of unknown lands to a wall built from Afryk to the Volcanoes, which keeps the Lowland from flooding by the True Sea.

"When you come to the shores of the Lower Sea, take ship eastward, and you will come to the mouth of the great river of Aegypt, for Aegypt lies all along the southern shore of the Lower

Sea. I know no more. All I would say is be careful, for I think this is the way the corsairs use for their traveling. Indeed," said Loick, with a discouraging pulling down of the mouth, "you should be careful from the moment you step off His Majesty's good granite road, for the forests are full of outlaws." He rose. "The horse's name is Sunbeam, and she comes with His Majesty's good wishes. And his farewells, and his hope that good fortune may attend you, and that you find your sister, so that he and the other Kings are able to join you to take back your kingdom."

"I am grateful," said Idris.

"It is a long and dangerous way, for one so young," Loick said discouragingly and left.

After he had gone, the Limpet family was grave and subdued. They sat at the table and talked of the old life in the Westgate, when everything had been simple, when the bell rang for the Hour of Thanks, and the town noises ceased, and the mica and fish scales made the air glitter in the sun, and Idris had been truly a child. Idris went to bed sad, but a King. He rose before dawn and gave Sunbeam a feed of oats. Then he slung on the saddlebags and kissed his family one by one.

They followed him to the edge of Ys and waved as he rode away from the town up a long, heathery hill, Kek, his gull, balanced on the wind overhead. He turned to look at them from the crest of the moor. The little figures were still waving. Then he spurred his pony, and they were out of sight, and he was riding on, down the granite road striped with the shadows of standing stones, toward the place where the South Road stopped and the three-moons' road to Aegypt snaked faint and treacherous into the trees.

TWO

*K*ek, said Idris's gull, mentioning its name.

He was riding high over the forest, tilting his wings to the wind that blew off the sea. Below him the wild lands trended south into a gray haze.

There was a sort of road in the trees — not a proper road like the ribbon of hewn granite knifing south from Ys, but a line of trodden ground crawling among the thickets toward a range of hills many leagues ahead. Kek had had a succulent lunch of bear's innards in the last village. Now he was drifting to and fro on the breeze, looking down at the person riding the pony far below.

The person wore leather boots, breeches of baggy wool, and a cloak. The horse carried saddlebags that the gull knew contained food for humans, forbidden to gulls.

There was movement in the trees a bowshot ahead. A bright dot of fire went suddenly out, leaving a smear of steam winding through a thicket of yews. Perhaps something had died. Kek paused for a moment on the wind. He was pretty full of food. But a gull could always get a bit fuller.

Kek, said the gull, gliding forward and down.

The breeze was on Idris's back. In his pack was the food Harpoon had given him for the long road south. In his mind were the farewells of his foster family. Between his knees was his tired horse, Sunbeam.

The trees on either side of the lane penned in a river of shadow. The sky was darkening. It was time to make a fire and lay out his sealblanket, for Darksolstice was a mere moon gone, and the nights were long and cold. The farther the road ran into this great wood, the more he felt his kingship falling away from him, and the more he was Idris Limpet, just a boy, hammering on the gates of the world, unsure what might answer him.

Something moved at the side of his eye. His hand went behind his saddle to the hilt of his sword. Now the thing that had moved was in front of him, but Idris could not see it properly in the half-dark, and he pulled Cutwater, but it snagged in the scabbard, and someone close to him grunted, and something smacked him painfully on the sword elbow. His fingers went dead. His heart was thumping, but the voice of Orbach, his old swordmaster, sounded in his head: *Someone takes a hand from you, well, you've got two.* So his right hand found the sword hilt, and this time the blade came out and flicked around at knee height, but the snag had given the half-visible thing in front of him time to jump clear and vanish. A twig broke behind him. Something walloped the back of his head. A million bees flew into his skull. Idris plunged off the saddlecloth and tasted gritty earth. A huge sadness overwhelmed him. I have escaped the Captains and the monsters and Armies of the Mount, he thought, and the fury of the weather, and the Aegypt corsairs. I have redrawn the sword Cutwater from its stone and met allies who will help me reconquer Lyonesse when I rescue Morgan. But now the rescue will not happen, and it will all end in this dusky wood not far down the Aegypt road.

"Let's s-strip him," said a voice, as if to itself.

The world went black.

———◆◆◆◆◆———

"He's not old," said a voice in the dark, still talking to itself. "S-serf by his clothes. Knight by his sword. Idiot by the fact that he was riding the Oak Road alone."

Idris opened his eyes to argue with this. He saw tree trunks, branches fan-vaulted against dusk-blue. There was no sign of whoever it was that had spoken. Blood was wet on his brow, and he felt deadly sick.

"You are a horrible mess," said the voice. "And you will be a worse one unless you t-tell me where you have put it."

"Put what?"

"The finegold."

"No finegold," said Idris to the empty night.

"Hmm," said the voice. "Nice s-sword, though. Nice scabbard and all. Should fetch big money—oi!"

Idris felt the slap of the sword hilt in his palm, and knew

that Cutwater and Holdwater had torn themselves away from the thief and come back to their master. As Holdwater touched him, the pain in his head vanished. He stood up.

Part of the twilight moved. Idris had a fleeting impression of a tall, thin figure wearing some sort of cloak that took on the dusky colors of the wood. He saw a pair of eye-whites, and teeth in a mouth that hung open. He put his mind out and felt youth and fear, not malice. "Let there be peace between us," said Idris, in the Manner.

"P-peace," said the voice, and Idris heard truth in it. He sheathed Cutwater.

"You had a c-cut," said the voice. "It just disappeared."

"I eat my greens," said Idris. *Tell 'em nothing,* Orbach the swordmaster had said. "Who are you?"

The tall figure bowed slightly from the waist. "People usually call me T-Tristan Smuggles," he said. "Seeing that I am a master of d-disguise. T-Tristan will do." Here he flicked back the remainder of the cloak and stood revealed in the dusk as a lanky youth with crossed eyes.

"You are," said Idris politely. "And a robber, too."

The lanky youth blushed and vanished again. Idris could feel that he was flattered, in a way that a real robber would not have been.

It was dark. The wind rustled in the trees. There were no stars. Quietly Idris drew Cutwater. "Where are you?" he said.

Silence. Gingerly he put his mind out. And felt a presence, waiting. He walked toward it, sword in front of him. "Tristan," he said, "peace or no peace, if you do not reveal yourself and give me back my horse, I shall believe you are an enemy."

"And I believe you are a spy," said the voice of Tristan, exactly where it should have been.

"Believe what you want," said Idris. He put his mind out and saw in Tristan's head a picture of a cave in a cliff with a hastily doused fire in front of it.

"Hey!" said Tristan's voice. "What are you doing?"

"Take me to the fire," said Idris.

"No." A scuffle of dry leaves, as if he was running away. But Idris felt the mind and followed it.

Trees passed. There was a slope, a glow, a smell of wet stone. He came out of the oaks into a clearing in front of a wall of rock. A boy came out of the cave carrying a burning log, and laid it on a flat stone with dry kindling and some other logs, and knelt and blew. The flames leaped and flared. Idris said, "My horse?"

The empty air shifted. The thin youth stood before him, looking surprised and displeased. "Gawaine has him." A whinny from the cave. Idris moved toward it.

"There are three bows in the cave," said Tristan. "They are all drawn upon you."

"There is no need," said Idris.

"You are a s-spy of Mark's," said Tristan.

"Mark is my friend. I come in peace. Do you not want to know why?"

"Not really."

"But I will tell you anyway," said Idris, making his mind firm, as if he were talking to a monster in the stables of the Great Ambrose. "I am the King of Lyonesse. I have been chased out of my country by a creature called Fisheagle and her spoiled son, who is called Murther and who loves to torture children. I am traveling to Aegypt to seek my sister, who has been stolen by corsairs. In a ninemoon I will bring her out of that evil land and King Mark will help me conquer my kingdom." He could feel the minds around him listening. Impressed, even.

But he could feel Tristan rallying against him. "D-dear King Mark," he said with sarcasm. The others laughed nervously. "G-generous as always."

"I believe he speaks the truth," said Idris.

Tall Tristan sighed. He took off his cloak and sat down on a stone by the fire and warmed his hands. "Which sh-shows you can be an idiot and a King at the same time," he said. "Do you really think he would have made the promise if he thought you could bring your sister out of this Aegypt place?"

Idris sat down, too, aware that an arrowhead followed him. He could have put out his mind and shown this Tristan things that would have made him believe. But he had felt something strong and independent in him, and he found he wanted to persuade him by argument, not monstergroom tricks.

Three dirty boys dressed in rags shuffled out of the cave and started rigging a spit over the fire. The one called Gawaine expertly hacked chunks from a deer carcass and set them to roast, while the others went meekly about gathering firewood.

Idris said, "It is a great thing I have asked, and a hard but fair test he has set. Why do you not trust him?"

"Because he sent me out of my tower," said Tristan.

"Why?"

"Plain wickedness."

Idris had seen wickedness in Lyonesse. Mark was not wicked. "And you had done nothing to offend him."

A pause, shifty. "Except take some horses."

"How many?"

"Fourscore."

"How took?"

Tristan seemed to catch Gawaine's eye in the firelight. "They s-strayed," he said. "Gawaine rounded them up. I helped. Gawaine's good with horses."

"Where are your parents?"

"Dead. Gawaine's, too."

"At the hand of King Mark?"

"Of the b-breathing plague. Gawaine's in a K-Kratabec raid. But that is not important. Mark has interfered in our lives. We are outlaws."

"Because you stole a mere eighty of his horses? It strikes me he has a reason to be a little put out. Perhaps you should talk to him and see if you can mend this...misunderstanding."

Tristan's face had taken on a dogged look. "Perhaps he should talk to me," he said.

"You could give him his horses back."

"We sold them," said Gawaine from the fireside.

Idris could feel that both of them were lonely and angry and lost, as if they would rather not have been skulking in this wood but did not know what to do next. But he could also feel that they were both fierce and brave.

They talked as they ate, glad of Idris's company but still suspicious. The deer meat was burnt on the outside and raw on the inside. ("As usual," said Tristan. "You cook it, then," said Gawaine.)

Idris passed around Harpoon's spelter bread; she would be glad he had shared it. None of the five outlaws had eaten bread for a long time, it seemed. They began to laugh and shout, happy with its fine, doughy fillingness. "Do the fire," said Tristan, at last. "I'm off to bed."

"Your turn," said Gawaine to one of the bowmen. He yawned and motioned Idris into the cave. Idris went into the thick dark. "I've got your blanket," said Gawaine's voice in the dark.

"Thief," said Idris.

"Do you want a fight?" said Gawaine.

"Certainly," said Idris.

"Maybe tomorrow," said Gawaine, rather too quickly. There was the sound of a blanket going around a body, a sigh. "Gosh, I'm going to sleep well." Idris saw him lie down between him and the cave entrance. Gawaine could have the blanket tonight; when you were dealing with wild people, it was important to approach them a step at a time. Tomorrow they would see. He raked together a pile of dry bracken, lay down, and for a moment watched the firelight waver on the roof of the cave. Then he closed his eyes and was instantly asleep.

He dreamed.

He saw himself from *below*: a thin thing, sprawled on a cave floor, arms outflung. But the mind that saw him asleep was his, too. So one part of him was in a cave, and another part was... *down here*, in a dark world of bitter water, full of things that flew slowly through... *darkgardens*, where red and blue lights danced long and stately. Here and there, shafts of brilliance pierced the dark. *Wells*. And toward these shafts enormous creatures shooed shoals of other creatures, as officers might shoo soldiers toward a castle for an attack.

There was a noise: a hum of thought. Some of it came from Lyonesse. Some of it was farther distant, but louder—a noise that in the human world would have been marching feet and the blare of trumpets. *They're breaking through*, said Idris, perhaps aloud, and in his dream his hand grasped Cutwater's hilt. And through the watery infinity a beam of hatred stabbed out, beak and claws and icy mind, and groped for him, jabbing closer and closer—

Idris woke. His hand was indeed grasping Cutwater, and he was shivering with terror. For the clawing mind belonged to his enemy Fisheagle, Regent of Lyonesse.

His breathing steadied. The vision faded. He lay, eyes open, and came back to himself.

And saw that there was no firelight on the cave roof. It was dark, and a penetrating cold had crept through the bracken and into his bones. In the wood beyond the clearing he could hear something thinking: red, lumpish thoughts. *Blood*, they said. *Crunch bone, rip meat. Blood.*

Idris scrambled to his feet, brushing off bits of dry bracken. Gawaine was awake, too. "Where d'you think you're going?" he said, drowsy under Idris's blanket.

"There's something out there."

"Nonsense."

A howl split the night. Idris's skin crawled.

Gawaine said in a high, urgent voice, "Harris didn't do the fire. It's direwolves."

Idris drew Cutwater from Holdwater. The sword came easily, as it always did when it would be needed in earnest. Gawaine was still gabbling. "You can't fight them," he said. "There are dozens of them. They're big. They hate fire. Without fire, they'll tear us to bits."

"Let me out of the cave."

Gawaine looked at him, opened his mouth to argue, shut it again, and stepped aside.

Outside the cave mouth a half-moon was squeezing silver light between black branches. *Blood*, growled the thoughts in the shadows under the trees. Idris put his mind out, but the direwolves' minds were like heavy blocks of muscle, too stupid to budge. He counted twenty-six of them.

Kill, said the loudest mind. A mind as stupid as the others but more powerful, passing the taste of blood and meat to the others in the pack.

36

No, thought Idris, as hard as he could. He felt the leader's mind stagger, its grip on the pack weaken. *"GO HOME,"* roared Idris, with his voice as well as his mind.

They were faltering now. *Home?* they were thinking.

"GO HOME," roared Idris again. He swatted the dull ashes of the fire with Cutwater's blade. Red coals arched into the inky shadows. A wolf voice screamed, then another. The minds were weakening now: *Here, hot, hurt. Home, good, warm,* they were thinking. But the leader was still there, its thoughts hard and gory, *Kill, crush with me,* working itself into a rage. Deep in the cave, Sunbeam squealed with terror. Suddenly out of the shadows there bounded a beast the size of a horse, the moon glinting in a pair of ice-blue eyes. Idris's feet badly wanted to run. But Cutwater was light and easy in his hand. He stepped away from the creature's pounce, smelling its rank pelt. Cutwater sang in the air. The snarl ceased. The head went one way, the body another, fountaining black blood in the moonlight.

Fear. Hurt, whined the direwolf pack. Bodies crashed through the undergrowth and were gone.

Idris stooped, took hold of one huge ear, and dragged the head into the cave. "Here you are," he said, yawning to hide the shake in his voice. "Why doesn't someone light the fire?"

Gawaine said casually, "This is yours," and handed him his sealblanket, as if he had discovered it lying on the cave floor. Idris found he was exhausted. He wrapped himself in the blanket, lay down, and went to sleep.

Idris was woken by the clink of pottery on stone. He opened his eyes. Gray daylight was creeping into the cave. A cup stood on the ledge beside him. Steam rose from it, carrying the smell of weedwater thickened with honey.

"Thank you," he said. He drank. Energy spread through him. He stood up, stretching.

Tristan walked across from a stone table, even skinnier in the daylight than he had been in the half-dark. He bowed. "What must I d-do?" he said.

Idris frowned, suspecting he was being teased. "About what?"

"You have saved the band, so it is yours to lead. I who was leader am now part of the b-band. This is the rule." He looked sleepless and depressed.

Idris smiled. He did not want any outlaw band, but he needed friends, and this meeting had the whiff of destiny about it. He said, "I live by other rules. But I would value you as a friend and companion, if you choose."

Tristan bowed. He took Idris's wolf-bloody hand and pressed it to his brow. "Then I thank you and will s-serve you as my liege lord, without whom we would all have died this night."

"Excellent," said Idris, somewhat amazed. "Then these are my commands."

"Sir?"

"My name is Idris, not 'sir.' You can think of me as your

liege lord if you like, but I prefer to think of you as a Knight, like me." Tristan's face relaxed. Idris went on. "As I told you last night, I am on a long road to find my sister and free her from those who have enslaved her. Any who want to come with me, come, and in time I will make your peace with King Mark. Any who want to stay as outlaws in the forest may stay. Nobody has to fight me."

"I shall come," said Tristan.

"Where are we going?" said Gawaine.

"To Aegypt."

"What is Aegypt?"

"You walk to the sun's left until the grass turns to sand," said Idris. "Apparently."

"Sounds rather interesting," said Gawaine, with a casualness Idris thought was an attempt to regain face after his fear of the direwolves.

"I have heard of it," said the youth who had failed to stoke the fire. "They definitely tear the guts out of children and offer them to their gods." He frowned. "My mother will need help with the lambing."

"And mine," said another voice.

"And mine."

Idris nodded and stood up. "Good-bye and good luck," he said. He watched with Gawaine and Tristan as the youths bundled up their gear and scuttled into the trees, casting nervous glances over their shoulders.

"Do you want to go with them?"

"No!" said Tristan, shocked.

Gawaine scowled at the forest. "I'm sick of trees," he said.

"Absolutely," said Tristan.

Idris sat down on the direwolf's severed head. "Then we must go, and soon," he said. "I must be in Lyonesse with my allies when the Dolphin comes of age next Darksolstice. For it is on that Darksolstice that I leave childom and enter the year of my fourteenth birthday, when I come of age in Lyonesse. Aegypt is far away. There is no time to waste. I have letters for the Duke of Kaldholm and the Overlord. We must find them."

"Kaldholm?" said Tristan. "At Eytgard? I kn-know the way."

Deep in his mind, Idris heard a voice say: *Well done.* It was a small voice, but it sounded like his old friend the Mage Ambrose, buried with dragons in the western mountains of Lyonesse. Idris felt a pang of affection and sadness. The affection remained: the sadness passed. For it was Ambrose who had taught him to recognize the tide of destiny. And now he felt that tide gathering under him, sweeping him on.

Gawaine had drawn a short sword and was busily sharpening it with a stone, as if the walls of Aegypt were within sight and he was about to fight his way in at the main gate. He tested its edge with his thumb, sheathed it, and said, "Ready when you are."

"Then we should go," said Tristan. "N-not a moment to lose, by the sound of it."

Idris was satisfied. They felt wild, but trustworthy and tough. He said, "There is something we must do first."

"Name it," said Gawaine, hand on sword.

"We're ready," said Tristan, sweeping his cloak around him.

"Brekfuss," said Idris.

Their laughter sent the rooks cawing high over the winter-naked oaks on the wild hills that divided them from the palace of Eytgard.

A cold drizzle was falling as the three travelers set off. Their possessions fitted neatly into the homemade panniers slung on Sunbeam's elegant back. It was clear that the pony did not think much of this arrangement. But it did not occur to Idris to ride while his companions walked. As a King, he was not big enough to be much of a fighter or old enough to be much of a governor. So fairness was the best tool he had.

The ground grew higher, the trees lower. Three days they marched south and east among scrubby hills, sleeping in caves and under fallen trees. The rain fell continuously, and they slid on greasy slopes of clay and fell into great standing puddles from which they rose with chattering teeth. Idris reckoned that in three days they had trudged as far as a horseman would have ridden in one. "This is too slow," he said to Tristan.

"All right," said Tristan. "Gawaine can s-steal some horses, next chance we get. He'll love it."

Gawaine heard but trudged on without answering, his head hooded in an old sack.

"Not from farmers," said Idris.

"Who could f-farm on land like this?" said Tristan. "The people who live up here are outlaws and bandits. Gawaine knows. He was born here."

"It's true," said Gawaine in a small, gloomy voice.

"They're all horse thieves," said Tristan. "Gawaine's lot, too."

"Horse *breeders*," said Gawaine. A long pause. Then, in a new voice, quiet and sad and entirely without the bravado he had shown since the direwolves, "We were raided by the Kratabec." His greenish eyes took on a glassy look, as if tears were close. Idris knew Gawaine was looking at the death of his parents. "They really are horse thieves. Murderers, too. They've got hundreds of horses, mostly other people's. Their country is over there a day's march." He pointed a little to the right of their course.

"In that case," said Idris, "would you like to pay them a visit?"

"Yes," said Gawaine, and now his eyes had turned hard and bright as green stones, and his fierceness was entirely genuine. "I certainly would."

<hr />

The following morning Idris, Tristan, and Gawaine stood in a gorse thicket at the bottom of a small stony hill. On top of the hill was a village in a stockade of pointed logs. On the hill's sides were paddocks walled with peeled tree trunks, in which little clumps of horses grazed peacefully in the drizzle. Sunbeam and the baggage were four hours' march away, in the care of one of Gawaine's family's old retainers.

Idris and Tristan dropped to their hands and knees and started to crawl through the gorse stalks. They wormed their way to the edge of the thicket. There were horse herders squatting around a fire in the top paddock. Tristan said, "Here I go." He pulled his cloak around him. Suddenly he was not there anymore. It was not that the cloak made him invisible, exactly; but it merged perfectly with the background, so he became a mere boy-shaped flicker of no-rain in the rain. Idris watched the flicker walk around one of the bottom paddocks, out of sight of the glum group around the fire, until it came to the slip-rail. The rail slid out of its slot. The paddock stood open. Now it was Gawaine's turn. As if on cue, Idris heard a whinnying from the thicket. It sounded like a horse, but it was Gawaine. Idris held his breath.

There were five horses in the paddock. They put up their heads to listen to the call. Then they trotted to the gap in the fence and turned down the hill, away from the stockade of the Kratabec village. The rail of the paddock replaced itself. A flicker started down the hill. Again the whinny, this time deeper in the wood. The horses broke into a trot. Up on the hill the horse herders squatted in the cold drizzle. Nobody had noticed them go.

When Tristan came to the forest's edge, Idris went to meet him. They began to trot along the line of hoofprints in the mud of the forest floor, stifling a glee so powerful it blotted out the fear of pursuit. After half a league the suppressed laughter faded, and Idris was able to put his mind back, listening for the spikes of attention that would become shouts. None came.

They found Gawaine under a mighty oak, feeding the horses bits of purple carrot out of his pocket. When he heard them he looked up. He said, "I've made some head collars. We can ride." He looked busy and useful, in his element at last.

Idris was pleased to have companions and to be able to rest his sore feet. He said, "This is well done."

"It is," said Gawaine grimly. "I recognize these animals. They are of my family's stock."

They scrambled onto the horses' bare backs and trotted into the trees.

That night they slept in the ruins of Gawaine's family tower. Once it had stood on its hill like a beacon of golden stone. Now it was a burnt-out ruin, stinking of bitter ash. Idris lay long awake, looking out of a window socket at a star that had appeared in a deep embrasure of cloud. Gawaine seemed happy to have annoyed the Kratabec, but no number of stolen horses would make up for the loss of a family. Idris thought of the tower on the Wolf Rock in Lyonesse, the home of his sister, Morgan, and her kind foster parents, burned, too. When he was King in Lyonesse, no towers would burn. Pulling the sealblanket over his head, he slept.

In the morning they rose before dawn and hurried on, always east of south. The horses went swiftly and well. High above, Kek rode the wind with Idris in his head, looking down over a world of wet, wooded mountains that on the sixth day after the night of the direwolves began to descend to a series of lower hills.

They passed a village, then another. The people greeted them without much curiosity; evidently they were used to travelers. They bought more bread in the third village, and rank mutton-ham from an autumn-killed sheep. Game was scarce in these populous lands, and what little they saw was jealously guarded by the people of the castles that frowned from the hilltops.

On the eighth day they left the hay barn where they had slept, exchanged messages of goodwill with the farmer, and set out across a low green plain. The flat fields were full of aurochs and sheep and big-boned goats, amazingly fat. The air was not warm, but there was a balminess to it, quite unlike the raw edge of the winds that blew in Ar Mor and the mountains. Across the horizon ahead lay a gray square-sided building.

Idris sent Kek forward. The gull swept over a wide reed bed, and Idris saw that the building was a huge castle on an island in a wide black river. Machinery lined the battlements, and from the topmost tower a yellow flag bearing the device of a crimson dragon drummed stiff in the breeze.

"Eytgard," said Tristan, with the smugness of a successful guide. "Home of the D-Duke of Kaldholm."

They crossed the river with their horses in a flat-bottomed punt hauled along a fixed rope by men in knee-length jerseys of rough wool. In Lyonesse under the Regent, the ferrymen would have been serfs or monsters, mute and terrified. These men grinned at the travelers with an openness that made Idris think they were free. His mood lifted. As for the dragon flag, he took it as a good omen, for he and Morgan had been saved by dragons in the Sundeeps, and perhaps a dragon would save them again.

They landed at a quay and passed under a portcullis. Gawaine's head was swiveling as he gaped at the dizzy towers and cliffs of wall.

"Shut your mouth," hissed Tristan, tapping his friend's jaw closed. "They'll think you're a p-peasant."

"And you're not?" said Gawaine, firing up. "As far as I remember, we both lived in the same cave—"

"Hush," said Idris. His mind was full of a great murmur of human thought. It held nothing as sharp as a monster. But there was an edge to it, as if everyone in this place was striving to get the better of someone else. He caught shreds of greed and desire: people buying and selling things. Perhaps that was it.

Tristan must have caught a corner of his thought without realizing. "Trade," he said. "This is the biggest m-market in . . . the West. Tin rings gold-plated. Old horses greased to look new. Salt that's mostly sand. Here!" He reached out and grabbed a herald by one scarlet sleeve. "Take us to the Duke."

"Who are you?" said the herald, curling his lip.

Idris touched his mind and said quietly, "The Duke."

46

The herald went pale, bowed deeply, and said, "My lords, follow me."

"How do you *do* that?" said Tristan.

Gawaine, glad to get his own back for the peasant crack, said, "I'm a horse breeder. You're a robber. He's a King."

The herald led them through stone passages into a room where people sat on benches, as if waiting. Beyond the window the castle buildings made a ring. But not a ring floored with grass, in the usual way of castles. This ring was floored with water. And on the water, packed like mullet in a box, were ships and barges piled with bales and sacks and barrels of goods from (Tristan said) all the shores of all the world.

Another herald ushered them along a passage floored with deep corsair carpets and into a great room with four windows. One looked north at the rain clouds smothering the mountains of Ar Mor. Another looked south over a plain splashed with green patches of sun. To the east the river wound into distant blue mountains, and to the west it ran thick and swollen to the far gray line of the sea. The room was empty except for a hill of cushions in the middle of the floor.

"Idris House Draco," bellowed the herald. "You are admitted to the presence of His Grace the Duke of Kaldholm."

Someone in the room uttered a gigantic belch. Tristan hid a giggle. The cushion-hill erupted and a head came out. The hair was dark and matted, the black beard clotted with spilt food. A body followed. It wore a robe of filthy fur, and in the dirty hand there flopped a slab of red meat. But the eyes under

47

the matted brows were bright and sharp. "Idris, is it?" said the apparition, belching again. "King Mark sent me a pigeon, told me you might come. Show me your letter." He sniffed through hairy black nostrils, chewing and reading, his fingers leaving greasy marks on the lambskin. "You're a King, eh?" He sniffed again and spat phlegm at the wall.

Idris was not sure what to make of this disgusting Duke. He bowed, in the Manner. "I thank Your Grace for receiving us," he said. "I ask you to help us on our way to Aegypt."

"I would be pretty stupid not to receive the King of Lyonesse," said the Duke, flicking a lump of gristle off a cushion and onto the ceiling. "And I would be even stupider to keep a Pretender of Lyonesse here any longer than I had to, that nasty Regent, don't want to get on the wrong side of her, wouldn't be clever." He bit at his slab of meat. Gravy ran down his chin. "But as for helping you, well, the idea is that you do it on your own, and if you succeed I help you, but until then you're on your own." The Duke chewed noisily for a moment, mouth open. Then he said, "Bors?"

A little door opened. A short, thickset youth came in, looking fed up. "I was listening," said the youth. "You'd better help him. Then you can tell the Regent that you sent him away, and it will be true. And if he conquers the Regent, he'll be grateful."

"Think so?" said the revolting Duke. He turned to Idris. "That's Bors. Very clever lad for giving advice. But won't tell a lie. Can't. Awkward person to have around. Say an enemy comes

48

to see you, you give him zupper, plan a poison pudding, and after the first course up pipes Bors, 'Look out, he's going to murder you!'" This notion seemed to put the Duke in a rage. "And what is to stop me locking this King up and telling the Regent he's here? Nothing personal, but I'd get a good price. By the Hill of Slain, you make me sick, Bors. Too clever by half." He tore at his meat again.

"All right," said Bors stolidly, catching Idris's eye and holding it with a blankness in which Idris read sympathy. "The Regent of Lyonesse and her monsters are bad for trade, though. But if you don't like my advice, you needn't have it. I've had enough of you. If King Idris is going to Aegypt, I'll go with him. By the way, your breath smells like a privy."

"How true," murmured Tristan. Gawaine made a snorting noise as he suppressed a laugh.

"Hah!" cried the Duke, spitting chewed meat. "Get out while I think what to do with you. Guards, take 'em to the Gaze Tower. Bors, too." He rolled back into his mountain of cushions. The audience was over.

"That didn't go very well," said Tristan, as two guards marched them through the stone corridors of the castle. "Was it a good idea to tell him about his bad breath?"

"It is better for him to know than not know," said Bors.

"Funny, too," said Gawaine. "And you didn't help, Tristan."

Idris found himself grinning, too. He put out his mind to touch Bors's and was astonished. It was as clear as crystal, without lies, or evasions, or mixed motives.

Bors frowned. "What are you doing in my head?"

"Getting to know you," said Idris, embarrassed at being discovered.

Bors looked surprised. "If you want to know something, ask, and I'll tell you. Well, zupper time. This is all rather exciting, isn't it?"

The Gaze Tower was not a bad prison, as prisons went. It was a round turret overhanging the water, with soft couches lining the walls. There was a table in the middle, bearing white bread, cold roast beef, and shallow baskets of apples. Tristan cast himself on one of the couches. "This is the life," he said, with the air of one born to luxury, not an outlaw from a cave.

Gawaine looked a little uneasy; he was too wild for confinement, no matter how luxurious. "I don't trust him," he said, in a voice muffled by food.

"Elegant beef," said Tristan languidly. "You going to have some, Idris?" Idris nodded and made himself eat. But he was too worried to be really hungry.

"Of course he may be testing us," said Bors. "He probably wants us to escape. If we don't, he'll think you're not worth helping, and tell the Regent. If we do, and he catches us, he'll still tell the Regent. If we succeed, he'll think we're worth helping."

"Even after all that about his breath?"

"He knows already. He likes the truth. That's why he kept me."

Idris reflected. It was the Wells all over again. If you failed, you died. It made the choice easier, in a way. He said, "Do you know where we find the Overlord?"

"In the mountains. Up the river," said Bors.

"Then we'll have to steal a boat."

"But first we get out of this cell," said Gawaine. "I'll shout. The guard'll open up. The rest of you can clobber him with the table."

"Excellent," said Tristan, squinting with pleasure at the prospect of action.

"But very noisy," said Bors.

"There's a quieter way," said Idris. "Listen."

They listened.

———⟨•⟩———

The guard on the door of the Gaze Tower was not a clever man. He was standing outside the great iron portal with a spear in his hand, thinking that it was an hour till zupper and that he was starving.

And suddenly he was thinking of cake. He could see it in his mind, sharp and perfect: a really beautiful cake, with Lowland fruits in it, and icing dyed shell-red. Beside it was a bottle of sweetest wine. And it was sitting on the table in the chamber in the turret.

"Cor," said the guard, licking his lips. He unlocked the door and started up the stairs. He was too stupid to ask himself why his mind felt odd, as if someone was pushing it.

Perhaps he should have.

When he walked into the chamber, he saw no cake and no wine. There were only three boys looking at him and a sort of flicker behind his right shoulder.

"Mf," said the guard as Tristan put a cushion cover over his head and upper arms and pulled the string tight.

"Oof," said the guard as cunning fingers took the key from his belt and tipped him into a chest. Dimly he heard laughter, feet running down the stairs, a door slamming, a key turning.

"Help!" cried the guard.

But he was inside a cushion cover, inside a chest, behind a locked door in a tall, lonely turret, which was now empty.

There was no one to hear.

Once down the stairs, the boys pushed their way through a throng of carts and people onto the quay.

The quay was a broad ledge of paving, lined with cranes, running around a basin crammed with boats. On the far side of the basin was the water gate into the river, a huge arch between two towers. Idris let his mind run across other minds like a stick along palings. *South*, he heard, *wine, money, swindle*. And then *don't like it, get away, freedom*. He stopped, his eyes traveling where his mind had been. Between two fat barges there lay a long, low boat whose bow rose to become a carving of a dragon's head. It was from this boat that the thoughts were coming: *Free, wild, the run of clear water.*

Idris was looking across at the dragon boat. A face was looking back: a pale face, framed with fair hair, the eyes dark-shadowed. *Wait,* said Idris. *If you please.* "Come," he said aloud.

The boys walked quickly around the quay and started out over the close-packed boats, jumping from deck to deck. The fair-haired person watched them come. He was not yet a man, Idris realized as they drew nearer. He was another boy, white-skinned, with bruise marks on his face, as if he had been beaten, and a quiet, wild atmosphere about him, as if he was not happy in the noise and crush of Eytgard.

"Greetings," said Idris, hurriedly but in the Manner, and named himself and his companions.

The boy bowed and named himself as Galahd. "Welcome aboard the *Firedrake*," he said, as politeness required.

"You are to take us up the river, Galahd," said Idris. "We go to Aegypt."

"Oh," said the white-faced youth, not at all surprised by this request, indeed hardly listening, his eyes searching the quay.

"He doesn't know where Aegypt is," said Bors the truthful but tactless. "He is a boat-kerl from the North. They don't know anything, except about boats."

Galahd shrugged. "This is true," he said.

"Can you help us?" said Idris.

Galahd's eyes passed from Idris to restless Gawaine and

53

stolid Bors, and narrowed a little as they settled on Tristan, whose cloak was half on, half off, so he was smiling kindly with a head set on a body only half visible. "I am ordered to wait for Ulf Tearingjaw to come back," he said in a gloomy singsong voice. "It is his boat. He will beat me, for he is drunk. So I must throw him overboard, as I have promised him I will next time he beats me. Which I do not wish to do, for it is killing, which is wrong. But I cannot break my sworn word. So what else can I do?"

"Take us up the river in your boat. We must leave. Soon."

Galahd raised his eyebrows and appeared to consider. Finally he said, "All right. We will move closer to the watergate."

Gawaine said, "What about the horses?"

"We need finegold. Can you find them and sell them?"

Gawaine cast a sharp green eye over the crowd of boats and the throngs of people milling on the quays. "Can a bear eat honey?"

"I'm w-with you," said a flicker in the air where Tristan had been. The pair of them ran over the boats to the land.

Idris, Galahd, and Bors began prying apart the boats' hulls so the *Firedrake*'s sharp bow could slide between them to a berth handy for the castle's watergate. Idris said, "The wind is blowing the wrong way. We will have to wait." And if they waited, they would be caught.

"No," said Bors. He pointed up at the battlements. Huge sheets of white cloth stood against the pinkening sky. They were stretched on frames. Men stood by the frames, tiny with

54

distance, beside big-toothed wheels and windlasses. "These are the famous harbor sails of Eytgard," said Bors, as if giving a lesson. "The sailmen work the frame-gear to tilt the sails so they funnel the wind in or out of the harbor. If they funnel it out of the harbor, the wind blows into the watergate. If they funnel it in, the wind blows out of the watergate. The harbor-master gives the sailmen their instructions. You need to talk to him."

Galahd shook his head. "He'll never let us out unless Tearingjaw asks him."

He may, said Idris in his head.

The low sun cast a flood of light over the boats and the stone of the castle and Galahd's face, turned awestruck to Idris. Then it sank behind a tower, and the shadows rushed in, and serfs lit torches along the quays.

They waited dry-mouthed, looking across clear water at the arch of the gate. A figure came jumping lightly from boat to boat: Gawaine, waving, then Tristan a flicker at his heels, uncloaking with a dramatic sweep of the arm, grinning with pleasure, Gawaine grinning, too. A heavy purse slapped triumphantly in Idris's hand.

"Feels like a lot."

"I may have sold a few that weren't ours," said Gawaine.

"It's a trick horse thieves, sorry, *breeders*, learn," said Tristan and dodged Gawaine's kick.

Idris said, "I'll go and see the harbormaster. Get ready." He shoved the purse into his tunic and threaded his way to the shore. As he jumped from deck to deck, he hoped Sunbeam had found a kind new owner; she had been a good little mare. But he could not regret her too much. Life was pressing ahead too fast for regrets.

He ran up a couple of steps onto the quay, made himself walk calmly to a lamplit arch bearing the Eytgard dragon crest, and stepped into a chamber lined with scroll niches. The yellow-tunicked harbormaster looked up haggard-eyed from his desk. "What is it now?" he said.

"I'm off the *Firedrake*," said Idris, harking back to the harbor talk he had heard in the Westgate as a child, making himself speak slow and casual. "We're sailing in half a glass. Would you ask the sailmen to give us a breeze out of the gate?"

"It's night," said the harbormaster. "They'll be closing the watergate any moment. What do you want to go for? There's stoves and warm straw here. It's blowing a gale outside."

"We'll go down to the sea on the current. We need to catch the tide north in the morning," said Idris, plunking down a handful of silver on the table. "Harbor dues."

The harbormaster shrugged and uncapped a speaking tube set in the wall by his desk. He had the vague feeling that he should have been asking more questions, but something in his head was telling him not to bother. "Young devils, too much hurry," he said. "You'll end up a pile of wreck. Not my problem, though." He whistled into the speaking tube. "Fill 'er up," he said to the sailman on the castle roof high above.

"Fill," said a faint, tinny voice. "Unfurling."

The harbormaster recapped the speaking tube. "And if they drop the gate on you you're not my problem," he said, handing Idris a pass with one hand and raking up the pile of silver with the other.

Idris made himself walk casually down the quay and skipped over the boats to the little knot of dark figures on the *Firedrake*'s deck. "Ready? Away," he said. "Quickly."

High on the battlements, the sail frames tilted. A puff of cold wind smacked his face. The moored boats shifted uneasily in the basin. There was a rope in Idris's hand. Bors was in front of him on the rope. "*Heave!*" hissed Galahd.

Idris heaved. The *Firedrake*'s sail rose, a dark oblong against the yellow-lit windows of the castle. It flapped, cracked full of wind, fell empty again. Someone shouted. The *Firedrake*'s side slammed into another boat. Galahd hissed something rude, leaning on the steering oar. The *Firedrake*'s wake roared, and the deck tilted. She began to slide toward the gate.

Suddenly there was another kind of shouting, deep and violent. "It's Tearingjaw," said Galahd, looking nervously at Idris. "The skipper."

"Keep going," said Idris. An angry skipper would attract the attention of the Duke's men. He saw Galahd swallow, his eyes narrow as he sighted at the gate. He turned to face the new threat.

The light from a cresset on the quay fell on a huge man in

a bearskin coat, bounding across the close-packed hulls toward them. A castle guard had stopped his patrol to watch.

The *Firedrake*'s dragon bow was cutting clear black water now. The men in the lifting room of the watergate watched it come. "Closing time," said the winchman, yawning. "I'm dropping it, boat or no boat." He started across the room to the release handle that would let the great oak grille fall into the water and lock in its groove in the bottom, sealing the gate.

A puff of wind raced over the harbor. Tearingjaw was on the next boat as the *Firedrake* slid past. Idris saw his mouth open, the light glint on long brown teeth as he jumped at them, and Idris gripped Cutwater with both hands, thinking, I do not want to kill this man, for he only wants what is his. Then the deck moved under his feet, and water roared on the steering oar as Galahd put his weight on it, and the *Firedrake*'s side swerved away from Tearingjaw as he leaped, so he landed not on the deck but a handsbreadth short, and crashed howling into the water.

"Well *p-played!*" said Tristan, clapping solemnly. Gawaine joined him, and even Bors nodded approvingly. And Galahd, expressionless Northern boat-kerl though he was, allowed a smile to touch his lips and bowed slightly. A new puff of wind filled the *Firedrake*'s sail. The boat slid under the arch and onto the broad bosom of the river. There was a crash as the gate came down a foot behind her sternpost; then they were free, heeling steeply, the wake tearing down the lee side, the castle of Eytgard a pile of lights shrinking in the distance astern.

"Upstream?" said Galahd, when they were out of view.

"Upstream," said Idris.

The stars wheeled. Stemming the current, the *Firedrake* began to glide up the river toward the hills to the east, and beyond them the mountains that held the palace of the Overlord.

THREE

Next morning, Idris woke in the sleeping-hay with the dank smell of the river in his nostrils. The *Firedrake* was moving strongly along a wide, smooth pool. He blew life into the embers on the hearthstone in the middle of the boat, scooped a kettleful of water from the river, and set it to boil. He made weedwater and took a mug back to Galahd, who stood hollow-eyed in the stern, steering from back eddy to back eddy to get the current in his favor. "Where are we?" Idris said.

Galahd shrugged. "Don't know." The river was slow and smooth, reed beds stretching away on either side. "But we'll need Flashers by evening."

"Flashers?"

Galahd took the mug and warmed his hands on it, steering with his hip. "To help with rapids. You'll see. I've never been brought a cup of weedwater by a King before."

Idris said, "A King without a kingdom is only a name."

Galahd's eyes strayed to the sword on Idris's back. "But Tearingjaw landed in the harbor. You've got a King's luck."

There was a general stirring. The other boys were waking. A smell of frying drifted aft from the hearthstone. "Put the boat up the bank," said Idris. "You need food."

"I don't want to waste this breeze," said Galahd. "Bring me something when it's ready."

So Idris left him, tall and fair, reading the River Lugh like a long scroll, putting league after league between them and Eytgard.

There was food on the table by the hearthstone. Tristan and Gawaine were already there, jaws moving hard. "I dreamed you s-stole the Duke's horse," Tristan was saying. "And you f-fell off. And I had to rescue you."

"Thank you, dear noble Tristan!" cried Gawaine, in a high, weak, sarcastic voice.

Tristan lifted up the loaf of bread to throw at him. Bors said, "I made that bread for eating, not throwing. Idris, there's eggs, sheepsteak, bread and honey and apples."

Idris realized he was very hungry. He took a board of food aft to Galahd, then started to eat his own brekfuss.

He said, "This is excellent. Who cooked it?"

"I did," said Bors. "You didn't want to eat raw flour, did you? And the sheepsteak tastes like sheepsteak because I put some things in it to make it taste that way, and the eggs are just eggs, only I didn't spoil them."

Idris ate, full of admiration for this blunt and talented person. He ate. And as he ate, he thought.

If he had not met Tristan and Gawaine, he might still be

trudging through the forest; or perhaps he would have been murdered by the horse-stealing Kratabec in the clay hills. And if it had not been for Bors and Galahd, they might be in a deep dungeon, waiting for the Regent. And to be fair, if it had not been for him, Tristan and Gawaine would have been torn apart by direwolves, and Bors would be serving the disgusting Duke, and Galahd would be still subject to the cruelties of Tearingjaw.

He came to a decision. Finishing the last delicious bit of bread and honey, he stood up, climbed onto the cabin roof, and said, "Gentlemen!"

Four faces looked up at him: Galahd haggard, an eye on the river; Gawaine with a crafty eyebrow raised; Tristan languid and half-visible; and Bors wondering what the fuss was about.

"Gentlemen, we are on our road to Aegypt," said Idris. "And each of us has helped the others according to our gifts and talents. If we had not, we would not be alive to eat brekfuss this morning. None of you has much to go back to in your home. But I have a kingdom, and it needs people like you. The first Knights of Lyonesse were chosen by the Old King to defend the realm. They were cunning and strong in battle, kind and fair in times of peace. I therefore invite you to be Knights of Lyonesse, and at the end of this hard road we must travel, you will perhaps find a home and a reward."

They looked at one another, then at him. "We'd be stupid not to," said Bors.

"Right, Bors," said Gawaine, with irony.

"But not very polite," said Tristan. "Idris, I accept with gratitude, and shall do what I can to defend your person and your realm. And that probably goes for Gawaine, too, though he is not likely to be much good at it. Ow!" For here Gawaine threw a bucket of water at him.

"Thank you, sire," said Galahd, ignoring the antics of Gawaine and Tristan and bowing in the Manner. "I am deeply honored and will do my best. Now will someone steer? For I must sleep."

Certainly these were not solemn speeches of acceptance or highly decorated words. But Idris was completely sure in his heart that these people without families had found a family with one another and him. And that in finding Knights like these, the kingdom of Lyonesse had been very lucky indeed.

After brekfuss he climbed the mast. The river wound among marshes. Ahead, a line of hills ran across the horizon. By the time the sun was at its zenith, the hills were higher than the dragon's head on the bow. The river had become faster and more turbulent. The wind had faded, and they were barely making headway against the current as they sailed around a headland and into a wide pool.

At the far end of the pool, the riverbed rose in a series of steps. Heavy water poured over them, white and rumbling so the deck shook. *Firedrake* would no more sail up that staircase than fly to the moon. Idris's heart sank. Their journey by river was over, and they had no map, and Aegypt was impossibly far away.

Galahd had been sleeping, but the change in the boat's mood woke him. He stood up and looked over the side. "Good," he said.

"Good?" said Idris. "We'll have to walk again."

"I hate walking," said Galahd. "Watch."

And though the other new Knights pressed him, he would say no more.

As they neared the rapids Idris saw a great sprawl of huts on the banks, enough to make a fair-sized town. Out of the huts there swarmed hundreds of little figures. Galahd leaned on the steering oar, and the *Firedrake* nosed between two rocks and into a patch of calm water at the rapids' foot. The swarm of little people of the town flowed to the water's edge. They were greenish-white, naked, entirely hairless, the lines of their muscles blurred as if by a layer of blubber under the skin. "These are the Flashers," said Galahd. "They speak with their minds. Their chiefs are called Margraves." A group of the greenish-white creatures swarmed onto the gunwale, grinning, showing little green teeth. One of them put out a hand.

Margrave? said Idris with his mind. The crowd nodded and gurgled. Idris laid a gold coin in the hand, which was webbed between the fingers.

"They live by rapids and river shallows all the way north to the Ice," said Galahd. "They build dams we call flashes, to help ships up places like these. When there are enough ships waiting, they break the dams and let them down. Hey!"

A small Flasher had jumped down from the gunwale and

trotted past the boat's hearthstone to peer into the sleeping shelter. It moved in a strange, clumsy scuttle, humming a high, excited tune. One of its long feet caught a wisp of the sleeping hay and sent it into the fire on the hearthstone. Suddenly the little creature was shrieking in the middle of an orange-red ball of flame. Bubblings of horror rose from the crowd. Idris picked up a bucket of water and flung it into the heart of the flames. It had only been the briefest flare-up, and the water put it out instantly. But the little Flasher lay huddled on the deck, black with hay-ash, moaning in a small, thin voice.

Idris bent over the creature. Its skin had been wickedly seared. Much of it had burned away, showing the pink blubber beneath, traced with little blue veins.

My son, my son, the Margrave was keening with his mind. Idris could feel Galahd's eyes on him. He pulled Holdwater over his head, drew Cutwater from it, and laid the scabbard on the Flasher child's body.

There was the sort of silence that happens when a thousand people breathe in and forget to breathe out.

For a moment, nothing happened. Then the shreds of skin lost their scorched look and took on a healthy glisten. Veins arrived and spread on the raw patches, and new, clean skin spread swiftly to cover them. Finally the Flasher child opened its eyes, as if waking from sleep. It gave the watchers a look of horror, dived overboard, and swam into the deeps with the fluent grace of a water creature.

You? said the Margrave of the Flashers to Idris. *How?*

Idris let his mind rest on the Margrave's. *King?* said the Margrave's mind, surprised. *Thank you, thank you. Welcome.*

Idris bowed, catching from the corner of his eye a glimpse of Galahd, openmouthed, and his other companions, frozen, watching. An idea came to him. He showed the Flasher a mental picture of Tearingjaw, bearlike in his coat. *Don't let him pass.*

But our duty, said the Margrave, giving off a sense of being shocked.

Do your duty, said Idris. *But do it slowly.*

He felt a moment's blankness, then a phlegmy, froglike chuckle. *Yes, King*, said the Margrave and was gone, issuing orders in his strange gurgling voice. His people hurled themselves into their work.

From great heaps on the banks they hauled logs and stones and pine trees with the needles still on them. These they piled across the bottom of the rapids until the whole width of the River Lugh was dammed, and the dam was rising higher and higher. The water upstream of the dam rose, too, lifting the *Firedrake*. A mere two glasses later, the rapids had become a smooth, shining pool. "We go," said Galahd. "Let fall the sail."

Down fell the sail. In punched the wind. And away slid the *Firedrake* up the river, watched by the entire town of Flashers, standing along the top of the dam, bowing.

"I've never seen them do that before," said Galahd with wonder in his voice. "You have made important friends, I think."

"He's from Lyonesse. Very magical place, apparently," said Bors. "Probably stuffed with magic himself."

Idris did not want to feel this distance between himself and his Knights. So he said, "Everyone's good at something. Bow to the Flashers." They bowed. With his mind, Idris said, *Thank you.*

A gift to one is a gift to all, said the Margrave in thought. *When you want us, call. We will come.* Idris felt the pride of his Kingship glow in his heart. The scabbard Holdwater had its power again. And he had the friendship of his companions, and now of thousands of Flashers. Friendship he had earned. Now he was truly a King again—

Something smashed into his mind: a freezing blast of beak and claws, tearing at his thoughts. He put his hands to his head and fell to the deck, muffling frantically, as he had been taught in the monsterstables of the Great Ambrose.

I am Fisheagle, Regent of Lyonesse, screamed the voice. *You are no King. My son, the Dolphin Murther, will be King at Darksolstice. I know you live, and I know you will surely die.*

The beak and claws tore, but the muffle fought them off. At last they went away. Idris lay shivering on the bottom boards, hearing the worried voices of his Knights.

He sat up and made himself smile into the anxious faces. He said, "My enemy the Regent of Lyonesse seeks me always. This time she found me by chance. But all is well."

And he and his companions put the Regent from their minds; yet Idris wondered exactly what chance it had been that had led Fisheagle to him.

Over the next six nights there were more Flashers. Word of the events at the first rapids seemed to have spread upstream, so they welcomed the *Firedrake* with enthusiasm. The hills gathered around the river as the boat rose. The wind blew from the west, driving them on. The Knights lay around and chatted. Bors talked politics to Galahd, and Tristan played Gawaine at an endless game of Dots with pebbles and an improvised board, bickering steadily over Gawaine's equally steady cheating. Idris sat a little apart. For somewhere in the back of his mind he could hear a roar of voices, and he could not think why. They sounded like monsters, but there were no monsters here. The hills did not shudder as the ground of Lyonesse shuddered. Still, he felt the voices trying to get into his thoughts—

Of course you do, said a voice in his head.

Idris froze.

Idris! said the voice. *How lovely to hear you! When I get out of this thing with your help I will take you to my darkgardens where the little fish swim red and blue and—*

"Monster, where are you?" said Idris, as quiet and cold as he could manage.

Close by, close by, said the voice, soft and cold. *We will be with you soon.*

"Away, thing," said Idris, his hair prickling with horror, and put up a muffle.

"Who are you talking to?" said Tristan.

"A monster," said Idris.

"A what?" said Gawaine, moving a pebble while Tristan wasn't looking.

"Cheat," said Bors.

"Me?" said Gawaine. "You're seeing things—"

"A creature from the Wellworld," said Idris. The river stretched ahead, gray and pocked with rain between banks now steep and wooded. "The most common kind they call burners. Men catch them for fuel in Lyonesse, for they live in the world of bitter water below the Wells, but they burn in air, hotter than wood or charcoal. There are other kinds that do not burn. But they speak directly from mind to mind, telling lies."

"And they are speaking to you?" said Tristan, frowning. "Here? How?"

Idris did not answer. He had been happy to be far from monsters, speaking with his voice to his friends, not his thoughts to monsters. Now he peeled away the muffle again and put his mind out to listen.

He heard the quickened drum of his own heart, the thoughts of his companions. He felt the quick thoughts of fish, the bright, top-speed lives of birds in the riverside woods. He put his mind wider, heard a wolf, the slow dreams of a hibernating bear—

Something screamed.

It was a terrible sound, horror and rage and despair, the sound of a living creature being burned alive. It was the dreadfully familiar sound of a burner in use.

But what was a burner doing in a wet forest a moon from Lyonesse?

He put his mind up to Kek.

The gull was cross. He did not like freshwater, and trees made him feel shut in, and it was hard to find the kind of food he liked. But Idris had no time for the feelings of sulky gulls. Through Kek's eyes he scanned the river's windings through the dark green hills. And saw what he had been looking for. Down there on the gray ribbon of water, five bends of the stream away but approaching at the tip of a white arrowhead of wake, was a boat. A boat tearing an effortless groove in the gray surface. A boat with no sails or oars.

The shriek of the monster grew louder in his mind. "What is it?" said Galahd.

"I see a boat with a monster to drive it along," said Idris.

"I have heard of this but never seen it," said Galahd, his eyes glinting with seamanlike curiosity.

"We must hide."

"Where?" said Galahd, waving a hand at the riverbanks, smooth and steep, and the boat, wide as a cart, long as a garden.

Idris said, "Get ready, then." He could feel disaster hurtling toward them. Gawaine was whistling quietly to himself as he strung a short, dangerous bow, and Bors was carefully laying spears into the rigging, where they could be mistaken for ropes.

He saw Tristan draw his cloak around him and vanish. Then the monsterscream tore at his head, and he put up the muffle, and the strange ship skidded around the next corner.

He had time to see that it was built of wood, intricately carved, with a blunt bow and a crew cabin that gave it the appearance of fierce, narrow eyes and a funnel on the cabin that jetted a dirty white smoke. He felt something batter at his mind, feel his muffle, and reel back amazed. He smelled the old monster-reek of burned flesh and brimstone. Then the boat leaped forward, aiming its nose at the *Firedrake*.

He saw Galahd put the steering oar hard over. But in a contest between wind power and monsterengine, monsterengine would always win. The boat's blunt snout turned after them and leaped forward. Idris heard Galahd shout "Hold on!" and drew Cutwater. Then there was the twang of Gawaine's bow, a scream, a gust of monsterstink, and a tearing crash, and he was sinking in water, dark, icy, bottomless.

He could feel the weight of Cutwater dragging him down. But when he tried to free his wrist from the loop, it tangled, and he heard himself think, Poor Morgan, poor Lyonesse—

Something grabbed his hair. He saw light. He gasped air. Someone had his tunic and was dragging him onto a platform on the side of the new boat.

"This one," said a voice. It belonged to a man with a deadwhite face and dead-white hair and eyes that were invisible behind a leather blindfold in which slits had been cut. "Take his sword."

Idris stood and coughed and spluttered and hung his head. He took longer about it than he needed, to give himself time to look around. The *Firedrake* lay capsized in the water. She wallowed, blew a long burst of bubbles, and sank. A silence in the ether. Then a screech and a roar, and the freezing mind of Fisheagle leaped at him. He muffled. Beyond the muffle, he heard her . . . *laughing.* The freezing mind roared away, leaving a hideous aftertaste of scorn.

"Idris?" said the voice of Bors.

Idris came back to himself. He was standing by a hearthstone on an outdoor platform close to the monsterboat's waterline. The other Knights crouched dripping by the hearthstone under the spear points of half a dozen men in leather armor and spiked helmets, one of whom (he was pleased to observe) had Gawaine's arrow sunk deep in his shoulder. He counted, pretending to cough. Galahd was expressionless, taking in the strange new boat. Gawaine's face wore an expression of injured innocence. Bors seemed to be making calculations. They were all there but Tristan. It was probable that Tristan was there, too, only invisible.

"The sword, or you die," said the albino.

"Who asks for it?"

"That is Earl Wulf of the Martenstane," said Bors in what he probably thought was a quiet voice. "He has a very bad reputation. He—"

"Silence, or I cut off your ears," said the albino Earl.

"Ooh. Painful," said Gawaine, as if to himself.

The Earl rounded on him. "Here," said Idris quickly. He drew Cutwater, holding the sword blade downward so it was no threat. He stepped forward, as if to hand it to the Earl. As the blade crossed the thick granite hearthstone, the hilt seemed to wriggle in his hand. He opened his fingers. The sword sank to half its depth in the stone.

The Earl's pink eyes swiveled at Idris behind the mask slits. He grasped the handle and tugged. A frown furrowed the brow above the leather mask. He tugged harder. Then he turned away, so no one could see his face. "Take them to the close-cabin," he said.

"Dearie me," murmured Tristan's voice encouragingly in the thin air close to Idris's ear.

And a few moments later there they were, locked in a little cabin beautifully built of hard, dark wood. "Well shot, Gawaine," said Idris.

"Not well enough," said Gawaine. He was too wild for small, dark places, and he sounded edgy and depressed.

The deck tilted under them. "We're turning 'round," said Galahd.

"Who is this Earl?" said Idris.

Naturally it was Bors who answered. "He is a servant of the Overlord," he said. "He will be taking us to the Wooden Palace, which is the home of the Overlord."

"If he can get us there," said Gawaine, defiant.

"He will," said Bors, matter-of-fact. "He is very cruel and very efficient."

"I have a letter to the Overlord," said Idris.

"Then give it to him, not to this Earl," said Bors.

As usual, the blunt speaking of Bors made perfect sense. Idris sat on the floor with his back against the cabin bulkhead and tried to puzzle it out. If the Earl was a vassal of the Overlord, why was he using monsters? He put his mind around the boat. He felt Tristan lurking on the afterdeck, wrapped in his cloak. His mind went into sleeping quarters, galley, cabins, saloon. There was a place he could not go, for it was walled with iron, beastbane. Through it he could occasionally catch the heavily muffled scream of the burning monster that powered the boat, and the thoughts of another, waiting, panic-stricken with the knowledge of its fate. Somewhere else on the boat was another mind, monstrous, too, but different. Idris stayed muffled, and waited, and thought about Fisheagle. Perhaps her last visit had not been mere chance. Somehow, she knew where they were. But she had not succeeded in entering his mind. Did she know where they were headed?

A nasty thought. Perhaps she knew in whose power they found themselves and considered she had nothing more to worry about.

Two days passed slowly as the unnatural boat forged upstream. Now and then it stopped to wait for the Flashers to dam the river, and Idris felt the little creatures' dim, loyal thoughts. To pass the time the prisoners did exercises, wrestling and shadowboxing, all against all, and Gawaine kept up his eternal game of Dots, with Bors instead of Tristan, though he complained constantly that it was no fun because Bors was impossible to cheat.

On what must have been the third evening, the door opened. "Idris," said a guard, and prodded him out of the cabin into the dark alleyway and down to the galley deck at the back end of the boat where Cutwater glinted in the lamplight, still deep in the hearthstone. Beyond, the river lay flat and black. "The sword," said the albino. "Move it."

Idris smiled as irritatingly as he could. "Not until you release us," he said.

Do as you are asked, said a voice in Idris's head. A woman stepped into the lamplight. Or what he thought was a woman; but as the light fell on her he saw absurdly long teeth and the fingers tipped with blood-red claws. Idris felt sick. He recognized the creature—not the individual, but the species. He had seen it first in *Of the Diversitie of Monsters*, the catalog of Wellworld creatures that Ambrose had given him; and again, in the flesh, in the catching room in the Old Well, where corrupt Captains of Lyonesse did their unholy fishing in the river of Wellwater that was drowning Lyonesse. It was an eelhag; there would be long fins running down its back from its shoulder blades.

"Mind your manners, creature," he said aloud. "Did Fisheagle send you from the Valley of Apples?"

"Valley of what?" said the eelhag, in a quiet, lazy drawl, spoken aloud, not in the mind. "I know no Fisheagle. I am of the Wells by the salt fires of the Lower Sea."

"But there are Wells only in Lyonesse," said Idris, frowning.

The eelhag sensed that he was off balance. A thick red tongue lolled around the jagged teeth. "A kinglet of Lyonesse would think his own Wells important and unique," it said. "Perhaps it comes as a blow to his pride to learn that there are also Wells by the Lower Sea. Many Wells, wide and deep, and many friends and Helpers and others of my world. And the men who made these Wells understand us better than you."

"We are not savages, you know," said the death-white Earl. "We trade with the Lower Sea. We understand the more refined life that only the Wellworld can bring. So we buy creatures like this for our use and pleasure."

This was wickedness itself, practiced in secret by the Captains of Lyonesse, punishable in others by instant drowning. Idris was so shocked that he dropped his muffle. The eelhag leaped into his mind, scoured his thoughts, and laughed at him. "There is a new world coming," it said. "You will get used to it, if we let you live, little King of Lyonesse."

"To the pit with you, slimething."

"Quiet," said the Earl. "Creature, is this truly the King?"

"It is. We know him. His blood is in the Well."

Idris said, "I demand to speak with the Overlord, your master."

The Earl smiled under his mask. "The Overlord is an old man, weak now, not much of a master. Lord Skrine, his nephew, rules in his place. And I have the honor to serve Lord Skrine, who is a man not frightened to deal with powerful creatures from other worlds."

The eelhag's tongue flopped out, and it purred. It was the most disgusting sound Idris had ever heard.

"Lord Skrine will be pleased to see you," said the Earl with an evil smile. "We have heard of the goings-on in Lyonesse, of course. Your fame goes before you. I expect he will keep you until such time as the Regent of Lyonesse may like to buy you from us. It will be a big price my Lord Skrine asks, but I am sure she will pay." He beckoned the soldiers. "Put His Majesty back with his friends." And they took Idris back to the Knights, his mind ringing with the scornful laughter of Fisheagle.

Day followed day, shut up in the cabin, hearing the shouts of the crew, and the screams of the monsters, and the clack of the Dots board, and the eerie Norn humming of Galahd, and the mind-whispers of the Flashers, and the boredom of Tristan, biding his time, wrapped in his cloak. All the time they drew closer and closer to the palace of the Overlord. And, as Bors pointed out, to Aegypt.

If they lived to see it.

Idris spent hours with his mind up to Kek, watching the river steepen and narrow as the hills closed in. Every now and then there came a distant babbling and shrieking from away to the south, as of monsters uncontrolled. The Wells of which the eelhag had spoken, perhaps. But why did the monsters make so much noise?

Other things were more cheerful.

Occasionally when he went out for fresh air, Tristan whispered in his ear. *Not yet*, said Idris in his mind. *Wait*. And once, he sent Kek far downriver to the first rapids. A ship was there, waiting. The Flasher dam had burst or been taken down. A man was stamping up and down on the ship's deck, a bear of a man with a nose like a strawberry and a dirty black beard. Idris recognized him as Tearingjaw. He was shouting for Flashers to build the dam. The Flashers only stood on the bank and watched him with their pearly eyes. And when Idris went to the mind of the Margrave, the Margrave said: *He will not pass yet.*

I thank you, thought Idris.

Flashers build up the right and break down the wrong.

The air grew colder. On the tenth morning the cabin door opened and a voice said, "Out."

Out filed the Knights, blinking, into the fierce light of a new world.

The ship lay alongside a quay on the shore of a brilliant blue lake. All around the lake huge mountains rose, gray crags beetling above slopes dazzling white. Idris had seen snow in Lyonesse, but he had never imagined that there could be this much.

Four men with a derrick were lifting the stone holding Cutwater onto a cart with runners instead of wheels. "What is this lake?"

"It is called Polkhorn's Eye," said Bors. "The Lugh flows out of it. So also does another great river, the Rhiann, I believe, that passes sunward into the Lower Sea."

Idris did not answer. Gawaine was looking at him sideways with his fierce green eyes, the prospect of freedom tingling in his blood, willing him to fight. He could feel the tug of Cutwater. He saw himself pulling it from the stone, the Knights seizing weapons and helping him cut a lane through the guards, taking ship for the Lower Sea—

Wait, said Idris with his mind. His duty to Lyonesse was to take Mark's letter to the Overlord, not to get himself and his Knights killed in a skirmish halfway to Aegypt.

The Earl's pale face turned eyeless toward them. "Get them horses," he said.

The horses arrived. Idris was given a shivering old mare, mere skin and bone and weeping sores. He thought sadly of Sunbeam. Half a day they rode, up, up, into the mountains. Gawaine was calmer now that he had a horse between his knees. He was laughing at Bors and Galahd blobbing uncomfortably along after him, followed by a pair of grim-faced guards. Behind the guards came a creaking sledge. When Idris put his mind out he could feel Tristan among the sacks it carried, cold in spite of the cloak.

Chestnut trees gave way to pine trees. Then the trees ceased altogether, so the road wound across the face of a steep snow-field with outcrops of rock. The snowfield climbed a roof-steep league to a great pile of walls and roofs and battlements, black and shining, leaking wood smoke into the pure blue sky.

"Behold the Wooden Palace," said the Earl. He had changed his blindfold for a full-face leather mask against the sun, but the sneer showed in his voice. As they drew nearer, Idris saw that this was indeed a marvel. The palace was enormous — bigger even than any of the mighty Welltowers of Lyonesse. The amazing thing about it was that it was made of wood: wood hard as mineral where it grew from the rock, heavy bark-faces above, and for the roofs bright shingles of cedar that spread a balmy smell down the pure mountain air.

They crossed a bridge over a chasm. Idris saw that where the timbers met the ground, huge, knuckly fingers of wood sank into the living rock. Roots. The palace was founded on a living tree, incredibly ancient.

They passed under an arch. A drawbridge thunked down behind them. Idris smelled pine tar and wood smoke. "I demand to see the Overlord," he said.

"I fear he is indisposed. The men will conduct Your Majesty to his quarters," said the Earl, with a bow and a smirk. "Take him away."

The prisoners were hustled across a yard and into a passage floored with polished wood. Hard hands dug into Idris's arms and dragged him away from his Knights. He heard Gawaine shouting at someone to get their hands off him, and Bors telling him to calm down. The voices faded behind him as guards hustled him up a flight of stairs and through a heavy door. Wooden bolts shot. He stood in the half-dark, alone.

And lonely; he had not realized how used he had become to the company of his Knights. To occupy his mind, he made a detailed inspection of his new quarters.

If it was a cell, it was a comfortable one. There was a stove, stoked from the corridor. There was a bed, a table with food, a chair. And there was a window, glazed with sheets of horn that cast a dim, yellowish light over the wooden walls. Idris went to the window and moved aside one of the panes.

The view was beautiful, but not encouraging. A wall of wood swept down from the windowsill, then became a cliff of living rock. The wooden wall was smooth as glass, polished by centuries of wind loaded with ice crystals. A fly would not have found a foothold on it. The cliff plunged into a gorge. Idris could not see the bottom, but he heard the faint boom of heavy water tumbling among boulders.

He went and sat on the bed and despaired. His sword was gone again, and without it he was a mere child, not to be allowed an audience with the Overlord. He was a fool to have started this journey. He was too young. His protector Ambrose was sunk in the Sundeeps. He had led his Knights straight into captivity. Being a King made no difference. Was a disadvantage, indeed. Skrine would send a message to Lyonesse, and the Regent would send Mountmen for him or arrange to have him murdered. And Morgan would be lost, and so would the kingdom—

A faint noise caught his ear. He looked up.

There was only the room, quiet, dim-lit, smelling of ancient wood.

The noise again.

Someone was drawing the bolts on the door.

The door inched open, and a face appeared around it. It was an elderly pink face, with mild blue eyes that blinked. It looked as if it spent a lot of time outdoors, doing something nonviolent, like gardening. It said, "Are you by any chance Idris of Lyonesse?"

"I am," said Idris, and found himself bowing, in the Manner.

"Good," said the face, pushing open the door and showing that it was connected to a small body dressed in a suit of brown overalls that seemed recently to have been in contact with a flower bed. He said to an invisible guard, "You can lock me in if it will make you happy." The door closed. "Permit me to name myself," he said. "I am Ulf Brightsword, whom men call the Overlord. And I must say I'm very glad you're here."

FOUR

The Overlord shuffled across to the table and said, "Do you mind if I sit down?" He sat and pawed at a floorboard with the toe of his right shoe, which (his legs being short) barely touched the ground. "Dreadful," he said, as if to himself.

"What is it?" said Idris.

"Rot." The Overlord shook his head. "The palace is falling to bits. Wicked shame. It's my nephew, Skrine. He hates it. Says it's old-fashioned. Now look. Are you the Idris Ambrose found?"

"I am," said Idris, feeling like a boy in a dark cave spotting a candle.

"How is my dear old friend?"

Idris felt a great warmth. A friend of Ambrose would be a friend of his. But his happiness cooled, for he had no very reassuring answer. "In the vault below his tower in the Sundeeps, where he is confined until he finds a means by which dragons may breed."

"Always up to something, dear old chap," said the Overlord, as if Idris had said that Ambrose had gone fishing. Idris handed him King Mark's letter. The Overlord read it. "Yes, yes, quite right, we'd love to help. Idris of Lyonesse, welcome to the Wooden Palace, planted by my twenty-eight times great-grandfather. Had you ever heard of it?"

"Never, to my shame."

"Pleasant Manner, pleasant Manner," said the Overlord to himself. "Planted as a seedling. It has grown, as you will see. I'm very proud of it, actually." He shook his head sadly. "But it's dying, you know. Awfully sad. It's that boy Skrine. He's my sister's son. She married a nasty chap who came up the river from the Lower Sea. They had Skrine, and then both of them died of the bright sickness. Skrine's twenty-four now, and he hates this place, so he fills it up with bandits like that Earl you met, and disgusting creatures and engines that come from the manufactories by the Lower Sea, and honestly sometimes I think I'm not master in my own house. And the worst thing of all is that he's trying to dig a great hole through the roots, a Well he calls it, even though the water here's perfectly good already. I think it is his hole that is killing the palace."

Idris bowed his head. He had seen the madness monsters could produce in men. He said, "Can't you stop him?"

"No time," said the Overlord, looking away, ashamed. "It's too awful. I spend all day every day with the gardeners, trying to cure the rot. Most of my people hate the new people, but a thug with a bow can rule a hundred good citizens without.

Besides, if I fight Skrine, he'll burn the palace, because he knows I love it. They're at it now. Listen."

They sat quietly. The wind sighed around the wooden eaves. And through the polished floorboards came a dim thumping and the shriek of burners.

"Barbarians!" growled the Overlord, grinding his teeth.

"I am sorry," said Idris and fell quiet, silenced by the pain in the old man's thoughts.

"It's falling to bits," said the Overlord. "It knows nobody cares. Oh, my poor castle." He pointed at a patch of floorboards that had a dull, blackened look, with a crisscross of cracks at its edges. "Dry rot," he said. "Nothing anyone can do."

Idris unwrapped the scabbard Holdwater from his waist. He laid the brightly worked sheath on the rotten boards.

There was a silence, short but deep. Then the Overlord slid out of the chair and dropped to his hands and knees over the rotten patch. Gently, Idris lifted the scabbard.

The cracks and dullness were gone. The board shone hard and whole and bright as new.

"Well, I must say," said the Overlord, eyes shining. "This is simply *marvelous*. What can I do to help?"

"You could set me and my companions free."

The Overlord swung his little legs and looked miserable. He said, "Skrine wants you kept for the Regent of Lyonesse. All these creatures from the Lowland, they listen to what you're thinking. There would be trouble."

Idris bowed. *But you promised*, he said with his mind.

85

"I'm not as young as I was, you know," said the Overlord.

Idris bowed his head. The Overlord was too old to be fighting monsters. There was no ally here.

"Can't get out of the palace now," said the Overlord. "I used to, even when the drawbridge was up. I used to put the ball down the hatch in the Flight Attic, you know, and get out that way." The blue eyes were watching Idris, not mild anymore, telling him something. "Nobody goes to the Flight Attic anymore. Certainly not you."

"Don't I?" said Idris. Perhaps the Overlord was not too old after all.

"And I can't just lend you one of the ships in the Willow Harbor to get down the river to the Lower Sea, because they don't belong to me. They belong to merchants. Some of them are very kind. Like Wollick, who has the *Sand Goose*."

"*Sand Goose*," said Idris. The Overlord might be old, but he was canny. He was showing Idris a way out.

"Well, then," said the Overlord, sliding down from his chair with a bump. "Good luck." He waved an arm at the wooden walls. "All green it was, in spring, and not a crack in it. Think of it," said the Overlord. He looked up, his eyes hard and bright. "Good luck with your sister. If you get back, you can count on me to find a way out of the palace and bring men to help you." He shuffled out of the room.

Idris heard the guard salute, the bolts slam to. He sat in the window and gazed at the blue-white peaks stretching away into the distance.

He had been given useful information. If he wanted to escape Fisheagle, find Morgan, and gain his kingdom, he must act on it. But first, he must get out of this room.

He put his mind out and found Tristan, hungry, lurking near the kitchens. A short wait, then a slither of bolts. The door opened. "Th-there you are," said an expanse of empty air.

"Tristan," said Idris, grinning at space.

The air flickered, and the lanky form of Tristan appeared, throwing his cloak over his shoulder. "Guard's in the privy," he said. "Got any food?"

Idris gave him some bread and a slab of strange boiled-milk cheese. Tristan sat down and started to eat like a starved wolf. "They fed the others," he said, through his mouthful. "Bors said it was disgusting, and Galahd said they had to make the best of it, and Gawaine sat on Bors's head to make him shut up before someone got speared. And they fed you. But the kitchen cupboards were all locked, and I couldn't get the key."

"Listen," said Idris, and outlined a plan. "Can you do it?"

"Of c-course."

Tristan stuffed the rest of the food into his pocket and was gone. The door closed. The bolts shot.

Idris waited, his mind up in Kek's. The gull sat sulking on a pinnacle of the Wooden Palace, looking disapprovingly over the miles of frozen mountains. There were other birds up there, red-footed choughs that danced around the spires and turrets like burned black leaves. Kek disapproved of them, too.

Idris sent him flying over the dizzy tangle of courtyards and towers. In one of the courtyards he saw the ship's hearthstone, with Cutwater sunk blade-deep in the granite. Over another, he spied a roof of cloth hiding something that emitted dust and noise. Skrine's Well, perhaps. It was not sensible to dig a Well in a mountaintop. There would be a great distance to dig, and no guarantee of a Wellworld portal at its bottom. It looked as if Skrine might not be a man of large brain. The thought was encouraging.

The day faded. A guard came in to light the lamps. Idris heard his feet go down the corridor. Silence fell over the castle, except for the steady thump of the Welldiggers. Then even that stopped, and there was only the sigh of the wind around the wooden walls and the deep, slow creak of the palace dying.

Idris dozed, the scabbard Holdwater wrapped around his waist. He was woken by the sound of the bolts. "Come," said the voice of Tristan from the shadows. Idris took off his boots, padded across the polished boards and out of the open door. "Two hours to dawn," said Tristan. "I have found the F-Flight Attic and let the others out and stopped Gawaine from shooting everyone in sight. They will already be there. We must hurry."

"My sword," said Idris.

"What about it?"

"I can't leave without it."

"But—"

"It's in a courtyard," said Idris. "I can take you there."

"No," said Tristan. "There are guards everywhere."

"We must," said Idris. "We'll use your cloak. Go ahead. Tell me if it's clear."

Tristan loosed a weary sigh, pulled the cloak around him, and vanished. Idris stood with his head out of the door, waited, watching the glow of the horn lamps reflected in the dark floorboards. The lamps blinked as Tristan passed them. Tristan's hand appeared in midair, beckoning Idris on. Idris closed the door carefully, shot the bolts, and padded after him, boots in hand.

They passed down staircases hewn out of the thickness of branches, through halls vaulted with roots, and past suites of rooms with fresh green leaves growing on their doorjambs. There were carpets underfoot now, and from a patio lined with galleries there came a waft of incense and the music of tuned horns. In the carpeted places the guards were thicker, and Idris found himself hiding for minutes at a time. But at last they arrived in the cloister surrounding a yard. And in the middle of the yard, driven into the hearthstone, the sword Cutwater gleamed faintly in the starlight.

The cloisters were dark; anyone could have been standing there, watching. Idris backed into an alcove and pulled his boots on while Tristan made a circuit. The wood here smelled ancient, with a mushroomy whiff of rot.

"Clear," said Tristan's voice from the air beside him. "Come under the cloak."

It seemed a long way to the middle of the yard, one foot in front of the other, bumping each other under the cloak, feet and elbows escaping from cover, skin crawling with the thought of eyes in the tiers of windows. Then they were at the stone, and Cutwater's hilt was warm and friendly to his hand, and he drew it from the stone as easily as a spoon from a cup, feeling the power flowing into him as Idris the furtive boy once again became Idris, True King of Lyonesse.

He turned and ran back across the yard, then out of the cloister, following the finger that Tristan held outside his cloak. He began to mount stairs. On the first landing he thought he heard a step, and stopped to listen. Nothing. Holding Cutwater ahead of him, he walked up into the dark.

He could hear something... *sniffing.*

And felt a thought. *Dear Idris,* it went. *Come, and I will drink your lovely blood.*

His flesh crawled. He said, low and urgent, "Back, Tristan!"

Another sniff. He could feel the monster in front of him in the black dark, a mere leap away, drooling fangs agape. His sword hand came around. Cutwater sang in the air as he brought it in a humming waist-high arc. It slammed into flesh and bone with a thud that jarred his arm. Something screamed, a terrible scream in the mind. A lantern shutter clanged.

There was light.

The eelhag was standing in front of Idris, blood pouring down its robe, red mouth wide and hideous. He drew Cutwater back and brought its blade around again. The dreadful head leaped from the body. As head and body fell, they changed from something human into something waxy and pale, tentacles and fangs coming and going until they hit the floor and bubbled, vanishing.

There was the sound of someone being sick. Not Tristan, though his face had a greenish cast. Someone farther downstairs. "Run!" said Idris, retreating up the stairs.

A rush of feet. "Halt!" said a voice from below.

He heard the hum of drawn bowstrings. A squad of soldiers stood on the lower landing looking up, dark-browed under their spiked helmets, eyes shifting nervously to the monsterflesh bubbling down the bare wooden stairs. Idris said, for the benefit of Tristan, "I will deal with this alone." But how? He turned. "I am Idris of Lyonesse," he said to the squad. "Your Lord Skrine will not thank you if you kill me."

A man stepped forward. No, not a man. A youth, with a little fair wisp of mustache. He said, trying not to look at the horror on the stairs, "Give me your sword."

Idris put out his mind. He felt the youth's disgust at the monster. "That is one of Lord Skrine's allies," he said, pointing at the monstermatter on the stairs, the wood beneath it scorching and dying. "And yours, too, if you serve him. They are killing the palace. They are killing my kingdom."

The youth nodded, frowning. "Idris?" he said musingly. "I have heard of you."

"I am pledged to fight monsters," said Idris. His heart beat more strongly. He could feel that the speaker loved the Wooden

Palace, despised Skrine, admired him as King of Lyonesse. Feeling as if he were taking a step in the dark, Idris said, "Join me."

Hesitation. A sense that the fair youth was weighing things over. On the one side, his duty to Skrine, friend of monsters. On the other, a plain and noble wish to do good.

Idris said, "Lord Skrine is killing your palace. If I live, I shall save it and your country and bring peace."

The youth's face had turned very pale, and he glanced at the remains of the eelhag. He said, "This is true. My ancestors loved this castle." A pause that lasted forever. Finally he said, "I am with you."

Idris said, in the Manner, "Name yourself."

"Lanz."

"Lanz, you may escort me to the Flight Attic. We will not need these men, for where could we go from there?"

"Nowhere," said Lanz, in his clipped soldier's voice. "Squad, dismiss."

"He was locked up," said one of the soldiers. "How did he get out?"

"Sorcery," said Idris, leering horribly. The soldier backed away hastily.

"I said dismiss!" snapped Lanz. The squad left, feet squelching in the remains of the eelhag. "After you, my lord."

Idris climbed. Behind him, Lanz said, quiet and urgent, "Lord Skrine had spies in the squad. He will come after us. There is no way out of the Flight Attic."

Idris nodded and climbed on. The stairs felt gritty under-foot, as if they were not much used.

"We will be trapped," said Lanz, serious but not (Idris noticed) nervous.

"Perhaps."

The air was becoming colder. The stairs made a spiral around a fat wooden pillar, narrowing, as if they were climbing up the inside of the great limb of a tree. At the top, the way was blocked by an ironbound door. "The Flight Attic," said Lanz. Idris battered on the door with the sword hilt.

"Who?" said the voice of Gawaine.

"Idris." Sounds came from far below: metal-shod feet, barked orders.

The door opened. Idris and Lanz stepped through. It was a big room, twilit. The rest of the Knights were there, their grins of relief at seeing Idris lit yellow by a single candle flame.

Idris sheathed Cutwater. He said, "This is Lanz. He was a soldier of the Wooden Palace, but now he is a Knight of Lyonesse." Lanz bowed stiffly. Idris could see that Gawaine was suspicious. It was not to be expected that a horse thief like Gawaine would approve of a soldier.

But Gawaine introduced himself, in the Manner. Lanz did the same and smiled. It was a wide smile, not at all military, and it seemed to cause Gawaine to revise his view. Bors grunted, and Tristan made an exaggerated bow with a sweeping move-ment of the arm, and Galahd made his greeting politely but absently, because he was studying the Flight Attic.

The place was icy cold. As Idris's eyes grew used to the half-light, he saw that this was because it had only three walls. Where the fourth wall should have been was emptiness, and beyond it a view of the dizzy upper branches and turrets of the Wooden Palace in the gray predawn. In the middle of the floor was a trapdoor. Beside it stood a wheeled trolley bearing a huge ball of metal, as round as Idris was tall. A fat rope ran from the ball, over a pulley in the ceiling, and into a channel between the rafters.

Boots thundered on the stairs. A sword hilt pounded on the door. Lanz raised his finger to his lips. "Who?" he said.

"Ordinant Grutt. Open, dog."

Lanz unshuttered a little slot in the door and thrust his blade through. There was a shriek, followed by the sound of a falling body. "An unpleasant man," said Lanz, wiping his sword with military calm.

"We should hurry," said Bors.

"Hurry to do what?" said Gawaine, yawning because he knew it would annoy Bors.

"To learn to f-fly," said Tristan.

"That's not funny," said Bors. "There isn't time."

"Hush," said Idris. There was no sound but the sigh of the wind in the rooftops and muffled voices from the stairs outside.

Put the ball down the hatch, the Overlord had said. Idris bent and opened the trapdoor in the floor. A chill, musty air

94

sighed up at him, with a feeling of enormous depth. He said, "Push that trolley."

Feet crashed on the stairs. Several sword hilts hammered on the door. Someone was shouting for axes and a ram.

Bors and Lanz went behind the trolley and pushed. As it came to the lip of the trapdoor, it tilted. The huge metal ball slid off and plummeted into the dark, taking the rope with it.

The rope ran over the pulley in the rafters and through the snow on the roof, down a special groove in the castle's wooden wall, and through a trench dug down the mountainside into the chasm, up the other side, and across to the little wood on the hilltop a full league away. The rope leaped out of the snow and tautened, shedding ice flecks, making an aerial runway a league long, spanning the chasm.

"I *see*," said Galahd, smiling with a seafarer's pleasure in ropes and pulleys.

"What's it for?" said Bors.

"I think it's a f-flying machine," said Tristan languidly.

"So let's go," said Gawaine, impatient for the open spaces, wild eyes swiveling at the door.

"I don't like heights," said Bors.

"Well, you're going to have to get used to them."

The metal ball reached the full extension of the rope with a twang that made the wooden tower vibrate like an Iber lute. And there it was, taut as a fiddle string, stretching from the Flight Attic to a little grove of trees on the skyline.

"Nobody has used this since my father's father's day," said Lanz. "How very interesting."

"*Interesting?*" said Bors, through chattering teeth. "We're going to *die!*"

"You frightened?" said Gawaine.

"Of course I am," said Bors, eyes closed to blot out the awful drop.

Lanz had gone to a rack on the wall and taken down a handful of slings, each topped with a grooved wheel. Idris wriggled into a sling and hooked the wheel over the taut rope. He watched the companions do the same behind him. Lanz said, "Nobody has used it for many years. The rope may be rotten."

Something heavy crashed into the door. There was the sound of splintering wood. The ram had arrived.

"It is p-possible that the rope will be rotten, but it is c-certain that the swords will be sharp," said Tristan. "Jump."

"There must be a brake," said Galahd, looking around. "Or our weight will pull the ball up again."

"Hurry!" said Gawaine.

"Patience," said Galahd and pulled a lever. A pair of metal jaws sprang in on the rope and clamped it tight. *Crash*, went the ram on the door. Splinters flew.

"I'll go first," said Idris, in a voice that threatened to become a squeak. "It's me they want. If the rope holds, come after me. Bors next."

"No," said Bors.

"Yes," said Tristan and Gawaine, smiling as each of them gripped one of Bors's arms above the elbow.

"I'm not jumping," said Bors.

"No," said Tristan, with a dreadful grin. "We're th-throwing you. Hook him on, Lanz."

Idris said, "If the rope breaks, give yourselves up and swear loyalty to the Overlord, not Skrine. If it works, last man bring all the slings left over."

Crash, went the ram.

"The lock's going," said Galahd.

Idris ran across the room at the empty wall and leaped into space.

And fell.

He thought, Here I am, and there is the blood-colored sun peering over the white mountain, and it will be the last thing I ever see, and my poor Knights will be captive—

The sling caught tight under his arms and the pulley wheel howled above his head, and the keen air was parting on his face, and he was yelling a long yell as he flew over the chasm, half a league under his feet, and hurtled at bird speed toward the grove of trees. Just as he thought he was going to smash into the wood like a slung stone, the rope was sloping uphill, and he was slowing, and the ground was rising to meet him, and there in the exact spot for his feet was a snow-covered step. He landed on the step, shrugged out of the sling, and shouted for joy.

He looked back. The Wooden Palace stood huge against the dawn-pink sky. Little dots were skimming down the rope. The first turned into Bors, his scream of terror becoming a long, wild war-yell. Then came Gawaine, Tristan, and Galahd, Lanz bringing up the rear. They piled into the snow and stood up, shaking and laughing and slapping one another on the back. The rope began to hum. The little figures of soldiers were approaching, slowly, on improvised slings without wheels. Idris put his hand on Cutwater.

Suddenly the rope went slack. Far in the distance, a tiny figure fell into the gorge, twisting as it fell. A thin scream, abruptly cut off. Bors turned white and looked away. Nobody was laughing anymore.

"I told you," said Lanz. "It was an old rope. Come." He led the way to a hut at the summit of the ridge. Idris followed, the scream ringing in his mind.

"Here," said Lanz, kicking snow away from the door and hauling out a long machine like a boat with runners.

"What is it?" said Gawaine.

"It's what we call a sledge," said Galahd. "Obviously."

"Oh," said Gawaine, abashed for a change.

The Knights hauled the machine onto the ridge. From the cornice of snow on top, Idris saw the long white slope fall easily to the brilliant blue lake and a group of log buildings, tiny with distance, on the shore. There were ships anchored off the buildings; the Willow Harbor, no doubt.

"In," said Lanz.

The sledge had four benches, each wide enough for two riders. They climbed in. Lanz said, "Go," shoved the sledge, and leaped on as it started to slide—slowly at first, then faster and faster, the broad runners bringing it up onto the icy crust of the snow, so the early sun made rainbows in glittering fans of ice crystals and the cold rush of wind pulled at their faces. Gawaine gave a long howl of joy. Down swooped the sledge, then up over a bump; it took air and flew over a little stand of pines, came down on the far side with a crash, and coasted across the flat shore of the lake, slowing as Lanz hauled on a lever that dug in a brake. They came to a halt under a stand of orange-twigged trees: the willows from which the harbor took its name, thought Idris as he laughed with the Knights, the danger behind them blown away by the wildness of the ride.

"They will be here in three hours," said Lanz, who had a sober, calculating way about him.

The laughter stopped. Idris climbed out of the sledge.

One of the buildings was a stable. The other was an inn. Idris loosened Cutwater in Holdwater and pushed open the inn door.

The room was cold and dirty, with straw on the floor and a fire of green logs leaking smoke at the ceiling. Half a dozen men were sitting at rough tables eating stew out of wooden bowls. Reminded of its own lack of brekfuss, Idris's stomach rumbled loudly. He said, "Merchant Wollick?"

A fat man sat with a fat boy at the table closest to the fire. He had not let Idris's arrival interrupt his eating. Now he looked up. His little eyes were bright and penetrating, and they rested on the rich hilt of Cutwater. "Yes?"

"I bring the compliments of the Overlord. We seek passage to the Lower Sea."

A thick silence fell. "Nasty place, the Lower Sea," said Wollick through his next mouthful. "Might I ask the reason?"

Idris said, "We are traveling to instruct ourselves in the world." Well, it was not quite a lie.

"A laudable thing in the young," said the merchant. "Don't you agree, Merk?"

His companion looked up, scowling. "I'm *eating*," he said.

"My son," said the man and sighed. "Even greedier than me. You hungry?"

"Yes," said Idris.

A bell started ringing outside. Lanz said, "That's the palace alarm."

An old woman put her head around the serving hatch. "Someone's escaped from the palace." She licked the end of her nose, squinting keenly at Idris and his companions.

"They're with me," said the rotund merchant. "That right, Merk?"

"Yes, Dad. Pass the bread," said his son.

"Do you know, Merk," said Wollick, "I think that seeing as the *Goose* is all loaded, it might be time to pull up the anchor and hop it? And perhaps this young gentleman and his friends might like to come along, and if I might venture a suggestion, take brekfuss on the ship, not here?"

"With the greatest of pleasure," said Idris, reversing toward the door.

"I'll be rearguard," said Lanz, drawing his sword and turning his handsome smile on the other eaters who were reaching for weapons in the manner of people who smelled a reward. Wollick rummaged in his capacious gown, produced a large battle-ax, and added his smile to Lanz's. The other eaters suddenly became more interested in their food than their weapons. "Merk, go to the larder and see what you can find."

Merk pushed his plate away and burst into action. He vanished into the back regions of the inn, returning almost instantly with a large basket piled with food and topped with a live cockerel. "Ham, bread, fruit, and this nice fat bird," he said.

"Excellent work!" cried his proud father. "Off we go, then."

And off they went into the hard blue light, nailing the doors shut behind them.

The procession named themselves in the Manner as they crunched through the snow to the foreshore, though Idris merely admitted to being of the Westgate. "The Overlord said you are very kind," said Idris. "He was right."

"Kind? No," said Wollick, looking upon Idris with his shrewd little eyes. "Rumors get around, and I know a King when I see one. I feel that in years to come you will be a useful person to have in my debt. Now. Let us get aboard the *Sand Goose*."

And out Galahd rowed them, through the brash-ice of the lake fringes to the ship, as stout as her owner, loaded down with mountain cheeses and seedling house-trees that would (given thousands of years and correct pruning) grow into palaces. Up came the anchor, jingling with ice crystals. Away she sailed, the Knights of Lyonesse standing in her bow, off the placid blue of Polkhorn's Eye and on to the ice-gray waters of the River Rhiann, which flowed into the Lower Sea, the river-road to wicked Aegypt, where Morgan lay captive.

FIVE

The young River Rhiann burst out of the lake like a gigantic child from a nursery, leaping and kicking, roaring down rapids and howling through gorges that dropped cart-sized clods of snow on the deck. The *Sand Goose* was built to be solid, not nimble. Wollick handed out heavy poles and stationed the Knights in the nose under the guidance of an old man with the blue whirlpools of the River Pilots tattooed across his brow. Galahd got the hang of it instantly, and Merk was an old hand, his mighty heft giving his pole plenty of power. The others watched, unwilling to make fools of themselves. Lanz muttered that this was no job for a soldier, and Tristan and Gawaine made jokes for each other's benefit and told anyone who asked them to join in that they were too sensitive for manual work. Bors had still not recovered from his terror in the Flight Attic, and was not about to risk further humiliation. But Idris seized a pole of his own, and got the hang of leaning with his feet planted on the deck and the far end of the pole firm on the rock. After a while he saw Lanz watching him. He could hear the officer thinking even without using his monstergroom skills of mind, If the King can do it, I can do it myself. Lanz picked up a pole, and put the tip on a rock, and leaned in on the word of command. As the *Sand Goose*'s clumsy bow came slowly away from the threatening mass of granite and into clear water, Tristan and Gawaine laughed more loudly. Idris paid them no attention; he guessed that they were not liking the fact that a Knight as new as Lanz was proving more willing than they were. Finally they each picked up a pole, and after a few tentative prods they began to like the exercise. And Tristan, seeing Bors leaning against the mast with his arms folded, said, "Get a move on, lazybones."

Bors looked offended. "I'm not lazy," he said. "I'm sulking."

"Which is not very clever," said Gawaine, conveniently forgetting that until a couple of glasses ago he had been sulking himself. "Is it?"

Bors thought about this. "No," he said finally. "It isn't." Grasping a pole, he spat on his hands and went to work.

So down the river the *Sand Goose* bounced, day after exhausting day, ship, crew, and cargo. They moored each night by the path that ran down the riverside. Idris sometimes saw Wollick's large head cocked, as if he was listening for sounds from upstream. But all he heard was the roar of the river and occasionally the bellowing of a team of aurochs towing a ship against the current, pace by agonizing pace, to beat the spates of the spring thaw.

Gradually the mountains drew back from the shore, and the river slowed and became more placid, and the night frost-nip gave way to a warmer air that smelled of resinous leaves and cooking smokes. And as they went south across Tyrrhen another smell made Idris frown and fall silent. It was only a whiff, but from time to time he thought he caught the stench of burning monsters.

On the eighteenth day out from the lake, the *Sand Goose* was moving slowly down a gray mirror of water under a gray roof of cloud. The forest on the banks was sparse, its floor grassy. An elk looked up, with its eyes only, for the huge antlers made its head too heavy to lift. The birds were not singing; everything was quiet. Wollick said, "Two more days and we will be in the Green."

"What's that?"

"You'll find out," said Wollick.

Idris bowed, as was mannerly, and went to eat nuncheon with the Knights.

The group was sitting on the boat's bottom in two lines, facing one another across the hearthstone. Merk was with them; nowadays he seemed to prefer their company to that of the crew. Idris went to sit in the middle of the row. "No," said Bors, blunt as usual. "You're the King. Go on the end."

If it had been Tristan or Gawaine, Idris would have expected a tease. But Bors never told anything but the exact truth as he saw it.

"If you hadn't come through the wood," said Gawaine, "we would still be stealing horses in the rain."

"Or eaten," said Tristan.

"And if you hadn't come to Eytgard," said Galahd, "I would be old Tearingjaw's boat-kerl, and Bors would be cleaning up after that stinking old Duke."

"And if you hadn't come to the Wooden Palace," said Lanz, "I would still be a Lieutenant of the Guard, doing things I did not like doing on Skrine's orders against the instructions of the Overlord, who was my King."

"And when you came into the tavern," said Merk, "when I was having some stew, I definitely knew you were a King."

"You d-didn't stop eating, though," said Tristan.

"Eating helps me think."

"You must do a lot of thinking," said Gawaine.

"Whereas you are remarkably thin, no-brains," said Merk.

"Idris has helped us all to b-better lives," said Tristan, his thin, freckled face unnaturally solemn. "This is because he is not only the rightful King of Lyonesse but a superior being all 'round."

Idris threw some bread at him, and the talk rumbled away to other subjects. But even in jest, such remarks made Idris uneasy. Certainly he was a King. But when there were people in high seats, people in lower seats started jockeying for position and seeking favor. He remembered the days when he and the other prentice monstergrooms had sat at the table in the Wrestler's Elbow. Morgan had been there....

Best not think too much about Morgan, yet.

The table in the Wrestler's Elbow had been circular.

Idris walked to the head of what would have been the table if there had been one. He said, "It is true that I am a King. And I am happy to sit at the head of the table. On condition that the table is round."

They stared at him, jaws hanging. Then Bors slammed his palms together and gave a great bellow of laughter, and everyone else started to laugh, too. And from that time forward they sat around the hearthstone in a circle, and were knit by the circle, so that the strength of one was the strength of all.

As they were finishing their nuncheon, Wollick cocked an ear. "Ah," he said. "The cataracts. Positions, please, gentlemen."

Idris realized that for the better part of a glass, the sound of voices had been backed by a heavy roar. He and the Knights stood up. The river was narrowing. The pilot was at the steering oar. The roaring grew louder, echoing from the walls of what was now a gorge. Suddenly the mirror of water bent and broke, and became a long, thunderous slope, heading downhill as far as the eye could see. And in Idris's nostrils was the unmistakable smell of bitter water and burning monsters. He had last smelled it in the Valley of Apples in Lyonesse. What was it doing here?

A whaleback of rock slid by. But Idris was gazing past the helmsman, at the base of the slope. Or where the base might have been, if it had not been hidden by a sheet of greenish vapor that stretched away southward until it became the sharp, curved edge of the world.

"There," said Wollick. "You started in Lyonesse and came to Ar Mor, you say. You went to Eytgard and came up the River Lugh into the mountains to Polkhorn's Eye, where it rises. And we've come down the River Rhiann, so you've crossed the mountains by water, and this last couple of weeks we've been coming down what you might think of as a shallow staircase with water a-running down it. And from here on, things keep going downhill. In more ways than one," he said grimly. "That fog is what they call the Green, and it is a dirty fog of Wellwater and monsterbreath and sunheat and mucky green-slime rottenness. Down there under the Green is the Lowland, which is a huge plain, full of nasty things, but it will come as no surprise to you, King Idris, because they are the same kind of nasty things as you get in Lyonesse, I hear, only worse and bigger. And the River Rhiann goes across the Lowland until it runs into the Lower Sea. And if we turn left on the Lower Sea and do not get murdered by corsairs, we come at last to Aegypt on its far or southern side. Which is the nastiest thing of all, because though they do not have monsters there they have worse things, by all accounts. I will not be going to Aegypt," said Wollick. "But you can't miss it. Go to the Lower Sea, get in a ship, and sail southeast until you hit the far side. If you hear screaming, that'll be Aegypt. Now all of you take a breath of clean air and remember what it tastes like, because with the wind from the south, chances are you won't get another for moons."

Idris saw his Knights grave-faced, taking that last clean

breath. He took one himself. A last view of fresh spring hilltops against the blue; then an eddy of vapor, and the *Sand Goose* and its crew dived into the Green.

There was little air in this world, and what there was made your eyes sting. The ship was still sliding down cataracts, but the river seemed to be slowing. At the end of a day of coughing and streaming eyes, she floated into a broad pool along whose margins stood blackened buildings, each with a pier jutting into the river and, alongside the pier, ships tied one beside another. There was the clank of machinery, and jets of smoke, and (when Idris opened his muffle a chink) a familiar shrieking in the mind.

Idris went to stand next to Wollick. He said, "They are burning monsters."

"That's what makes the Green," said Wollick.

"They bring them from Lyonesse?"

"What would they do that for, when they can get as many as they want in the Lowland?" asked Wollick.

"They've got Wells?"

"Thousands of 'em," Wollick said. "Monsters spilling out like sausages from a sausager's parlor. And a very filthy mess they do make. My grandfather said when he used to trade here, this was all green grass and trees, all the way down to the shores of the Lower Sea. But it's sunk, and the rivers flow filthy, and the Masters don't mind, so long as they get rich."

"Masters?"

"Monstermasters. They dig Wells and tell the monsters what to do. Though to tell the truth, I think the boot's on the other foot nowadays."

Idris nodded grimly. The Masters sounded like the Captains of Lyonesse, becoming rich as they ruined the land.

"Well, here we are, gents," said Wollick, as the pilot steered them toward a wharf. "Rosebud Creek. We'll stop for the night."

"Where do you go from here?" said Idris.

"Not to Aegypt, like I said," said Wollick, wobbling with horror at the notion. "We will be working our way downriver to the northern banks of the Lower Sea, trading as we go, you know how it is. We'll be hoping to meet ships from the other side of the Lower Sea. There's a desert over there, the Great Stone. The closer you get to the Great Stone, the better the price you get for mountain cheese. Though you have to stop before it melts, of course. Terrible place, the Great Stone. Goes on forever, heat fit to boil your brains, but they do love their cheese."

"So to get to Aegypt?" said Idris.

"We'll take you to the sea," said Wollick. "Then you can take one of the stone boats from the Volcanoes. They unload at Thbee. Now, then. Tie her up alongside, then zupper."

They ate in the circle, as usual nowadays, making it big enough for Wollick and the crew.

"It's like this," said the whirlpool-tattooed pilot. "The snow'll be melting up there with the spring wind coming off the Lower Sea. So the river'll fill up, and anyone trying to get down the cascades will get killed, and that will include little Lord Skrine and his lads. Unless they ride down the towpath, and who would come by road if they could come by water instead, eh? Nah. If we don't get trouble in the next couple of days, we won't get trouble at all."

He was right. There was no trouble in the next couple of days.

The nights were different.

———⋖⋗•⋗⋖———

As he unrolled his sealblanket in the *Sand Goose*'s bottom that night, Idris heard the clink of wine jugs from the tavern on the quay, and Wollick and the pilot singing in harmony, celebrating the safe threading of the cataracts. He pummeled his cloak into a pillow, made sure that Cutwater was a hand-stretch away, and closed his eyes.

But sleep did not come. He heard the shouts from the shore, and the gurgle of the river past the hull, and the coughing of the Knights as the monster-tainted air caught their throats. And then another sound...

He drew in a breath and held it. He could hear many hooves, the jingle of harness, and the clink of armor. Then the crash of a flung jug from the direction of the tavern, and Wollick's voice, bellowing. Idris's heart slammed him upright. Then he was up, shaking the Knights awake, Cutwater naked in his hand. He ran along the quay by the *Sand Goose*, casting off all the mooring lines except the last. And here came Wollick, a

111

lumbering shadow in the lamplit murk, and the pilot, tumbling aboard in a gust of wine.

A voice from the murk cried, "Halt!" And there in the torchlight stood the White Earl, like an unhoused hermit crab without his mask, a shadowy throng at his back. One of Gawaine's arrows clanged off the Earl's helmet. Idris brought Cutwater down on the last mooring line. The current swung the *Sand Goose* out into the river. "Archers, draw!" barked the Earl.

"Down!" said Idris and flung himself into the bottom of the boat as a fleet of arrows sang overhead. Against the vaporous lamp glow he saw Gawaine stand again, notch, and loose, heard this time the shriek of a voice that sounded like the Earl's. "Shoot!" he said. Another fleet of arrows. Then a freezing blast, beak and talons, and the mind of Fisheagle lanced out at him and saw him groveling in the *Sand Goose*'s bottom and laughed a scornful, infuriating laugh, as if she was certain she had nothing to fear from him. Idris pushed his head into the ship's rough planks, muffling for all he was worth. At last the mind-beam left him.

When he looked up he saw the shore far away, the quay lights, haloed with murk, glinting on a last shower of arrows falling short. And Wollick's voice. "Pilot!" it was roaring. "Make me a course downriver!"

"Aye-aye!" said the pilot. "Oars, lads!"

The Knights and the crew set the oars and started to row. The wharf was a great distance astern now, a blurred line of lights hanging in space. "Perfect," said the pilot in a strange, fuddled voice. "Took a bit of a bang on the head back there. But I have our position exact. Lashings of water, next stop—"

Nobody ever found out where the next stop was supposed to be. For at that moment there was an enormous crash, the *Sand Goose* lurched sharply to starboard, and Idris felt icy water pouring over his feet.

"I expected that," mumbled the pilot. "I know zackly where we are."

Idris did not believe him. The water was at his knees and getting deeper. All around him, people were shouting as they realized the same thing. "Abandon ship!" cried a voice.

The ship's punt was alongside. Everyone tumbled in. Idris found himself squashed up against Wollick, who seemed to be weeping for his cheese.

"Where to?" said a voice.

"Don't worry," said the pilot. "I know zackly—"

"Your wits are mazed," said Wollick from behind a large handkerchief. "Lads, row away from the lights unless you want an arrow in you."

They rowed. After three glasses, the punt's nose grounded on sand with a faint *crunch*. Everyone piled out.

The night was starless, as black as a squid's ink-cloud. Idris found he was tired, and cold, and hungry. But Morgan was burning in his mind. He said, "I am sorry about the *Goose*, Wollick. We will just have to walk to Aegypt. Agreed?"

"Agreed," said voices in the night, six of them, by the sound of it. Tristan, and Gawaine, and Bors, and Galahd, and Lanz. And...

"Merk?" quavered the voice of Wollick in the dark. "Are you leaving?"

"Father," said Merk, "I love you dearly. But there is more to life than cheese."

"There's a living in cheese," said Wollick.

"I may come back to it," said Merk, strong and proud. "For now, I go with my fellow Knights to Aegypt."

"Good boy. Silly boy," said Wollick. There was the thump of two large people embracing. Then he said, in a voice thick with tears, "I would have done the same when I was your age. When they lock you up in Aegypt, think of us here, diving for the cheese."

"I will," said Merk. "Cheer up, Dad."

And the Knights of Lyonesse filled their water bottles from the clean river and walked into the dirty night.

⊰•⊱

They slept huddled in the lee of what seemed to be a sand dune and woke at dawn, mouths dry in the hot wind still blowing from the sunward. The ground shook. The light grew. Sand stretched away on all sides, sheets and dunes and dust devils. "On," said Idris. And on they walked over the shivering ground as the pale disc of the sun rose on their left.

After an hour, Merk said, "I'm hungry."

"There's no food," said Galahd.

"Oh yes there is," said Merk. From the folds of his merchant's robe he pulled three loaves of coarse river bread and a block of boiled cheese and laid them on Lanz's shield.

The companions sat in a circle, with the shield in the middle. Once, Gawaine would have swiped more than his share, and Bors would have told him what he thought of such behavior, and Tristan would have mocked them both, and Idris would have kept the peace while Galahd thought his own Northern thoughts and waited for the wrangling to end. But now nobody took more than his share, and they ate in silence. Not a tense silence, though: a thoughtful silence, grim and full of purpose. After brekfuss, Idris bowed to Merk and said, "Thank you."

An expression of pleasure flitted across Merk's large features. "Foraging is my specialty," he said, slapping his belly.

On they went. The sun climbed the sky. At noon it stood well to their right, the land still low and sandy, the wind harsh and dry. Every now and then, curious shapes loomed out of the fog: ruins, and dead trees ghostly in the eye-aching haze, their bark hanging off in strips. And always the monsterstink and the shuddering, as if the land were being shaken from below. It reminded Idris of the Poison Ground of Lyonesse, only dry where the Poison Ground was wet.

A glass after the sun had passed the meridian, they came to a river. It was a welcome sight, for they were thirsty, and the heat was fierce. Merk pulled out his water bottle and took a deep swig. "Might as well empty it before we refill," he said.

"Don't finish it," said Idris. The river looked too slow and too black.

"Why not?"

Idris walked up to the margin. He bent. The acrid smell of it stung his eyes. "Wellwater," he said.

"So?" said Merk.

"Not the kind you are used to. Poison. That's why nothing grows here."

They looked for a ford, found one, and waded across, then scraped the stinging water from their legs with sand and set off once again. That evening they camped in some ruined buildings by what had once been a wood and finished Merk's bread and cheese, leaving only enough for a sketchy brekfuss. The next morning they walked on, stiff and sore, with empty water bottles and emptier bellies. Merk was too tired to complain, and even Tristan and Gawaine made no jokes.

Toward the middle of the morning, Gawaine said, "Look." A few moments later, Idris made out a line of shadows hazy in the mist. The shadows grew bigger. Soon it became clear that they were some kind of animals, kneeling to rest. Men moved among them.

As the Knights came up to them, Gawaine spoke to the animals in a low, kind voice. A man ran from between the beasts. He was a small man, stooped, carrying a spear. "Halt or die!" he said and doubled up in a storm of coughing.

Tristan's voice sounded in Idris's ear. "Keep him talking and I'll r-rob him," he said.

"We are not robbers," said Idris. The little man had finished coughing. His face was yellowish and sweaty. It looked more scared than ferocious. Idris bowed deeply, in the Manner. "Allow me to name myself. I am Idris of the Westgate, and I travel with my companions."

The small man seemed taken aback by this civility. But he bowed and said, with worried looks at the Knights from under his brows, "And I am Alkzah of the Plains, and I trade with my dromals. But the dromals are sick, for we had bad water, the Tyrrhen Springs having been spoiled by a Well since we last visited them. All the Lowland is poisoned by these Wells."

"Let me see," said Gawaine. He moved among the coarse flanks of the couched animals, murmuring to them so they seemed to murmur back. "Yes, they are sick," he said. "But if they have fresh water, the poison will pass through them."

Alkzah's worry seemed to lift a fraction. Idris put his mind out, felt the little man's anxiety and loneliness, and said, "We will travel with you and protect you, for the Wellwater has weakened you, and we are strong."

"I have no coin," said the small man quickly.

"We will pay well for bread and water untouched by Wells," said Idris.

"And any other food you've got, obviously," said Merk.

"Where are you going?"

"To Aegypt. To keep a vow. Can you show us the road?"

"Better, I will take you along its beginning. But you will die." Alkzah frowned. "I think you saw my mind. You are not a creaturefriend?"

"Creaturefriend?"

"One who talks to the things from the Wells."

"Monsters, we call them. I talk to many people and things. That does not mean I agree with them."

"Good," said the little man, swaying with exhaustion and fever. "My father and my father's fathers traveled these plains. Stories have come down to me of a time when there was clear air and forests of cool trees around springs where men and dromals drank unharmed. But men came and found Wells where monsters lived, and it seems that the Wells were gates into a world of poison, and the men used the monsters, but as they used them the land sank, and poison spilled out, and the world is as you see it now. It is a bad fate for the Lowland."

"My own country of Lyonesse has suffered in the same way," said Idris. "We will travel together, and you will show us the road, and we will do what we can."

***

So the Knights journeyed along the Aegypt Road with the caravan of Alkzah Fixx, consisting of Alkzah, his four wives, his twelve children, and a herd of stamping, belching, three-humped dromals, which under Gawaine's doctoring soon returned to health. It was not a prosperous caravan. Its business was to call at the little villages that somehow managed to scratch a living from the shuddering soil of the Lowland, and buy their flabby vegetables and bitter milks, and sell them to the dwellers in the shanties outside the Welltowns, escaped serfs for the most part, who drew from this fare a little nourishment and a taste of home. Galahd and Gawaine helped with the animals, so they gave more milk. Merk did prodigies of foraging, and Bors cooked what he found into dishes that astonished and delighted the children of Alkzah and gave his wives some rest. And Idris and Tristan and Lanz steered the little band through the mobs of rovers that prowled the Lowland stealing what they could and wrecking what they could not steal.

As they forded stinking rivers of Wellwater—no burner licenses here, not even the consoling fraud of an Hour of Thanks or a Treaty—they drew ever closer to the land of Aegypt. And all the while the land shuddered, and when Idris unmuffled, monstervoices roared, fierce and triumphant in a way he had never heard them before, as if the Lowland would bulge up and the Wells would burst through.

On the tenth evening, the Knights sat as usual around a little fire of dried dung and listened to the coughing of scavenging animals. Gawaine and Tristan were singing an Ar Mor dancing song for the children, with Bors joining in the choruses out of tune. Idris felt an unease in Alkzah. He said, "What is it?"

"We are coming to Bitter River," said the little man. "It is a city, with Wells and much evil. I go to the little houses at its edge to sell what I have, but I will not go to the river bridge that carries the Aegypt Road, for the town is full of monstrous things, and many who go in do not come out. After the market I am turning the caravan back." He paused. "If you try to cross the bridge in Bitter River, you will certainly die. You are good people, kind and noble. It would be a waste if you were merely killed by monsters or their Masters. Come on with us."

Idris was touched that Alkzah valued the Knights' protection so highly. He said, "We will cross this bridge or find another, for to Aegypt we must go."

"There is no other bridge."

Idris shrugged. "Then we will find a way of crossing this one." He threw another dromal-pat on the fire, rolled himself in his sealblanket (too hot in this desert, but saved from riverwreck and captivity, a reminder of home), and slept well.

Next morning, the serfs from the town's edge came across the dirty sand to the market Alkzah and his people had laid out among the couched dromals. Idris watched from the shadows of a tent. They were a poor lot, eyes dark-circled, dressed in rags, many with weeping sores on their legs and arms, as if they spent too much time in Wellwater. As the serfs began to straggle home with their little bundles, the Knights bade a courteous farewell to Alkzah, refused all payment, and spread out among the returning serfs, seven more figures added to the twoscore.

Idris heard Gawaine's voice, then Tristan's high and droll, and a couple of little boys laughing at what they had said. He found himself walking next to a woman carrying a bundle under her clothes. From among the strands of her dirty black hair a pair of gray eyes looked out, red and sore but remarkably sharp. "Who are you?" she asked, in the harsh croak of the Lowland.

Idris shook his head. They were not talkative, these serfs, and silence would be more convincing than lies.

"I don't know you," she said. "You a spy from the Masters, then?" Her face was twisted and fierce, the way faces in Lyonesse twisted when people talked about the Regent and the Captains. "You—" She stopped. From her bundle came the sound of coughing, small and thin, but with a rending sound that sounded as if the cougher was being torn apart. The fierceness on the woman's face turned to pain. She pushed back her cloak, revealing a tiny baby, froglike and pale except for a thread of red blood running from the corner of its tiny mouth. "Look at that," she said. "Dust, poison, famine. Go back and tell your Masters that if the babies are dying there won't be nobody to work for them, and monsters don't plant corn or sew clothes."

Idris and the woman had stopped walking. The Knights had stopped, too. The serfs from the market trudged past, hazy in the Green, without the energy to look around at the two ragged figures facing each other over the limp body of the child.

Idris said, "I am not from the Masters."

"That's what they all say."

He looked at her steadily, watching the anger in her eyes turn to something like curiosity. "Give me the child," he said.

She hesitated. Then she handed Idris the tiny bundle. It smelled sour; not dirty, but ill. He looked down at the face. The skin was bluish, the bones high. Not just ill. Dying.

He squatted on the ground, laid the baby on his cloak, and shrugged out of the baldric that held his sword. He said, "Get better, baby." He drew Cutwater and laid Holdwater gently over the infant's ribs, finding a bright pinpoint of life in a dark sea of pain.

The pain vanished. The pinpoint grew into a huge, brilliant universe of hunger and wanting. For a split second he saw his own face looming, felt the panic in the baby's mind, saw the mother's face beside his own. Then Idris was back in his own head, watching the pink tide rise in the child's skin, the blood at the corner of its mouth dry and vanish, the eyes open, the little arms reach for the mother . . .

"*Waaah*," yelled the baby, demonstrating that its lungs were perfectly healthy again.

"What?" said the woman, gathering up the child and clasping it to her.

But Idris could not answer. For as he had opened his mind to the baby, other things had come in: a babel of monsters, screaming and churning, and a feeling that here the monsters were terrifyingly close, a mere skin of earth away. Then the freezing roar of Fisheagle, searching, tearing other minds to get at his, screaming, *You're here, I hear you drawing your sword. Helpers of the Lowland, he's here, break through and drink blood—*

"Lord?" said the woman, hugging her baby.

Idris forced himself to smile, Fisheagle's screech still ringing in his mind, feeling the ground pressing upward under his feet. He slipped the baldric back over his head and drew up his rags to hide the sword. He said, "It is not safe here."

"I will leave," said the woman. "I will take my baby and go into the mountains."

The ground seemed to bulge under Idris's feet, as if they were walking over a mere bladder that might at any moment burst, spewing monsters. "Perhaps that would be wise," said Idris. He pressed a finegold into the woman's hand and bowed to her. The Knights stood watching, blurred by the Green. There were no jokes now, no discussions. They had seen what he had done, and they were proud to be part of it and to protect him now that they felt his weakness after Fisheagle. Idris rested a moment, taking comfort from their protection. Then he said, "On," and resumed his march over the shuddering ground, followed by the woman's cries of thanks. The Knights marched with him.

Idris half expected the ground to open and monsters to pour out and devour him at Fisheagle's bidding. But they did not. Perhaps her power was less than he thought.... At any rate, he knew now that she could hear him draw Cutwater. That was how she had found him when he had used Holdwater to heal the little Flasher. Any time he drew the sword, she could find him.

Well, he was Aegypt bound. Aegypt was a place of terrible power, by all accounts. But at least the power was not Fisheagle's.

On trudged Idris and his Knights. The road led at first through little clusters of huts. The hut-villages soon gave way to a sprawl of buildings, half-visible in the dark, which Idris decided were manufactories. Above them flares of light jumped and coiled, poison-violet and bile-green and raw red. When he opened his mind a chink, the scream of burning monsters was so fierce that it made his brain sore. Behind them crooned other voices, soft but monstrous. *IDRIS*, they cooed. *IDRIS, WE KNOW YOU'RE HERE*. By the flicker of the light he saw the faces of the Knights, set and strained. Their minds were less open than his, but they had no muffle, and the pain must be fierce.

They walked till their feet got tired, and still they were passing through the manufactories. The light ahead brightened, and Idris felt a hollowness in his stomach that had nothing to do with hunger. For against its flicker stood the shapes of tall towers, all the same height.

"What are they?" Tristan said.

"Chimneys," said Gawaine.

"No smoke," said Galahd.

"Peasant," said Bors.

"Palace rat," said Gawaine.

"Welltowers," said Idris, before a quarrel could develop.

"What are they f-for?" Tristan said.

"Catching monsters. The land has sunk so far that the Wells must be built up so they don't flood it out. They are the reason the Lowland is as it is."

Lanz said, in a tight, hard voice, "I am glad I turned against Skrine the friend of monsters, then."

The towers of Lyonesse were at least in good repair. As they drew closer Idris saw that these had a broken and neglected look. The air was full of the harsh stink of Wellwater. In a flash of sick-pink light he saw one tower broken off halfway, and a fat black torrent pouring out of it.

"What's *that*?" said Gawaine, as a huge, lumpy shape wriggled away into the darkness, leaving a thought like a whiff of foul gas: *I have arrived, and here I will breed and spread to cover the face of the world and spoil it utterly.*

Lanz said, "This cannot be allowed."

As in the Wellvale, the city was clustered around the bases of the towers. Here in the center there was a jostling throng of people, well-dressed and rich-looking, and dromals and horses richly caparisoned, and torch jugglers, and a man on a street corner playing a flute, accompanying a dancing lizard. A troupe of acrobats was performing in a square. At first, Idris thought they were human. Then he saw that each of them had three legs.

"Monsters," said Bors. The acrobats bounded together, became one many-tentacled beast, which leaped house-high into the air, split into a dozen creatures that tumbled, landed, bounced, recombined, and resumed their dance.

"Seen 'em before," said Merk. "The keepers buy 'em from the Masters. Highly profitable. All monsters are."

"It's not natural," said Gawaine. "What are they *for*?"

"Fun," said Merk. "These ones, anyway."

"Nothing is just for fun," said Gawaine, shocked. "Horses want to run. Wolves want meat. What does this thing want?"

"To come into our world from its world, and drink blood, and wreck everything," said Idris.

"So we must stop them," said Lanz, who saw everything in black and white. "Starting now." He put his hand on his sword hilt, started to draw, and looked down when he felt Tristan's hand grip his sword wrist.

"This m-might not be the perfect moment," said Tristan, smiling a lazy but not altogether genuine smile.

"We'll get our chance in Lyonesse," said Idris. There were Guardians about, big men in sea-green metal breastplates and spiked helmets, drifting through the crowd like sharks through mackerel. "But first we must go to Aegypt, or we have failed."

"Which means," said Galahd, "we have to find this bridge."

Idris was glad to hear the practical Northern voice. To tell the truth, he was deeply shocked. Such a profusion of monsters could not have arrived here without a very flood of Wellwater. And once Wellwater was in the world, there was no way of getting it out again.

Not that the Bitter River crowd cared.

It wandered down the streets eating and laughing and throwing silvers to the mountebanks, the women wearing jeweled fangs, hair braided and waxed into tentacles, imitating monsters. And some of the crowd were sucking the blood out of small live animals they bought from vendors who stood by piles of cages: Crosses, flaunting their monstrousness.

"Give us silver?" said a voice. Idris looked up. A lanky, mean-eyed man was rattling a tin mug of coins in front of him while a small, ill-smelling monster hovered over his head, shooting fire from its eyeballs. "For the Amazing Blazeo?"

"Go away," said Idris.

"Oh," said the mean-eyed man. "Too snobbish for entertainment, is it? Too pure, my lamb?"

Eyes were beginning to swivel at them. Idris rummaged in his purse, forcing a smile. They must not draw attention to themselves.

But Bors could not tell a lie. "You heard what the lord said," he snapped. "Go away. Your creature is an abomination. We hate it."

"Lord?" said the man, the mean eyes narrowing. "We? Who is this lord, and who are we? Eh?"

Idris saw that one of the Guardians had stopped and was watching him and his Knights with cold eyes. Outside the muffle, monsters called, *IDRIS! IDRIS!*

He shoved a couple of silvers into the hat. The mean-eyed man made a deep, sarcastic bow. "Bless you, my lord," he said. "And your companions. 'Scuse our great wickedness, too. Oh dear, yes."

Then there was a shout, and Idris looked around, and his heart sank. Bors was holding a rat-faced man by the scruff of the neck. The rat-faced man was kicking. "He was trying to pick my pocket," said Bors.

"I was not!" shouted the rat-faced man. "This geezer caught hold of me and tried to nick my purse. Look!" And he held up a purse that Idris knew belonged to Bors.

"Don't be silly," said Bors, incapable of guile.

But the rat-faced man had friends in the crowd. "Thieves!" they cried. "Footpads! Spies!" Lamplit faces closed in. Idris's hand went to Cutwater, though he knew that seven against seven thousand were odds that even Cutwater could not beat. Then someone shoved him violently in the back, and he was flung off his feet, and his head banged a corner of carved stone. His vision darkened. As it cleared he struggled to his hands and knees, catching a glimpse of his Knights standing back to back in a tight circle, facing outward, a ring of spiked helmets closing in on them. He thought, They are dead. Then he frowned. The spiked helmets were not using the sharp ends of their spears but the handles, as if to capture, not kill. Above the crowd, his eye caught Tristan's. The tall boy was not wearing his cloak. But as Idris watched, he fended off a blow with a curiously blurred left hand, and winked at Idris.

Then Idris knew what had blurred the hand. He put up his own. Tristan made a flinging movement in his direction. Idris's fingers closed on cloth. Tristan went down, leaving Idris staring and holding his cloak.

Faces were turning on Idris now. He ducked into a deep doorway, heart thudding, swung the cloak around his shoulders, pulled up the hood, and slid into the crowd. Bodies banged into him. Voices swore, surprised. He grasped Cutwater's hilt and began to creep toward the rumpus. But he could hear that the fight was over, and when he put his mind out to Tristan's, he felt windedness and anger and confusion. There were spiked helmets around the Knights. Some of the helmets were binding their hands. He drew closer.

A sallow man with a red turban and rotten front teeth had sidled up to one of the helmets. "Six of 'em," he said. "I'll give you ten silvers a nob."

"Twenty," said the helmet. "You'll get a hundred each in the city."

"Like you've been there and you know," said Red Turban, in tones of deepest scorn. "There's the feeding, and the transport, plus they look like troublemakers; not much demand for troublemakers. Fifteen, and if you don't like it you can sliddle their neckses and slip 'em in the Bitter as monstermeat."

"Pirate," said the helmet.

"Happy to be called so," said Red Turban. "Bring 'em to the ship any time you like as long as it's now. Cash on delivery."

The helmet made a disappointed sound and beckoned a donkey cart. His fellow Guardians picked up the Knights and slung them in like so much firewood. Idris watched. Holdwater had cured his head, but he felt heavy with despair. They would never find Morgan now.

The cart set off down a side alley. Idris wrapped the cloak around himself and trotted after it. The alley sloped downward, dark and empty except for the cart. He could hear water at the bottom, and the shouts of men, and the creaking of cranes. The stink of Wellwater was strong enough to make his eyes burn.

At the bottom of the hill, the lane arrived on a quay. There were ships alongside it, receding into the dark downstream and upstream. The bridge was a stone's toss overhead. In its center was a pair of guard towers. Idris could see people up there, brilliantly lit by monsterlight. There were guards examining what must have been passes that let you through a barrier. If they had tried to cross, they would have been caught....

They had been caught anyway.

Men were pulling the struggling Knights out of the donkey cart and shoving them up the gangplank of a ship. There were shouts from the bridge, a sudden glare of monsterlight from a monstermaster's retinue. By the light Idris saw that the hull of the ship was painted a deep blood-red, and that its bow ran down to a long, sharp ram tipped with a bronze skull.

Idris stopped, hearing his heart thunder in his ears.

A ship like this was burned on his mind. He had seen it alongside Penmarch's *Swallow* in the storm after the escape from Lyonesse. He had seen it in the last dying flash of Penmarch's loyal mind. It was a ship like this that had carried his friend and sister, Morgan, away into slavery.

The ship up whose gangplank the slavers were driving his Knights was an Aegypt corsair.

Idris found himself grinning a cold, dark grin. They had lost one Aegypt road. Now it seemed they had found another.

He wrapped the cloak around himself and ran lightly up the gangplank.

The guard at the top looked up and blinked but missed the flicker in the glare and shadow of the bridge. Idris walked down the deck. He could hear voices from below, the clank of a spoon in a cooking pot, Merk wondering aloud what the food was like. "Aegypt fare," said a harsh voice with a heavy accent.

"These are beans. With worms in 'em."

"Beans are good. Shut your mouth." There was the crack of a lash on a body.

"Beans? Mm, nice," said Merk, voice tight with pain. Idris was down the steps now, pressed into a corner, invisible in the cloak. He saw the Knights with a great crowd of other captives in a barred enclosure like a cattle pen. Merk was hiding a yawn with an arm that bore the weal of a many-thonged whip. The barred gate clanged, and one of the guards turned a key in an iron lock, and the whipman lashed the bars instead of Merk.

"Welcome to our voyage to Aegypt," said the harsh voice. "Some people find sea travel healthy. I do not think you will be among them." The guards clumped onto the deck, taking the lantern with them. There were the sounds of unmooring. Idris wrapped the cloak around him, slid the door open a crack, and went on deck.

The corsair ship was moving. Wells and manufactories were sliding by. Black monsterbacks heaved in the dark flood. *Good-bye, Idris*, said the monstervoices, huge and soft and cruel, taking what was in his mind and using it for their own purposes.

You are going to Aegypt where we cannot come. You will never be seen again, farewell, farewell!

Idris sat in the shadow of the ship's forecastle, watching the corsairs with their fierce faces pad sure-footed about their work. He was tired, and the Green burned his throat. His Knights had been made slaves, and there was no way he could see of rescuing them.

But he was heading toward Morgan, which was what he had set out to do.

·PART TWO·

The Helpers had been spiraling for long ages. Now they clustered tight around the pillars of light that lanced down from the Wells.

*Among the throngs she flew, dancing among their mountain-sized immensities, brushing their slimy flanks with her leathery wings. She rubbed up against their cold monstrousness, and bathed in their thoughts (*rend, tear, *went the thoughts;* blood, flood, never burn*), and reveled in the knowledge that when it was finished above, she would rule below (*yes, yes, *boomed the Helpers in their soft, cruel voices,* you will rule, you will rule*). While up in the tower her body lay, the pulse ticking slow in the white throat, the lids closed on the pupil-less eyes. And below her the land lay in perfect subjection, from Kernow to the Westgate, from the Southgate to the Sundeeps. Things that had been turbulent were still. The Welltides blew filth into the land, and the Captains caroused with the dreadful things that offered themselves in the river that flowed through the Old Well. And Lyonesse worked energetically to sink farther into the trap that had sprung at the first discovery of the first seep from the Wellworld.*

And she had heard the hiss of the sword being drawn, and she knew that now the last obstacle was far off in the Lowland, going to Aegypt to be crushed.

Something stirred in her — triumph, perhaps. The tick in the neck vein became a pulse. Fluids gurgled. The taloned fingers twitched. The lungs heaved and crackled.

She sat up. She walked to the window. The bronze shutters wheezed open. She screamed as the light burst in on her eyes. She looked down on the land.

Away it swept, Wellvale, lake, Poison Ground; and beyond it the woods, and the downs, and the moors, and on the horizon the line of the Wall, and above it the bright-burning sea.

The upper lip drew back. The yellow fangs dented the scarlet cushion of the lower lip. The land was green, the moors blooming, the oaks in full leaf, and even the stunted bushes that would persist in growing in the crannies of the Mount showed twisted flowers. Summer was coming to Lyonesse.

The last the kingdom would ever see.

The shutters wheezed to. Fisheagle, Regent of Lyonesse, lay down on her bed of stone and plunged back into the cold, bottomless, lovely dark.

SIX

The days passed. The corsair ship plunged southeast through the black waves of the Lower Sea toward the shores of Aegypt, Kek the gull riding effortlessly in the backwind from the sails. The breeze was hot, always from the southwest, and it lifted the Green from the sea and rolled it in billows over the deck.

Idris spent the days wrapped in Tristan's cloak behind the anchors in the cable tier. In the graveyard watches he stole food from the galley and made his way down the companionway to the slave pens, where he talked to his Knights through the bars. In the days, the Knights sang songs of home—Gawaine and Tristan at first, then Bors, much more in tune now, and eventually even Merk and Galahd and (last of all) Lanz, though Lanz had trouble with the harmonies. The corsair crew was big and powerful. There was nothing to be done until they were on land; perhaps nothing then, though Idris did not allow himself the thought.

The days dragged on. No land showed itself.

Then one morning while Idris was lying under the cloak with his chin on his hands, gazing at the bronze ram-tip cutting the black water, a puff of wind hit his face. A new kind of puff; not sour and sickly, like the wind from the Well-tainted Lower Sea, but hot and sandy, with a hint of wood smoke.

The wind puffed again. Then the Green writhed and was torn away. And there across the horizon lay the land.

It was a low, brownish-yellow land, dotted with clumps of trees — odd topknots of greenery perched on long brown stalks, but trees nonetheless, wonderfully soothing after the nakedness of the Lowland and the black roll of the sea. Beyond the trees was a platform of cut stone. On top of the platform, buildings rose in steps to an enormous height, windowless, as if whatever lived in them walked in darkness. At the foot of the buildings were more trees, miniatures of the ones by the shore.

Not miniatures. They were as tall as Lyonesse oaks. But the buildings were so huge that they dwarfed even the hugest of trees.

And somewhere in that monstrous place was Morgan.

As the sun sank, the wind changed and blew from the sea. Soon the ship was sailing up a broad river, with towering banks of smooth stone a league distant on either side. Three days they sailed up the river. Just after noon on the fourth they arrived at a city that crowded down to the smooth brown water in man-made cliffs of stone. Two rowing boats came out from the land, crammed with men, catwalks down their middle, and on the catwalk a man with a whip. The corsairs dropped towropes to the rowing boats, and the rowing boats dragged the ship toward the shore. Idris crept out of the cable tier; the anchors would soon be needed. He went and put himself on top of the fo'c'sle and watched.

The anchors plunged into the soup-brown water. The singing in the slave hold stopped. A bowshot to starboard, the river walls loomed high. The sun glinted from the red-raw patches on the rowers' shoulders and the flies that crawled on them. He had been brought up next to the walls of Lyonesse, the greatest in the world. But beside the walls of Aegypt, the walls of Lyonesse were no better than garden hedges.

He swallowed, dry-mouthed. He opened his mind, cautiously, for fear of monsters.

There were no monsters. There were only the hard thoughts of the crew and a cloud of fear from the slave hold. He was pretty frightened himself.

A crash of weapons. Two corsairs came and stationed themselves on either side of the companionway. They were in what must be shore armor, with helmets wrought to look like skulls, and breastplates in the form of rib cages, and bronze breeches like thighbones, entirely different from their corsair sea clothes of cotton and wool. Idris put his hand on his sword hilt. Cutwater would take care of them, and then...

And then what?

In his mind he saw the slaves coming on deck, himself attacking the guards. And the guards and corsairs hurling themselves on the slaves helpless in their chains. And a massacre that would leave the Knights dead, and Morgan in captivity, and Lyonesse kingless, a filthy waste like the Lowland.

There was the sound of shouting. Idris peered out of his hood. Another boat was alongside: a barge, this one, its superstructure a cage of bars. The corsairs were hauling it tight against the ship's side. A sliding gate in the bars opened. A section of the corsair ship's side flopped out like a trapdoor, making a gangway into the barge. And Idris understood that the Knights were not going to come on deck to be saved or massacred. They were going to be transferred from one cage to another. Aegypt handled its slaves as efficiently as the grooms of Lyonesse handled their monsters.

Idris saw the Knights herded across the gangplank, blinking in the glaring noon. He sent out a thought to Tristan. *Still here*, he shouted with his mind, too loudly, for the guards by the rail shifted uneasily, feeling the thought. *I'll come*, he thought, felt the flush of hope that warmed Tristan's mind, then muffled again as the skullhelms turned, searching.

He moved back among the barrels. The barge crawled away toward a towering stone wall. It passed through an arched portal. A grille dropped behind it. Idris unmuffled, put his mind out, and searched beyond the walls.

Thousands of voices poured into his mind. Most of them sounded agonized, desperate; those would be Aegypt's slaves, wanting above everything to be free. Behind the slave minds were others, chittering like insects—normal people, who did not care whether they were free or not as long as they were fed and entertained. And behind them again were other minds, huge and awful, the minds of vast mad creatures lumbering in pits like tombs. As bad as monsters, but entirely different from monsters...

No Morgan. It was ridiculous to have expected Morgan to be there, waiting.

He must get ashore.

The sun was sinking. It fell straight down, quite unlike the sloping roll that took it below the horizon of Lyonesse. One moment it was a bloody ball behind the enormous buildings. The next it had gone, and night had fallen like a black cloak.

A dinghy rowed out from the land. People came aboard the corsair ship. There were voices from the stern cabin where the crew lived. There was the clink of glass, a woman's giggle, a strange, sliding song.

Idris crept aft. The voices sang on. He padded over the cabin roof. The visitors' dinghy was tied to the taffrail, the river gurgling along its planking. He untied the painter, dropped into the dinghy, and cast off. The current bore him swiftly away.

When he was a safe distance from the ship, he began to row. The exercise made him sweat. The Aegypt night was hot, and he had scarcely moved for a week. He rowed to the quay nearest the arch through which the slave barges had passed. There were stairs behind the quay, heading up into the thickness of the wall. He started to climb. The stairs went on and on, flight after flight, lit by strange glowing sconces in the walls. He stopped counting steps after ten hundred, for his heart was hammering in his ears and his lungs felt like fire. Just as he thought they would never end, he stepped onto a flat stone pavement. He heard voices and smelled smoke. Pulling the cloak around him, he peered around a corner of masonry.

At the far end of a little courtyard, two men sat by a brazier, the flames dancing in their bronze armor and skull helmets.

Feet sounded on the steps below. Idris tugged the cloak around him and pressed back against the wall. A man walked past him and into the courtyard. The empty eye sockets of the guard's skullhelm turned on him. "Show," said the guard.

The man showed a sort of plaque attached to a chain around his neck. The skullhelm nodded. He handed the man a token from a little stack at his side. The man fitted the token into a slot in his plaque and passed on.

Apparently Aegypt was not a country you could just stroll into.

Idris took a deep breath and wondered what he should do. He found his hand on Cutwater's hilt. And decided.

<hr />

High on a smooth stone ledge the gull Kek opened his eyes in the dark. Far below, the figure of his master walked into a pool of light. Thanks to the cloak, it was invisible to the human eye. Not to the gull eye, though; Kek could see it perfectly.

The figure moved toward the two men in metal suits. The sword flicked out. It was too far away for sound, but it must have hit, because the figures went over sideways and lay still; and the Idris figure bent and took something from the neck of one of them, then something else from a table, and pushed the two things together, and hung it around his own neck, and ran through the gate between the fallen soldiers.

Kek had half unfolded his wings. But his acute gull senses told him that there was no death down there. So he folded them again. As Idris walked into Aegypt with the sentry's plaque at his breast, Kek put his head under his wing and went back to sleep.

<hr />

The first journey in Aegypt was a square lined with fat columns. Above the columns the stone flanks of buildings sloped away smooth and windowless into a black sky crusted with stars. Idris felt tiny in this vast place. But he knew that tiny was the way Aegypt wanted him to feel, so he strode out, whistling. After all, he was King of Lyonesse, which was a better kingdom than this or any other.

And suddenly this square was merely big. Big, and bullying, and smelly, as if nobody came here much, and when they did they used it as a lavatory. The man who had passed the soldiers in front of him was an indistinct figure walking down the dark center.

Idris walked after him.

The stored heat of the day poured up at him from the stones. It took most of a glass merely to cross the square. On the far side was a pair of doors, six men high, closed, lit from above by the same wall plaques that had been on the stairs from the quay. The doors had no handles. Idris put out his hands and pushed.

The doors did not budge. A chill ran through Idris. Soon someone would find the unconscious soldiers. How had the man ahead of him gotten through?

He noticed a little rectangular dent in the door at eye height. He thought of the plaque around his neck and pulled it out. It fit into the dent exactly. This time when he pushed, the doors moved smoothly open. When he took back the plaque he saw that the token was missing from its slot, absorbed by some mechanism in the door. He stepped through into bustle and noise and smoke. The doors slammed shut behind him.

He was in another huge square. This one was busy, with cooking fires blowing smoke over a moving throng of people, and the wail of musical instruments mingling with a roar of voices. "Honored sir, welcome to Thbee," said a voice at his waist. When he looked down he saw a figure squinting up at him from under a wig of straight black hair. "May I lead you to your majestic lodgings?" said the little man in a guttural version of the North Tongue.

"I have no lodgings," said Idris. Four other little men in wigs tugged at his tunic, offering him food, jewels, lodging, and a wig. The first little man screeched at them, flailing at them with his stick. They scuttled away. The little man twisted himself to look up at Idris. "What you need?" he demanded.

Idris was beginning to come to his senses. He had stolen a boat, landed against the law, flattened two soldiers, and burst into this old and angry country under false pretenses. Soon people would be looking for him. He was very hungry and extremely tired. He did not like the look of the bent man, nor could he risk looking into his mind. But the bent man was all he had. So he said, "Food and lodging."

"Allow me present self," said the man, bowing until his nose brushed the cobbles. "I Sith. Merchant, guide, and general dealer — specialist in goods of foreign origin."

"Smuggler, then," said Idris.

"If you insist," said the small man, looking pained. "I was saying. Welcome through Aegypt Gate of Thbee. I find you food and lodging, you give me money?"

"If I am satisfied," said Idris.

"Follow," said Sith. His bent-double lurch was surprisingly fast. Idris followed him across the square at top speed. As they passed the food stalls he glimpsed a wheel-sized dish of blood-red rice, a green lizard turning on a spit, and people, people, people, all wearing wigs, all staring at Idris. "Must buy hair," said Sith, stopping at a wig stall. Idris bought a wig and put it on over his real hair. The staring stopped. Then they were on the far side of the square, and going through a door into a filthy hallway and up into a room with a gallery overlooking the square, and on the gallery cushions and a low table. "Food here," said Sith, sitting down on the cushions and gesturing Idris to do the same. He clapped his hands. "Now we eat," he said.

It seemed that Sith was eating, too. Idris had no doubt that he would have to pay for both of them.

"So," said Sith. "Where you from?"

"Lyonesse."

"Never heard of it."

Idris did not answer. He was gazing at the fires and crowds in the enormous square. At the far side, the doors through which he had come had burst open, and a crowd was gathering.

"Dear, oh dear," said Sith, whose clever black eyes were rolled in the same direction. "Looks like trouble. Old Ones hating trouble."

"Who are the Old Ones?"

A servitor arrived with a huge round of flat bread and a dozen bowls, each containing a stew or some vegetables. Ripping off half the bread, Sith scooped food from a succession of bowls and began shoveling it down as if he was afraid Idris would take it away. "Old Ones are very huge, very powerful, rule the minds of all men," he said through a mouthful. "In Lowland beyond Lower Sea there are Wells, with monsters. Here in Aegypt there are no Wells, no monsters. Instead we have the Old Ones, most powerful of the powerful." Sith's face turned a nasty yellow, and Idris thought that if his mouth had not been so full his teeth would have chattered. "They live in lovely palaces dug in ground, and never die, may soft rain wet their kind, kind hearts. For we love them, we do, and they punish us as kind father punishes child that errs. By crushing, mostly."

Idris could feel Sith's terror. He said, "And they are not monsters?"

"Oh no," said Sith. "Quite different. Old Ones more powerful. Much more. They have heads of very big animals and plants, and bodies of very big people. Nobody sees them, for they too big to see, and maybe they live in a place where mortals cannot see. They tell us their desires in our mind. Sometimes they desire better palaces, so we send slaves to build them better palaces. Sometimes they want to eat souls, so we send their priests the bravest and most beautiful souls to eat. The most beautiful souls of all go to the New Palace. Which is a palace," said Sith, "with many trees, and where lives the Holy Morrab the Child, who is the servant and priest of the Old One called the Tree, very terrible, very, very old. Seven thousand years. Old as one thousand old, old people one after the other." He looked at Idris from the side of his eyes.

Idris had been half listening, taking advantage of Sith's stream of talk to do some eating himself. The food was good, once you learned to avoid the fiery red pastes. He hoped his Knights were being well fed. Now he looked up. "Where are the slaves sold?"

"In the market. At dawn." Sith frowned. "Hello. What this?"

Men were shouting in the square. Someone threw a handful of something onto a fire. The flames flared up and shone in the bronze bone-armor of many soldiers. "Looking for someone," said Sith. Then, with a roll of his malignant eye, "Would be you, perhaps?"

The comfort of the food left Idris. He felt suddenly alone and scared. He said, "I don't know," delved into his money belt, found a finegold, and laid it on the table. "But I seek lodging. *Safe* lodging."

Sith's eyes devoured the gold. "Yes," he said. His hand swept the coin away.

Idris said, "And tomorrow I will give you another two finegolds. Provided I am not disturbed. By soldiers or anyone else. Because if I am asked questions I will have to give answers. About guides and general merchants." He put his mind out. Sith jumped. Idris caught a whiff of terror but an even stronger whiff of greed.

Sith said, "Come." He led Idris into an upper room, pulled back a section of heavily carved paneling, and shooed him into the little compartment inside. It smelled strongly of mice, but no smell on earth could have stopped Idris from falling asleep.

At some time in the night he heard what might have been the crash of doors and the bump of searching feet. But he was muffled and wrapped from head to toe in Tristan's cloak. So he slept on. And the next thing he knew the panel was rattling again, and a voice was hissing, "Dawn comes. Hurry. Where finegold?"

Idris rolled out of the compartment. He was stiff and sore and very thirsty. He stumbled down through the dark house to what seemed to be a kitchen, Sith squeaking like a rat in his wake. A jug of milk stood on the table. He had a swig and caught the thick, musty taste of dromal.

"Two finegold," said Sith, putting out a claw of a hand. "Plus reckoning for zupper and bed."

"One," said Idris, taking it out of the belt and handing it to him. "The rest later."

"Later?" said Sith, writhing with disappointment. He sighed. "Come along, then, mustn't be late." He handed Idris the wig they had purchased yesterday. "Must remember to wear. Old Ones say so. In wearing, we worship."

Idris thought that was ridiculous, but he put the wig on anyway. It prickled. Sith grabbed him by the sleeve and dragged him out into the square.

The cookstalls had gone, and so had the aimless crowds of last night. The only human presence was a crowd at one end, half-visible in the pre-dawn grayness. "What you go do?" asked Sith.

"Buy some slaves."

"Huh," said Sith. "Hope you got plenty finegold." He hustled Idris toward the crowd, which was gathered by a gate in the inland side of the flat-topped pyramid into which the slave barge had rowed last night.

"Quick," said Sith, barging through the press of bodies. "Must get good places."

The crowd passed through two barred gates and into a huge, dim room. A stone stage ran along its far wall, separated from the audience by heavy bars. To the right was a small unbarred platform. A man in a heavy gold wig climbed up to it, wheezing slightly. There was a table with a handbell. "Salemaster," said Sith. "He sell slaves; highest bidder win. If you bid finegold you no got, they sell you, too, ha-ha." He looked down the rows of buyers. "Quarrymans buying stone haulers," he said, pointing out a group of bull-necked men with short, bristling wigs. "Building man." This one had a long, thin nose and a wig cut away to show a bald patch. "House mans and womans. Dance peoples, fun peoples." These were heavily painted, with wigs of many colors, drenched in scent. It was not just the scent that was curdling the dromal's milk in Idris's stomach. It was the knowledge that any one of these people could have bought Morgan. She could be working twenty-five paces from here, or twenty-five leagues from here . . .

Or be dead.

Idris said, "I think a friend of mine was sold here. Is there any way of telling who bought her?"

Sith said, "Can read records. Go back five years. Prices, ages, description. If you want."

Idris said, "I want," then discovered that he hardly did want, for fear of what he might find.

Sith towed him through the crowd to a little room where a bored-looking clerk in a moth-eaten wig sat in front of a wall of pigeonholes tight with scrolls. "What you want?" hissed Sith. "I pretend you looking for slave to make matched pair."

"A girl. Thirteen years old. Reddish hair. Pretty, with a

nose like a small bird's beak. Freckles on it. Green eyes. About five moons ago."

"Not many like that," said Sith and croaked something to the clerk. The clerk rolled his eyes wearily. Idris slid a finegold across the desk at him. The clerk's weariness vanished. He pulled scrolls from a pigeonhole, calling out a series of names. None of them meant anything to Idris. The clerk went to another pigeon-hole, this one with fewer scrolls in it. More names, none of them right. Then another pigeonhole, with very few.

"Oh dear," said Sith. "Hope not this one."

"Why not?"

The clerk pulled the scrolls down, leafed through them, frowning. Idris found he could not breathe.

"Those ones bought by Morrab," said Sith. "She who eats souls for the Tree."

"Ah," said the clerk, smiling brightly. Idris felt a freezing wave of goose pimples. "Margan."

"Morgan," said Idris, his heart fluttering. "Morgan Wolf Rock."

The clerk nodded. "Margan Wafrack," he repeated.

"Where?" said Idris.

"I told you," said Sith. "Morrab. So your friend dead."

"No," said Idris. When Sith had talked about Morrab, he had been too busy eating to listen properly. "Why?"

Sith shrugged. "Morrab only buy to put in Sacrifice Engine. Trust me, she dead."

"Dead?" said Idris, not believing it.

"No question."

Idris stood and stared and felt as if he might faint. All this way, buoyed up by the thought of seeing Morgan again.

And all along, she had been dead.

It was over.

He would never be able to prove to King Mark and the Duke and the Overlord that he was a true King and a worthy ally, deserving of help. His noble Knights had come into slavery in vain. And worst of all, by far the worst, his dear friend and sister, Morgan, was gone forever. He would never laugh with her again. She would never boss him around again. She would never need his help again....

He wanted to weep, but he was too empty for weeping.

He found himself next door, in the crowd in the auction room. He noticed a sort of alcove at the back of the room, masked by a screen of pierced marble worked in the likeness of a flowering tree.

"That place for New Palace, where Morrab live," said Sith. "That where they bid for your poor friend. If New Palace want slave, they show hand there."

The stone tree was beautifully made, its branches sinuous and elegant. But it was not beautiful. It felt cold and evil, like the vast creatures he had sensed in the pits. He hated it. He hated this whole disgusting country.

Oh, Morgan.

He would not cry. Not here. He would buy his friends, and they would leave. If King Mark would not join them, they would fight Fisheagle and her armies with the other Knights of Lyonesse, and if necessary they would die in the attempt.

A red beam of light lanced through a window in the building's end. "Sun come up," said Sith. "Begins."

The man in the gold wig blew a whistle. A file of people shuffled onto the stage behind the bars. Idris watched them dully. The first few dozen were men, heavyset field workers, bewildered-looking, dressed in bits of sack around their middles. "Stone haulers, stupid," said Sith scornfully. And sure enough, the bristle-wigged quarrymen were raising fingers. Gold Wig rang his bell, the heavyset men were sold, and more came. "Quarries again," said Sith. Idris felt a dull fury that people could be bought and sold like this. Calm, he told himself, echoing the words of Orbach, his swordmaster. Anger is no good unless you use it. "Fun people," said Sith casually. Sure enough, the people in colored wigs were bidding now, and the numbers of fingers raised was getting bigger. Gold Wig rang his bell. "What price?" said Idris.

"Sixty for all."

Idris had seventy finegolds in his belt—sixty-eight, once he had paid Sith.

Next came a long stream of quarrypeople and cooks and builders. The bell rang again and again. Everyone seemed bored. Idris's disgust grew. Was he the only one who could see that these were people, with mothers and fathers and children?

And Morgan had been through this. How would she have felt when she had passed onto that stage with the chain between her ankles, peered at like a prize calf, on her way to be killed?

Control the anger. Use it.

The auctioneer had started to shout, as if excited. "Says new, pretty, brave," hissed Sith.

And onto the barred stage walked the Knights.

They looked small and young and not at all pretty. They had been fighting, for Tristan had a black eye, and someone had hit Merk on the nose, and he had failed to scrub the blood off his top lip. Idris's heart filled with pride at the defiant looks they cast through the bars.

They stood squinting into the sun that streamed in through the window at the back of the room, brave and true and ready to fight anyone who came near enough. Idris could not keep quiet. He put his mind out to them, all at once, and roared cheerfully, *Here I am, lads.* They rocked, blinked, and grinned. Tristan recognized him under the wig. The Knights waved and nudged one another. Gold Wig frowned. Idris said, "I want to bid."

Sith said, "How much?"

"Ten for the lot."

"Not nearly enough," said Sith, but barked a guttural word. There was a flurry of other bids, then a pause. "Sixty now," said Sith.

"Go on," said Idris.

"Got the finegold?" said Sith.

Gold Wig was looking expectantly around him.

"Yes," said Idris, dry-mouthed. Sith bid again. So did someone else. Sith again. "How much?" said Idris.

"Seventy." Sith would just have to put up with what he had already been paid.

Silence. Gold Wig's hand strayed toward the bell: going, going...

A pause. Idris looked around the room, expecting eyes to be on him, the winner. They were not. Everyone was looking at the deadly alcove with its beautiful stone screen. For the first time, Idris noticed that there was a hole in the screen between the roots of the stone tree. From the hole there now projected a hand, white-gloved. The hand that had bid for Morgan. His heart thundered. The hand made signs: five fingers, spread twenty times. A hundred.

Gold Wig bowed. So did Sith.

"Bid!" said Idris.

"Against New Palace?" said Sith, between lips white with fear. "Not never."

"A hundred and ten!" shouted Idris, in the North Tongue.

The gloved hand rested for a moment on the sill of its hole, the fingers tapping. Then it took on life, like a white spider. It gestured a hundred and twenty. It pointed at the Knights, then at Idris. It made a beckoning movement to Gold Wig. Then it was gone, and the hole was empty, and the carved tree looked down, impassive and lovely and horrible.

Skullhelms were moving through the crowd. "She bought you, too. You dead," said Sith, lids blinking earnestly over his bulging eyes. "I like you. But Morrab know you bid too much, so she take you. So you dead. Is a pity."

The skullhelms were very close. Idris saw there was no escape. He had to draw Cutwater. But it caught in the scabbard, and the hilt snagged on Tristan's cloak. The skullhelms were a pebble toss away. Well, they would not get Cutwater. He did not altogether trust Sith, but half a fish was better than no zupper. He slipped the baldric over his head and wrapped it in Tristan's cloak. "Keep these safe," he said and thrust the bundle into the bent man's hands, following it with a handful of finegold.

"You dead."

Idris said, "I promise you, you will hear from me." He said it for himself as much as anyone else. Sith faded into the crowd as if he had been wearing Tristan's cloak, not just carrying it. Then there was the clash of armor, and something hit Idris shockingly hard on the back of the head. As the sunlight faded, he heard the clang of bars.

SEVEN

He woke. His cheek was on gritty stone. At first, he could not think where he might be. Then memory flowed back, and with it despair. There was the breathing of other people around him. He tried to speak. The first attempt came out as a croak. He tried again. "Who's there?" he said.

"Us," said the voice of Merk. "But not for long."

Lanz spoke, slow and precise. "They say we are young and perfect and brave, so now we must go to the New Palace."

Idris struggled into the sitting position. His head hurt, but his heart hurt worse. He said, "Tristan. I lost your cloak." And Morgan. And everything else.

He heard Tristan laugh in the dark. "No need for cloaks in the New P-Palace," he said.

"Or anything else," said Gawaine's voice, unusually gloomy. "Why?"

"What he means," said the calm voice of Bors, "is that they will sacrifice us to their gods, that they call the Old Ones. We should be proud, they say. The method is crushing."

Idris let his head hang. So it would all end very much as he had begun. A year ago he had been condemned to death as a Cross by Captain Ironhorse, petty tyrant of the Westgate. He had escaped by the kindness of Ambrose, his friend and guide. Everything that had passed since then, the training in the Wells of the Valley of Apples, the discovery of his destiny, the burying of Ambrose, the flight, the quest: All that had been in vain. He might as well have stayed in the Drowning Cell under the Westgate.

But at least he would be following Morgan, and in the company of his brave Knights. He raised his head. He said, "You have been true companions. I'm sorry I brought you to this."

There was a silence. It was Lanz who broke it. He said, in his soft, precise voice, "Excuse me, Idris, but this is foolish talk. We came of our own free will to this most nasty land of Aegypt. And have promised to help you take back your kingdom of Lyonesse and do good in the world. And if it is granted to us, we will come with you, and the monsters will go back to their place, and the Wooden Palace will sprout leaves again, and the world will be cured of unpleasant diseases like Skrine and your Regent."

"We will," said the other companions, with voices that did not on the whole shake too much.

Idris was deeply moved by this loyalty, even though it was based on things that could never happen. He felt the sting of tears, and behind the tears an enormous pride. It was not the ancient pride that flowed through the hilt of Cutwater from the stones of Lyonesse. It was simpler than that. It was the pride of having gained six friends so loyal that they uttered no word of complaint that they must die in his company. His shoulders straightened. He said, "Dear companions, thank you. One way or another, we will show these savage Aegypts what it is to be Knights of the Table Round."

Then the cell door burst open, and hard white light glared in, and soldiers in armor made to resemble the bones of men dragged them into the noonday for sacrifice.

———❧•❧———

At first the glare made it hard to see. As Idris's eyes cleared, he saw that there was a cart waiting, big, caged with bars, with dromals harnessed to it. The soldiers pushed the Knights up a ramp—not harshly, but with an odd, impersonal gentleness— almost (Idris thought, his stomach sinking) like butchers leading prize animals to slaughter.

Here in the glare of the sun it was less easy to be calm. The dromal cart left the slave market and the square and wound (endlessly, it seemed, but still too quickly for these last minutes of life) through the broad streets of the city. The crowds in the streets glanced at them, then looked quickly away, making signs against the Evil Eye. Soon the buildings fell back, and the cart was trundling along a wide road that ran arrow-straight across a treeless plain of brown sand to a group of palaces on the horizon.

The size of the buildings meant they were farther away

than they looked. One was in the shape of a vast crouching beast. Another was an enormous globe sunk in the sand to half its height. Others were still being built, with tent camps for the slaves and plumes of dust rolling off the outcrops where the quarrymen burrowed for stone. But the palace toward which the dromal driver directed the cage-cart was long and low, painted purest white, with towers and spires rising from its middle. As they drew nearer, Idris could see a crowd of people gathered by the wall.

Kek, he said in his mind.

And there he was, behind the gull's eyes, soaring free above the land of Aegypt, as over so many lands before. Down he glided toward the enormous white palace. There seemed to be yards inside it, courts, perhaps gardens. But Idris's mind was not on gardens. He was looking at the outer wall of the palace, where the crowd was gathered; looking at it closely, because Kek was zooming down toward it with an enthusiasm that meant only one thing.

Food.

Idris saw that a patch of the wall was not white. It was stained a nasty brownish-red, as if something had seeped down it from a complicated arrangement of stone blocks and scaffolding built against it.

His mouth was dry, his knees trying to knock. He did not want to think about what had made that stain. He knew he was going to find out soon enough.

They should have died fighting in Bitter River, not allowed themselves to be led to their end like animals. He felt himself about to weep.

Morgan had made the same last journey. She would not have let herself have thoughts like this.

"Anyone got any food?" said Merk. "I'm starving."

And suddenly Idris laughed. You could choose to die like an animal, or you could choose to die like a Knight. Dying would hurt, probably, but not for long. And whatever came after death could not hurt, for there was no one there to feel it. "Driver!" he shouted. "Food!"

And to his astonishment, food came: a basket of fruit, flat bread, and sour white cheese, with water that had a sweet, musty taste, very good. The Knights sat on the floor of the cart in their circle and ate and drank pretty cheerfully, careful not to look at the palace and the grisly machine that stood against its wall.

The dromals came to a halt by the machine. The leader of the soldiers marched up to the cart, his skullhelm blank. "Now then, gentlemen," he said, in a harsh version of the North Tongue. "You have eaten and drunk. Good. At this time it is my sad duty to explain to you the workings of the Sacrifice Engine. As far as you are concerned it is not too complicated. You will all stand on that ledge on the wall." He pointed with his short bronze sword. "Then that big slab of stone that is leaning away from the wall will slam in your faces. It is very quick. And your souls will go to feed the Old Ones, or perhaps live with the souls of the other brave young ones in the New Palace." A pause. Morgan listened to this alone, thought Idris. Poor, poor Morgan. "If you make a fuss, it makes it worse for everyone. You do understand, I am sure."

Idris looked at the Knights. Even their lips were pale. Tristan said, "I'm glad we came."

"Yes," said Gawaine. "Before, I was alone. Now I know what it is to have had friends."

Bors said, "It hasn't been much fun. But I have liked it."

"We have lived," said Galahd. "Everyone must die."

"And you have shown us our true natures," said Lanz. "For which we are grateful."

"Though the food has been horrible," said Merk.

Idris smiled and said, "Thank you all." A strange... absence... was creeping over his mind. He said, "Courage, my friends." And they all smiled, a weird, dreamy smile, and touched hands.

Things happened quickly after that.

The iron grilles of the cart clashed open. Idris felt himself grabbed. His wrists were bound, a bag whipped over his head, and he was carried away by strong hands in hard armor. He would have struggled, but the feeling of absence had become a cloudiness in his mind. The drinking water, he thought, fighting soft waves that tried to blot out his ideas. He put his mind up to Kek. The gull was sitting on a projection of the New Palace wall, looking down. Through the gull's eyes, Idris saw that the projection was a skull, carved in stone. And he saw the seven hooded figures carried to the ledge, placed facing outward, and chained upright, facing the monstrous slab of stone pivoted out from the wall. Somewhere in his dreamlike thought he felt that same wall against his back, the very wall against which Morgan had stood. He knew that the slab of stone was out there, ready at the pull of a lever to slap in and squash him flat....

The clouds in his mind swirled. He concentrated, determined to think his last thoughts clearly.

Good-bye, Kek, he thought, mind spinning slowly, throat full of the rotten smell of the old blood on the wall, fighting an image of Wollick in whale-sized bathing breeches diving for cheese in the Rhiann. Good-bye, Harpoon and Ector, the Boys and the Stones. Farewell to my people and my land of Lyonesse and my Knights. And worst of all, farewell to Morgan, poor Morgan, who had traveled this very way, stood in this very place. Died this very—

A click.

A terrible impact.

Darkness.

He was falling. So this is it, he thought.

He landed on something bottomlessly soft. Then he was not falling, nor sinking, but lying. Lying in great comfort, with clouds rolling in his mind. And the chains at his wrists and ankles were falling away, and the bag on his head was drawn off. He had not expected this. Perhaps now there would be flowery meadows, or old friends, or monsters, or Old Ones. The clouds made him not care.

He opened his eyes.

He was looking at a pretty girl with brown hair and freckles. He had never seen her before. "Are you all right?" she said. "You're being fantastically brave."

"Fine," he said. "Thank you for asking." He sat up.

He was sitting on deep grass, amazingly soft, very green. Around him he could dimly see the forms of the Knights, each with someone talking to him. He said, "Who are you?"

The girl said, "I was chosen for the Tree. Like you. I wasn't as brave as you, though. You're still alive, by the way." Idris stretched his fingers and his toes. He still had all of them, and by the feel of it, everything in between. Eventually, he decided that he believed her.

The girl said, "All that stuff about the Sacrifice Engine. Nobody gets squashed. When the slab comes in, the bit of wall you're chained to pivots back, and you fall into the palace. All that nasty muck on the wall is animal bits from the kitchens. The worst that can happen is that you fall badly. You *are* all right?" she asked anxiously.

"Fine," said Idris. He was not, though. There were a couple of hundred questions he wanted to ask, but his head was still cloudy, and something in him made him want to weep, or perhaps laugh, so he wept anyway.

"Poor you," said the girl, with great kindness. "You are feeling bad because you have had a horrible shock and because

Morrab always has poppy juice put in the water, to make the blow less cruel, you know. Just go to sleep, and in time it will fade."

Idris shook his head. "I am busy," he said. Something was trying to dawn on him. "I have come to find Morgan Wolf Rock, who was brought to Aegypt a slave."

The girl's face seemed to swim a little. "Come?" she said. "Not been brought?"

"Come," said Idris. The fog was thickening. He felt uneasy, agitated. He knew what it was. If Morgan had been through the Sacrifice Engine, Morgan might not be dead. "I must make inquiries," he said. "Find her. She must be here. Do you know her?"

"Later, perhaps," said the girl. She said it kindly, but all this kindness was becoming annoying. Somehow it annoyed Idris to sleep. But as his eyes closed, he seemed to hear a murmur run through the palace. *He has come*, said the murmur. *He has come.*

He slept.

When Idris awoke he felt clearheaded and full of energy, as if he had been asleep for a very long time. He sat up on the bed.

He was in a bright room with a fretted window looking out into a courtyard full of green trees. It seemed to be morning. Birds were singing, and there was the splash of a fountain. He was wearing a robe of pale cloth, light and cool. He opened his mind and listened. A murmur of human thought: no monsters. He stood up and pushed the door. It was not locked. He walked down the corridor, looking into all the rooms. In each, one of the Knights lay sprawled, dressed in a robe like his, asleep.

"Lord," said a voice behind him.

He turned and saw the freckle-faced girl again. She bowed. "You are to dress, if it please you," she said. "Then you are bidden to audience with Morrab the Child."

Idris felt his spine crawl at the name. Behind the fountain and the birdsong were the awful pits of the Old Ones and the Tree that Morrab served.

But he had died once. What else was there to be afraid of? "Very good," he said.

The girl showed him a bathroom with a great marble tub. Servants appeared and cut his hair (nobody in the New Palace seemed to wear the horrible prickly wigs). They scoured his finger- and toenails, and scrubbed him until he thought he would have no skin left. Then they left him to wash off the soap in a warm waterfall, and finally to swim in a huge pool of fresh water. When he got out, he found, laid on the bed, a tunic and breeches of the kind worn in Lyonesse and a cloak of feather-light night-blue material. He put the cloak around his shoulders and fumbled for the brooch. His fingers made contact with a familiar shape. For a moment the world became quite still. For there over his heart was a snakelike creature, its tail in its mouth so it made a circle: the device of the Devouring Eel of House Ambrose, that he and Morgan had worn long ago in Lyonesse.

"Sir?" said the girl's voice at the door. "I am to take you to Morrab."

"What does this mean?" said Idris, pointing to the brooch.

The girl frowned, puzzled. "It is to fasten your cloak." And try as he would, Idris could get no further information.

He followed the girl down sun-striped corridors, through great halls thick with incense and across green gardens shaded by trees of cherry and almond. Once he thought he caught the whiff of Wellwater. But this was Aegypt, where there were no monsters, only slaves. So he put it down to his imagination.

At last they came to a set of bronze doors. The girl spoke a word. The doors swung open. She motioned him forward. He walked in.

He heard the doors close behind him. There was a white marble strip down the center of a black marble hall, flanked on either side by red columns that rose into darkness. Idris expected floors to give way, or slabs to fall, or the columns to clash and crush him. The scuff of his bare feet filled the hall with whispers as he advanced. Seven thousand years old. Old as one thousand old, old people, one after the other, Sith had said. He tried to swallow, but his throat was tight with dread.

A house stood at the white strip's end. A house of plain Northland design, with yellow light shining from its windows: oil lamps, warm and friendly, not the hot white glare of the Aegypt sun. Idris put his mind out a little way, to touch whoever was in that place. And found his heart beating like a smith's double hammer. The door in the house in that vast and pillared hall was opening, and the light was streaming out, and a figure was coming to meet him, veiled from head to foot. It moved slowly, stopped. Then it began running toward him.

And suddenly he was running, too, and they were standing within touching distance, and he could see the weave of the cloth veil that hid the face, moving with its rapid breath.

He said, "You are Morrab the Child?"

The figure bowed.

Idris put out his hand and took the veil and moved it aside, so that the face glowed in the golden light that seemed to be shining all around him.

For the face unveiled had pale red hair, and a little beak of a nose, and green eyes half awash with tears. It was the face he had traveled three moons across the world to see: the face of Morgan ni Uther of the Wolf Rock House Draco of the Vanished Children, his dear friend and sister.

EIGHT

They hugged each other for a long, long time. Finally Morgan said, "Where have you *been*?", wiped the tears from her face with the hem of her robe, took both his hands, and pulled him into the house. Idris looked around him, laughing, shaking his head. The room was like a Lyonesse room, with mosaics on the wall portraying a maiden rescued from sea monsters, and a wooden table piled with food. "Seal cheese and honey," she said. "Sunapple juice." She looked at him, almost nervously. "I wanted you to feel at home. Is that all right?"

Idris said, "Better than that," and hugged her again, to make sure she was real. He hardly trusted himself to speak. It had been four moons since he had left Ar Mor, full of belief in his quest. A mere day ago, he had thought it lost, and Morgan dead. But here was the quest fulfilled, and his bargains with King Mark and the Duke and the Overlord sealed, and his kingdom saved. And best of all, here was Morgan.

"What are you waiting for?" said a voice. And there stood a creature like a scaly melon with fins, winking, as far as you could wink with only one eye. "Go on, tuck in."

"Digby!" cried Idris, bowing in the Manner to his sister's pet monster.

Digby bowed back, then grew himself a large pink mouth and used it to beam upon the reunion.

Morgan piled his plate with food, and Idris told his story as fast as he could. She watched him eat as if she thought he might evaporate. He could feel her mind like a friendly hand on his, clenching sometimes, with the death of Penmarch and the capture at Bitter River. He examined her as he talked, printing her again on his memory. Her face seemed thinner, the green eyes bigger, with a darkness behind them that was new. But she was Morgan, and that was all that mattered.

When he had finished she said, "Goodness, how brave." She smiled, looking down. "I've missed you. I was longing for this. I knew you'd come. But ... well, I thought you might not. Because it's not an easy place to get to, is it? But I was always ... looking out for you. Watching the slave market, just in case. And you were never there. Until yesterday, when your friends were up for sale. I just had a feeling. And I put my mind out and there you were. That was me bidding against you. I'm so sorry. I wanted to shout and hug you, but I had to make it look natural." She smiled, as if she was happy for herself and proud of him, both at the same time. "The last I saw you, they were dragging me off the deck of the *Swallow*, and I saw the sword go overboard and your head go down and your ... heels go up, and into the sea you went." A tear ran down the side of her nose, and she squeezed his hand hard enough to hurt.

"And then?"

"Oh, I kicked and I screamed and they locked me in their slave hold and I was so, so sick. And I suppose they must have turned straight 'round and headed for here. Because the sea got calmer and the weather got hotter and they let us up on deck to breathe sometimes. They were horrible," she said. "I mean, they didn't hurt us or anything. But it was like being...I don't know, a sheep heading for the market at the Southgate Revels. They looked after us very carefully, but only because of the money we were worth. It took the wax of a moon to get past Iber and the Pillars and into the True Sea. Then seven nights from there to the Afryk Wall, which is to the west of here, and another four up the Lower Sea in that disgusting Green. You would have liked the embankment, though. The last thirty leagues of the Lowland has sunk, oh, half a league, so the water is held in by great walls on either side, and the land is so far below that you can't see it. Not that you'd want to," she said. "So many Wells! Even Digby hates it."

"Low and vulgar," Digby said. "Most unpleasant."

Morgan took Idris's hand and squeezed it. "At any rate. They put us in at the slave gate, and we came up in the market and were sold. I don't need to tell you about that."

Silence. Then Idris said, "It is a long way from being a slave in the market to being Morrab the Child, a servant of the Tree."

She looked down, almost as if she was ashamed. "I was on that stage behind the bars." Again the squeeze of the hand. "I was listening carefully. To people's minds, you know. I've gotten better at that. A woman came and sat in the Alcove of the Tree, in the auction hall."

"Morrab the Child."

Morgan nodded. "She...heard me listening. Digby went and talked to her."

"A few words was all it took," said Digby, with charming false modesty. "A song. A little dance. She was an old, old, old woman. Very powerful. But very lonely." He grew eyelashes and batted them. "How could she fail to notice how lovely I was?"

"Darling Digby," said Morgan fondly. "So Morrab got interested in me. And when the rest went to the building and the quarries or the funhouses, she had me and Digby brought to the New Palace." She smiled, a smile haunted by terrible memories. "Not by the Sacrifice Engine, though. That was when the Sacrifice Engine really did kill. She had me taken out of the prison in the night. I thought that was...the end of me. But she had me smuggled in at the side gate. She was horrible, half nightmare and half silly old woman. She tortured her servants and she smelled disgusting and she talked to herself. But when I arrived she made me her pet and talked to me instead." She made a face, turning her head, as if she did not want to look at what was in her mind.

"There is no dishonor in being a pet," said Digby, sounding offended.

"Quiet," said Idris. He had caught a glimpse of Morgan's thoughts: fear, a great dark hall, a single lamp reflected in four eyes, two bright and green, two dull and slate-black. Four hands playing cat's cradle: two ancient beyond age, slow and clawed; two young and strong, frightened, but trying not to shake. And as the evenings passed, the ancient mind taking the new mind and binding it with an invisible web as intricate as the cat's cradle, using the young mind's sympathy and kindness to strap it to its age and misery. He caught a rumor of the horrible confidences the old mind whispered, a knowledge so dreadful that it would bend a young mind forever —

Unless it was a mind as strong and self-willed as Morgan's.

"So I talked to her," said Morgan, making light of the horror Idris had glimpsed. "And Digby amused her, and she made me Morrab the Child and showed me to the things that rule Aegypt." Idris saw the huge, mad Old Ones stooping to inspect this insect-sized Morgan, perhaps stir her with a giant fingertip. "There is one called the Tree, whom she served. I serve it now." Her voice was matter-of-fact, but she shuddered. "First I was her toy, and then I was her friend, and then I was her heir, and two moons gone it was time for her to pass down, so she went." It seemed a strange way of putting it, but Idris let it go. "I had argued with her about the lives in the Sacrifice Engine, so she made her people rebuild it, so it was as you saw it." She smiled, again with the haunted look. "All that business about eating souls is rubbish." She cast her eyes down. "I think."

Idris found himself grinning. Trust Morgan to prick the bubble of nonsense.

It's not all nonsense, said her delicate thought in his mind, and he felt the terror behind it and knew that there were things Morgan was not telling him, because she did not want to upset him.

"But that's enough of that," she said, returning to her old no-nonsense briskness. "Now I am Morrab the Child, and I can do what I like. How can I help you and your friends?"

"Knights," said Idris. "My allies need to know we have found you, and you are safe. Then we will go back to Lyonesse for Darksolstice, and tumble old Fisheagle down the Mount."

"Yes," she said. "Sometimes I think I feel her mind."

"Even here?"

"There is a Well."

"But there are no monsters in Aegypt."

"Morrabs grow old and bored and wish to know forbidden things."

"Morrabs?"

"There have been many. The Well is sealed. But sometimes you can feel the Regent knocking at it. She feels safe in Lyonesse, now you are gone."

"She's in for a shock," said Idris grimly. "When the Kings of Beyondsea meet you, they'll come to Lyonesse and we'll kick Fisheagle into the sea. And you and I will clean the Mount and live in the Kyd Tower—"

"I can't," said Morgan.

Idris stared. "But you've got to."

For a heartbeat the queenly manner slipped, and Idris saw she was desperate. She said, in a voice that sounded as if it were being pressed out of her, "I am bound here."

"Bound?"

"There are curses for me on the borders of Aegypt. I serve the Tree. The arches of Realmgates, the gates of the country, bear his sigil. If I cross them, the Tree draws my life out of me."

Idris said, "I have made a four-moons' journey to find you. Without you the Kings of Beyondsea will not help me take Lyonesse."

"I am sorry you were troubled," she snapped, with a flash of the old Morgan.

Idris knew her well enough to know he could not push her any farther. The only person who could persuade Morgan was Morgan. And that took time.

So he bowed, and said, "Come and meet the new Knights of Lyonesse."

She stood up quickly, flushed and excited at the prospect of company. Then she remembered to be stately, and they walked back through the colonnades and cloisters of the palace to the quarters of the Sacrifice Engine's victims.

The Knights were sitting by a pool in a garden, around a table piled with Aegypt bread and bowls of fruit. Gawaine's sharp green eyes saw Idris and Morgan first. He said something, and they all rose and bowed.

"Morgan," said Idris, "these are the Knights of Lyonesse who have come with me to find you."

The Knights looked at Morgan with intense curiosity, but could not in the Manner ask questions. They rose, and named themselves — Tristan first, blushing, for he had met few girls since he had been outlawed in the forest; then Gawaine, glancing up with his green horse-thief's eyes as he bowed; and Bors, who stared openly at this strange red-haired creature in Aegypt robes. Galahd smiled his open Northern smile. And Lanz, better used to life in palaces than the rest, took Morgan's hand and bowed over it gravely. When he straightened up, his eyes locked with Morgan's and did not seem to want to let go.

Morgan looked into Lanz's face. Idris saw a delicate pink blush touch her cheeks and the shadow fade from her eyes. She said, "Lanz, all of you, I am glad you came."

Lanz bowed deeply, without dropping his gaze, and for a moment it was as if Morgan and he were the only people in the garden. Then Merk, who had been casting glances at the food from the corner of his eye, said, "And I am Merk, and it is very kind of you to lay on this fine nuncheon, but I am extremely worried that it might spoil."

"It won't get a chance if you're anywhere near it," muttered Gawaine.

Morgan looked at Merk's moon face and laughed and said, "Sorry to have interrupted. Sit down, everyone."

So they sat down and finished nuncheon, Morgan between Idris and (somehow) Lanz. Tristan and Gawaine made sure to offer Merk ridiculously large quantities of food, all of which he ate. Morgan laughed until the tears ran. After nuncheon, Merk got up and said, "Thank you for a pleasant snack."

Morgan bowed, her face solemn, except for the eyes. "I am glad you thought it was worth the trip."

"Indeed," said Merk, frowning slightly, for he had the sensation of being laughed at.

"M-may I help you to your room?" said Tristan.

"I can — wahey!" cried Merk.

This was because Gawaine had crept behind him and dropped to his hands and knees by the side of the pool, and Tristan had converted his helping hand into a shove, and Merk had tripped backward over Gawaine and hit the water with a huge splash. As he came up spluttering, the Knights of the Table Round flung off their outer clothing and hurled themselves into the pool, bombing him. As Idris shrugged out of his tunic, he saw a slim figure pound past him, leap, and land in an explosion of water, and knew that Morrab the Child had faded into her ancient shadows, and that his sister Morgan Wolf Rock was back.

Then he hit the water, and sank, and came up, and grabbed the edge of the pool, because in Lyonesse nobody swam on pain of death, for swimmers were monster or Cross. Morgan was swimming, though. So he tried it himself. And found he could; that the water was kind and silky, and that he moved in it easily. "Fun?" said Morgan.

"Fun," said Idris, and thought, When I rule in Lyonesse,

all will learn to swim. Then Bors bombed him, and he forgot about ruling and concentrated on swimming.

When at last they got out, servitors brought huge, fluffy towels and dried them, and they played Dots around the table. Morgan was happy and bright, and sat next to Lanz, who taught her the rules, while Gawaine played cunningly, and Tristan bet enormous sums of imaginary finegold, and Bors lost because he was completely unable to bluff, and Galahd set sunapple-leaves sailing across the pool, and Merk devoured a stream of snacks brought by giggling servitors who seemed keen to test if he would explode. The Knights were somewhat surprised by Digby at first. But they soon got used to him, and he watched the proceedings from a carved throne, making disapproving noises when someone cheated and blowing elaborate fanfares to celebrate cunning strokes.

As the sun dropped in the western sky, the shadows of the palace fell in the courtyard, and another kind of shadow grew in Morgan's face. She drew away from Lanz, said something about her duties, and vanished into the palace.

All week they lazed, gathering strength after the hard moons of traveling. Morgan walked the enormous gardens, sometimes with Lanz, sometimes with Idris. Only one thing she would not discuss, and that was her home. The Wolf Rock was a burned-out shell, and her parents had vanished under the ashes. It was as if she could not bear to think of the glories of Lyonesse, its green softness, the kindness of the people, the cry of gulls in the clear air that came from the sea.

One day as they were sitting by the pool in the Great Court, Idris said, "We must find a way to leave soon."

Morgan shook her head wearily. "I told you. The Tree will not let me pass the gates."

"Are you sure?"

She said grimly, "Come with me." Idris felt something cold and ancient and very frightening in her. He followed.

They passed from the green courts into an older part of the palace. The years had eaten the joints between stone and stone, and the paving of the halls was worn into ditches by the passage of millions of feet. At the end of a court even more worn than the rest was a stepped pyramid, the edges of the steps blurred with age, a stone door set in its base. Idris greatly disliked the look of the pyramid. He found his heart cold and his feet reluctant to go forward. But Morgan dragged him on. As they drew nearer to the door, he saw it was carved with the likeness of a vast skull, with eyeballs of white crystal in whose deeps lurked a glitter of pure evil.

Morgan spat a word at the door. It sighed open. Steps plunged away inside, lit by the uncanny Aegypt glow. An icy breath came up at him. "Come!" said Morgan, yanking him down the stairs.

It was a long descent. A smell of musk and spices gathered around them, thick and disgusting. At the bottom they entered a chamber filled with long, narrow boxes, each on a stone plinth. "Here," said Morgan.

There was a sound from one of the boxes: a creaking, like a voice, but no voice Idris had heard before. He put out his mind....

And found weariness. Such deep, awful weariness as he had never imagined could exist. He walked to the box, which had no lid, and looked in.

Two eyes looked back at him: ancient eyes, terrible, in a face crumbled to rags through which the white bones showed.

"This is Morrab, who took me in," said Morgan in a blank, careful voice. "She will live forever, by the mercy of the Tree. But she will keep getting older, by the malice of the Tree. I have been made Morrab now, by the power of the Tree. This is what waits for me."

Idris forced his mind to be still, though it wanted to scream and run. He said, in the Manner, "It has been a deep honor to meet you, great Morrab. I name myself Idris of Lyonesse, King, Brother of Morgan, whom you call Morrab the Child."

Then go home and reign and leave this awful place, said the mind in the corpse. *You will have to leave the girl, for she has become Morrab, servant of the Tree, and is confined by the sigils that the Tree has set on the Realmgates.*

I thank you, murmured Idris with his mind. *I wish you rest.* He turned his back and started to walk up the stairs.

"Don't you want to look in the other boxes?" said Morgan, in a voice with a horrible edge of madness.

"No," said Idris, keeping his own voice steady with a great effort. "I suppose they are the ones who came before?"

"One hundred lifetimes," said Morgan. She was walking up the steps, slow and weary as an old, old woman. "The first of them is covered in hair. There is nothing else left of her. Just hair and tiredness. Seven thousand years in a box." She put her face in her hands, and the tears streamed between her fingers.

Idris put an arm around her shoulders. He said, "I will take you back to Lyonesse."

She shook her head impatiently. "You can't. So shut up about it." They walked back in silence through the blind courts of stone to the trees and the pools and the Knights.

When Morgan saw Lanz, she looked brighter. "Now," she said. "You need to escape from Aegypt."

"And you with us," said Lanz, bowing gallantly.

Morgan went pink. She gave him a quick smile. Then the shadows swept in again, and she turned away and clapped her hands and gave orders in the harsh Aegypt tongue. Servitors wheeled into the garden a great roll of the smooth reed cloth the Aegypts used for writing and unrolled it on the green lawn. The scroll bore a picture of the land of Aegypt and its surroundings, scribed in gall and ashes. The Knights gathered around.

From the corner of Aegypt that would be closest to the summer sunset, a line went across the Lower Sea to join a range of mountains with painted fire spewing from their summits. The western side of this line was colored blue.

"What's that?" said Idris.

"The wall," said Morgan and smiled, as if she caught in memory a whiff of the fresh salt air of Lyonesse. "It stops the True Sea from flooding the Lowland. The Lowland is sinking because of the Wells. So now the western end of the Lower Sea runs between great embankments through the wall and into the True Sea; embankments like the rivers of Lyonesse, but much, much bigger. The wall south of the joining of the True and Lower seas belongs to Aegypt, and north of the joining belongs to the Lowland. The Aegypt half is kept up by slaves, the Lowland half by monsters." She began to sound excited. "Nobody goes there much, except smugglers. I will send you across the wall to the Volcanoes, and you can go to the Northland from there."

"But you must come with us," said Lanz.

"I can't. Idris knows why. There is a curse."

"Curses can only hurt you if you believe in them," said Bors, ever practical.

"A few glasses ago, Idris didn't believe in people living seven thousand years."

"Seven th-thousand *years*?" said Tristan, stirred from his languor.

"That is the age of Morrab the Child," said Idris, in a voice that discouraged further questions. There was silence, except for the steady chomp of Merk's jaws on a dromal steak. Idris's eyes rested on the coast of Aegypt. His hand went to his side, seeking the pommel of Cutwater. Which of course was not there, because it was in the keeping of Sith the smuggler...

A thought came to him.

He looked at Morgan, who was standing close to Lanz, gazing on the map with a face of stone. He said, "The sigils of the Tree are on all the gates of Aegypt?"

"Every one," she said in a low, flat voice.

182

Tristan said, "S-sigils?"

Idris held up a hand. "And if we left the land without passing a gate?"

"It cannot be done. The Tree hears everything—hey!"

For Idris had run at her and scooped her up and was hauling her toward the pool. He threw her in, and she came up spluttering and laughing, and Lanz threw Idris in and went to save Morgan, and Gawaine, seeing an outlet for the wildness in him, threw Galahd and Tristan in with a crafty wrestling hold. Upon which, Merk picked him up with one hand and slung him in, then jumped after them, tucking up his heels so his vast bulk hit the water with a stunning *whack*, throwing up a sheet of spray that half drowned the occupants of the pool.

And everybody was too busy spitting out water to entertain thoughts of the gates of Aegypt or the sigils of the Tree. Or anything else that might cause thoughts that could be overheard by a vicious Tree-being in a vast, dry pit.

Later, Idris said to Morgan, "The man who has my sword is called Sith. Can you find him and tell him to bring it to me?"

"Of course," said Morgan and gave orders to a servitor. Later, she was playing Check with Lanz when the servitor came back. "Your Sith is here," she said. "This man will take you to him."

The servitor led Idris to the slave quarters of the palace. A forlorn figure sat hunched on a stool in the corner of a small, bare room. Beside it a long bundle leaned against the wall. "Sith," said Idris. "Welcome to the New Palace."

"No hurt," said Sith, falling on his face. "Loyal, worshipping, given things to keep, not stolen them, promise, promise."

"I know," said Idris. "Up."

"Your sword," said Sith, pointing to the bundle.

Idris put out his hand. As always, he could not tell whether Cutwater had jumped into his grip or whether he had reached out and grasped it. Whichever the case, here was his sword in his grasp, and the scabbard at his hip, and flowing through him the power of Lyonesse.

"Now," he said. "I am very grateful, and I am going to give you a chance to be useful to Morrab the Child."

Sith went the color of dirty dromal's milk and sat down suddenly on his stool.

"I know you are a clever man and a brilliant smuggler," said Idris coaxingly. "So I want you to find us a way out of Aegypt that does not use the Realmgates. My gratitude will be large, and so will that of Morrab, cruel and wicked though you know her to be."

Sith groaned theatrically. "Gratitude will be so nice, when Old Ones have torn out my poor insides."

"—and there will also be a great deal of finegold."

"Piles of it. Heaps," said the voice of Digby, who had soared around the corner, using his favorite winged-melon shape.

"What's *that*?" said Sith, shrinking into the corner.

"An ordinary demon, which I will prevent from eating you if you agree to help," said Idris, putting out his mind and resting it threateningly on the little smuggler's.

"Help? Agree? Of *course!*" said Sith, through teeth that chattered. "What do we do, and when do we start?"

It was still dark when the train of dromals set out from the New Palace ten days later: a group of grooms and servitors first, then the Knights gathered around Morgan, and finally Idris, with a hand on his sword hilt and an eye on Sith. All wore wigs. Sith grumbled in a small, high voice about the discomfort of his saddle, the many profitable business deals he would miss, and the appalling danger, until Digby grew a set of fangs and bared them at him. After that, the smuggler fell silent.

The horizon grew a line of scarlet and the sun bounded up huge and bloody, throwing the leggy shadows of the dromals across the sand ahead. The servitors opened sunshades. From the pools of shadow they made, the Knights watched the vast palaces of the Old Ones follow them along the horizon. At last the palaces fell behind. They were lulled into a comfortless trance by the jog and sway of the dromals' trot, and the heat of the air, and the strange bagpipe-like song that Digby sang as he hung from Morgan's sunshade, transformed into a scaly green fan to cool his mistress, but keeping the draft away from Lanz. Lanz rode beside Morgan, and Digby was exceedingly jealous of him.

At dusk two days later, the caravan threaded through a tangle of stony hills and saw the Lower Sea stretching away under the dirty haze of the Green. Next morning, they started down a road that wound along the bottom of a gorge of dusty stone. The ground quivered, and boulders cracked loose from the cliffs. As the sun began to decline toward evening, they rode into the streets of a little port with ships anchored in the offing.

The quays were of marble, cracked, and some of the buildings were piles of rubble, for down here where Aegypt met the Lower Sea the earth twitched like the skin of a horse tortured by flies. "Once a great port," said Sith. "But the Realmgate fell down in an earthquake, and nobody built it again."

Which was why they had come here. Would the Tree's sigil function if the gate was ruined? No, Idris told himself. Certainly not. But he was not entirely sure he believed it.

The harbormaster came out of a building. Sith said to Idris, "Give me fifty finegold." Idris handed him a purse, and Sith went and spoke to the harbormaster. The man bowed and conducted the party to a ship waiting alongside, a strange thing, long-bowed, top-heavy to Idris's eye. The party walked up the gangplank between two files of skullhelms. Two servitors carried a large basket after them.

"Quick, quick," said Sith, his dark little face greasy with sweat as the bearers stowed the basket in the cabin. "We go." The officer of the skullhelms was deliberately not looking at him. Idris had a very good idea where some of the fifty finegolds had gone, but he did not allow the thought to form, for fear of the Tree overhearing it.

The Captain bellowed orders. The sail unfurled. The mooring lines came aboard. The south wind wafted the ship onto the Lower Sea. As soon as the land had fallen into the horizon, Morgan came out of the basket, with Digby wrapped around her neck in the form of a scarf. "See?" said Idris. "There was no Realmgate to pass, so no sigil. You're safe."

She nodded and smiled. But he was worried to see that the darkness was back in her eyes.

That evening on the cushions of the luxurious stern cabin, Idris explained to his Knights what they would do. "We are short of time," he said. "It is five moons since I left Ar Mor. We can't travel back the way we came. So each of us must carry the news of Morgan's rescue to a different ally. I will put my mind into the Kings and show them what has taken place."

"We s-separate?" said Tristan, with a sadness that made Idris realize how close he and his Knights had become, these past moons.

"For a while. Tristan, you will carry my letter to Mark of Ar Mor and make your peace. Bors, to the Duke, for he will believe you. Gawaine, to the Lords of Eirinn, for they love horses. Lanz, to the Overlord, for he trusts you. Merk, to the Thains of Albion, for they love their food. And Galahd to your people, the Norns. You will promise these Kings alliances. And they will be glad to have them, for I shall go into their minds and show them that we have found Morgan, and the terrible doom that awaits if they do not join me. You will tell them to be with their men on the Heights of Albion above the Mount of

Lyonesse seven days at the latest before the Darksolstice that is coming. Tell them that on Darksolstice a white smoke will rise from the Ambrose Well, and Lyonesse will rise against Fisheagle and Murther, and at that point their help will be needed."

A murmur of pride went around the cabin. Only Tristan remained silent, gazing into the deeps of his weedwater, his hair hanging over his face. He said, without looking up, "Mark of Ar Mor thinks I am an outlaw."

"You were once," said Idris. "But now you are a Knight among Knights, and we will bring peace and kindness and law without cruelty. Well?"

Tristan looked up, and Idris saw something in his face had changed, so now it was solid and confident, without the doubt and languor it had had when they met. Mark would see it, too. Even Gawaine seemed able to see it, for he passed up this excellent chance of teasing his friend. Tristan bowed. He said, "You are right, and I will g-go. Dots, anyone?"

And the eternal game of Dots started again, with the usual cheating and banter. But tonight there was an extra warmth to it. For the Knights were more than friends now, more like family, but with a noble cause uniting them. And they knew that soon they would be parted, and that dangers lay ahead of them, and that perhaps there would be no more games like this, for there are no games beyond the tomb.

At nightfall, Idris went into a little cabin on the ship's quarter, and bolted himself in, and closed his eyes, and began to prepare the way for the Knights.

First, he put his mind up to Kek. The gull was far away, gliding over the northern margins of the Lower Sea. The sea stretched black to the horizon. Nearby, a broken Well belched scummy water, and an object with tentacles around a fanged mouth-hole slashed at a seal. A man with dark eye sockets and blue-white skin was plowing a field. The plow moved jerkily through stony sand in which a few brown weeds grew; before the coming of the monstermasters, all this had been green woods and fertile fields. A child stumbled across the field, bringing its father his nuncheon. The child looked thin and sickly, the nunchbag small and ill-filled.

The gull settled on the branch of a dead tree, and folded its wings, and watched the Well-slimed waters of the Lower Sea break oily on the beach.

Idris took all this in and stored it in his mind. This was what his country would become if the monsters of the Wellworld triumphed in Lyonesse as they had in the Lowland. And after Lyonesse, Ar Mor, Eytgard, and the lands of the Wooden Palace. Now he must send the picture out as a warning to his allies.

All was in readiness.

Idris put his mind out six ways. He had not done this before, and it was hard. He found the Overlord, and the Duke of Kaldholm, and King Mark of Ar Mor, and the High Lord of Eirinn, and the Thains of Albion, and the Norn of Norns. And each of them — the Overlord in the warm pantry of the Wooden Palace, the Duke in his pile of gravy-stained cushions, King Mark among the lace curtains in his hollow mound by Ys, the

High Lord among his harpers, the Thains in their smoky hall, and the Norn of Norns in his log house — dreamed awake, and dreamed the same dream.

In the dream, each was looking over his own familiar lands. Where once they had been green and living they were brown and lifeless. Each looked on his house and saw that it was crumbling, flooded with filth. Through this filth each King waded until he came to a room that each recognized as his own high room of state. Steps led up to a dais, on which were two blood-red thrones. On one of them sat Murther. There was a little child on his lap. It was screaming, and Murther was gouging at it, giggling. On the other throne sat Fisheagle. A delicate smile played over her blood-red lips, as if the screams of the child were beautiful music. From time to time her mouth opened, and from between her fangs there lolled a pointed green tongue.

BEHOLD YOUR MASTER AND YOUR MISTRESS IF YOU DO NOT ACT, said Idris in the dream he was making. *ONE WILL COME TO YOU AND EXPLAIN WHAT MUST BE DONE. HE IS A KNIGHT OF LYONESSE. HEED HIM. AND LOOK WHAT THEY HAVE ACCOMPLISHED ALREADY IN THE LOWER SEA, THESE DWELLERS IN DARKNESS.*

Here, Idris showed the sleepers what Kek was seeing. The effect was much improved when Kek planed down from his tree and began rending at a maggoty lamb carcass, the flies lifting in a cloud around his jabbing beak. Idris left them with that view and returned to himself in the cabin on the ship, exhausted and wet with sweat. He slept long and deep, without dreams.

It was a seven days' cruise westward down the Lower Sea as it flowed between its embankments across the Lowland to the True Sea. The Knights exercised in the rigging, Galahd leading them through the spiderweb of rope, swinging and leaping like the apecreatures of the jungles south of the Great Stone. Morgan seemed tired and distant. The river flowed high above the surface of the Green, but there was little to look at—the water was wide and brown and boring, the banks out of sight on either side. So Idris watched through the eyes of Kek, who floated above the dirty Lowland, dodging jets of vapor and jutting buildings. He had ever more strongly the sense that the earth was bulging upward, pressed by monsters from below, ready to burst.

On the fourth morning of the voyage, a line seemed to cross the horizon ahead. As the day wore on, the line grew thicker and higher until Idris could see it was a wall like the Wall of Lyonesse, but mightier. Something was happening to the air above the wall. Kek looped and soared around the ship's mast and yard, stark white against a clearer blue, happy and excited.

Idris called the Captain and the Knights and Sith into the stern cabin.

"We are nearly at the True Sea," he said, when they were gathered. "We will sail into it, turn to starboard, which is to say north, along the wall, and land at a place Sith knows near the Volcanoes. There we can go ashore and continue our journeys by land. Sith will explain."

The Knights were quiet. The feasts were over, and there would be no more games. Morgan was sitting close to Lanz, but not looking at him. She nodded slowly, as if her mind was elsewhere.

Sith wound his little fingers together, the picture of shiftiness. "Yes, Sith have heard of a place, a little, little bay at the foot of the Volcanoes. It is called Roadsend. Because a road ends there. Good road. Useful road, that leads north. The roads are all watched, but not this one, no." He looked around, saw the many grave eyes upon him, spread his hands. "I hear this by rumor," he said.

The Captain put his head around the cabin door. He said, "My lords and my Lady, we are entering the True Sea."

The ship passed through a vast cloud of gulls, swooping and shrieking over the place where the murky brown waters of the Lower Sea thrust into the deep blue of the True Sea. Then the horizon spread away in front of them, and they turned north, the Aegypt Wall a low, dark line beyond the taffrail. Such joy to be free! thought Idris, as he felt the sea breeze on his face. To feel the ship's rise and fall in the True Sea! Such delight to leave terrible Aegypt for the sea road to Lyonesse and the crisp salt air!

Tristan and Gawaine were playing a last game of Dots. Gawaine's face had settled into the mask with which he hid his cheating. He was pleased to be bound for the open road, wild and lawless. He could see Tristan was cheating, too, but for once said nothing. Bors had pulled out a sharpening stone and was putting a shaving edge on his sword. Galahd was back in his element, moving around the ship, trimming sails, conferring with the helmsman. But Idris saw that not everyone seemed delighted. Lanz and Merk had turned a dirty green and were sitting on the deck gazing at their feet. And Morgan had disappeared and was now a mere bump in the rich blankets of her bed in the stern cabin.

Idris let her lie. He rode the air behind Kek's eyes as the ship tore a white groove in the water north, ever north, heeling to the wind from the southeast. Looking through Kek's eyes, he saw great mountains on the horizon ahead, mountains with cities sprawled at their bases and a glow of fire under the plumes of smoke they vomited from fiery craters under their peaks.

These were the Volcanoes, and somewhere at their feet lay Roadsend. A perilous journey for the Knights; but at least the danger would come from men, not hideous Old Ones immortal in dry pits.

On they sailed as the sun went down and the stars pricked out. They ate zupper on deck, sitting in the usual circle. It was a quiet meal, for the minds of all were already on the road they must travel. But they sat as friends, and each of them knew that his strength lay in the others. And when they had finished eating, Idris raised his horn mug of sunapple juice and said, "To the meeting in Lyonesse, and the life thereafter." All of them raised their mugs, and all of them drank; all except Morgan, who seemed weary and had stayed in her bed to gather strength for the journey to come.

Tristan said, "Long life and success to Idris our K-King." Then they raised a great cheer, and Idris knew they meant it from the bottom of their hearts, and hid his proud tears in a bow to them all, his friends and companions and faithful Knights.

Next morning's dawn pinkened a little bay with a beach of white sand between horns of black rock and a long, low building to one side. The slopes of the volcano above were dark, except for the pale line of a road wriggling down to the beach.

"Roadsend," said Sith. The anchor went down. The sailors pulled a rowing boat around to the entry port. The Knights shuffled along the deck with their bundles, Merk complaining that it was early and he was hungry. Idris counted heads. There was one missing. Morgan's. She hated getting up in the morning. He went back to the cabin. She was a still shape in the bed; it was as if she had not moved since last night. He put out his hand to touch hers where it showed above the covers.

It was cold.

His heart beat once, like a drum. He pulled back the blankets.

Her eyes were open. The marks of dried tears were on her cheeks.

The Tree had kept its promise.

Morgan was dead.

NINE

There were the sounds of people and baggage moving over the side. Water clucked at the ship's hull, and dawn birds sang on the slopes ashore.

Morgan was dead.

Idris felt that a handful of sand had trickled between his fingers and onto the beach, and there was nothing he or anyone could do to pick it up again. He felt the tears pour over his face. He put his mind out to Morgan's.

There was nothing there; not even a place where something had been and from which it had now gone.

With shaking fingers he pulled Holdwater's baldric over his head. The scabbard had brought her back once before. It would do it again.

Someone was calling his name from the deck. He brushed the sound away. If he drew the sword, Fisheagle would find him. Well, let her. He drew Cutwater and laid the scabbard on Morgan's body, and put his mind out once more—

INFANT, roared a huge voice. Not Fisheagle. Something else. *I AM THE TREE. I AM NOT DEFIED.*

He crouched rigid at the bedside, gazing with his mind at the darkness where bright Morgan had once been. And suddenly his mind fell through darkness, and he saw the thing whose voice it was. It writhed and bellowed in its dry pit, gigantic, driven insane by its immortality, on the edge of being and not being. It had a body like a huge man's. But instead of a head it had a tree, a tree like the one in the fretwork on the screen in the slave market, and instead of arms it had roots. Roots that went to the remotest gates of Aegypt's Kingdom. Roots in whose hair-fine outer fibers something lay tangled. And when he looked at it closely, he saw that the thing was the figure of a girl who looked at him with sad green eyes and gave him a helpless smile.

The figure of Morgan.

Lanz put his head into the cabin. "I must say good-bye," he said.

Idris stood. Lanz was trying to see around him, to look at Morgan. Idris wanted to sit down and weep and howl for grief and despair. But in a clear, cold corner of his mind, Idris knew that if Lanz knew Morgan was dead, he would not take the road to the Wooden Palace, and there would be no Overlord to help in the conquest of Lyonesse. He heard himself say, "She is sleeping. She is not well. She was saying she would see you in Lyonesse."

Lanz looked unhappy. "You are not coming?"

"We will follow."

Lanz bowed his head, ever the dutiful soldier. He took a

gold chain from his neck. "When she wakes, give this to her. It is mountain gold."

"I will," said Idris. "Good luck. We will meet on the Heights of Albion."

"Good luck." A final glance at the figure in the bed, and Lanz was gone.

Idris went on deck. Numb with grief, he watched the Knights land on the beach. He saw them find horses at the inn by the wood and ride away up the road, little figures shrinking as they approached the first ridge of the Volcanoes. He saw them turn and wave, and waved back. Then they were gone. He turned away, eyes clouded with tears.

The ship picked up its anchor and turned its bow down the wall toward the coast of Aegypt. Idris left the scabbard Holdwater upon the body of Morgan, for whatever good it would do. He double muffled, so when Fisheagle found him, cold and scornful, he hardly heard her. When she had gone, he put his mind out and quietly wished each of his Knights a prosperous journey.

Then he and his dead sister drifted back toward the past, where the Old Ones sat monstrous and unchanging at the dry heart of their hideous Kingdom.

⇌•⇌

For two days and nights, Idris sat by Morgan's side while the ship sailed back along the wall to Aegypt and little Sith bit his fingernails on the deck. The world was full of noise from the

Lowland, on the far side of the wall. It was more than the usual chatter. It was a roar of monstervoices, each striving and ambitious, shouting about something that was about to happen; though in the dullness of his grief, Idris could not be bothered to find out what.

He muffled against the racket, plunging deep till all he could hear was the heavy thump of his pulse and the terrible stillness of Morgan's. Between some sunset and some dawn, he did not care which, he was sitting torpid and silent when a small voice said, *Idris*.

And suddenly he was not torpid anymore. For the voice was tiny and remote, but bright and sharp. And it was a voice he recognized: the voice of his friend and teacher, whom he trusted more than anyone else in the world. *Ambrose?* he said.

Of course. I have been watching. This was only to be expected. Believe me, things are always better than they seem. Visit the Wall Mage at the Aegypt Gate.

Meaning?

If a person can succeed with the breeding of dragons, no cause is hopeless.

And have you succeeded?

A small chuckle, infinitely distant, fading.

Ambrose?

Nothing.

"Ambrose!" roared Idris and opened his eyes.

"Sir?" said the sailor standing in the cabin door. "Captain says Aegypt Gate in sight."

"We will go ashore," said Idris. A warmth remained in his mind. Ambrose, after all this time. There was hope in the world after all.

Then the present grasped him, and he called, "Sith!"

Sith scuttled in, wringing his hands. "They will take us and gut us," he said. "Oh, oh—"

"Quiet," said Idris. "When we go ashore, you will lead us to the Wall Mage."

Sith shrugged. Idris caught a fleeting thought in his mind. *Run*, it said. *Away, flee.*

"With Morrab," Idris warned, "you are protected from the Old Ones. Without her, you are not."

Sith reflected. Then he bowed and said, "Yes." Sith's only interest in life was Sith. Idris knew he would not flee.

Half a glass later, the ship came alongside the stone quay of the Aegypt Gate of the True Sea Wall.

Idris had been making preparations at top speed. Morgan's body was on a litter, with a powerful seaman at each handle. They traveled at a jog-trot down the quay and set the litter down in the square in front of a low, cube-shaped building just outside the vast arch of the Aegypt Gate.

"Here," said Sith.

Idris pushed open the door and ran in. A man looked up from the table at which he was seated: a very small man, with eyes the color of deep water. "I beg your pardon," said Idris. He explained quickly, the words tumbling over one another. "I have a friend who is ill."

The small man sat looking at his hands on the desk in front of him. "It is a straightforward case," he said. "As you surmise, your friend who is Morrab belongs to the Tree, and she passed his sigil, oh yes, there was one, as you sailed on to the True Sea, through a Realmgate of a sort, so her life remains with him."

"And if I take her back through the gate?"

"Her life may return. Slowly, though. Moons of care, moons. They are petty and jealous, these Old Ones. He will have racked her." He sighed. "So now you will go." He looked up suddenly, eyes bright, head on one side like a bird's. "You have been schooled by mages, I think."

Idris bowed, his feet itching with impatience, the Manner holding him. "By Ambrose of the Devouring Eel," he said.

"Ah, Ambrose." The little mage smiled, and Idris suddenly saw that he was very ancient. "An old friend. We do what we can to keep the balance. I am in charge of the walls, you know." He gestured to a great bronze hammer hanging by the door and fell silent. Idris could not tell what he meant. He started to inch toward the door. "Wait," said the mage. "There are dark things afoot in the Lower Sea." He leaned forward. "If I were you," he said, "I should keep to the high ground."

Idris bowed again and said with what patience he could muster, "I thank you, Master," all the while thinking, Morgan, the Gate, I must go.

He ran out into the burning sun and shooed the litter toward the Aegypt Gate. The shadow of the enormous arch passed over them. They came into the light on the other side.

"Down," said Idris.

The bearers put the litter down.

The sun glared out of the sky. Morgan's face was pale and still. Then something in it seemed to flicker. Idris's heart boomed in his ears.

Her eyes opened.

He hugged her. He felt her shivering. She said, in a tiny voice, "That must never happen again."

"What?"

"There was a pit, and One with a tree for a head, and I was caught in the roots, and I am caught forever. Oh, a disgusting place." She began to cry.

Idris stayed with her, feeling the warmth of life return to her hand. But what kind of life? If she left Aegypt, she was condemned to die. If she remained, there was the crypt in the New Palace, and the boxes beside the other Morrabs, so old that they had fallen to pieces, until she fell to pieces herself, and would still be alive. He reached in the pocket of his tunic and found the chain Lanz had given him. Carefully he put it around Morgan's neck. "From Lanz," he said. "Mountain gold."

She smiled, a smile that squeezed a tear down each cheek. "And so is he," she said. "I'll never see him again."

He said, "Oh yes, you will," knowing that his voice had the heartiness that people use with invalids. He waited till she fell asleep, her hand wound in the chain. Then he left her and ordered dromals and guards and supplies for a journey in the desert, and they set forth. The Wall Mage had advised him to stay on high ground. He had a notion of what this might mean. As his dromal plodded across the hot brown hills of Aegypt, an idea, horrifying but necessary, was beginning to grow in his mind.

On they rode, while the monsters from the Wells of the Lowland shrieked a triumphant chorus, louder and louder. On the tenth day, the gigantic buildings of the Old Ones rose on the sunward horizon. On the eleventh, they entered the New Palace, and everything was quiet and sunny and dappled with the green shade of the trees, as it had been for seven thousand years.

Week after week, Morgan lay on a daybed, gathering strength, while Digby fanned her with a large spotty tail modeled on a peacock's. Slowly she gained color. The year was passing. The New Palace filled with hopping throngs of little birds that arrived, rested, and flew on. Some were strange to Idris; but one day there were swallows overhead, and warblers in the sunapple trees, and a nightingale, too tired to sing. These were the birds of the northern summer, returning to their winter quarters. The Knights would be with the Kings. In three moons it would be Darksolstice. Idris was eaten up with impatience.

One morning, Morgan beat him at Check and laughed, and Idris judged her strong enough to begin putting his plan into action.

He set off in the direction of the sunward wing, towing Sith in his wake. The little smuggler had been reluctant to leave the palace since the voyage to the Volcanoes and had turned into Idris's interpreter—Idris was getting by in the Aegypt tongue, but he still lacked the formal speech required for dealing with officials or, as today, librarians. After a journey of two glasses through courts and cloisters and echoing passages, they came to the Library, a great building like an enormous pigeon house whose inner walls were pocked with alcoves filled with scrolls instead of doves. High on the walls, tiny figures scuttled like spiders among the alcoves.

Idris clapped his hands. The spider-figures froze. Then one of them ran down the wall and stood panting before him. "Ss?" it said.

It was a man, dark-skinned, tiny, with bright, intelligent eyes. The Librarians of Aegypt originated in the hot forests south of the Great Stone. Their tribe passed its days studying ancient texts in their own libraries, which were built high in the treetops, so they were used to climbing. This one crouched before Idris on bandy legs and long, sensitive fingers. "Kk?" he said impatiently.

"Tell the Honored Librarian that I seek knowledge of the Realmgates and the power of the Tree," said Idris.

"Ff," said the Librarian, as if these were subjects Idris should have mastered some time ago. Then he bounded away and scurried busily up a wall.

A glass later, he returned with an armful of scrolls. Idris took them to a table and bent over them. "All the gates are marked," said the Librarian in a small, high voice. "Look. The sigil of the Tree is on all of them."

And sure enough, the map showed there was no entrance to Aegypt without the sigil of the Tree. But in all the New Palace itself, there was no sigil marked. Idris's heart began to beat hard with hope.

"What?" said Sith, squinting at him.

"Nothing," said Idris, muffling hard. He thanked the Librarian, who knocked his brow civilly against the desk. Then he walked back through the palace to Morgan's chambers.

"Well?" said Morgan, weary on her daybed, not really interested.

When Idris put his mind out to hers, it was the merest flicker of warmth. He sent her a strengthening thought, then drew back. As he did so, he felt an eye on him and a mind in his. He looked up and saw Digby watching him. "You're not *serious!*" said Digby. "How *thrilling!*"

"I have no idea what you are talking about," said Idris and slammed his mind shut.

"Ooh," said Digby. "Touchy!"

Fewer than three moons to Darksolstice.

Lyonesse was three-moons' journey away.

By normal roads.

There were others quicker. But they were deep and dark. And very, very dangerous.

It was black night when Idris got out of bed. He shrugged into a cloak against the night chill and slid out of his room.

The moon printed the shadows of the pillars black on the paving of the colonnades. He ran, swift and silent. Once a skull-helm guard walked by, and he stepped back into the shadow of a pillar while the skeleton-figure crunched on its rounds; not that he had anything to fear from the palace guards, but he did not want to be remembered. The ground trembled a little, even here in the solid land of Aegypt. The sense of pressure and movement from far away in the Lowland had been increasing these past weeks.

The guard passed. Idris began to run again. At last he came into the older part of the palace and caught the whiff of Wellwater he had smelled faintly on his first day here. From there on, he followed his nose.

The way led through quadrangles long abandoned. The moon shone on a chaos of fallen masonry. And suddenly he was standing in front of a great drum of blackened stone: the sealed Well of the New Palace.

For a moment he stood and shivered. Then, gingerly, he put out his hand and touched the smooth black surface of the tower. It was chill and dry, and voices flowed out of it. *Idris,* they said. *The time is at hand. Oh, the things you will witness as we kill the lands around the Lower Sea!*

Be still, thought Idris and muffled, feeling their shock as the bolt slammed home. He began to walk around the Well.

The Wells of Lyonesse were tall as mountains, built ever upward to stop the Welltides from flooding the sinking land. Their walls were double, full of rooms, and they were bound in intricate work in stone and mosaic tile. But in Aegypt slaves did the work, and there were no monsters. So no monsters were caught, and the land did not sink, and the tides were lower in relation to it. By the standards of Lyonesse, the Palace Well was a low, squat thing, unornamented, workmanlike: a back door out of the world of air into the Wellworld. A disused door, unregarded.

Or so Idris hoped.

He walked around the side, picking his way over the rubble at its base until he came to a short flight of steps. From the top of the steps, iron rungs led up the barrel of the tower. Grasping the iron, he began to climb.

Last time he had climbed a Welltower, the corroded rungs had torn his hands. These rungs were solid; metal lasted forever in the dry Aegypt air. Idris rose steadily. When he looked sideways he saw the upper towers of the palace bone-pale under the moon, and beyond them the grim temples of the Old Ones spread across the desert under the billion stars.

After two hundred and thirty-one rungs, he heaved himself onto the top. There was a narrow platform around the mouth of the Wellshaft, which was sealed with an iron plate; iron was beastbane, proof against monsters. The catching apparatus was man-powered, where in Lyonesse it would have had a monster engine. It was ancient, but still in place. Idris drew aside the iron plate and leaned over the hole, catching the distant slosh and boom of water far below. He walked around the machinery. The catching gear did not interest him. But he paused over the winch that opened the sluice shutters. It seemed to be in good condition. He gave the windlass handle a turn, listening intently. There was a faint grinding in the deep.

Good.

Then he sat on the Welltop and dangled his legs down the hole, and let the terrible thoughts march through his head.

By now the Knights would have met their Kings. They would either be in prison, or ignored, or approaching Lyonesse with their retinues and their armies, waiting for the proclamation of the new King at Darksolstice.

And the rightful King of Lyonesse was in Aegypt, a three-moons' journey away, two moons and a wane to go before Darksolstice, dangling his feet into a Welltower and thinking impossible thoughts that must become possible if his kingdom were to live—

Something happened.

It was an explosion in the mind: a dark burst of monster-thought that would have blown Idris's head off, had he not been muffled.

A great roar of triumph in the mind. *THROUGH*, it screamed. *WE BURST THROUGH, WITH THE DARKNESS. TODAY THE LOWLAND. TOMORROW THE WORLD.* The tower shook, and Idris heard the crash of falling masonry from elsewhere in the palace, and the mind-roars of the Old Ones. He wrapped his head in a double muffle and sent his mind out to Kek.

Sleep, said Kek.

WAKE, roared Idris. He heard the surprised squawk of the gull as it grabbed air with its wings and lofted into the sky, away like an arrow to the shores of the Lower Sea.

And through its eyes saw horror.

———————⋊•⋉———————

The Lower Sea lay spread under the brilliant moon. The gull was high, higher than it had ever been, a morning's march straight up, vertically above Bitter River, so it could see the great sheet of the Lower Sea, and the lands that lay around it, gray in the moonlight.

The lands were changing.

As Idris watched, the center of Bitter River bulged upward. The earth seemed to stretch, then crack and break, and through the rents there welled a dark ocean. There were things in the water, things that flopped and writhed and wriggled and swam, gigantic things the size of mountains. And as they burst up from the Wellworld into the moonlight they screamed, a huge, terrible scream of agony at the light, and joy that they would take possession of this new world, and that it would be theirs to spoil. The monsters and the Wellwater they lived in filled the river, overtopped it, so the high, scummy wavecrest of the Wellworld raced across the land, tearing down hovels and palaces and manufactories, until it joined the wave fronts from the other Wellbursts and crashed down on the Lower Sea. And Idris knew that what was happening here in the Lowland was an invasion long prepared. And that unless he could stop it, the same kind of invasion lay in store for Lyonesse.

He sat consumed with horror, beaten down by the howl of triumph from the Wells. *It is ours*, cried the voices. Then he heard another, in memory: the little Wall Mage of Aegypt Gate. *If I were you, I would keep to the higher ground.*

Suddenly he knew what had to be done.

He sent Kek sailing down the wind, a long, long glide, following the line of the Lower Sea as the Lowland fell away on either side and the embankments rose, carrying the water to the wall that kept back the bright waves of the True Sea. The sun was rising.

From this height, the river embankments were slim, dark lines, with a clot of darkness where the embankment met the True Sea Wall — the Aegypt Gate, beside which the Wall Mage sat. Idris put his mind down into the town. He found the Wall Mage sleeping in his little tumbled bed, and shouted in his mind: *The Wells have burst up!*

He felt the old man's shock as he woke. He felt him tumble out of bed, stagger to his writing room, seize the bronze hammer that hung there. He felt him swing the hammer over his head with the last of his ancient strength, and slam it down on a bronze peg that protruded from the center of a stone in the floor.

Idris saw into the mage's mind as it followed the bronze peg deep into the wall, where it crushed a crystal brace, so that a stone fell, and a thin stream of water poured in, and melted the salt that cemented a block, so the block fell out, and a seep of water appeared around it, and the seep became a trickle, and the trickle a runnel, and the runnel a gush, and the block shot out into space, tumbling down the wall face, and its neighbors after it, end over end, the water bursting forth in a great wet fist, matched by another fist of water on the northern shore of the river, and the walls that kept the sea out of the Lowland began to crumble away.

Thank you, said the Wall Mage. *Farewell*. A confused vision of bursting masonry and crashing rock and tumbling water, then darkness. Through Kek's eyes Idris saw that part of the Wall was gone, and the True Sea was pouring through the hole, clean and salty, so Idris's head rang with the bellowing of monsters smashed and buffeted, and the awful terror of the Lowland people, merchants and monstermasters and tenders of the salt fires of the Lower Sea as the bright waters tore them away.

All over the Lowland, people flocked to higher ground, and salt-seared monsters perished in their thousands. In the New Palace, Idris resealed the Well, climbed down the tower, and walked to the chamber where Morgan and he would meet for brekfuss.

Morgan was already at the table, alone except for Digby, who was perched on her shoulder. Idris sat down. He poured himself some weedwater, took a slab of Aegypt bread, and said, "The Wells of the Lowland have burst up. The walls are down. The Lowland is drowned."

"I saw it in my dreams," said Morgan, pale and wan.

"We must go back to Lyonesse."

"You go back. I can't." Her voice was weary, as if she stood at the far end of eternal life, not its beginning.

"There is a way."

She shook her head, stirring her weedwater. "Why should I? My foster parents of the Wolf Rock are dead. There is nobody there for me."

"There is me," said Idris. "And Lanz."

Her face pinkened. "Yes," she said. "But I am no good to any of you if my body is dead and my soul is caught in the...roots."

Idris said, "Do you want to stay here until it is time for you to go down into one of those boxes? Or do you want to see home again, and Lanz, and fight the monsters who want to make Lyonesse into a Lowland, and get justice for the people of the Wolf Rock and Angharad our mother? There is a way. A dark and risky way. But a way nonetheless. Perhaps we will die. But at least it will be a true death."

Morgan looked up. She held his eyes a long time. To his joy, he saw the dullness had left them, and that in them was now a trace of the old wild Morgan, breathless with hope. She said, "What is this way?"

Idris drew breath carefully, feeling the world balanced on a knife-edge. He said, "You remember what Ambrose told us about our ancestors?"

"I do."

"In particular about Kyd Draco, who had in him the blood of Captains as well as Knights." Idris saw again the face of Ambrose in the Iron Room, the night he had drawn the sword Cutwater from the latches of the Old Well. "Strange blood, Ambrose said, that came from who knows where. Well, I do know where."

Morgan was gazing at him, expressionless. "Where, then?"

"There are things that have always seemed odd," said Idris. "One thing in particular. When I fell from the Fort of Westgate, I told you about that, I was under the water for half a glass at least, yet I lived. When you are in water, what do you see?"

She shrugged. "A sort of blurred bluish light."

"Nothing else?"

She frowned, remembering. "There was a time, when I was little, and I fell in the horse pond at the Wolf Rock. I thought I was drowning. You know what the monsters in the stables at the Ambrose used to say? Come with me into the darkgardens, where the little red fishes swim, all that? Well, it was dark, with little bright flashes. They said I was in the pond for a long time, a whale's dive, they said. They couldn't understand why I wasn't dead. And of course nobody wanted to talk about it afterward."

Idris was back in the school at Westgate on the day his life had changed forever. It was the Hour of Thanks, and the great bell was booming in the mica-glittering air. *That which swims is Cross and must die. Thou shalt not suffer a Cross to live.*

He shivered. "In case anyone thought you were Cross," he said.

"I suppose so."

"Well, you are," he said.

"*What?*" said Morgan, now looking quite unlike the high priestess of the New Palace and very much like her pink, annoyed Lyonesse self. "Me? Cross? How *dare* you?"

"It's sooooo obvious," said Digby, butting in. "You speak with your minds. You can live in water —"

"Shut up!" snapped Morgan.

"All right, you can choose," said Idris. She was so stubborn, thought Idris. Oddly, this made him feel extremely close to her, the way he had felt when they had been monstergrooms in the Great Ambrose. "Choose," he said. "You can live here until you fall to bits like those horrible old things in the boxes. Or you can admit you're Cross, and we'll go back to Lyonesse and do our duty or die in the attempt." He took a deep breath. It was time to say what he had come to say. "I have been in the Library and studied the maps. There is no Tree sigil on the Palace Well."

There was a long silence, during which she tried to stare a hole in him. Then she said, "Oh."

"At best, we can travel home through the Wellworld —"

"I'll guide you!" cried Digby, thrilled. "You'll never manage without me!"

"— and at worst we drown or get eaten."

"Go back and destroy Fisheagle and Murther," said Morgan. "Or stay and wither over a million moons." She straightened her shoulders and looked at Idris with a bright green eye. "The Well it is," she said.

"*Excellent* decision!" said Digby.

Idris bowed and took her hand, which was warm again. He could feel the huge blunt mind of the Tree in its pit, shoving at these ideas, trying to grip them, but fumbling, like a person with enormous fingers trying to pick up a little shell on a beach. It would find a way, in time, even if it meant picking up the beach, too.

So they must go before it could grasp their intentions.

"Digby," he said. "Are you sure you can do it?"

"Easy as falling off a chair," said Digby. And he fell off the back of Morgan's chair, to demonstrate.

<hr />

A little later, Sith came into the palace. He looked harassed and ragged, as if he had been pulled and torn by crowds. "Terrible out there," he said. "The sea's come up a thousand steps. Storms, thunder, rioting. All the ships are lost. All the ports are drowned. The tide's in, and I don't think it'll ever go out. How am I supposed to smuggle across two hundred leagues of sea?"

Idris shrugged. The big blunt fingers of the Tree were still fumbling at his muffle. If they pulled his head open, their owner would see what lay within and put the sigil on the Well. . . .

"Sith," he said, "you have been a good servant. What would you like me to give you?"

"Finegold," said Sith.

Idris called a servitor and arranged for Sith to be given as much finegold as he could carry.

"Where are you going?" said Sith.

"We are not leaving the palace," said Idris. "It is just that it is time you got on with your life."

"True," said Sith, whose mind was on the enormous amount of finegold, not his loyalty to his master. "All right. Have a nice life." And he was gone.

Idris went to his room. The night was hot, but he could not stop shivering, and the fingers of the Tree were fumbling harder.

A voice sounded, small and clear. *For goodness' sake get on with it, boy.* The blunt fingers were snatched away from his head, as if someone had driven a sword into them. *Now look here, Idris,* said the voice. *Head for the Ambrose and come straight to me. You know where.* A pause. *Oh, by the way. You've done pretty well. So don't spoil it by being idle. Move. Now. This is urgent.*

Ambrose? said Idris.

Who did you think it was? said the voice, small and clear and silvery. *I can't hold this nasty vegetable off forever. Hurry.*

Idris found he was grinning. Suddenly the New Palace was only a palace, the Old Ones were mere nasty spooks, and it was time to leave.

He took Cutwater from the wall and slung it about him. The serving maids parted drowsily as he marched through the anterooms to Morgan's chamber. "What?" she said from the bed.

"We are leaving. Now. Digby?"

"All present and correct," said that cheerful monster.

"Leave?" said Morgan.

215

He took her hand. "Don't think. Just come."

The hand went rigid in his. "Tomorrow. Maybe."

"Ambrose sent word. The Tree is trying to get into me. Don't think."

IT IS NOT PERMITTED, said the voice of the Tree through Morgan's mind.

Idris battered it with his own mind. The thing withdrew, surprised. "Muffle," said Idris. The huge blunt fingers came back, started to fumble again. "Sing a song," said Idris. "Anything. Keep it out."

> *"O the walls of the land go all the way 'round*
> *all the way 'round*
> *all the way 'round*
> *And the King built the walls so we won't drown*
> *all of us in the morning,"*

sang Morgan, in a small, quavery voice.

"Out!" said Idris, pushing her through the anterooms. "Sing!"

The waning moon hung low as they marched through the courts and gardens and colonnades into the zone of ruins, blotting out the whispers from the dark with the silly children's song. *"All of us in the morning,"* they sang, marching over the tumbled masonry to where the fat chimney of the Well towered black against the stars. "Climb," said Idris. "Digby. Can you manage?"

"Of course," said Digby huffily.

"*All the way 'round*," sang Morgan, coming up the rungs behind him. His confidence was wearing off now. They were going to jump into a Well. His knees were knocking.

The Tree was still fumbling at his mind. Don't think, climb. "*All the way 'round*," he sang, and Morgan with him. And there they were on the Welltop, under that last-quarter moon. The Tree was a heavy hammer in his head as he hauled at the sluice lever. It would not shift. "Help me," he said. Morgan came next to him and heaved. He could smell the sleepy sweetness of her hair, feel her hands beside his on the lever, smell the Wellstink rising from the deeps. Heave. Nothing. *Heave.* Suddenly, far, far below, iron grated on iron. "*All the way 'round*," she sang, as the lever came over.

"Sluices free," said Idris, going back to the routines of the Welltops of the Valley of Apples, where they had worked as monstergrooms. He pulled Cutwater from Holdwater and raked it across the iron seal-plate — let Fisheagle find him if she wanted; he no longer cared. The blade sliced the metal like cheese. The two halves fell into the dark. There was no splash; the Well was too deep for that. He said, "Digby? Hold on." He took Morgan's hand in his. She wanted to pull it away. He knew how she felt.

WHAT? said the huge Tree voice, suddenly in his mind. *THE PORTAL TO THE OTHERWORLD? I HAD —*

But they never found out what it had done. For Idris had taken a deep breath, said, "One, two, *three*." And on *three*, he and Morgan leaped into the Well.

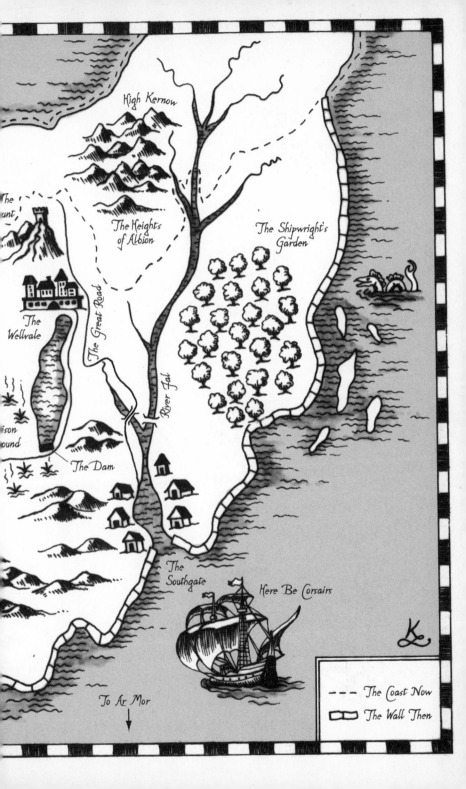

·PART THREE·

Oh, the triumph. Oh, the glory. Oh, the soundless cheering that rang through the Wellworld deeps as the Wells of the Lowland burst upward, and the Helpers swam out into the light to destroy!

She watched what happened with her mind, hovering in a far, dark place, at a safe distance from all the rushing and the upbursting and the yells of triumph. She must watch and see how it was done, for they had promised that when she had given them Lyonesse she would rule them, and she needed to know about their nature and tactics.

She saw the reason the invasion failed. It was that on the margins of the Great Colony (for so the monsters called the Lower Sea) there had been a power that controlled the walls and had a way of breaking them down (she shivered with rage, and the scales on her body rattled, and the leathery wings she used to swim in the caverns of darkness trembled raw and angry).

But nobody controlled the walls of Lyonesse; nobody but her, that was, now that nasty little Idris was drawing his sword in Aegypt. And if by any chance he did return, she would welcome him back. And having welcomed him, she would usher him and his pathetic allies into her trap.

She sent her mind to her son, her darling son. She felt him stir in his blood-red bed, sip delicately at the cup of blood beside it, running the delicious fluid through his dear sharp teeth. You are nearly of age, she said. Go, and defend yourself and your rights, if these people come.

She felt his mind; sluggish and cross, the mind, but he was only young, and young people needed their rest.

When the time came, he would spring the trap. And darkness, lovely darkness, would fall, and she would rule above and below.

TEN

The fall. The long, long fall, turning slowly in the air. There was time for Idris to hear Morgan shout, "Good-bye, Idris." Time for Idris to shout, "Courage, my sister." Then the huge crash into bitter water, the sinking, deep, deep, Morgan's hand in his, struggling, wanting to go upward, and his lungs were bursting, but he knew that up to the surface would be no help, for they would merely be trapped in the chimney of the Well, the high, high chimney, with a vengeful Tree hastening to plant its sigil....

No point in surfacing.

Idris held Morgan, tight, even as she kicked and battered him and his body told him to struggle or he would die.

But he did not rise. Something was pulling him down. A voice in his head said, *Come on, what's wrong with you? Don't be silly;* the voice, he realized, of Digby. And he felt Morgan's hand go limp in his and his mouth open and the bitter water flow in to choke him. The world turned to darkness, with little red and blue lights swimming in it....

Idris breathed Wellwater.

And was still alive.

Everything changed.

He was flying, swift and weightless. He could see; but the thing that let him see was not light but darkness, rich and beautiful. He was in a place too big to be enormous: a void without edges, filled with the deep, musical echo of a million thoughts, in which he flew hand in hand with a person he knew to be Morgan.

Beautiful, said Morgan with her mind.

Idris agreed. There was the sensation of a sigh next to him, and the voice of Digby in his mind. *I told you so. Just be careful what you say. Thought travels here. Would you like to visit a darkgarden?* The word filled Idris's mind with a feeling of home, warm bread, the pride of pulling Cutwater from the stone: a huge, powerful satisfaction. *That's how they make you feel*, said Digby. *Come.*

Idris fought away the strangeness of that huge floating darkness. *We go to the Ambrose*, he said.

Hush, said Digby.

Ambrose, Ambrose, went the echoes of the thought into the infinite distances. *Ambrose? Ambrose?* it came back from a billion minds, echoing, changing, until there was the hint of an angry buzz behind it, like a beehive attacked by woodpeckers.

Oh dear, thought Digby. *Fly.* And Idris knew that whatever he was had grown huge, leathery wings and was indeed flying through the harmonies of the void, the harmonies that were now touched by menace. There were other things flying after them, faster and faster. In his mind, Digby was saying *Don't think, don't mention your name, your blood is in this world, oh dear, we will all be devoured...ah. A darkgarden. In here.*

The sense of flying toward a great sphere, swooping very close to its surface, flying at terrifying speed along its huge curves, its hills and mountain ranges, into a valley, a valley of beautiful darkness, with at its end a looming cave mouth from which flowed harmonies sublime, a cave mouth that was an entrance; and in, swooping, wings folding, plummeting in free fall through an even deeper darkness.

Blackness deep and velvety, with a vast, low harmony pouring through it, so you did not know where you stopped and the music started, and streams of darkness different from the velvet darkness, of no color, but in Idris's mind red and green and starburst-blue, floating around you and through you and in you, bringing peace.

Beautiful, thought Morgan, only the word sounded like a chord from a perfect stringed instrument.

And they watched, calm, washed by music. But that was not what made Idris feel brighter and happier than at any time since he had left the stonefields of Ys. It was that in Morgan's thought he had heard not the corsair slave nor Morrab the Child, but his dear, true friend and sister, Morgan. And things were normal again — or as normal as they could be, given that they were in unhuman form, luxuriating in a darkgarden in a universe of bitter water inhabited by monsters.

He floated, feeling Morgan near him, lapped in the velvety black, with the dancing red lights flowing through him in whorls and arabesques, beautiful as music made visible. He felt himself slide into the dark glory of it, dissolving, until he was part of the huge smooth blackness, happy. And the pursuit had passed them by, and the danger was past.

But somewhere, he was still Idris. And Idris began to lose count of how long they hid there; it was impossible to tell. But he did know that time was passing in the world of the... *gasfaces*, he found himself thinking... and the arc of the sun was sinking toward Darksolstice, when he must be on the Mount for the coming of age of Murther. His kingdom of Lyonesse was tiny, compared to these dark immensities. But it was home.

Go, he thought at his companions.

They tore themselves out of the great harmony, and they went.

With his darksenses Idris saw himself and his companions flying through the watery void, passing throngs of other creatures, huge, indescribable, surrounded by flocks of smaller creatures.

The Helpers, said Digby, as if out of the corner of his mouth. *With their servants, which you call burners. The Helpers send them up the chimneys to you gasfaces. On. Quick. Food!*

And away he powered, mouth vast and gaping, heading for a shoal of little things swimming in the black. Idris found himself doing the same, his mouth a great pit bristling with fangs, plunging into the heart of the shoal. And a crunch, a really good crunch, then the taste of something absolutely and completely delicious. *Good?* cried Digby in his mind.

Excellent! said Idris.

What is it? said Morgan. *I want more!*

Blood.

Oh.

There is a thing we say, thought Digby. *A poem, you would call it*:

Give me blood in the music
Give me music in the blood
Give me more, quickly

Ah, said Morgan. *Delightful.*

Indeed, said Idris. He knew perfectly well that it was a ridiculous poem, with a disgusting message. But the part of him that was a monster did think it really, inspiringly, beautiful.

Away they flew, on and on. It seemed to Idris that they picked up a current, and that the current hurled them across the world. At last, Digby's voice in his mind said, *Coming near.* Ever since they had been in the current, he had been singing more of his bright tunes in praise of darkgardens and blood. Now he fell silent.

Idris knew why.

Something was wrong with the darkness ahead. It was . . . spoiled. From high in it there descended shafts of brightness, agonizing to monster senses, like the pillars of a great building. Around those pillars, in spirals that merged into a huger spiral, there drifted a throng of monsters.

What is that? wondered Idris.

Chimneys.

A monster's chimney is a man's Well, thought Idris with the human part of his brain. Great shapes slid past, mouths vast as sea caves, tentacles fat as trees: the huge monsters called Helpers. Then they were in the throng spiraling around the pillar, in a darkness thick with leathery fins and slimy flanks and teeth, elbowing toward the middle. Voices began to speak in his head.

You go.

Must I?

It is good. There will be blood without end.

But if they catch me I will be dry and frizzle and burn.

Blood, as much as you want. Look.

And down the pillar of light there drifted the faintest stain of pink.

The Well's open, said Idris. *They're groundbaiting.* High above on the Welltop, the catchers would be pouring copper buckets of blood into the Well.

They swam on. Now there was a tightening in Idris's chest, as if it was becoming a chest again. *Tide coming,* said Digby.

Take us to the Ambrose Well, said Idris.

Please don't say that name. Oh, I hope they didn't hear. Follow me.

They flew on through the dark, past one light column, into a group of others. Idris saw in his mind the Welltowers of the Valley of Apples rising above this watery void, the hookmen and grooms nervous on the Welltops, fishing for monsters.

Idris, hissed Morgan. *Listen.*

The music of the world was full of a bee-buzzing again, getting louder. *Ambrose?* it droned. *Idris?* Puzzled. *Idris? Ambrose? Idris?* The puzzlement turned to rage. The music became mere furious noise, rose to a buzzing howl.

They heard. Swim, said Digby, urgent, frightened. *Swim, swim.* Idris caught Morgan's hand and followed their guide into a pillar of light, zigging and zagging to avoid teeth and claws and flanks.

A slow cloud of blood drifted in the light. A monster lazed in it, licking up particles in a delicious daze. Suddenly there appeared from above a cluster of globes like an enormous bunch of grapes. Idris was puzzled for a moment, then realized that these were the blood-bladders that baited the hook. The ground-bait blood hazing the water around the bladders drew the monster part of him with the promise of dizzy pleasure. The lazing monster seemed to wake up and powered toward the bladders, jagged mouth gaping. There was a roar, a sense of upward movement, and he knew that the tide was washing him up the Well. A new current of water beat at him. *Behind you*, shrieked the voice of Morgan, and Idris felt his monstrous flesh crawl with the knowledge that something was close on his heels, felt a mind screaming *Blood, blood*. Idris turned back and found himself looking into a great mouth, open, roaring. He tried to hit it with his mind, but there were changes in him, and his mind was confused, too weak, so the mouth came on, jagged with dagger-teeth, screaming. And Idris's body was changing, muscle and bone writhing under the skin, bitter water in what was now a throat; but as well as a throat he had an arm. He twisted away. The jaws clashed shut on the place where Idris had been. The thing turned with a horrible muscular wriggle and darted at him again. But now there was a hand on his arm, and something in the hand, and he knew that something was Cutwater. As the mouth came in for the next lunge, he sliced the blade across a rubbery something that screamed, agony this time, not rage, thrust again, felt the blade drive into something that writhed and juddered and roared in his head, while a great tide of water whirled him upward. Then there was a dazzle of light, and a crash, and he was human, lying naked in cold iron railings, his eyes blinded by light, and he let out a huge breath that was a spout of bitter Wellwater, coughed, breathed air, and croaked, "Hookmen! We are man, not monster!"

A stunned silence fell, while the dazzle of brightness little by little became shapes he could recognize. There were figures in brown boiled-leather armor, visors down: hookmen and bait-men. Another in red armor, visor down, too: a monstergroom. This was the familiar Welltop of the Great Ambrose; but all the people bore the barbed-squid badge of the Brassfin Spouter. Alongside him was Morgan, wedged in the railing, a white sprawl of arms and legs wearing a small green tunic. In Idris's left hand was Cutwater, sunk deep in the black body of a monster like a giant wicked shark. On the stones of the Welltop lay a burner, beginning to fume as it dried.

"Get rid of that burner before you kill us all," snapped Idris. "We are human, not shapechanged."

"Avaunt, Wellworm," said the groom, not believing him. Morgan gave a great retching cough, spewed two lungfuls of Wellwater, and began to breathe. The hookmen hauled the burner to the monsterchute and hustled it down.

Idris pulled Cutwater from the shark-thing's head. "Put this thing back down the Well," he said, gesturing to the creature. The groom in red armor was advancing on him, iron spear in hand. Idris said, fast, "Know that I am no shapechanger or foul beast of the Otherworld, and that if you come to kill me or my companions, you will have to fight me first."

The groom came on. Idris lifted his sword to the guard position. Then the groom stopped. "Idris?" it said. It pushed up its visor, revealing the pale face of his old friend Kay.

Idris's heart beat warm with relief. Kay, who had been a prentice groom with him. Who had rivaled him, and betrayed him, and repented too late, and become his friend and ally. He sheathed Cutwater in Holdwater, waiting for the silent lash of Fisheagle's mind. But he felt nothing. "Idris," said Kay and fell to his knees, tears pouring down his face. "What joy to see you, what happiness, my liege lord, my King."

Idris stood naked on the stones of the Welltop as they rocked with the heaving of the Wellworld. These were the stones of Lyonesse, and the power of them flowed through his bare feet and into his soul. Like a bird in the air or a fish in the sea, he was once again part of his Kingdom.

"Get up, get up, Kay, do," he said, between chattering teeth. The sun stood at the noonpoint, shining over the forest of

Welltowers inside the walls of the Valley of Apples, and on the rainbow scum of the lake, and his lands of Lyonesse beyond: a winter sun, low and cold in the deep blue sky. "We are very happy to see you," he said.

Kay rose and bowed low. "I see the dead walk," he said in a small, wondering voice. "Forgive me."

"Oh, of course you are forgiven," said Idris, white and shuddering. "But if we don't get some clothes we shall be truly dead. And so shall we be if the Mount knows we are here. So can we go and get a bath and would it be possible to have some horses? There is a lot to do."

"Nobody will tell the Mount," said Kay. "I shall make sure of that. The Ambrose is leased by Brassfin. The apartments are empty. Nothing has been touched since you left." He started snapping orders. Servitors wrapped Idris and Morgan in furs (Morgan's green tunic turned out to have been Digby, doing a little shapechanging for modesty's sake). They hurried down the familiar staircases and into the quarters once occupied by Ambrose, now sadly grimy and spiderwebbed. Here they bathed and dressed in clothes nobody had bothered to move from their old chests in the Goldfinch Chambers. The clothes were now much too small, but they did the best they could. From here they went to the Iron Room, proofed by the metal against the mind of Fisheagle and her spies.

"Well?" said Idris, sitting by Morgan at the table. "Tell us what has happened since we have been gone."

"The kingdom is in trouble," said Kay. A tremor shook the floor, and from somewhere in the Welltower there came the crash of falling masonry. "The Regent has taken the land from the Knights and the Yeomen and given it to the Captains. Fisheagle has decreed that no licenses are needed for monster-catches, so the Captains catch monsters day and night, and the lake overtops the dam. The Poison Ground is double what it was when you left, and anyone who raises an objection is thrown down a Well. There are more Black Mountmen, and nobody dares speak his mind. But people are unhappy, and even Fisheagle cannot kill them all." He looked down at his hands so as not to have to meet Idris's eye. "If you can live forty days until Darksolstice and show them the white smoke, they will rise."

Idris knew Kay was remembering last Darksolstice, when out of petty jealousy he had as good as betrayed Idris. *I told you then*, said Idris, with his mind. *It is forgotten. And now you will be my Knight.* He watched Kay's face clear. "How many can we raise?" he said.

"Of Knights, perhaps a hundred, each with thirty men. There are a hundred hundred Mountmen, well armed. Fisheagle has ordained that only Mountmen may carry bows. She says it is to make the land peaceful for the coming of age of the Dolphin." Kay made a face.

"We do not want her peace," said Idris, thinking of the darkness of the Wellworld, the passionate thirst of monsters for blood. "My allies will be on the heights of Kernow seven days before Darksolstice. And they will bring men with bows and more besides."

A knocking came on the door. Kay opened it a fraction. Into the gap came the face of Ambrose's dwarf, Cran. "Greetings, Lord Idris, Lady Morgan," he said. "There are spies. There is a squad coming from the Mount. They'll be here in half a glass." Idris knew then that Fisheagle had indeed heard the drawing of Cutwater. Suddenly he missed Kek.

Kay stood. He said, "Would you travel in a monstercart?"

"We've done it before," said Morgan.

Idris thought of the small, clear voice of Ambrose in his mind before he had leaped into the Well. "We will go west," he said. And that was all; for if Fisheagle tore into Kay's mind, he did not want her finding them.

"I will arrange the horses," said Kay, and gave brisk orders to Cran. Then he and Idris and Morgan hurried down to the loading bay, eating as they ran.

———⇌•⇋———

As the sun sank toward the distant blue line of the western hills, a horseman galloped out of the western gate of the Valley of Apples. Half a glass later, a monstercart left the loading bay of the Great Ambrose and started down the street toward the barge-wharves. It was drawn by a team of six aurochs and was in the charge of a tall monstergroom whose tunic bore the barbed-squid badge of the Brassfin. The monstergroom's name was Kay, not that most people cared, for a monstergroom was a monstergroom, and everyone had their lives to be getting on with. A squad of Mountmen separated to watch the cart pass, shrinking away, for they were hired thugs from Albion, and they did not feel easy with monsters.

The cart did not go down to the barge-wharves; few did, now that the currents in the lake had become strong enough to swamp a barge. Instead, it turned out of the northern gate, where the groom showed a pass. "Cut monster," said Kay. "Taking it up to the Equinox Predictor site."

"Pass," said the gateguard, waving them through. And the cart rumbled out of the gate of the city, heading west.

Inside the monstercart, Idris and Morgan sat in a tiny dark compartment under the false bottom of one of the tanks. (During the past nine moons, the Regent had made a lot of things illegal, the main result of which had been great improvements in the arts of smuggling.) They huddled close together to stay warm, and to keep from bumping into each other as the cart jounced over the uneven road. Another tremor. "I'm sure the ground never used to shake this much," said Morgan.

Idris remained silent. She was right. Not only was the ground shaking more, but it had a new urgency—the kind of urgency he had felt in the Lowland just before the Wells had burst upward. Though it was hard to be sure. Since he had come out of the Well, the monstervoices around him seemed to have grown fainter. Not that the monsters were talking more quietly;

it was as if he was no longer able to hear them as clearly as before.

On they clattered in the dark. It was good to be with Morgan. He missed Kek, though—

Shouts from outside. The jolting stopped. The side of the tank clanged open, and light poured in. "Out," said Kay urgently. "If you please, sire, that is."

They tumbled blinking into the road—no more than a track here, running through a grove of yews that sheltered it from inquisitive eyes. Ponies stamped and snorted in the shelter of the trees. "Here is Arquil with the horses," said Kay. Arquil had a pointed beard and (despite the Regent's ban) two bows, one of which he gave to Morgan, with a quiver of arrows. He swept off his broad-brimmed hat and bowed deeply.

"He will take you where you want to go," said Kay. "Be careful. Things have changed. Hup!" He cracked the whip, and the cart rolled on.

Idris mounted his pony, said, "Ready?" to Morgan, heard her say, "Ready" in return. "We go to Castle Ambrose," said Idris to Arquil. And they were away.

Oh, the glory of that first Lyonesse hillside! The close-cropped turf scattered with the year's last daisies, the drum of hooves, the air parting on the nose crisp and bright, the burble of a curlew...

And the smell of burning stone.

Idris drew rein, and Morgan halted beside him. On the next hilltop was a group of men with a monstercart, and a machine with two great wheels and a pottery nozzle. The nozzle was pointed at the heelstone of an arrangement of standing stones. From it there roared a jet of blue fire. The stone flared and bubbled and melted into a white-hot puddle that sent a foul brown smoke bowling across the turf.

"Come," said Arquil, edgy.

"What are they doing?" asked Morgan.

"Melting away the old stones. They say it is progress." Arquil clapped spurs to his pony and thundered away over the green downs, with Morgan in his wake and Idris bringing up the rear.

That night they stayed in the barn of a farmer called Dorrin, and Arquil put his head close to the farmer's as he explained something. Later that night, the door of the room Idris was sharing with Morgan inched open, and a small face under a black mop of hair peered in. "Come," said Morgan.

"Mustn't," said the child.

"Why not?"

"Because you are very important and you have come to save us from the wickeds and you are not to be 'sturbed because you need your sleep."

"All this is true," said Morgan. "But if you come here I will tell you the story of Great Idris the rightful King and the voyage to Aegypt. If you promise to go to bed straight after."

"Promise," said the child, leaping under the covers beside Morgan. "See?" said Morgan to Idris when the story was over and the child had gone to sleep. "Legend in your own lifetime."

Idris carried the child to her own bed and went to his own narrow cot beside Morgan's. When he woke, the dawn was slanting in at the window. They broke their fast with oats and weedwater and set off west again.

Once, the three riders stood in the shadow of an unmelted stone circle watching a Mountman squad pass, glinting like blackbeetles under the sun. Idris could hear the Mountmen's hard, crude thoughts, driven always on by terror of Fisheagle. They seemed muffled; he did not know why. But the dimness was a mercy, because he knew he was the object of their pursuit. As the morning wore on, Idris's mood darkened. He had made the three-moons' voyage, found Morgan in Aegypt, and leaped into the bitter world of the Well. That had been difficult, but not as difficult as this. Morgan's family tower was destroyed by Fisheagle, and her foster family with it. And he was back in his own country, only to see it being destroyed around him.

As the sun rolled westward, they stopped inside a grouping of tumbled stones. Last night's farm had packed nuncheon for each of them, aurochs pies and last year's apples, shriveled but delicious. The good Lyonesse food spread around Idris, and the ghosts of his despair drew back into the dark corners of his mind. "One more day to Castle Ambrose," said Arquil, mouth full. "Mountmen'll get thinner on the ground as we go west. They get nervous out there."

Idris was thinking of the dawn he and Morgan had spent in a pine tree in the beautiful Sundeeps, watching the Red Dragon and the White destroy the armies of the Mount with their raging blue-white breath. He did not like to think of the desolation that would have replaced those balmy woods and meadows. The shadows closed in again. To distract himself, he rummaged in his bag for a final apple.

His fingers found something hard, like a small, shallow cup. He drew it out and found that he was looking at the conical pyramid of a limpet shell. He thought of the limpets that clung to the rocks of the Westgate, immovable.

Arquil was watching. "That was the Dorrins," he said.

"Why would they be putting limpet shells in our nunch-bags?" said Morgan, impatient as always.

"The people give them to one another as a sign that they will stick close to the land. But that when the True King comes, they will show his enemies their sharp edges. Just about everyone's got one."

Idris stared at him. Then he laughed and tossed the shell into the air so it hung a moment at the top of its arc, a small, hard mountain against the blue sky of Lyonesse, with the Sundeeps under their clouds far beyond.

"Weren't you called Limpet once?" asked Morgan.

"I still am," said Idris.

Later that afternoon they rode past a farmstead. Now that he knew to look, Idris saw the limpet shell stuck over the door so that everyone entering the house must pass under it. He rode on over the drumming turf with a rejoicing heart.

The sun set. Stars came out, and the air was sharp with frost. The outlines of the hills were familiar now, for this was where he had done his training under Ambrose's soldier Orbach. Still, for old times' sake, Idris raised his hand so the stone on his ring caught the light of the Flake of Mica, a dim star winking on the western horizon. When Orbach had first given him the ring it had been too big, so he had had to wear it on his thumb. It was too tight for his thumb now, so he wore it on the middle finger of his right hand, the hand that he now raised so the ring caught the light of the star; and a line of marker stones blazed pale on the summits of the low hills ahead, making a glowing road to the horizon.

Over that horizon they rode, and at midnight saw in the valley below the dark bulk of a building.

"Castle Ambrose," said Idris. "I'm surprised they didn't ruin it."

"They tried," said Arquil, "but it's built so strong it near to ruined them."

No lights glowed in the windows, and as they passed under the arch in the courtyard Idris saw that the portcullis hung askew, and the yard itself, once carefully swept, was strewn with rubbish and smashed roof slates. Arquil sprang from his horse and hammered on the nailed door. Looking around, Idris thought he had never seen a place so obviously derelict—

He heard something.

It was a murmur of thought, instantly gone. From inside the castle? He glanced at Morgan. She was dark and shadowy on her horse, but something about the alert tilt of her head made him think that she had caught it, too. Suddenly a door slammed open and light flowed into the yard.

And hulking against the light stood a Black Mountman.

Idris's heart seemed to roll in his chest. Then the Mountman raised his head, and the light fell on the face below the rim of the helmet. And Idris drew in his breath. For the face was the face of Orbach, his old friend and swordmaster.

Orbach's eye settled on Idris. It widened. Then it winked, and its owner bowed deeply and laid a mighty finger to his lips. "Yerse?" he said, in a harsh, grating voice.

"Travelers," said Arquil. "Asking shelter, in the name of the hospitality of Lyonesse."

This was perfectly in the Manner, and not even a Mountman would be expected to refuse. "One night only," said Orbach. There was the sound of nailed boots behind him. "In the stables. For this is a Mount fort, occupied by order of the Regent, and the public is not admitted."

He hustled Idris, Morgan, Arquil, and the horses across the yard and into the stable door, shushing them as he went. They stabled the horses and gave them nets of hay. Then Orbach shooed them into a tack room, through a door by the bridle racks, and into a room at the back of the stables. It was sparsely furnished, with a big stone bed, a rack of swords mounted on the wall, a table and chairs, and a hearth of stone under a chimney hood.

"How are you here in that uniform?" asked Idris.

"There are many who wear it," said Orbach. "And not all of them think as they are supposed to. Sire, this is a great day." His eyes went to Morgan and crinkled with a vast inner grin. "Greater than you know," he said. "Have a seat."

They sat down at the table. Beneath his joy at seeing Orbach, Idris was tired, and there were deep black hollows under Morgan's eyes.

"The castle is in the hands of the Mount?" said Idris.

"You could call it that," said Orbach, still with the secret grin. "We've got one stupid Ordinant whose uncle is a Captain and got him the job. No brains there. And we've got three Black Mountmen that would fillet their grannies for a silver. And, oh dear, if only they knew!"

"Orbach," said Idris, too tired for secret jokes. "It is very, very good to see you. But we are hungry and we need news."

"News!" said Orbach, his armor clattering as he laughed. "Get on and have a look down there." And he pointed at the hearthstone.

It was an ordinary granite slab. In its center was the gray ash from a peat fire, and at one corner a limpet shell. Idris felt a curious prickling chill. He knew what he should say next without knowing why. He said, "Morgan, pick up that shell."

"Ha!" said Orbach, hugging himself.

Morgan made a tutting noise, shrugged, bent, and grasped the shell. At first it seemed locked to the stone. Then it moved in a complicated double sliding. Suddenly the fire had vanished into the wall, and there instead of the hearthstone was a flight of steps leading down into the earth.

"Go on!" said Orbach, snorting with glee.

They walked down, Idris first, for he could feel that Morgan was thinking of that descent into the crypt where the Morrabs crumbled undying. The steps went down to a gallery, which led to a confusion of passages and walkways across great arches spanning spaces whose edges were invisible in the flare of the torches. It felt as if they were very deep under the earth. At the end of a last dim gallery was a doorway. From the doorway came the warm glow of torchlight, and the clink of knives on plates, and the hum of voices...

Of familiar voices.

Idris heard Morgan's feet hesitate behind him. Then he felt himself shoved aside as she ran past him, and he heard the voices again, and put out his hand to stop Orbach coming past him, and waited.

He heard Morgan give a great cry. He heard a clamor of voices, weeping at first, then settling into a steady, joyous hum. And finally Morgan again, a new Morgan, full of happiness, calling, "Idris! Oh, Idris! They're here!"

And Idris went down the remaining steps and in through the door.

ELEVEN

It was a large, round room with a domed ceiling, box beds lining the walls, and a table in its center. It must have held three- or fourscore people. But the ones Idris noticed were Morgan, fast in the arms of a woman with long dark hair and a tall, thin man: her dear foster parents, whom she had thought buried under the ashes of the Wolf Rock Tower.

Idris waited until their first paroxysm of joy had passed, and Morgan turned toward him, shining-eyed, an arm around the waist of each of her foster parents. Then he bowed in the Manner to hide the fact that his eyes were pricking with tears and said, "Uther Wolf Rock and the Lady Nena. I hope I see you well—oh, for goodness' *sake!*"

For Uther and Nena, who had acted as his own foster parents and made him part of the family circle at the Wolf Rock, had fallen to their knees. Idris felt his face hot with embarrassment. Then he remembered that Uther and Nena were in the presence of the True King, and acting in the Manner. So he said, "Rise, dear friends," and Morgan pulled them to their feet, laughing and crying at the same time, and Idris shook hands with Uther and kissed Nena on her cheek, which was soft and powdery as ever.

"Sire," said Uther, "I thank you for bringing Morgan back to us from the place where she was taken. If ever we needed a greater reason for thankfulness than that you were our King, this would be it."

Idris smiled and nodded, noticing that all trace of the Aegypt shadow had left Morgan's face, which was bright as a sun. He did not intend to tell anyone about Aegypt, or that he and Morgan had passed through the Well; as far as the Knights of Lyonesse were concerned, a Cross was a Cross. So he said, "It is a great happiness that we are all back together again."

"You must be famished!" said Lady Nena. "Zupper's on the table. Eat!"

Idris ate, and so did Morgan, chattering away with her mouth full, while Orbach stood by the door with the smug look of a mountebank who had just produced a longtooth cat from an empty basket. When Morgan's joy had settled into a steady happiness, Uther told in a quiet, half-amused voice the story of what had happened since Morgan and Idris had fled the Valley of Apples.

"It was last Darksolstice, when you pulled the sword out of that stone," said Uther. "We were in the tower. Couldn't be bothered with all that nasty Mount ceremonial stuff. After zupper one of my tenant farmers, Evan Hamza, came runnin' in and said half an army of Mountmen was comin' down the road over the Poison Ground and he didn't like the look of them.

Then I get a…" He frowned. "Well, a sort of message, you'd have to call it, like a dream really except I seemed to be awake, from old Ambrose, to say we should leave sharpish. Which we did, and took a cartload of stuff down to Hamza's barn, and ourselves, too. And when we were a league out of the door we saw this big orange light in the sky behind us, and that was the poor old Wolf Rock goin' up in smoke." He paused, his bushy brows low over his clever eyes. Idris suddenly noticed that his face was drawn and papery, as if in a single year he had grown old. "So we stayed with Evan for a bit, helpin' on the farm and whatnot. But the filth was spreading out of the Poison Ground. And believe it or not, in three moons the trees were dyin' and a nasty sort of fog was killin' the corn, and there were Mountmen everywhere stickin' their noses where they had no business. And of course no sign of you."

Morgan was clinging to her foster father's hand, tears sliding down her face as she relived that day of flight and despair. "There was no way of telling you," said Idris, feeling that he should have found one.

"No, no, message in wrong hands very bad thing," said Uther. "Anyway, Ambrose got a message to us that you were safe, and that it would be a good idea for us to come to Castle Ambrose. And old Orbach had made the place look ruined and pretended to go over to the other side, and of course the other side didn't know about the undercastle. So we told some other people, friends, tenants, anyone who wanted to come, and brought them down here." He waved a hand at the other groups around the walls of the room, who had fallen silent and were listening intently. "And here we are." The eyes were bright again, drilling into Idris. "What now?"

"The people will rise."

Uther made a doubtful face. "I hope so," he said.

Idris had a moment of uncertainty. He saw blackbeetle squads of Mountmen roving the land, flames jumping through houseroofs, weeping families. Then another picture, hot on the heels of the first: Fisheagle and Murther in the Kyd Tower of the Mount, and below it the Valley of Apples and the lake pouring filth into the Poison Ground, scummy tendrils of water threading through village and field and wood. He saw the black backs of monsters writhing in Lyonesse as in the Lowland, raging for blood and chaos. He shrugged. "There will be trouble whatever we do," he said. "So on Darksolstice I shall be in the Valley of Apples, and the white smoke will rise. I have summoned the allies. They will wait with their men while the Dolphin leaves childom. But Murther is not the only one who leaves childom this Darksolstice. I leave it myself. And with my allies beside me I will take my kingdom. Will you help me raise the people?"

Uther's face had stayed completely still. Now he rose from his chair, bowed, and turned to the other people packing the room to the walls. "Dear friends and people of Lyonesse," he said. "We know that this youth went to the Kings of Beyondsea and promised that he would rescue Morgan, who like him is of my foster family. You have heard how he kept that promise. And you have seen that he has brought Morgan back from the wicked land of Aegypt, a thing never done by mortal man, let alone mortal boy. And now he wants to lead us against Fisheagle and to take the throne. So, what do we think of this Idris House Draco, sometime Wolf Rock, once Limpet?"

There was a general roar of approval. Idris saw Morgan's proud smile and felt strength flow through him, a strength like the one he had felt when he had first laid hands on the hilt of Cutwater and the power of the stones of Lyonesse had flowed into him. But this was sharper and stronger—the power not of stones but of people.

They came up to him one by one, an ordinary-looking bunch—farmers, blacksmiths, shepherds, carpenters, women from the Fishers' Guild with cat-whisker face tattoos like those of his foster mother, Harpoon. He shook hard hands and returned fierce looks. And he was very glad that these ordinary people of Lyonesse would be fighting for him, not against him. For they were tough and resolute, which made them dangerous. But more dangerous still, they had nothing to lose.

He raised Cutwater aloft in Holdwater, and cried, "People of Lyonesse, I bring you the sword of vengeance in the scabbard of healing. Spread the word that your King is here, and that his name is Idris House Draco, but that he will be known until our victory as Limpet." And once again, their roar of approval battered the roof stones of the sunken castle.

"Well done," said Uther, after Idris had shaken hands with each individual person in the undercastle. "Now. Sleep, and onward."

The next day slid away in the joy of reunion. Deep into the night the harpers sang, but more delightful to Idris than the lays of old Lyonesse was to watch Morgan happy between Uther and Nena. Next morning he rose early, splashed his face with cold water, and made his farewells. Orbach was in the round room. "Orders?" he said.

"I must go to the Sundeeps."

Orbach raised an eyebrow. "Well, you know the way. We'll find you a horse."

Idris followed the swordmaster through a maze of stairs and galleries to a stable lit by shafts from above. "Never knew all this was here, did you?" he said. "Loves an undercastle, does the Master. There's a lot of iron in it, so no one can hear what we're thinking. Proof against everything but flood, he said. If you take that passage there it'll bring you out of an old mineshaft in the White Valley." He hesitated, clearing his throat. "One other thing, if I may make so bold."

"What?" Idris was impatient to leave.

"The Ordinant was saying in orders of the day from the Mount that there are dangerous people on the loose, and the worst of them all is a youth, ugly, big sword, meaning you. Kill on sight, is the orders. I don't know how you got back to the kingdom, sire," said Orbach, "but that Regent knows you're here."

"Good."

"Hm," said Orbach, looking less than impressed. "As your swordmaster, I would like to remind you of what I always told you: In battle never do from in front what you can do from behind. So would you wear this?" He held up a black tunic and a black helmet.

"Mountman gear?" said Idris, who after last night felt invincible. "Never."

"Not Mountman. Mountmessenger. Sire, I beg you, you're no good to anyone if you're taken. Today's watchword is a question: Who are the Helpers? Response: They who will come. And sire, I put on this nasty uniform my own self. And I beg you reflect that if I hadn't, you would have been in trouble."

Idris was forced to admit that Orbach had never yet been wrong. He swallowed his pride with an effort. "Very well," he said and took the tunic and put it on over his own. It was made of hard, coarse stuff, with the silver emblem of the Mount over the heart. Below the emblem, the cloth had been patched.

"Chap who used to own it had an accident," said Orbach.

Idris could guess what sort and who had caused it. He came to a decision. "When we fight the Mount, I want you to be my General."

Orbach frowned. "Very kind, sire. But you've got plenty of Knights."

"True. But I want a cunning fighter, not a Knight. So please do as you are told."

Orbach's face became unnaturally still as he hid a grin of pleasure. "Yessir," he said. "Nicely done, sir, if I might say. Now here's your hat." He handed Idris a Mounthelmet. It was hard and heavy and smelled of sweat and leather, with a visor that hid the wearer's face. Idris swung into the saddle. "Anyone asks, you're carrying dispatches for the North Dog Fort Garrison," said Orbach. "Sealblanket behind the saddlecloth. Food in the bags. Go!" He slapped the horse's rump, driving it out of the stable.

The hooves rang in the upsloping tunnel. Light appeared, gray at first, then a pinpoint of brightness, then the mouth of a cave looking into the gorge of quartzy rocks that was called the White Valley. Idris paused, dismounted, peered out of the cave. White stone, green grass, a red stag grazing. He jumped back onto the saddlecloth, trotted out into the world, and headed west.

The hours passed with the drum of hooves and the chill of the winter wind on his face. The grass of the Downs gave way to heather. Idris was solitary in a great disc of wild hills. He found himself missing Kek.

On he rode, under a cold sky ridged with rain squalls. In the middle of the day, Idris came over the crest of a hill and straight into the middle of a squad of Mountmen. His heart beat hard, and his hand went to Cutwater. But the sword felt dead and tight in its scabbard. An Ordinant on a horse wheeled toward him. "Who are the Helpers?" he roared, hand on sword.

"They who will come!" shouted Idris back.

"Pass," said the Ordinant.

And Idris passed on, grinning with delight behind his visor.

As the Sundeeps crept up the western sky, a thought began to nag at him. He had run into the Mountmen without knowing they were there. Why had he not heard their thoughts? He was muffled against Fisheagle. That must be it.

Strange, though.

He slept in a looted passage-grave. All next day, Idris rode on, the Sundeeps rising jagged ahead. Another night he spent in the burrow of a longtooth cat, the cat (by the lack of smell, and by the calmness with which his horse approached it) being absent. Toward noon on the third day of traveling, thirty-three days before Darksolstice, he came to the foot of the mountains.

He stopped his horse, dismounted, and looked at the road that wound into the dizzy heart of the crags. This was the place where the first Kek had been killed protecting him from the greatgull. Idris's confidence had been worn thin by solitude. He missed his Knights. He felt uneasy, and worried, and too young. The dragons had ravaged an army among these crags. There would be terrible things to see. Well, there would be many terrible things from now on. Young or not, he had better start getting used to them.

He took a deep breath, wrapped the reins around his hand, and took a step onto the path.

High above, he heard the cry of a gull. Not a thin mew, like the cry of Kek; this was a deep, roaring yell. He saw the creature that had made it glide stiff-winged over a cliff top, then another, then another: huge white creatures with bodies the size of an adult seal's, terrible war beaks, and yellow eyes as big as goose eggs — greatgulls, no doubt fat with the carrion of last year's horrors. The flock began a long, purposeful downward glide.

Idris pulled his pony into a thicket of thorn trees and burrowed under the trees himself. The vast birds planed down at him, slashing with their beaks. If he had been on the bare hillside, they would have torn him and his mount to bits. But gulls great or small are not made to deal with trees, so batter as they might, they could not penetrate the thorny canopy of branches. So he crouched under the tangle, buffeted by the blasts of air from their huge wings, and in time they lost interest in this thorny problem, and their cries faded as they flapped off in search of easier meat.

Idris crawled out of the trees, drawing the pony after him. A flight of hedge sparrows watched him, heads cocked to one side. The sun was behind the hills now, sinking. Well, thought Idris, gulls did not fly in the dark. So he must make the passage of the Sundeeps crags by night. And a good night it would be, for the sky was a pure and deepening blue, and the moon was already up, a pale ghost of its nighttime self, huge on the eastern horizon.

As the last sun patch winked out on the Downs far behind him and the sky above the crags ahead turned from shell-pink to an angry meat-red, Idris loosened Cutwater in Holdwater and started to walk uphill, leading the pony.

The evening was quiet. Up the path wound, up and up. The moon shone full on the slopes, and he saw that he was walking through the rubbish of war. It gleamed palely from a helmet

255

rolled under a rock. It made deep pits of shadow in holes that had once held eyes, and coated long bones with cold silver. But this was the Sundeeps, home of the old magic of star and stone, which was not to do with fire and monsters, but with things growing. And things had grown, grown amazingly, as if the Sundeeps had decided to bless the evidence of massacre by clothing it with life. So the effect was not like walking through a boneyard, but more like walking through a tangled but harmonious garden.

An odd harmony, though, and one to chill a traveler to the marrow. So Idris sent his thoughts to dwell on the old Lyonesse, the warmth of the Wolf Rock, the cries of his friends, the shift of the light over the Westgate sea. All these things he would restore.

Up he climbed, up and up in the gray moonlight. The woods sank far below. He passed through valleys where the rocks that pierced the grass had an odd, melted look where the dragonfire had caught them twelve moons gone. It was tiring; he thought he might stop and sleep. But there were too many up here in the sleep of death, and Idris feared the dreams that might come. So he went on over the pass between Hanjague and the Hedge, and began to descend into what had once been the Sundeeps woods, thick and green.

He had expected the woods to be a burned-out graveyard of trees. But they were as dense as ever. New saplings had grown uncannily fast around the charred stumps of the old Sundeeps giants. They wrapped around him, warm and friendly. No harm could befall him here. He was so tired he could scarcely keep his eyes open. He hobbled the horse, crawled under a big-leafed bush, rolled himself in his sealblanket, and fell instantly asleep.

There were no dreams. But as he came up from his first sleep, he heard voices. There were hundreds of them, all murmuring to one another; not the voices of the dead, agonized and savage, but kind voices, like friends who had crept into your bedroom but who did not want to wake you up. There was something breathless about them, as if they were in awe. And something gossipy, too. *It be him*, they said, in deep country accents. *Three cheers for 'im. Oh no, you doan cheer Kings, you be loyal, thazz what you be. Three cheers anyway. Hup, hup, hoorah.* Up went the cheers, odd and squeaky.

Idris awoke.

It was still dark, but the eastern sky was gray beyond the branches. The little voices did not go away altogether. They stayed, happy, awestruck. *Look*, they said. *He's a-moving. Stand back!*

Idris sat up. The forest floor rustled. He realized that it was entirely carpeted with animals. Most of them were tiny, shrews and moles and wood mice. But on the outskirts of the crowd he caught sight of something much bigger, the size of a small bear, except that around its eyes were pale stripes of fur: a badger.

Brock, he thought, putting his mind out with an effort.

Kingg, said the badger, with a deep, humming grunt. *We takes you as Kingg.*

We do, we do, said the little country voices. *But mind where you puts your feets if ee please, zur.*

Idris felt very tired. But he knew that as a King he must do what his subjects wanted. So he crawled out of the bush (*Look, not too proud to walk proper fourlegs like uzz,* said the voices), found his horse, unhobbled it, and clambered onto the saddlecloth. And through the forest he rode, with the creatures of the Sundeeps galloping proudly around him.

Two hours he rode, and came at last to the meadow by the lake. The sun was up now. The animal voices were shriller, doubtless ill at ease in daylight. Mice and rabbits were trying to keep their distance from a couple of longtooth cats. The cats were yawning and licking their fur, eyeing half a dozen huge badgers, while the badgers were watching one another, for badgers are private creatures, with a strong sense of home and a fierce dislike of social life. Beyond the two great standing stones where the horned stagmen lit their dancing fires lay the lake with the island on which Ambrose's tower had once stood.

Idris turned to the animals and said gently with his mind: *Dear people of the land, it is very kind of you to have escorted me this far. I am proud to be your King and happy that you came. Please do this for me if you meet the people of the wicked Regent: Mice, eat their corn. Rats, gnaw their spear shafts. Moles, make hills to trip their horses. Longtooth cats, frighten them with your screechings, and badgers, dig your setts in their paths. And I want you to be good to one another, by which I mean do not eat one another, however hungry you may be.* Here he felt the first whispers of disagreement. Some things not even a King could change. *Go, and thank you,* said Idris.

The moving carpet rippled into the forest, and he stood alone in the green meadows by the lake. The only sound was the whisper of wind in trees, and the tiny sub-song of a wren practicing against the coming of spring, still a couple of moons away even in the balmy Sundeeps. Idris slid off his horse, slung his saddlebags over his shoulder, and walked into the lake.

The first time he had done it, he had held up the ring, and the Flake of Mica had lit the stepping-stones. This time his feet found them without difficulty, and he strode across the dark surface to the green island.

Once Ambrose's tower had stood here, on a daisy-starred lawn. The tower had gone, and the lawn was ringed with new trees—not seedlings of a year's growth, but real trees, with trunks as thick as his leg. All around the edge they grew: oak, ash, willow, rowan, elder, birch, hazel, pine, twined with old man's beard. These were the nine powerful woods of the old magic of star and stone, pulling energy out of the sky and into the ground. Idris pushed aside a curtain of leaves and walked across the short grass to the ancient yew tree that stood where the tower had been. The center of its trunk had rotted out, so that it was less like one tree than a circle of trees. Goodness knew how long it would take a tree to grow so big. Certainly more like a thousand years than one. But it was a mere eleven moons since Ambrose's tower had occupied this ground.

Idris walked into the middle of the yew. There was a stone there, big and flat, like the altar stone of Carnac. In the middle of the stone was carved the device of the Devouring Eel.

"Ambrose," said Idris.

Silence. Only the sigh of the wind, and the lap of the wavelets, and the tiny song of the wren. Not song. Speech.

Idris, King, said the wren in its sub-song, *lay your sword on the seal.*

Idris pulled the baldric over his head and laid sword and scabbard on the device.

The stone started to turn.

It turned slowly and steadily, like water swirling out of a tank. It rose a foot in the air, shifted to one side, and laid itself gently on the grass. The hole from which it had unscrewed itself was a shaft, circular, with stone steps spiraling down into a pale light. *Loves an undercastle, does the Master.*

Idris caught his breath. A figure was walking up the steps; a figure in a dark red tunic bound with leather at the cuffs, trousers cut off above the ankle, and embroidered boots of soft doeskin. The hair was dark, cut short. The beard was short, too, the face thin, the eyes bright and clever, young at first sight, but after that wise and ageless, seamed with little lines at their corners. "Winter," said the voice, in a reminiscent tone. It hugged itself and shivered.

"Ambrose," said Idris, pierced with happiness. This mage had saved his life, and told him who he was, and taught him everything he knew, and been a kind, brave, loyal friend to him and Lyonesse.

Ambrose's eyes locked on his, looking deep into his mind. "Good morning, sire," said the mage, as if Idris was just back from a fishing. "Cold, isn't it?" He nodded and smiled. Idris might have thought him simple in the head, if he had not felt the eyes going into his mind, gentle but piercing. "Would you like some brekfuss?"

"Very much," said Idris.

"Still got the sword, I see," said Ambrose, leading him down the stairs. "You've grown."

Like most people, Idris did not like being told he had grown. Still, he found himself nodding as he walked across the big, comfortable room to a chair in front of a round table that bore a plate and a knife and a dish of ham and eggs and bread. "I heard you coming, of course. You've done very well, all things considered." Ambrose waited while Idris gave himself some brekfuss. Then he pulled the dish toward him, scraped the remains of the ham and eggs onto his own plate, and began to eat as if starving. "In fact," he said, looking up under his eyebrows, "you're nearly ready to begin."

Idris had been thinking that this brekfuss was the most delicious thing he had ever tasted. Now the food turned to beach sand in his mouth. "*Begin?*" he said. He had fled Fisheagle, rescued Morgan from the Tree, sent the Knights to the Kings of Beyondsea, returned to his kingdom through the Wellworld, and proclaimed the Sign of the Limpet. Begin? He had nearly finished.

"That's what I said." Ambrose dabbed his lips with a linen napkin held in long, ink-stained fingers. "But it's all right; I'm going to give you some help. Luckily I've made some progress down here these last few centuries ... years ... one loses count, time passes differently in the Sundeeps, you saw the trees, grown well, eh? So the dragons have given me some time. They've got an egg, so they're happy. Let's hope it hatches. Meanwhile, you've got to get the people behind you and throw those monsters out."

Idris said, "The Kings will come. The people wear the Limpet. The white smoke will rise, and I will ascend to the Mount and take the keys of my kingdom."

Ambrose frowned impatiently. Idris was left with the echo of his own words ringing pompously in his ears. "A sword in a stone and a limpet shell on the doorpost is a start," said Ambrose at last. "But it isn't enough. You must go out and show these people you're a King. There is going to be fighting. And dying. Blood. Guts. Loyalty and friendship. Real stuff, not magic swords. If you've got magic, people will rely on it and they won't fight properly and they'll die. You need people to go into this with their eyes open."

Idris found himself about to tell Ambrose he was talking nonsense. Then into his head there came again the troops of Murther flinging torches on thatch, and scummy tongues of Wellwater licking at the cornfields and orchards of the land. His ill-temper faded. He bowed his head. He said, "Great Ambrose, you saved me from the Westgate. Now tell me what I must do to save my people."

"Spoken like a King," said Ambrose. He pronged the last egg on his plate, posted it into his mouth, and chewed for a while. "You're not going to like it," he said at last. "But here goes anyway. What do you know about your people?"

"Much. They are poor. Oppressed. I have been one of them. I have——"

"You were fostered by specially chosen parents. *Carefully* fostered. And watched, and brought on, and rescued, and trained by me and Orbach. Not, in fact, one of the people at all. By the way, have you noticed anything about your mind lately?"

"Noticed?" Idris's anger had returned. "I didn't come here to talk about minds——"

"You can still speak with your mind," said Ambrose, interrupting. "But the speech grows dimmer. True?"

Idris opened his mouth to snap that he was not used to being talked to like this. Then he remembered the puzzlement he had felt when he had nearly ridden into a Mountman squad the day before. "Yes," he said. "Well, perhaps."

Ambrose nodded and gave him his kind smile. "They told you when you were training," he said. "Your gifts of mind come upon you when you are ten or eleven. But they fade as you turn from boy into man; in you not completely, but what were once shouts will in time become mere whispers. And you have used the Wells to your advantage; but now you must have done with the Wellworld. To be a King of men, you must be a man yourself."

"I don't see why," said Idris, put out. "Extra powers will make me useful to my subjects. To fight monsters I need to understand them."

Ambrose sighed. "You understand them already," he said. "Special powers will merely set you apart from your subjects. Fisheagle was an ordinary little girl when I first knew her, and look at her now. No. What I am saying is that you must shed the things of the Wellworld and become one of your people. Then you can rule them."

Idris stared at him stonily. "And how am I supposed to do this?"

"Give the sword Cutwater back to the Lady. It has served its purpose. The scabbard Holdwater you can keep. I will give you another sword."

Idris was shocked. "Cutwater? Never."

Ambrose shrugged. "Then drown in the Wells and take your people with you. The choice is yours. But might I explain?"

Idris shrugged. "If you want."

Ambrose looked at him kindly. "The sword Cutwater was forged by the Old King with the breath of monsters. Why do you think it spent seven hundred years blocking up a doorway instead of cutting up enemies? And came through the Wellworld with you? Because it lives half in mansworld and half in monsterworld. You must have noticed that when it doesn't want something to happen, it thinks for itself. It threw itself into the sea when the corsairs took Morgan. If it doesn't want you to fight someone, it catches in the scabbard. And you know perfectly well that when you draw it, Fisheagle can hear it leave the scabbard, and she knows where you are."

"But I have mastered Fisheagle," said Idris. "She sends her mind, I muffle. She is only a creature."

Ambrose sighed. "So she has allowed you to think. Now listen. If you are going to be a King, you will decide what your sword will do, not the other way around. You can kill a monster with any sword, as long as it's got iron in it. By carrying Cutwater you are drawing attention to yourself at a time when that can be very dangerous. Eh?"

Idris bowed his head. Ambrose would not be saying this if it were not true. And he remembered Mark of Ar Mor: *Swords and scabbards do not make Kings. It is the other way around.* But he found himself standing up, full of indignation. He heard himself say, "Cutwater is the sword of my fathers."

Ambrose sighed, reached over to a workbench, and picked up a spoon. "This was the spoon of my fathers," he said. "It is made of copper, which has turned bright green and is now poisonous. It is good to own it. But nowadays I use a spoon made of silver because it does a better job and it won't kill me."

Idris said, "Ambrose, it is a joy to see you, and I am always grateful for your excellent advice. But I cannot yield up the sword Cutwater."

"Spoken like a true pompous thickheaded King." Ambrose pointed to a rack in the corner. "There are a couple of good ones there. One of them belonged to the Old King, too, if that helps."

"No," said Idris, feeling his stubbornness increase. "I will have Cutwater, and let Fisheagle do her worst. I go to raise my people and join my Knights. Thank you, and farewell."

Ambrose raised a satirical eyebrow. "Where will you start?"

But Idris had turned his back and was walking up the stairs.

He walked slowly. For to tell the truth, he had no idea where to start. Well, he would go back to the castle, and take counsel with Uther and Orbach and Kay, Knights all. They would know what to do.

He drew Cutwater, admired the play of light on its blade, razor-keen as the day it had been forged seven hundred years ago. He put his mind out far, far, looking for consolation, and touched Morgan's.

Idiot, said Morgan's mind, faint, like all minds now. *Do as you're told. Give up the sword. Count on your Knights and your allies and your people. Be yourself.*

I am King, said Idris stubbornly. *I decide.*

Silence.

At first, he thought it was the silence of Morgan failing to reply. Then, as he came out of the spiral stairs and onto the greensward by the altarstone, he realized that it was more than that. The Sundeeps were always full of a warm, cheery hum of little voices. Now that had gone, as if all the talkers had ceased in mid-remark.

Something roared. He found his face in the turf, grass in his mouth, but he could not taste it because the thing in his mind was burning cold and shrieking: *There you are, I see you, keep the sword and fight us with it, and we will tear you fiber from fiber*

in the dungeons of the Mount and suck up your blood as you come asunder.
He clutched his head and rolled and tried to muffle, but Fisheagle was in his head with a power of which he had not dreamed, and he realized that she had been lulling him into a sense of false safety, and now she was levering thought from thought with cruel claws and a hooked beak, and the thoughts behind the thoughts came spilling out in a dreadful tangle that the talons ripped away, and a voice was shrieking and he knew it was his own.

Then peace.

He lay on the greensward and heard the little breeze sigh in the branches of the nine trees, and the quack of a mallard, and the lap of the lake. The ugly tangle in his head moved gently, as if it had been stretched out of place and was now returning to its old shape. He watched an ant pick its way through the grass stems and wondered if he was going to be sick.

"*Stupid* boy," said Ambrose's voice, cross but affectionate. "What's your name?"

Idris tried to tell him that he was Idris, King of Lyonesse. But the words would not shape themselves. Instead he heard that voice speaking on its own, so remote that he could not make it do anything but tell the truth. The voice said, "Idris Limpet."

"Thank goodness for that," said Ambrose, helping him to his feet. "I had to bump her out of the way. She nearly tore you to bits. Wanted you to keep the sword because she knew the trouble it would cause you. Now come back down, and you can try some other swords, and we will talk about this sensibly."

Idris jabbed Cutwater into the turf and followed the mage meekly into the ground without looking back. His thoughts were confused and stumbling. Ambrose gave him a sort of milky soup that made him very sleepy. "Go to bed for a bit," he said. "You will need to think straight. A lot hangs on it."

"Bed," said Idris. He lowered his head to the table and fell into darkness.

When he woke up, he was in a large, comfortable bed. There was a glass by the bedside. He drank what was in it: another liquid, this one sour, oddly refreshing, that chased the cobwebs from his mind and set his thoughts running in order. All doubt had left him. He knew exactly what he must do. He swung his feet out of the bed, climbed into his clothes, and went to look for Ambrose.

The space under the island seemed to have grown bigger since he had last been here. There were storerooms and work-shops and places full of tubes that bubbled and jars in which swam things that Idris preferred not to look at too closely. From the last room a staircase led steeply down to a gallery overhanging an enormous cavern. It reminded Idris of the monsterstables of the Wellvale—except that in the monsterstables there had been a chemical stench that got up your nose, while here the smell was more like a stable for horses, with a faint whiff of brimstone.

Ambrose was on the floor of the cave, dwarfed by distance, shoveling, up to his knees in straw. "Idris!" he cried, waving.

268

"You remember Enys and Caradoc?" He waved a hand, introducing in the Manner the two gigantic dragons that lay on either side of him, flanks towering into the shadows of the cave. "There has been an egg, you know."

THERE HAS, rumbled two gigantic voices in Idris's mind. *SOON THERE WILL BE MORE OF US.*

I look forward to that day, said Idris politely with his mind. *It will be a great one. Ambrose, when you have a moment?*

Ambrose leaned his shovel against a rock pillar. "Excuse me," he said to the dragons.

YOU ARE EXCUSED.

Idris watched the mage climb the stairs to the gallery. He thought Ambrose looked bent and tired. But the voice came brightly from the haggard face. "Sleep well?"

"I did," said Idris. "I have been thinking. You are right. There are other swords."

Ambrose's eyes lost their sarcastic glitter and began to burn with a grave fire. He bowed. "That is true, and you are brave to admit it."

They walked up the steps and onto the island. Idris plucked Cutwater out of the turf and slid it into the scabbard. Ambrose hauled the punt with the seats of polished tree branches from a hidden boathouse. "Come," he said.

The boat slid wakeless across the peaks reflected in the lake. Clouds moved in and hid the crags, and a fine gray rain wept down, so it was not possible to tell where the water began and the air ended. A dark shadow loomed: the cliff of black stone, bearing the carved sign of the Devouring Eel. A stillness settled over the world. After a while, Ambrose took Idris's arm. "Look!" he said. "The Lady!"

As before, the water was heaving and roiling. From the swirl there rose a woman's arm, sinuous and beautiful, tattooed with a pattern of mistletoe leaves and berries and a bracelet in the form of the Devouring Eel. The hand opened. The bones were fine, the fingers long, the tips upswept like the feathers of an eagle's wing. An eel ring encircled the third finger.

Idris drew the sword, held it at the balance point in the blade, and put the hilt in the hand. The fingers closed. For a moment Cutwater stood upright above the surface, pointing at the sky. Idris gazed at it, burning it into his mind. Then the arm slid smoothly down, and two tiny wavelets clapped together over the sword's point, and it was gone. Idris felt as though part of him had gone with it.

"I know," said Ambrose. "But something now has room to grow in you that is completely your own."

Idris nodded. But he ached for the power that had flowed from the sword's hilt. How would anything ever take its place?

"Look," said Ambrose.

A speck rode the sky high above. It grew until it was a bird, huge and dark, with white head and breeches. Its wings were the size of palace doors. The sky darkened, and the wind howled in the finger-feathers of its wingtips as it stooped, settling on the fist Ambrose held out for it, glaring at Idris from its hard yellow eyes. "This," said Ambrose, "is the natural Sea Eagle, one of the creatures of your kingdom. Unnatural Fisheagle stole its name. But soon she will be gone, and he can live in peace. Friend Sea Eagle, this is Idris, your King."

The eagle drilled Idris with its fierce golden look, as if fixing him in memory. Then it spread its enormous wings, wafted up, up, became a speck, and vanished into a cloud. "Now," said Ambrose. "We will find you a sword, and you can raise your people and throw Murther and his mother off the Mount, and be the True King of Lyonesse."

 TWELVE

mbrose led him down winding stairs into a room with a stone fireplace, its walls lined with swords. "Wake up!" said the mage.

A figure started up from a chair by the fire and bowed deep. "Orbach?" said Idris. "What are you doing here?"

Orbach bowed again. "I have come to help you choose a sword. Seeing that you asked me to be your General."

"Come on, then," said Idris. He walked to the rack and sorted through the weapons. Three he kept out: one with a hilt beautifully made in enamels and violet leather; another with a blade of Eastern make, rainbowed in the light; and a third with a handle of gray stone and a straight, slim blade of iron, not excessively big, but of a balance that made his hand feel lighter bearing it than not bearing it. "What do you think?" he said, tossing this last sword to Orbach.

Orbach caught the weapon by the hilt. He pulled a silk handkerchief from his sleeve, threw it into the air, and let it float down. Just before it hit the ground, he brought the blade under the falling handkerchief, edge up. The handkerchief fluttered to the flagstones in two halves. "Good," said Orbach.

"Look on the pommel," said Ambrose with a faint smile.

The pommel was a sea-green jewel. Engraved into it was the seal of House Draco, a device of a dragon's head blowing an inlaid ruby cloud of fire.

"It was the sword of Kyd Draco, your true father," said Ambrose. "Cutwater chose you. This one you chose yourself."

Idris slid the blade into the scabbard Holdwater. It fitted perfectly.

"Your horse is at the landing stage," said Ambrose. He handed Idris a pack. "Provisions," he said. "No magic. The time for magic is gone."

Idris knelt. He said, "Ambrose, you have saved the people of Lyonesse and me with them. I shall do my best."

"I should hope so, too. As for Lyonesse, it's not saved yet, and you've got a moon till Darksolstice. Now ride, and find an army, and ride some more. *Look* out."

There was the silence again, as if the world were holding its breath. Idris felt the icy scorch of Fisheagle. But he was invisible to her now, and her mind passed over his and went to burrow elsewhere in the kingdom.

Ambrose said, "A woman like that would no more imagine you could give up Cutwater than clean her own privy. Now fare well, and we will see each other at Darksolstice. And if I am not there and things go ill, go to the Fort of the Westgate, where this began, and do what you must do."

"The Fort?"

"You saw what the Wall Mage did at the Aegypt Gate when the monsters broke through to the Lowland." The eyes came up. "There is a nail in the Fort like the one at the Aegypt Gate, to use in case of need. Though perhaps the need will not arise."

Idris's mind went back to that terrible vision of bursting stone and flying water. He bowed his head. "I will do my best to make sure it does not."

"You will," said Ambrose.

As Idris led Orbach across the water to the land, the altar stone in the giant yew was screwing itself back into place.

All the creatures of the Sundeeps were assembled at the landing, from the smallest shrew to horse-sized longtooth cats, and on the outside of the group prowled the horned figures of the ancient stagmen, bellowing their fealty to their King.

But some of the party were not from the Sundeeps. Morgan was there, and Kay, and half a dozen men in Mount uniforms without helmets. Orbach introduced these. "Good lads," he said. "Joined the Mount to feed their families."

"Where are your families now?" asked Idris, feeling as he spoke the absence of his Knights.

"Hiding in the Marshes inside the Broken Wall," said one of the men, jerking a thumb southward. "Lot of us down there."

"Then we will ride to the Marshes," said Idris. He turned and spoke to the creatures of the Sundeeps. "My people," he said. "It is a long way, and there is no need to follow me, for you are best off at home. But come to the Valley of Apples at Darksolstice. It will be a dangerous place, but I should like to see you there." Hauling his horse's head around, Idris Limpet and his band rode south to raise the country.

⸺⸺⸺❖⸺⸺⸺

As they passed the lonely farmsteads and villages, the inhabitants looked up from their work. "What is it?" they said, for life in the west of Lyonesse was a quiet affair.

"Idris Limpet," said someone in the band.

The farmers and smiths and hunters narrowed shrewd eyes, and felt the shudder of the ground under their feet, a shudder more powerful and sinister with every passing day. And more than a few went back into their yards and pulled swords out of the thatch, and spears out of the ricks, and hammers from the tool racks in the forges. So that by the time the band was clattering down the Old Road to the Westgate they were ninety strong.

The weeds grew thick between the paving stones, and the guardhouse window was broken. A squad of four Town Guardians came out of the door. "Halt!" barked their Ordinant. "Who goes there?"

Idris looked down at the straggle of men in their grubby brown uniforms and felt no need to answer. Eighteen moons ago, they had towered over him, locked him in a cart, and dragged him off for execution. But they were only Town Guardians. Idris had fought Black Mountmen and won. Next to the Mountmen, the Guardians were rustic and feeble. To Idris, they looked stupid and slovenly and frightened.

He rode forward from the band. "Halt!" said the Ordinant again in his flat, official bark. "State your name and business."

"I am Idris Limpet of the Westgate," said Idris. "And you are Diph Artegus, and you hit your children and beat your wife."

The Ordinant's face grew red and heavy. Recognition dawned in his eyes. The red turned to a terrified gray. "You were drowned," he said. "You are Cross."

Coward, thought Idris. "On," he said.

"Wait!" said the Ordinant.

But his voice was lost in the drum of hooves as Idris and his band rode into the town.

The tired and shabby town. The eighteen moons since Idris's leaving had not been kind to the Westgate. Tiles had slid, and paving had cracked, and the roosting gulls had expanded their range as more houses had fallen into ruin.

"Hey!" said a voice at his stirrup.

Looking down, Idris saw a spotty boy about his age, small, with a slightly nervous grin on his face. "Cayo?" he said.

"That's me. You're Idris, aren't you?"

Idris's old friend looked as if he was not getting enough to eat. His eyes, once bright and brave to the point of foolishness, had a worried look. "You want to watch out," Cayo said. The ground shuddered.

"We will," said Idris. "After we've beaten the Mount. You wait."

"Wait? No way," said Cayo, sticking out his chin. "I'm coming with you."

Idris remembered him as having been remarkably small and remarkably brave to make up for it. "Come, and welcome," he said.

The procession clattered on, raising a cloud of dust that glittered with mica in the clear sealight. A crowd was gathering. The faces were closed and nervous, but in some of them Idris caught a flicker of recognition and excitement. The uncertain hollow in his belly left him. He began to feel warm and confident.

In the middle of the square stood the granite plinth for the market, empty now. Idris slid off his horse. He jumped onto the dais, drew his sword, and clanged the side of its blade on a stone till it rang like a gong. Somehow, the square filled with people. At the back he could see a brown knot of Town Guardians. Orbach could see them, too. His dark, bright eye caught Idris's, and he slid into the throng like a seal into the water.

"People of the Westgate!" cried Idris.

The crowd fell silent.

"People of the Westgate, I am your King," he said. "I have come to lead you out of the slavery of Fisheagle and the Captains." He paused. A ripple of horror ran through his listeners. He could feel their minds shrinking away, thinking of torture and death. He was thirteen years old. How to convince them?

As if in answer to his thought, a great bell rang. It was the Hour of Thanks. Silence spread from the tower, filling the streets of the Westgate like the shadow of a cloud. The crowd looked at its feet and began to mutter. *Thanks to the Well and the waters therein*, they buzzed.

"Consider," said Idris, interrupting in a low, powerful voice. The crowd looked up, appalled at this sacrilege. "What good have the Wells done you, and the waters therein? They are spreading in the land. They are poisoning it. Is not food more expensive?" Murmurs now. This was undeniable. "Captains draw their power from the Wells. I used to live in the Westgate. Captain Ironhorse was a bully then, and I suspect he is one now. Which of you has he helped, unless you are a Guardian?"

He could see the Guardians pushing forward through the crowd toward him. A black helmet was heading toward the Guardians. Orbach, in his Mountman uniform.

"You have been told the Wells are the salvation of Lyonesse," said Idris. "But it is the Wells that caused the land to sink, and their only use is to supply monsters to pump out the water, and the catching of the monsters causes the very water to enter that they pump out. We have all learned of the Treaty between men and monsters. Well, the Treaty is a sham. There is no Treaty. The Regent and her brat will open our land to monsters and make all of it a Poison Ground." The black helmet was blocking the brown Guardians. "So I tell you. Refuse the Guardians. Refuse the Captains. I am Idris Limpet, whom Ironhorse tried to crush, but I lived, and I am your King."

In the crowd, the black helmet had met the brown

helmets. There was the sound of metal on metal. The brown helmets turned and ran.

"Now listen," said Idris. "Murther, so-called Dolphin of the Realm, leaves childom on Darksolstice and will become King. But I am your King in the true line. I promise to help you fight the Wells. Murther will throw you into them. Choose which of us you will follow." Another movement in the crowd. A boy Idris's age, leaving. A puffy face looking back over a richly cloaked shoulder. Spignold, son of Ironhorse. His feet pounding the cobbles, heading for the Castle. Two men started after him to pull him down. "Leave him," said Idris.

The world filled with the dark stillness that preceded the mind of Fisheagle. Idris muffled. There was the roar in the ether, the freezing scorch, dark and terrible. The mind passed over. The crowd rocked. Idris said, "People of the Westgate, what you just felt is the sign of her fear. Now I must travel my kingdom. If anyone wants to join my army, bring food and a weapon. If you would like to come but cannot, then stay at home and do what the Mount tells you, but slowly, so as to waste their time. And if you do not believe me, well, as a citizen of my Lyonesse, you are free to believe what you will. You will hear of me. Keep your ears open. Farewell."

Someone cheered, then someone else. He saw Daft Alb out there giving him the thumbs-up, and even his old school enemy Mawga, with tears sliding out of her crossed eyes. And behind the cheering, the tramp of feet. He put his mind out...

And was above, looking down at the streets of the Westgate. "Kek!" he cried, filled with joy.

Kek, said the gull, mentioning its name. Wearily, though, for it had been a long, long flight up the coasts of Aegypt and Iber from the Lower Sea.

"Now we ride," said Idris. "Come with us if you will." And the King of Lyonesse, without his Knights but with his gull, Kek, and his band, which numbered a hundred and fifty now, took the South Road out of the Westgate and moved swiftly into the first reed beds of the Marshes behind the Broken Wall.

There were islands of dry land in the Marshes. One of these, accessible only by hidden paths through the deadly swamp, was the farm of Scorrin, the farm of Arwal Hamza, cousin of the Hamza who had sheltered Uther and Nena after their flight from the Wolf Rock. There was a low white house looking into a courtyard of reed-thatched barns. Around the buildings were the paddocks for Farmer Hamza's small black cattle, and just now the reed shelters of the followers of the True King, whose numbers had increased to ninetyscore.

Seven days after his speech in the marketplace of the Westgate, Idris sat in the end of Hamza's barn. On the beam above his head perched six robins. A small group of rats sat to one side, cleaning their whiskers, undisturbed for the moment by the cat and the dog that lay in a peaceful heap by Idris's right foot. Like the other creatures of the land, they seemed to recognize him as their King and had given up their constant feuds out of something like loyalty.

As Idris watched the world outside, he saw another little group come out of the reeds — a man, a youth, a woman, and a girl and a boy too young to bear arms. He saw them ask directions and nod. They approached him with eyes lowered and bowed deeply. "Your Highness," they said. "We have come to join you."

Idris motioned them up. "No need to bow," he said. "I am Idris your King, but an outlaw according to the Mount. If you join me you will become outlaws, too." The ground shivered, rattling the winter-dead reeds. "Where are you from?"

"We were farming under Worple Down. The illwater come, and the cattle died, and a bad thing came to live in the illwater and ate our youngest," said the man. "Why should we worry about being outlaws when we got nothing to lose?"

"Then welcome to my army," said Idris. "Any who cannot fight must walk to Albion, for the Mountmen will use your family against you if they find them. Any who will fight should stay here, and we will go to the Mount and fight for our country."

"Me and the boy stay," said the man.

Again the shiver of the ground. "Orbach, look after them," said Idris. They bowed and walked away. Idris put his mind up to Kek: not as easy as it once had been, but a familiar, comforting thing in this strange world of marshes and armies.

Through the gull's eyes he saw the Marshes, laced with creeks and gullies. Here and there in the reeds, groups of people were approaching, led by Marshman guides. The gull was high, high enough to see the edges of the Marshes, and beyond to the Downs and the Hundreds and the oak forests, naked with winter, blackened at their edges by the advance of the Poison Ground....

And on the Marshes' northern fringe, the blackbeetle crawl and shift of Mountmen. There were boats there, square-ended punts that would slide over swamps and reed beds. There were monstercarts, and engines with long nozzles that he guessed would shoot jets of flame at the reeds, sweeping away the screen that guarded his little army from the world, and then perhaps sweeping away the army, too.

He said to Morgan, "It is time we were going."

Morgan looked reluctant. Uther and Nena had come to Hamza's, and her time here had reminded her of the safe, happy life in the Wolf Rock. Digby, sitting on her shoulder, was keener. "Hooray!" he cried. "Off we go!"

The army left that night, slipping out of the Marshes by secret ways. The women and young children set off across the southern plain, skirting the huge spread of the Poison Ground, heading for the distant blue mountains of High Kernow, joining the thousands of other families trudging northeast with their belongings on carts.

At dawn eight days before Darksolstice, Idris and his army camped in the dunes inside the Broken Wall. "Where now?" said Morgan.

"The Southgate," said Idris. "We will take the port. We

will raise the town. And we will go to the Mount for Darksolstice."

"And they'll let us in," said Morgan, with sarcasm.

"They will invite us in, to show they do not fear us," said Idris. "And we will accept, and show them that they should."

They slept with the boom of the sea in their ears.

After brekfuss, Idris held a council of war, with Orbach in the chair, General Orbach now, with tired circles under his eyes and an air of brisk authority. "I see it like this," he said. "The enemy will come down the west bank of the Fal. There's only one bridge north of the Southgate. If we break it, we shall have the east bank to ourselves. We can get up through the Shipwright's Garden, if there's a road, cross at the ford by the Falls, and link up with the Beyondsea armies on the Heights of Albion. But we need to find someone who knows the Shipwright's Garden. What?"

Kay was standing up, pale and stiff-faced. He said, "I will break the bridge."

"Me, too!" said Cayo, bouncing.

Orbach looked at the two boys, one eyebrow up, and opened his mouth to tell Kay he was too young.

"Wait," said Idris. "Kay should go to the bridge. Give him a Lieutenant and two hundred men. The Lieutenant will advise him. Kay will accept the advice. As for Cayo...Cayo, have you ever been in a battle?"

"Yes," said Cayo, tiny jaw stuck out.

"Or was it more like a fight?" said Idris.

"A bit."

"You could get killed."

Suddenly Cayo was not cocky anymore. "My mum and dad have gone," he said. "They were in our house when the blackbeetles burned it. I want to get my own back."

"Later."

"No," said Cayo. "Now. Just because you rescued me from Spignold in the Fort doesn't mean you have to look after me for-ever. I'm fourteen next year. Out of childom this Darksolstice. I want to fight." A look of extreme cunning crossed Cayo's tiny features. "Without me," he said, "you wouldn't have fallen into the sea and none of that stuff would have happened, and you wouldn't be here."

Idris sighed. "All right," he said. "Go. As a messenger, though. Not a fighter."

"Whee!" cried Cayo, in a most un-grown-up manner. "I'm going to be a hero!

"Fisheagle, we'll kick your bridge in
and I'll be Idris's carrier pigeon!"

he sang in a high, tiny voice.

"Good luck," said Idris. "Kay, take him with you. The bridge is yours."

Kay flushed with happiness. As the army formed up for the march, Idris could hear Cayo's singing, fading in the distance.

Then it was lost in the clank of weapons and the scuff of feet and the clatter of hooves. The Army of the Limpet was on the march.

Kay and Cayo headed north, toward the bridge over the River Fal. Idris's army moved out of the dunes behind the Broken Wall and headed along the coast to the Southgate.

For three days the army marched east. Every day it grew, swollen by men and boys from the quaking farms of the hinterland. The shaking of the ground grew more and more savage.

"They're bulging up," said Digby.

"What?"

"There are monsters pushing up from underneath," said the small monster. "The big ones. The ones they call Helpers. Very unpleasant. They want to break through."

At last the Southgate straggled out to meet them.

Once, the city had sparkled in the sun. Now its granite was blackened with a sooty mold, and the blue-flowered trees that used to bloom in the streets stood stark and dead. Thin-faced people watched from windows and doorways. There were no Mountmen.

"They've run away," said Idris, feeling the beginnings of triumph.

"Listen," said Orbach.

Idris listened. "I hear nothing," he said.

"Quite so," said Orbach. "The pumps have stopped."

The pumps took water from the low land of Lyonesse and spewed it into the sea. They were driven by monsters. If nobody was catching monsters, there would be no means of getting rid of the water. . . .

His eyes met Orbach's. They were dark and very serious. Idris realized with a chill that the land he ruled would be very different from the land he had been born into.

⋘•⋙

The arrival of the Limpet army and the distribution of food had a powerful effect in the town. The feeling of darkness lifted. People came out into the streets: housewives to sweep doorsteps, children to play soldiers, and most of all men and boys, sidling along to the headquarters Idris had established in a warehouse by the granary, to offer their service. To each one, Orbach, on Idris's instructions, said the same thing. "We will win. But it may not do any good."

And most of the men replied, "Anything's better than sitting here waiting to drown in Wellwater." And all the while the ground shook, and the sky was strange and bulging with thunderstorms.

Next morning Idris was sitting on a stone mounting block by the quay, receiving the men who came to offer him their service. He heard the clatter of hooves and smelled a gust of hot horse. A messenger flung himself on his knees before him. "I come from Kay," he said. "The west bank is full of Mountmen, thousands. He has had losses. But he has broken the bridge."

Idris tried not to think what these losses might mean. He said, "Then we march up the east bank!"

The messenger bowed, hiding his face. "But the enemy have used monsterengines to destroy the road through the Shipwright's Garden. No man can use it, let alone an army."

"What else?"

"Kay is retreating on the Southgate. The enemy presses him hard."

There was a silence. "We will go by ship," said Idris at last.

"There are not enough ships."

"We will use what we have."

The quartermasters started to assemble a ragtag fleet of barges and punts. Idris thought it looked far, far too small. The distant clash and shout of fighting could be heard from the northern part of the town. Orbach sent troops to reinforce retreating Kay and sat in front of a maptable on the quay, giving his orders. His face grew grimmer as the morning wore on. "How are we doing?" said Idris.

Orbach looked up from the table. "Nicely," he said. "As long as we get a miracle."

The miracle came.

As the sun passed the zenith, a fleet of white sails appeared on the horizon. They swept through the Seagate and tied up at the quays. The Captains came to Idris, six dark men, heavily bearded, with gold rings in their ears and bag-shaped hats of blue cloth. "Orders from King Mark," said their spokesman, who wore the Sun and Stone of Ar Mor as his cloak brooch.

"We are to give you help. His armies set off two moons gone and will be on the Heights of Albion at the time appointed."

Idris felt his blood warm with joy. So the Knights had won and made their cases, and the Armies of Beyondsea were on the Heights. "Brave Captains," he said, "you have arrived just in time. Please put yourselves at the disposal of General Orbach and be ready for battle."

The Ar Mor Captains grinned, their teeth sharp and white in their beards. "We are always ready," said their leader. "After nuncheon, that is." And away they went, as if it was the most ordinary thing in the world to eat nuncheon, sail up the Fal from the Southgate, and topple a tyrant.

It did not feel ordinary for long.

Late in the afternoon, Idris was on the afterdeck of the first of the fleet as it headed up the Fal bearing his army. A fast scout-boat had gone ahead of the fleet. Astern, hidden now by the Fal's great embankment, lay the Southgate, a Southgate changed beyond recognition since the morning. The harbor was empty, except for two ships ferrying families to the east bank, away from the wrath of the Armies of the Mount, who were still driving southward through the streets, resisted by a small but ferocious rear guard commanded by Kay. Idris stood looking upriver at the Fal as it wound across Lyonesse to its source in High Kernow, where the allies were waiting. The rear guard came aboard in a fleet of small boats. Idris saw Kay heading toward him down the deck of the ship, pale and bloody. Someone shouted from the nose of the ship. Something bumped down the side. Idris saw a tangle of lashed timbers, scorched-looking: the debris of the bridge. Something was caught in the tangle below the water's surface, waving, like a piece of cloth. As it waved it rolled, and Idris saw a face. Not a rag, a body. The face was grayish-white and very, very small. It was the face of Cayo. His heart lurched in his chest. Idris said, "No."

"Who?" said Morgan, beside him.

"We were at school together," said Idris. Cayo's face looked very peaceful. He had died doing what he had begged to do. Idris hung his head. He would have liked to weep, but no tears came. In reclaiming the land, they would lose friends. Weeping would come later. . . .

But Cayo was different. Idris had saved Cayo's life, in the Fort, at the beginning of all this. And now he was dead. "How did it happen?" Idris said.

Kay was with them now. "He said he was a fighter, not a carrier pigeon. He was the last on the bridge. I told him to come, but he would not. He cut the lashings and took eight with him. Without him many more would have died."

Idris had saved his life. Now Cayo had returned the favor. The sunlit world of the Westgate school was far away, in a different country. The tears fell. At last Idris lifted his head and put his mind to what must be done. "Make sure he is brought to land," he said. "We will bury him with great honors."

Kay bowed. The ships ran on up the Fal, pushed by the

brisk southerly breeze. They passed pumping stations and manufactories, silent now. At sunset, they came up to another bridge: an improvised bridge, this, the last before the Falls that brought the Fal down from the high ground above Trur. It spanned high-banked narrows. Below it, the river spread into a broad pool with sloping grassy sides. It would have been a beautiful spot, with the croak of a heron and the slide of the water. But this evening the quiet was spiky with shouts and the noise of weapons clashing. As they rounded the curve of the river, they saw a swarm of Mountmen at the western end of the bridge, their black armor bloody with the light of the sinking sun. The eastern end of the bridge was stoppered by a wall of unarmored Limpetmen, crouched behind shields. These were the skirmishers from the scoutboat, horribly outnumbered. From behind the shield wall, a sleet of slung pebbles howled into the blackbeetle throng of Mountmen. Idris saw the shapes of monstercarts, heard the savage thoughts of monsters.

The Ar Mor Captain said, "Permit me to help."

"Go on," said Orbach.

The Captain bowed and gave orders in his own language. Sailors milled around a device on the deck, a wooden cradle bearing a long gray stone. There was a Stonekeeper among the sailors, dressed in the order's robe of undyed wool, with a sickle in his belt—

BLOOD, said a voice in Idris's mind. His nose was full of a stink that suddenly rose from the water. People around him were coughing.

The Stonekeeper said a word. The thing on the deck made a deep, soundless twang that hurt Idris's head. The stone that had been lying in the cradle drifted into the air and flew away over the water, gathering pace, spinning like a great sycamore seed. It hurtled into the crowd of Mountmen with a crash. Black-clad figures were flung in all directions. Through them it spun, clearing a lane....

BLOOD.

Something broke the water upstream: a black thing, shiny. It rolled and dived, leaving a powerful swirl. Idris realized what the monstercarts were for. "They've put a monster in the river," he said to the Captain. "And Wellwater. Smell." The surface was thick with the corpses of fish. Idris felt rage at the filth and waste of it. "I need an iron hook," he said. "Land me. Over there." He pointed at a low slope of bank.

"Land?"

BLOOD. IDRIS.

"It's me it wants. It knows my blood. It's been sent. Go." He took the hook a sailor brought him.

"I'm coming," said Morgan. She took a hook of her own.

The Captain shrugged. Idris and Morgan dropped into a ship's boat. Four Ar Mor sailors rowed them ashore and pulled back to the ship. The stone-throwing machine spun another huge stone over the water.

BLOOD.

Screams rang out from the far shore as the stone thrashed its way through the Mountmen. There was grass under Idris's

291

feet now. He was standing on the bank of the river, a shallow slope leading into stinking water, the narrow beach piled with dead salmon. Morgan was beside him.

"What do you want to do?" she said.

"What we were taught. Over here," said Idris, moving to a place where there was a hollow behind the riverbank.

"Monstercatching?"

"Yes," said Idris. He nicked the ball of his thumb with his knife. Blood welled. He cast a drop into the river, and sucked the cut clean. "Now," he said.

His heart was thudding. Out there on the broad river, something was speeding toward the ship. Something that threw up a wave of black water twice as high as a big man, a wave that roared at its edges. Then a black head rose out of the wave, a head too terrible to describe, and a mouth opened in it, big as a palace doorway, full of teeth like sword blades, towering above the ship, yawning at it, ready to bite it in half—

Hey! said Idris with his mind. *Get over here, you dirty eel, and I will introduce you to the King of Lyonesse.*

The roar of the mind of Fisheagle. *Hence, slimecrow,* said Idris, batting her away with his mind. *Oi! Swamp-herring! Over here!*

The monstermind came at him. He let it probe him, so it could see he spoke the truth. He felt it taste the blood-drop. *Thank you,* it said, purring cold and slimy. *I know the blood of Idris. I will taste it all.*

Try, then, thought Idris. He stood, legs braced, gripping the hook shaft, in the position he had learned on the Welltops of the Valley of Apples. *Latrine leech.* He laughed.

Monsters do not like being laughed at. This one was angry now, crazed for blood. "Steady," said Idris, watching the huge wave turn away from the ship and roll toward the shore.

"Who are you telling to steady?" spat Morgan between her teeth. "I'll take its left."

"Good. Here we go."

The wave burst on the grassy slope with a roar. Suddenly they were up to their thighs in water, and something vast and black was between them, slippery skin and teeth and tentacles blotting out the sunset, and in the sudden chill of the shade Idris said, "Hooks," and dug in the iron hook.

The monster screamed with its mind at the touch of the iron, beastbane. "Weight!" cried Idris, and heaved on the ash shaft of his hook, and felt Morgan doing it, too, and stepped aside, and huge teeth slammed a handsbreadth from his face, and the monster was sliding up the slope under its own momentum, thrashing and snapping and screaming with iron-agony, until it topped the rise. "Loose!" cried Idris and let go the hook. The creature slithered into the hollow, where it lay writhing, the hook shafts clattering as it struggled.

Kill, it roared in the mind.

Idris drew his sword. He skirted the depression, going in behind the monster. It grew a tentacle and slashed at him. Idris jumped the tentacle and ran in, carving a long slice out of the monster's flank. The monster screamed. Something whipped Idris's face, but he paid no attention. The terrible jaws opened. He sidled up to them until he could smell the disgusting vapors from its innards. The teeth slammed shut. But Idris leaned away, a mere bending of the body. And while the creature lay stunned by the violence of its own bite, he ran up its flank and drove his sword into its eye. Something gushed out and over his wrist, cold and stinking, and the monster gave one last terrible shriek, shuddered, and lay still. The Mountmen had retreated from the far bank. Idris wiped his sword on its skin, slid down its flank, walked to the river, and washed himself. He heard a long, low sound and looked up. His people were standing on the ship's decks, stark black cutouts against the bloody sky. They were cheering.

"Let's get on," he said. He raised his voice. "Destroy the bridge," he said.

He and Morgan stood by the river waiting for the ship's boat to pick them up. It was quiet, except for the gurgle of the river and the distant burble of a curlew. Behind the silence, a mind-something was shrieking and blubbering with grief.

"You know what you have just killed?" said the voice of Digby, who was disguised as Morgan's hat. "That was Most Beautiful Darkness, and it was a pet, special friend, and blood relative of the Regent. She sent it after you to give it a treat. Well *done!*" cried Digby. "*Such* a bully it was!"

Idris nodded. He was thinking. Monsters could not live in ordinary water. They needed the bitter stuff from the Wells. The Mountmen must be pumping it up from the Valley of Apples: a fearful task, reckless of the health of the Fal. If there had been one monster, there would be more.

THIRTEEN

They made camp on the east bank of the river among the crags and boulders and oak trees of the Shipwright's Garden. The Garden was in fact a mighty forest. In its deeps, trees grew for a thousand years and died of old age untouched. It was an eerie place, perilous with longtooth cats and giant wolverines, where small farmers lived whole lives without seeing their neighbors. The road that ran beside the Fal had once been its only communication with Kernow to the north and the Southgate to the south. It had never been a very good road. Now it was a jumble of boulders and mangled trees, wrecked by the engines of the Mount.

Night fell, blacker and blacker. The pickets lit watch fires by the river. On the hills to the northwest other lights blinked green and blue and red: Mountmen signals. Those hills rolled up to a great flat-topped, windswept moor, whose other side sank by a series of valleys into the Wellvale. Idris and Orbach sat in the wood above the anchored ships in a tent pillared with the trunks of great oaks. They ate and drank, but not much, discussing their plans by a hissing fire of oak branches. Their conclusions were not encouraging.

Idris's army among the trunks of the Shipwright's Garden numbered a mere two thousand. The Mount had tens of thousands, wading toward them through the filth that the Wells had spewed into Lyonesse. And from the Wells there would come monsters, thirsty for blood, wild to make colonies in the poison swamps.

"The way I see it," said Orbach, "is that they won't want us to join up with your Knights and the allies in High Kernow. So they will send monsters down the river at us, chase us out, and finish us off on the west bank if we go that way. And if we stay on the east bank, well, we can't travel in the forest, so we can't get anywhere near the Mount, so they're safe. We can only get as far as the bottom of the Falls in the ships, the Falls being rapids. From there, we'll be walking. And to walk from there to High Kernow, over this" — he waved a hand at the tangled forest and the wrecked road in the dark outside — "it'll take till next Darksolstice, never mind this one. So how do we get up the Falls?"

Idris opened his mouth to answer. But no sound came out. He saw Orbach's face frowning, the striped material of the tent, the red eyes of the fire, perfectly familiar. But something odd was happening. He found himself pricking with goose pimples. For a mind was brushing his: a mind unfamiliar, chill, wet. A mind tense with ... *duty*. And he knew that deep in his own mind he had asked for the way up the Falls. And that he was being answered.

The sentry put his head in at the tent door. Until the day before yesterday he had been a carpenter, so he was not very good at stamping and shouting and saluting with his spear. Instead, he said, "'Scuse me, Idris, there's a thing out here got webbed feet." The head vanished, then came back in. "Actually," said the sentry, "there's thousands of 'em. Oi!" This last because he had been pushed gently but firmly aside by a throng of small greenish-white people. One slightly taller than the rest raised a hand. His comrades came to a halt. The leader stepped up to Idris and bowed.

Idris smiled, returning the bow, happiness growing in his heart. "Flashers of the Lugh, you are many times welcome," he said.

This was the cue for an avalanche of thought, in which he got the idea that these were not only the Flashers of the Lugh and some other rivers, but also of the Fal, these last living in the marshier parts of the Shipwright's Garden and furiously angry about the burnfilth (Wellwater, presumably) that was being tipped into the river. They had detected from Idris's thoughts that he was in need of help. This was too much to be expressed in thought alone. Speech was necessary. Idris's ears filled with the gurgling chatter of several hundred amphibious throats. *Flashers build up the right and break down the wrong*, they said. He held up a hand and said, "Margrave, explain yourself, if you please."

The Margrave explained at length and in detail what he and his people proposed to do.

"Yes, yes!" gurgled his people, when he had finished. "The Falls, the Falls! And after that the City of Illwater. How we will sweeten it!" And they laughed, a long, hilarious gurgle. Idris laughed, too, and Orbach with him, astonished by these creatures. Then the Flashers trotted off into the night on their long webbed feet, slapping one another on the back.

Idris slept in a little cabin of his own on the ship. He was lying there, going over the day in his mind, filled with happiness by the coming of the Flashers. He felt someone come into his cabin and sit on the bottom of his mattress. "Morgan?" he said.

"Yes. Who were those . . . creatures?"

Idris explained.

"What can they do?"

"Get us up the Falls," said Idris. "And do other things. Wait and see."

"Swine!" She flung herself on him and shook him, laughing. Then suddenly she was not laughing but crying.

"What is it?" he said.

"Nothing. I'm being stupid." She had herself under control again. Her voice was level and dark and cold. It reminded Idris of the Aegypt desert at night. "I'm frightened."

"We all are."

"Not of the things you're frightened of."

"Is it the Tree?" said Idris.

"I don't think so," she said, agitated again, though. There was a long pause. "Oh, well, yes. I can see all of you getting older. Nena and Uther have. You're growing up. You can't hear thoughts the way you did. It's natural." A deep breath in the dark. "But I can hear thoughts better than ever. I am afraid that if all this goes wrong, I won't be able to die, and you'll all leave me behind. Idris, it's so lonely being me."

And me, thought Idris. Not that he would have any trouble dying if Fisheagle had her way. It was not an amusing thought, but he found himself grinning anyway. He said, "Perhaps you should ask Lanz what he thinks."

"I know what he'd say. He'd tell me everything is all right and I should stop worrying."

"So trust him."

A sob.

Idris put his arm around her shoulders. He said, "A year ago you would have wanted to fight Lanz. Now you just want to talk to him. So you're changing, which is a fair start. As for whether you can die or not, there's a good chance we'll find out one way or another in the next few days."

Again, it was the opposite of funny. But this time they both laughed anyway. Then Morgan went back to her cabin, and Idris fell asleep.

Four days to Darksolstice.

·PART FOUR·

She had been a child once. A human child. She remembered a little girl, thin and weak in a clouded metal mirror. Herself. She remembered her father, squat and red on his golden throne, triple crown looming, breath sour, as he told her how she could rule. Befriend them. Betray them. Suck their blood.

Then the descent into the Wells, the changing of her tongue and nails so that she was beautiful. And later there he had been again, her father, white on the ground, sucked dry, and the delicious taste on her teeth. Oh, they had given her so much below the Wells, and she had taught them so cleverly!

She could feel the Helpers as they swarmed thicker, ever thicker around the Wells, pushing upward. She knew that the hour was at hand. The silly little armies of landcrawlers were ready to fight her dear child for the kingdom. Well, she would suck them into her trap, and they would die and bloat and drift away.

And then the Helpers would come, and the promises would be kept; and she, Fisheagle, would rule in Darkworld, and the Helpers would make what wreckage they wished, and have their fill of rich, thick blood. It had been promised....

Someone was laughing. What?

She had no time to find out. She folded her leathery wings into a fast-swimming delta and rushed from the bitter infinities into living rock, built stone, hewn tunnels, and into her tower on the Mount. In the next tower, the dear child was giggling as he munched living bone.

She sat upon the black stone bed and flung her mind into the world.

FOURTEEN

The Falls, three days before Darksolstice: a long roaring slope of water and rocks winding upward into Kernow. At the bottom of the Falls a pool, with a road to its west bank. Where the road reached the bank was a group of long, low buildings Idris instantly recognized as a wharf, where monstercarts unloaded their cargoes into barges for transport downriver to power the pumps and manufactories of the Southgate. A raw scar ran beside the road. Through his bringemnear Idris saw the mouth of a pipe, new-laid. Carrying Wellwater, no doubt, to support monsters in the clean Fal.

He was standing on the beakhead, in the very nose of the ship. It was a couple of glasses after sunset, and the sky was a sad gray, without stars. Except for the distant murmur of the Falls, the world was quiet....

Not entirely quiet. Above the sound of the Falls there came the gurgle of bodies passing through water. When Idris looked closely, he could see that the smooth black surface was pocked with the heads of swimming Flashers. Then another sound, from the road behind the wharf: the creak of a cart axle, and the scrape of a drag as the driver applied the brakes.

His cargo would be a monster. He would put it in the river. And it would tear into the Flashers and gargle their blood.

"Captain?" said Idris.

"My lord," said the voice of the Ar Mor Captain behind him.

"Could we put a stone through those buildings?" he said.

"Aye." Feet padded on deck. He heard the *whum* of the stonehurler. The stone flailed across the water. A huge crash as it hit the sheds. Dark buildings collapsing, the bellow of frightened aurochs. A sudden flare in the blackness, a lamp knocked into the hay, perhaps, lighting a tangle of aurochs and the smashed monstercart lurching sideways into the ruins. A crackle of thatch, then the long, terrible shriek of a drying monster.

And later, the tramp and clank of an army of Mountmen, black armor gleaming dully in the first glints of dawn, as they marched down the road to the smoldering ruins of the wharf at the Fallsfoot pool and made ready to launch their assault on the ships of the Limpet army come to destroy their Regent and her Dolphin.

After midnight, a shoal of Mount scoutboats slid onto the black water, paddles silent in the night. The Ordinant in the lead boat loosened his saw-edged sword in its sheath and watched the other boats, forty of them, slide across the dark water toward the Limpet ships, to take them by surprise and slaughter them while they slept—

The Ordinant frowned. The dark shape of the nearest scoutboat had vanished, leaving only a widening circle of ripples, bent by the current. The Ordinant put his hand on his sword hilt.

The side of his own scoutboat was suddenly covered in fingers: pale fingers, webbed, with pads at the end. The world spun. The sky vanished. Instead of air in his mouth, the Ordinant felt water. He struggled. But hundreds of cold, slippery fingers pulled him down into the dark.

One moment, forty scoutboats had been sliding across the surface. The next, the river flowed smooth and empty toward the sea.

The Flashers, having gotten rid of the interruption, went back to work.

<hr/>

When the new day dawned gray and clammy, the ruins of the monstersheds were at the middle of a huge city of Mountmen tents. The sentries on the quay peered into the morning mist seeking their scoutboats. They saw none. They blinked and peered again.

The Falls were gone. And so were the ships, and the Army of the Limpet. Where once the river had rattled down rapids, it now stood gray and smooth and empty, filling its gorge from side to side, blocked by a great dam of trees and boulders.

The trees stood thick in the hills between Lyonesse and High Albion. Animals called, and herons labored up from the shallows. The Limpet fleet lay alongside a low cliff in a pool far upstream of the Falls, its masts and spars perfectly reflected in the quiet water. The air was full of a deep, settled peace. To begin with, Idris could not think why. Then he realized. This place was in Albion. It did not shudder like Lyonesse. Year after year it grew lower, certainly; but what made it lower was rain-run and frost-flake, not constant undermining by the greed of Captains and the lust of monsters. Lyonesse must have been like this before the coming of the Wells.

The thought made him sad. He had not even taken possession of his kingdom, and already it was spoiled. He was sitting on the beakhead of the ship when Morgan found him.

He felt her mind on his like the faint pressure of a friendly hand. She said, "I'm not barging in. I wanted to show you something. You can't see much with your mind, can you?"

"Not as much as before." It seemed to be as Ambrose had said. Boys lost the gift, or at any rate it was replaced by others. Girls kept it.

"I've been practicing. Look," said Morgan. He felt her take his mind with hers, swooping dizzily upward.

And suddenly he was seeing the land from above. This was not as Kek showed it to him, hazed at the edges, a patchwork of moor-path and field-wall. This view was from high, high above, as a mapmaker sees his subject in his mind; yet he saw its details, too, houses, flocks, individual people, even. He saw the Valley of Apples pouring Wellwater into the escape channels. He saw that the lake had overtopped the dam, so it had become a waterfall over which the Wellfilth poured in a torrent.

The land beyond the dam was the Poison Ground. Once it had been a mere patch of filth in the green land. Now it had spread from the dam and seeped into the Marshes inside the Broken Wall, and up to the western banks of the Fal, so that only the Stone Downs and the moors and the Sundeeps still stood green and proud above the filth. And beyond it all, outside the wall, lay the huge metal glitter of the sea.

Idris's heart was a stone in his chest. His kingdom was ruined.

Look, said Morgan.

The Stone Downs were crawling with people. Some were Mountmen, their black armor gleaming in the gray light. But most were the ordinary people of Lyonesse: the women and children driving flocks of sheep and herds of aurochs and shambling bands of ground sloths; the men and youths separate, in groups that sent up the glint of metal, heading, as everyone was heading, for High Kernow and the Heights of Albion.

Morgan took Idris on to the Sundeeps. A man in a red robe was riding out of the mountains on a bay pony with a long, pale mane. The man lifted his head and looked up, as if he could see the watchers. To his astonishment, Idris saw that it was Ambrose.

In the storm of despair battering him, Ambrose's face brought a ray of calm. Suddenly Idris saw that Ambrose knew he was being watched. He felt the mage's affection and respect. He heard his voice.

You are on the right lines, said Ambrose. *Get on with it.*

And Morgan brought them back to themselves, on the beak-head of the ship in the anchorage in the high Fal. On deck, a servitor cleared his throat. "Excuse me, my lord. The High Margrave of the Flashers is here. You wished speech with him?"

"I did," said Idris, climbing on deck and bowing to the greenish-white creature in its ceremonial crown of jade-colored fish spines.

Tomorrow was Darksolstice Eve.

It had begun.

Next morning Idris rose early, put on a tunic and breeches of dark blue cloth, and pinned around it a dark red cloak with two pins, one the Dragon of Lyonesse and the other the Devouring Eel of House Ambrose. Then he slung his sword around him and went ashore.

A party was waiting on the close green turf: Kay, a small handful of men heavily armed, and Morgan. Morgan, too, was dressed in dark blue with a deep red cloak bearing the badges of the Eel and the Dragon, and carried her bow and a quiver of arrows fledged with crows' feathers.

As they cantered up the hillside above the bend in the Fal

where the ships were moored, Morgan saw that the river was far above its normal level, high enough to lap at a meadow that had once been a saddle between two hills. From the saddle the land declined in a long, greenish-dun slope toward the distant plain of Lyonesse. At the end of the slope, tiny with distance, stark against the background, stood the tower-crowned crags of the Mount, and beyond it the murky huddle of the Wellvale.

Morgan opened her mouth to comment. But even as she did so, Idris was spurring his horse toward a little group of horsemen cantering down the slope ahead. There were half a dozen of them, clad in bright colors, brandishing swords in the air. At first she thought they were attacking. But they did not look like attackers. They shouted, and their voices were full of joy and relief.

And she saw that Idris was smiling, too, the way he smiled when he was trying not to give away how very pleased he was. "My Knights," he said. Then the world was full of drumming hooves and familiar faces, laughing and shouting with happiness, and Morgan found that she was laughing, too, blushing as she greeted Lanz; and Idris was surrounded by his Knights, and she knew he felt that though they were not yet in Lyonesse, they had come home, and she felt it, too.

"All right!" cried Idris, and the racket stilled. "What joy to see you, my Knights! What news?"

"My father's in charge of the supply train," said Merk. "We've brought brekfuss. There's some pretty good venison, a couple of big pies, and some fruit. As for drink—"

"Lay it out, whatever it is," said Idris. Grooms came and took the horses, and servitors spread corsair carpets. Morgan sat first, Lanz beside her. They ate, everyone talking at once. The grooms were accustomed to courtiers listening to their Kings with a deep respect. This was different. The respect was there, but this youthful King and his Knights sitting in a circle were more like a group of friends than a royal court.

"So tell me," said Idris, when the first edge was gone from his hunger. "Who is here of our allies?"

"King Mark, of course," said Tristan, as if there had never been any doubt. "Very nice man, as it happens."

Gawaine had been tearing at a partridge with his teeth. "The High King of Eirinn's sent five hundred horses. Excellent animals, I have to say." He pushed his hair out of his bright green eyes. The eyes had lost their restlessness now. They were fierce and steady. Gawaine had grown up. "And wild men to ride them, very savage and tricky. They'll be handy."

Galahd was looking at his hands. He had finished eating and now he was tying an elaborate knot in a length of sinew. "The Norns are with you," he said. "The King sent twenty dragonboats to Kernow, each with twenty shieldmen."

"The Duke took a little persuading," said Bors. "He is a dirty man and thinks only of himself. But he came, and four hundred freemen with him. They're not the best, but they are free, so they are here because they want to be. Which is something, I suppose."

"More than something," said Lanz. "These are good men. They are all good men, indeed, though the Eirinn cavalry are not so disciplined. The Overlord has sent three hundred; there has been trouble, you understand, and the kingdom is divided against itself, so he may need your help when you have finished your work here."

"He can have it," said Idris. "Well, this is great work. Who'd have thought we'd ever get here when we were in the slave market in Thbee." All eyes went to Morgan, who turned slightly pink and smiled, reserving the best of it for Lanz.

They were silent for a moment. There was no need for words, for the friendship ran among them like ropes of steel, and each felt strong with the strength of all the others.

"And now," said Idris at last, "we will go to the Kings."

Servitors came to clear up the debris of brekfuss. Idris and his Knights mounted and rode. Lyonesse spread below, far and hazy, black-centered with poison. Along the hill in front of them, riders stood dark against the sky.

The armies were camped beyond the first ridge of the Heights. Idris and his Knights rode along the tents among travel-hard men in battle gear, who stood up and bowed, staring from under their helm brows at the cause for which they had come so far.

The Kings sat around a fire in a cone-shaped tent. They had been talking with Orbach, and looked up as Idris came in. They did not rise.

Idris said, "This is my sister, Morgan, whom I and my Knights brought from the land of Aegypt, where she had been taken. I had promised to do this, and I have kept my promise. And I showed you what became of the Lowland, and what threatens Lyonesse now, and perhaps all of you if we do not act. I thank you for coming."

King Mark was dark and unreadable. The Duke of Eytgard smiled greasily and shifted a goose leg to his left hand so he could wave to Morgan with his right. The Overlord nodded and smiled and looked pink and said, "We managed to get away after all!" as if he was talking about a picnic. The merchant Wollick, a strangely thin version of his former self, bowed deeply and told Morgan that any time she wanted to sell her bluestone ring he would give her the best price west of the Rusmont. The Kings of Norn and Eirinn and Albion bowed and made polite noises. Idris thought that the shock of what he had showed them in their dream had worn off. Now, they looked like men who were doing favors and might expect one day to have them returned. They made Idris feel ridiculously young. He had very little experience of this side of Kingship. He hoped they would not ask him any questions he could not answer.

He said, "It is good that you have come. You will be wanting to know what benefit there will be in it for you. Well, I promise you this. When you are vexed with monsters, I and my Knights and my people will help you get rid of them."

King Mark bowed, his dark eyes straying to the canker of

the Poison Ground gnawing at the land's heart. "A good thought," he said. "Let us hope there is not the occasion."

"Absolutely," said a small, diffident voice. It was the Overlord, swinging his heels in his chair. "But actually you've been jolly useful already. You said to stop Skrine, and I did, and filled in that nasty Well of his, and most of my men were delighted. I hadn't realized."

"And the White Earl?"

A shadow crossed the Overlord's pink face. "He's down there." He pointed with his thumb toward Lyonesse. "With four hundred of my worst men. Worst, as in nastiest. Cruelest. If they survive and get home, there will be trouble."

"We will beat them. If they live and cause trouble, I will help you against them. Duke?"

The Duke was slouched in his chair. For a moment, the only sound was his jaws sloshing chewed goose leg around the inside of his mouth. Eventually he wiped his jaws on his fur cuff, belched, and said, "Trade." Then he fell silent.

"Quite right," said Wollick.

"Trade?" said Idris.

"What His Grace wishes to say," said Bors, slipping into his old role as the Duke's truth-teller, "is that Eytgard in Kaldholm is a rich place, in good land. But its true wealth is in trade. And the alliance of men with monsters causes trouble, in the form of earthquakes and wars and the coming of seas where there were none before. So he has chosen to fight with you against the monsters and their friends."

"For business reasons," said the Duke, through another mouthful.

"Very wise," said another voice. It was a quiet voice, but it caused everyone in the tent to become quite still. Its owner was a man in a hooded cloak, standing by the fire, holding out his hand to the flames. The fingers were stained black and green, as if with copper and ink. Nobody seemed able to remember how he had gotten there.

The hood went back. And there was the dark, aquiline face of Ambrose, beaming upon all present. "Permit me to name these monarchs," said Idris, in the Manner, and named them.

"It is good of you to come," said Ambrose to the Kings. "You will not lose by it."

There was a general easing of tension. The High King of Eirinn and the Norn of Norns and the Thains of Albion might have doubts about allying themselves with a mere boy. But Ambrose spread confidence around him.

The mage held out a sheet of skin, folded and sealed. "I met a Mountmessenger on my road. He gave me this for you."

On the front fold was written in blackest squidink *Idris Limpet*. Idris knew what it was already. He broke the seal.

We command our subjects Idris Limpet and Morgan late Wolf Rock to attend us on the Mount on the Occasion of the Darksolstice, it read. *We offer safe conduct.* The squidink had been scattered with gold dust. There was a signature, jagged and spluttering, as if what had made it had claws instead of fingers, which was no more than the truth, for this was the signature of Fisheagle.

Idris reflected. The allies were something over four thousand men, and Idris had brought another two thousand. The Mount had three men to the allies' one, and everyone knew it. Idris was sure of what he must do. He took a deep breath and said, "I will go and meet the Regent, and tell her she must go, or I shall call my allies down from High Kernow to push her out." There. It was said, in front of six Kings. There was no backing out now.

"I shall come, too," said Morgan.

"And so will we," said Lanz.

"Only as far as the border," said Idris. "For now, take care of the Kings you have brought. For Darksolstice, I have a job for you."

"She means to humble you," said Ambrose.

"My sister and I are Knights of Lyonesse," said Idris. "We are written on the Skins of the Realm. How can we be humbled in our own place? As for Fisheagle, I do not think her dignity will be greatly helped by my Knights."

"What does that mean?"

Idris caught his Knights' eyes. They looked away, innocence itself. "You will see," said Idris.

"Make sure you know what you are doing," said Ambrose. The smile was gone, and his gaze was clear and hard.

"I have made preparations," said Idris. But even as he spoke, he thought: We must walk through the Wargate of the Mount and meet the enemy face-to-face. And he felt for the first time the true chill of fear.

Idris, Morgan, and the Knights took nuncheon with the Kings, serenaded by a choir of men of Lyonesse singing the dark harmonies of winter. Morgan was pale and silent.

Idris beckoned the choirmaster. "Sing us the Spring Song," he said. "We are going into a dark place."

So the choir sang the ancient Spring Song of Lyonesse, and its harmonies moved over the winter hillside like a green breeze, bringing a whisper of warmth and hope.

After nuncheon was over, Idris parleyed with Orbach and Ambrose and the Kings, and had a particular conversation with the Knights, in which there was a good deal of laughter. Then he took leave of his allies and his people, and mounted his horse, and rode down the narrow lane that led out of the Heights of Albion toward the Valley of Apples. Morgan went with him, Digby, disguised as a necklace, at her throat. Behind him rode his Knights, Kay now among them, come to escort him as far as the borders of his country, but not beyond.

The lane opened into a broad valley. At the bottom of the valley stood the Mount, and beyond it the Welltowers of the Valley of Apples jutting from the town walls like bottles from a box. "The border is at the white stone," said Idris to the Knights. "Leave us here. Do what we have planned. When you see white smoke over the town, come down. Orbach has the orders."

The Knights bowed, for once entirely solemn. Idris spurred his horse to a trot, swallowed to clear a throat suddenly tight, and said, "Now or never."

"Is this wise?" asked Digby.

"Shut *up*," said Morgan, in a voice that was very nearly a squeak.

So on Darksolstice Eve, the King of Lyonesse and his sister, both dressed in dark blue with the Devouring Eel cloak brooch of the Ambrose and the Dragon of House Draco, escorted only by Kek, his gull, and Digby, her monster, pressed forward down the road to the frontier of Lyonesse.

As they passed the white stone, two files of Black Mountmen closed in behind them, like a royal escort.

Or perhaps even more like the jaws of a trap.

<hr />

The road past the Mount to the city shivered with a side-to-side movement. At the city gates the Black Mountmen guards eyed the cloak brooches blank-eyed. One of them bowed, realized what he had done, and turned bright red.

The streets of the Wellvale had changed. They were slimy with mud that stank of Wells. The towers were blackened. The crowds looked tired and unhappy. A couple of Captains went past, triple crowns gleaming. Thirteen moons ago they had been carried in open chairs. Now they traveled in closed litters, protected from the city they had made by thick sheets of mica, with a little pane of priceless glass to allow them to see straight ahead.

As Morgan and Idris passed the entrance to the Old Well Square, Idris saw that a stage had been set up to frame the Old Well porch, where a year ago this day he had drawn the sword Cutwater from the stone and taken it for his own. The inside of the porch was illuminated by monsterlight, every detail crisp and clear.

And there, driven through the hasps of the forbidden door and into the stone, was a sword. The sword's pommel was richly worked, the decorations of its blade exquisite.

Too rich. Too exquisite.

"Cutwater?" said Morgan. "How?"

"Not Cutwater," said Idris. "It's a Captain's idea of what Fisheagle would want Cutwater to look like. Today's the day the Dolphin must draw it from the stone." His eyes met Morgan's. They locked. "I wonder if he'll manage," he said, for at that moment he had understood how he was to be humbled. And he smiled.

Morgan's face had been pale. Now some color came back into it, and she smiled, and Idris felt her in his mind, warm and comforting. "He will certainly try," she said. "And I will certainly watch." She turned. A squad of Black Mountmen waited behind them in the road, elaborately not watching. "Listen, jackdaws," she said. "We're going to the Ambrose. And tomorrow to the Mount, to do our duty to our kingdom. Any objections?"

Judging by the silence, there were none.

The dwarf Cran was waiting in the Goldfinch Chambers, which were as beautiful as ever. Every now and then the ground shook, hard, as if something had it in its teeth and was trying to worry it apart. They ate, and slept in their old beds.

Next morning Idris sat waiting for Morgan to finish in the bath, his eyes resting on the exquisite mosaic of goldfinches on thistle heads. There were new cracks in the tiles since he had been here a mere moon ago.

"Cran!" he said.

In came Cran, the eyes bright and intelligent in the long dwarf face.

"Today when the procession comes from the Old Well we will have the white smoke," said Idris.

"And about time, too," said Cran. His lower lip jutted, doubtful. "Lot of them blackbeetles about, though."

"It's sink or swim," said Idris.

Another shudder of the ground. The dwarf seemed to be listening to something. Idris heard it, too: the scrape of iron sluices deep in the Well. "Catching a lot of monsters," said Cran. "The stables is full to busting. Gettin' ready for something."

For war, thought Idris.

And here came Morgan, pale but beautiful in her ceremonial robes with the blue cloak over all. Idris went and splashed his face with water (a faint whiff of the Well even in that). The Well fired as he was in the bathing room, a shudder and a roar, then a fading boom of water in the channels. "No grooms up there anymore," said Cran in his harsh squawk, trotting after them down the Grand Stairs. "Just blackbeetles. I dunno what the world's coming to, really I don't. Wouldn't have done for the mage, oh, dear me, no." They were in the Wellporch now, the horses waiting outside and the stink of Wellwater heavy in the street. Idris drew his sword and gave it to the dwarf for safekeeping; there would be no weapons permitted at the Mount. He wrapped the scabbard Holdwater around his waist as a belt. Then he walked across the porch to the iron door that closed off the stairs down to the stables.

"What are you doing?" asked Morgan. She had always hated the monsterstables.

Idris opened the door onto the dark stairs down.

The darkness roared with monstervoices. *Come*, they yelled. *Be with us. Join our lovely darkness, oh, here we come with the little blue fish, oh joy!*

Idris grasped a torch from a cresset and started down the stairs.

He had traveled only ten steps when he saw in front of him light reflected on slopping black water. He backed away. A tentacle slapped on the stone, and monstrous laughter cackled in his mind. *No cages. Soon it is you who will be in the cages, waiting for the draining of your blood. We will be free, in darkness—*

He slammed the iron door, cutting off the mind-voices in mid-shriek. He looked at Morgan. Morgan looked back, wide-eyed with horror. The Wellwater in the monsterstables was carefully regulated to stay at the level of the cage-traps.

The regulations were gone. The waters were almost at the iron door, two bowshots above their correct level.

No wonder the lake had overtopped the dam.

"The horses are waiting," said Idris.

As the sun stood four glasses before the zenith, he and his sister started through the streets of the Valley of Apples toward the looming towers of the Mount.

FIFTEEN

The year before, the Valley of Apples had greeted Darksolstice with the sense that it was going to a party. This year it was a quiet, even glum procession of the noblest, the richest, and the most violent remaining in the land who rode out of the east gate of the city and started up the hill that led to the Wargate of the Mount.

The Wargate had always been terrifying. Now it felt shadowed by the very wings of death. The steep gulley of the approach had been swept of its last trace of greenery. The nets of boulders bulged more horribly than ever from the barbican, and burners shrieked, fuming half-dried behind the fire ports, cooled with water sprays, not submersion, so as to be ready for instant use. No birds sang.

Idris rode with his shoulders back, looking straight ahead, refusing to let himself think that all this deadly force was aimed directly at him, unarmed, riding into the heart of his enemy's power.

Inside the gate Mountmen took the horses. Morgan hissed. "We shouldn't have come."

"They won't break the safe conduct yet," said Idris. "Fisheagle wants Murther to be King. So the year must turn, and he must leave childom and take the sword from the stone in my presence. And then he will think of a good reason to kill us. If he can catch us."

"What?"

"Monsters hate clean water," said Idris.

"*Huh?*"

But now halfhounds were yelling behind kennel bars, and they were walking with the crowd through a scowling gate, then another, gate after gate, eighteen in all, each guarded by Mountmen. Last year, they had given their names to a Mountman on the first and last gates. This year, the Mountman's eyes landed on them, and he waved them past with a faint, sarcastic bow. Idris exchanged a glance with Morgan.

They were known.

The eighteenth gate clashed behind them, and they were in the Court of the Apple Trees, the garden at the base of the Kyd Tower. There were tables of food and drink, and a fountain in the middle.

There was a throne in the center of the fountain. Last year, it had held a monstrous creation for the amusement of the guests. This year, it held an old man: an old man in red robes, his face hidden in the folds of his hood. Idris's heart bumped in his chest. "*Ambrose?*" said Morgan in a horrified whisper.

Then the hood turned toward her, and Idris's head filled with a sound like the hiss of a lizard. The hood fell back.

325

And he saw with huge relief that it was not the real Ambrose but a monstrous caricature, the eyes burning with a hot red light, the teeth a confusion of barbed spines between jewel-green, scaly lips.

People were not looking at the creature in the fountain, though. People were looking at Idris. An old Knight caught his eye, and inclined his head in a faint but noticeable bow.

Nothing must be allowed to happen yet.

"Goodness, I'm hungry," said Idris, leading Morgan to the food. There were snipes and salmon and lobsters and Iber wine and sunapple juice, things that usually gave rise to a great roar of conversation. But since Idris had come into the courtyard the sound of talk was muted. Eyes had turned away from the doorway in the tower in the corner and toward Idris. Respectful eyes, but eyes aware of the danger of seeming to notice him too much.

There was another reason for the quietness of the crowd: Through the garden there spread like cold air the mind of Fisheagle. Idris felt it touch his, hard as beak and claws, but without rending. It had recognized that he was there and was pleased that he had come and brought Morgan with him.

And that they were in its power.

Idris felt someone looking at him and turned. His eye fell on a little group of Captains—two from the Valley of Apples, smooth and sleek, and another more uneasy and countrified. The countrified one was his old enemy, the Captain of the Westgate.

"Ironbottom!" said Idris and started toward him.

As Idris drew near he was interested to notice that he was now half a head taller than the Captain of the Westgate, and that the Captain walked with a limp, a result of Morgan having shot an arrow into his buttock twelve moons ago. The notion filled Idris with optimism. "Ironbottom!" he said again.

"Er, Ironhorse, an' it please Your Worship," said the Captain, with something between a bow and a writhe. "I don't think we've met?" he said, still avoiding Idris's eye.

"Idris Limpet," said Idris. "How is your boy Spignold? Not very well, I hope."

"Aha-ha," said Ironhorse, writhing.

"So will you fight for me or the monsters?" said Idris.

"Fight? Oh, surely not," said Ironhorse. And all the Captains laughed. But Idris, looking into their eyes, saw that they knew and feared him, and that what was looking back at him were not men, but hollow things turned by greed into mere bladders of terror.

The Captains named themselves in the Manner, but mechanically, as they weighed up the advantages to be gained by supporting Idris against the Regent. Idris could see their minds working without going inside them. He and Morgan were alone in a hostile city. The Regent had thirty thousand men. The face of the sleeker of the two creased in a confident smile. He leaned forward, breath smelling faintly of rotting lobster. He said, "In a moment we will go down to the Old Well, where the sword Cutwater abideth in the stone. As far as I—"

"We," said the other two Captains.

"—we are concerned, the True King of Lyonesse will be he who draws the sword from the stone and casts open the gates of the Old Well."

"Thank the Well," intoned all three Captains.

Idris smiled. He saw the Regent's whole scheme now, and it was exactly as he had expected.

He went to find Morgan and took her hand. The fingers felt cold and dry. "Well?" she said, low and grim, but not at all nervous.

"We will be presented," said Idris. "The Dolphin will sit in the High Seat. There will be the sacrifice of the burner and the bull to make the sun come up again, though it will come up anyway without wasting good cattle. Then we will go into the town and there will be the business with the sword. And then the smoke."

"And then?" She was distracted as something caught her eye. "Look at that mouse," she said.

It was sitting in the corner of the courtyard, brushing its whiskers with its paws: a small gray mouse, perfectly ordinary. But it was not behaving in an ordinary way. It was watching the crowd with bright, beady eyes. As Idris looked, the eyes turned to him. The mouse gave a small start. Then it bent its head in a perfect miniature bow, turned, and scuttled into a cranny of the wall.

"Master Idris and Miss Morgan House Ambrose!" cried a herald.

"That was once my name, but no more," said Idris in a loud voice. "Now I am Idris House Draco, called Limpet." The words rang in the stone courtyard. As the echoes died away, an appalled silence fell.

The crowd parted before them as they crossed the stones. They mounted the steps to the door at the base of the Kyd Tower. The Chamberlain was waiting there, his black tin hat of office pulled low to hide his eyes, the snot-diamond on the end of his nose blazing in the low Darksolstice sun. "This way," he said, but Idris and Morgan were already ahead of him, through the point-arched door carved with biting beasts and onto a flight of stone stairs carved with more beasts in hard black stone. Another mouse touched its forelock and scampered to its home in the mouth of a basalt wyvern. Then the Chamberlain shoved past them, puffing and clanking, and the bronze double doors wheezed open. And there in front of them loomed the chair of blood-red stone, and in it Murther, so-called Dolphin of Lyonesse, and behind it the Regent Fisheagle.

"Kneel," hissed the Chamberlain.

"Silence," said Idris, without looking at him.

The Chamberlain opened his mouth to argue, thought better of it, and scuttled away to lurk by the doorpost.

Murther was slouched in the red chair. He was dressed in a robe of deepest black that made dark rainbows when he moved. His burnt-black eyes looked somewhere to the right of Idris's head. Their rims were pink and nervous. Behind his chair stood his mother.

Fisheagle was thin, with a beak of a nose; long, narrow eyes stone-black without whites; and teeth that dented a lower lip painted the same scarlet as the throne. A spiked fin like a mullet's stood on the crown of her close-fitting black hood. The hand on the back of her son's chair had red nails thick as claws.

Idris said, "Well, Murther. Today we come of age, you and I."

Murther yawned, showing a thick gray tongue. "Why should I be interested in that?" he said. "The land is mine, and that's all there is to say."

"You will have to fight for it."

"Fighting I leave to my servants," said Murther, pretending boredom. He giggled. "But I like killing. You'll find out." He turned his dreary eyes on Morgan. His fingers plucked at his flabby lower lip. "You're getting prettier," he said.

"If only the same could be said of you," said Morgan coolly.

Murther's face slackened with surprise. The jaw fell open, revealing tiny sharp teeth, like a fish's. It was true that he had not grown more beautiful. Last Darksolstice, the mice of the Kyd Tower had revealed to Idris that Murther had fins down the backs of his legs. Since then, he seemed to have become more fishlike. His nose had gone back, and his lips had come forward, and his sallow skin now had a suspicion of slime. A hiss came from between the jaws. "When I am King you will come and live in my palace and I will hurt you," he said.

"But you will never be King," said Morgan gravely. "My brother, Idris, is the King, and you are a mere creature."

The black robe shone wonderful rainbows as the body inside struggled up from the chair. He said, "I will hurt you *now!*"

330

Fisheagle's hand fell on the shoulder. The skin was the color of rotten milk, with blood-red nails. "Hush, darling," said a voice like an icy razor. "Later." Kyd Murther subsided, hissing, into his chair.

I am surprised you came here, said the cold voice of Fisheagle, in his mind or his ear Idris could not tell.

"It is my palace," said Idris. "Though the company is not what I would choose."

Your life has not been what you have chosen.

"Nobody's is," said Idris. "Destiny drives us all." He took a deep breath. He was in the heart of his enemy's power, surrounded by her hired thugs, in the presence of her cruel and stupid son, who was about to steal the throne. He said, "Fisheagle and Murther—"

"Call her Regent Sea Eagle, and him Kyd and Dolphin," said the Chamberlain in a frantic whisper.

"The Kyd of Lyonesse is head of the reigning family," said Idris. "The Dolphin is the eldest son. So the Dolphin is me, not this nasty-looking fish-boy. And this other creature is not my Regent, nor is she a Sea Eagle, which is a noble creature of my realm. She is a fisheagle, or eelhawk."

There was a long, rending hiss. Careful, thought Idris. Do not push them too far. He said, "Fisheagle and Murther, it is the Manner for me to thank you as caretakers of my kingdom for holding to the custom, and receiving me and my sister at Darksolsticetide, and granting us safe conduct. This I do. But why have you asked us here?"

The red lips did not move. The voice sounded in his head. *Because it is no pleasure to me to have my victory without hearing the lamentations of my enemy defeated.*

"We will watch you wriggle and squirm," hissed Murther. "Shriek and bleed. Beg and seep——"

Yes, yes, my darling, said Fisheagle. *But first we want these little children to watch the ceremonies of noon, when my son brings up the sun again and so leaves childom, and in the porch, when he draws the sword from the stone and is proclaimed by all.*

Idris smiled. Fisheagle loved anger nearly as much as blood, and he would not feed her. "Playacting is always amusing," he said, though he felt it sounded weak and lacking in conviction.

I do so agree, said Fisheagle. *This is why I have been so amused to see your little army gather on the mountains. And why when the sword is out and the land is ours and my dear boy has played with you, I will put you and your sister side by side on iron thrones, and strap burners to your bellies, and enjoy your deaths, which will last a long, long time.*

Idris found this much easier to deal with. "I do hope you're wrong," he said. "We'll just have to see, won't we? Now. Come on, Morgan, I think she's finished."

He turned. The Chamberlain's teeth were chattering like a baby's rattle. "They were *rude!*" said Murther's voice from behind him. "They were *rude* to you and me, and that's not *allowed!* Why doesn't someone snip off their *noses?*"

There, there, my darling, said Fisheagle, stroking his greenish hair with her blood-red claws. *Someone will.*

Idris knew he should be darkened by Fisheagle's threats. Instead, they made him feel strangely cheerful. He moved through the throng in the Court of the Apple Trees, greeting Knights, laughing as Captains edged away from him. After a while he squinted up at the sun. "Time for the nonsense on the tower," he said to the people around him, and began to walk to the steps.

It was evident to everyone that Idris House Draco called Limpet was a dead man walking. So nobody wanted to be seen to accompany him, except, of course, Morgan.

So the two figures in their dark blue clothes, Eel and Dragon brooches glittering over their hearts, walked together up the wide stairs to the tower top. The fact that they walked alone should have made them look hunted and condemned. Oddly it made them seem regal; and many waverers accepted the appearance for the fact, and were converted.

As they reached the tower top, the bell struck for the Hour of Thanks. The court assembled on the circular roof and turned their eyes to the Dark Tor, a cone-shaped hill covered in stony winter-brown grass and scrub, crowned with an outcrop of granite on which stood a circle of standing stones. The shadow of the tower lay on its slope, creeping toward the stone. When the shadow of the tower entered the circle and touched the white quartz rock at its center, it would be noon, and Darksolstice would be here.

In earlier times there had been a bonfire lit on the Dark Tor at Darksolstice noon, to signal the sun's lowest zenith of the year and to summon it back. But no mere bonfire was enough for Fisheagle. So she had invented a new version, in which a burner, which she said represented day, was tied to a black bull, which she said represented night. The burner dried out and roasted the bull alive. The only thing it represented to Idris was shocking cruelty.

There was a stir. The heralds were shouting, "Part, Court!" Idris put his mind out to Kek.

The gull was hovering over the Dark Tor. Idris saw the gray circle of stones, and beside it the black helmets of a group of Mountmen, seeming nervous, as well they might be. For the Dark Tor was on the very border of Lyonesse, and among the crags beyond, gray plumes of smoke announced the cooking fires of the armies of rightful Lyonesse and Beyondsea.

Beside the Mountmen were a burnercart and a cage on wheels for the bull, which was flinging itself from side to side and raking its horns down the bars and bellowing. The shadow of the tower was edging across the hillside. By the sounds behind Idris, Murther and the Regent had arrived on the tower top, and Murther was struggling into the Solstice Seat, so his own personal shadow would be the first part of the tower to touch the Noonstone.

Something was happening on the Dark Tor.

Idris's Knights were there.

Idris saw a boy in a greenish-dun jerkin hiding behind one of the stones on the last slope before the summit. As Kek swooped, Idris saw another boy behind another stone, and another in a patch of fern. One of them looked up. The face was familiar: pale eyes, reddish hair. Kay.

Kay got up and started running over the close-nibbled grass to the circle. Half a dozen more went for the party around the bull's cage, swords flashing in the sun. Five of them attacked the guards, while another leaped onto the bull cage. "Gawaine," said Idris, gripping Morgan's hand. "It's Gawaine!"

The gate flopped open. The bull bounded free, pale horns hooking. It tossed a Mountman, looked around, and saw the straggle of men around the monstercart. A spear raked a bloody gouge out of its shoulder. The bull charged into the Mountmen, flattened two, and stood hooking left and right. The green jerkins stood back. One of them was clapping, as if at a game: Tristan. Idris tried to hide his laughter. Then Tristan and Gawaine and Kay took advantage of the confusion to point the monstercart's wheels downhill. Someone seemed to give an order. "Lanz," breathed Morgan. "Be *careful!*" The green jerkins withdrew, heading for the far side of the tower. The monstercart was rolling, picking up speed.

"The Solstice comes!" cried the voice of Fisheagle, who must not have been watching.

The shadow of Murther on the Solstice Seat was moving across the stones of the Quoit.

"Behold!" cried Fisheagle, spreading her cruel claws.

The Court of the Valley of Apples turned its heads. What it beheld was a lot of little black figures scuttling after a monstercart bounding down a hillside. The cart hit a rock and bounced into another boulder with a crash. Something shot out of the tank and landed in a grove of scrubby elder trees. On the crest of the hill the bull tossed another Mountman and trotted over the horizon into Kernow.

There was a hiss and a roar as the burner in the wood caught fire. A heavy plume of brownish smoke rose toward the Mount, carrying the sickly reek of burning elder.

Well, Kay, thought Idris. Any wrong you have done me you have undone, and thank you all, my Knights.

In the silence, somebody laughed.

Fisheagle turned, flailing a furious mind across the gathering. She heaved Murther out of the seat. "Owww!" he whined, writhing as the thick red nails dug into his flesh. "We go to the Old Well," she rasped. "My son is of age, and the people who have made mistakes will die horribly. Now the Dolphin will draw the sword from the stone. And with the sword he will be King, not Dolphin, and my work will be done."

But the Knights were not watching Murther. They were watching Idris. Many were bowing discreetly. For the Dark-solstice sun had passed the zenith, and Idris was of age, too.

Fisheagle stalked by, raking the crowd with her angry mind like a longtooth cat raking a deer's flank with its claws. She stank of Wellwater and rotten seaweed. But, thought Idris with a flare of triumph, most of all she stank of fear.

Idris stayed till he was among the last on the tower. An old Knight whose mind Fisheagle had torn was lying with his eyes rolled back in his head, only the whites showing, his Lady kneeling by his side.

"I beg your pardon," said Idris. "If I might help?" He unwrapped the scabbard Holdwater from his waist and laid it on the old man's brow.

The eyes closed, then opened again, bright and steady. "What was that?" the Knight said. "Horrible. Better now." The eyes focused. "Limpet." Confusion. "I beg forgiveness. Majesty, I should say."

"Limpet will do very well. Watch for the white smoke. Prepare the other Knights." Idris caught the old eyes of the Lady. "Discreetly."

"He will," she said grimly.

They joined the procession.

<hr>

There were crowds lining the streets now, coughing in the smell of Wellwater. "Cheer!" said a Mountman as Fisheagle went by on a moving platform hauled by serfs. A thin, ragged cheer rose. But it seemed to Idris that the real answer was the tremor of the ground underfoot, a long, continuous shudder, strengthening sometimes to a twitching, as if pressure was rising, ready for something bigger and worse.

Down the road they went, not speaking. He knew Morgan could feel the pressure, too, because her fingers were tight on his arm. A babel of monstervoices battered at the edges of his mind. It reminded him of the feeling he had had as he had crossed the Lowland with the Knights: like a wave gathering to break.

They passed the porch of the Ambrose. Cran was there, standing on the shoulders of his usual servitor. A long, weary shuffle later, and they were in the Old Well Square. There was a honking of trumpets and a shouting of heralds. The Mountmen made a semicircular wall to keep people away from the Old Well porch. The sun had gone in, and the square was winter gray, except for the porch, which was brilliant with light from a burner in a lantern. The ancient beasts carved into the porch's stone seemed to writhe faintly. The doors of the Well stood massive and immovable, because of the sword driven through the lock hasps and into the stone beneath.

Idris heard a voice in his mind. It was small and clear: the voice of Ambrose.

It is not the sword, said the voice. *It is the stone.*

The stone lay in its place, carved into the rough likeness of a monster. You could not see from this distance, but it was smooth as glass, blood-red, with little green lights in it that came and went.

Starlights, said the voice of Ambrose. *Not monsterlights.*

"Behold!" cried a voice from the stage. "The Dolphin approaches the sword!"

Idris found himself being pushed toward the front: pushed not by hands, but by his right to the throne of Lyonesse, and his coming of age and leaving childom, and the rising of his people, and the presence of his allies.

He found himself hard up against the line of Mountmen standing with linked arms to keep back the throng. He could smell sour uniforms. Between two black shoulders he could see Fisheagle thin and upright, sinister as an eel. He felt her eyes lock on him, heard her voice grate: "Let that one through."

The Mountmen parted. Idris walked across the empty paving to the porch in a silence that made the clack of his metal-shod heels ring in the square's blind cliffs of stone.

"So," said Fisheagle, in her loud, harsh voice, so the crowd could hear. "Who are you, and why do you come?"

"I am Idris House Draco, True King of Lyonesse," said Idris. "I am of age today, and I come to claim my kingdom."

A rustle in the crowd, dying away to silence again, only this time not quite silence, for behind it there was a strange, massive scurrying and a wide liquid rumor.

The small sounds were lost in an earsplitting shriek. For a moment Idris did not know what it meant. Then he realized it was the sound of Fisheagle laughing. "Well," she sneered. "A child rises to take the place of his King. Child, you will perish miserably, for the King of Lyonesse is not mocked like this. But first, so all may see that this is an imposter who takes in vain the True King's name, this bold child may draw the sword from the stone, if he can. Bring him here."

Idris found that there was a Mountman on either side of him. He felt his knees weaken. He had given this monster the excuse to squash him like a beetle and not be blamed.

But Lyonesse was his kingdom, not Murther's. And the

people were his friends and subjects, to whom he owed the duty of truth. And that great rustling was becoming louder.

His courage returned. He strode forward, outpacing the Mountmen, toward the doors of the Old Well. Murther looked at him sideways with his dreary eyes and ran his tongue around his purple lips. With an effort, Idris put his mind into the stone and knew instantly that something about it had changed. It was still red and smooth, with lights in it. But the red was dull and angry, the lights monster-blue, not star-green as they had been before. The sword stood sunk in it, bright and beautiful and entirely false. He could feel a mechanism in it that gripped the blade, simulating magic. He closed his eyes a blink and pushed the jaws of the machine with his mind. They stayed solidly closed. His heart began to hammer. He had lost his powers of mind. *Help*, he thought and heard the laugh begin again in the icy soul of Fisheagle. Then he felt a warmth, as if other shoulders had joined him and were beginning to push. Morgan's shoulder. And Ambrose's. He heard Fisheagle's shriek of rage, but it was drowned by a great, joyous warmth. He pushed again, laughing for joy. They all pushed. The mechanism yielded, clicked back. He grasped the sword's hilt and pulled.

It came out of the stone as easily as a spoon from a cup.

SIXTEEN

I dris held the sword aloft. There was a moment of stunned silence.

Then the cheering started.

The new sword felt awkward in Idris's hand. The sky darkened. He looked up and saw an enormous bird hurtling out of the sky at him. Its wings were the size of palace doors, the beak and talons yellow. The wind howled in its feathers as it dived. It was a sea eagle, flown from the dizziest crags of the Sundeeps. Its amber eye swept the porch entrance and fell on Idris. It swooped toward him. From its talons there dropped an object that flashed as it turned in the air: his own sword, nameless, ordinary, but his own, bearing the dragon of his House on the pommel. Behind the sword was the blue sky, with heavy black Darksolstice clouds riding the fierce wind. And between the sword and the sky, another cloud: white smoke, purest white, great clouds and billows of it pouring from the spout on the Ambrose.

The signal was in the sky. The moment had come.

Idris put out his left hand and caught the sword of his fathers.

There was a harsh scream of rage from the dais. Fisheagle reeled, blown over by the wing-draft of the great bird of prey. The hem of her skirt flew up. The crowd gasped. Her toenails were claws, her toes joined by webs of skin. "Kill him!" she shrieked as the bird soared away. "Kill them all!"

Something huge started battering the bronze Welldoors from the inside. Idris slammed his shoulder against them and thrust the false sword back through the hasps and into the stone. The battering grew louder. Splinters of bronze sprang from the doors and flew humming across the square. One of the panels burst outward. Something huge and greenish-gray snaked out, something between a fist and a mouth and a tentacle, making horrible sucking wails. Idris hacked at it and ran toward Morgan, who was in the middle of a ring of Knights, facing outward at an advancing group of Mountmen.

"Loose the Helpers!" shrieked Fisheagle's voice. A roar of huge monstervoices answered. Idris thought: It is too late, things are not happening in the right order, we are too few, they will sweep us away. Then he heard a shrieking and saw the Mountmen fighting the Knights begin pawing at themselves and beating their faces and tunics. As Idris ran toward them, he saw five rats run up a Mountman's leg and into his breeches, saw the man scream and fall and roll on the ground, and knew that the scuttling he had heard as he faced Fisheagle at the Wellporch had been the sound of the creatures of Lyonesse, risen to help their King.

"Well done, my people!" cried Idris, hacking his way toward the Knights of Lyonesse as they defended his sister. Suddenly there was water on the ground, up to his ankles as he ducked inside the circle. "On!" he cried, joining the perimeter of swordsmen.

"It's wet," said Morgan. "But it's not Wellwater."

"The Flashers dammed the river," he said over his shoulder, lunging at a Mountman. "This is Falwater. Sweet water." The circle was edging through the crowd toward a pair of horses wearing red cockades between their ears.

"Long live the King!" cried someone, then someone else.

"Head for high ground!" cried Idris. They were at the horses now. "Get up!" He took the instep of Morgan's foot and boosted her into the saddle.

"Helpers!" shrieked the voice of Fisheagle. "Come from your Wells and smash these gasfaces!"

"Helpers?" said Digby, in a voice lacking his usual confidence. "We really don't want to meet any Helpers. We should hurry."

Idris and Morgan swung into the saddles. The sound of the horses' hooves thundered up the Wellwalls. Mountmen and Captains were spilling into the street. The water of the Fal swirled hock-deep over the cobblestones. On every ledge and projection, a moving tide of mice and rats and shrews and voles was flowing in the direction of Kernow, swarming over Black Mountmen as they ran. "Thank you, all!" cried Idris. "To high ground!" For the ground underfoot was trembling, bulging upward through the Falwater.

Thick white smoke was still rising from the Ambrose, though the Welltower itself was rocking. The dwarf Cran was in front of the porch with a crowd of servitors loading chests onto a cart. Idris and Morgan reined in their horses to help.

"No!" said Cran. "Hurry on! There's going to be trouble."

Digby said, "To say there will be trouble is like saying the Tree is a garden shrub — oi!"

Morgan wrapped the overexcited monster in her cloak, muffling his sarcasm. Idris saw a throng of Black Mountmen splashing up the street toward them. He leaned over, grasped the loyal dwarf by the scruff of his tunic, and pulled him up behind him. "Ride!" he cried.

They rode.

They thundered through the streets of the Valley of Apples, Falwater splintering left and right in the winter sun, the ground shuddering and twitching underfoot. From behind them came a crash and a roar. Glancing over his shoulder, Idris saw the Brassfin totter, crumble in on itself, and descend into a thick upsurge of Wellwater. Behind him, the pursuit was bogged down in the deepening Falwater. The horses splashed around the last bend. The Kernow Gate came into view.

It was closed. A black storm of arrows whipped out at them from its flanking towers.

"Here!" shouted Idris, though he hardly knew why, and pulled his horse's head down a narrow alley. There were voices in his head. One of them was Fisheagle's. She was screaming: partly in rage, but also in terror. But beyond her shrieking, dwarfing it, was a voice huge and warm, that held in its vastness sun and rock, and beach and tide, and farm and oakwood, and a skyful of stars; warm but ancient, this voice, and tired by constant struggle. *Idris, my son, my King*, it said. *I am the land. I am old and weary and you are young. My time is gone. Yours begins. Look!* And deep underfoot, the land of Lyonesse shook its tired bones.

Idris found tears were streaming down his face. *Farewell*, said the huge voice. The land shrugged. A section of the city wall crumbled and fell. The dust cleared. Beyond the breach, Idris saw the first upsweep of hill, and beyond that the Heights of Albion and the crags of Kernow. And halfway up the hill his Knights, in bright war clothes now, thundering toward the gate, banners floating in the wind from the sea.

"What is it?" said Morgan. "What's the *matter*?"

But Idris only shook his head, unable to speak. So Morgan took his bridle and led him through the breach in the wall, and up the hill to safety among his friends.

—•—

It was dark when Idris and Morgan and the Knights rode into the camp on the scarp overlooking Lyonesse. The army was camped there, rank upon rank of tents neatly laid out inside a palisade, cookfires burning, horses stamping.

The Kings of Beyondsea must have heard what had happened this day, for this time they rose to their feet when Idris entered at the head of his Knights. Idris said, "We must be at the borders of Lyonesse by dawn. The land has risen against the Mount." He sat down at the table, Morgan on his right and the Knights around them, Ambrose looking on.

"I wonder," said Merk, "if there is anything to eat."

While they waited, Idris and the Knights recounted in detail the story of the day, laughing in the telling; though Idris said nothing about the land, for only he had heard it, and he wanted to consider what it meant. Food arrived. "My dear friends," said Idris, raising his jeweled mug of sunapple juice. "Without you, none of this would have happened."

"And without you," said Ambrose, "none of these people would have met. So, you people of the Round Table. Each of you has come through danger and faces more. But what is to come may be less than what has been."

"My land is threatened," said Idris. "What could be worse than that?"

"What is that chair you are sitting in?" said Ambrose.

"Chair?" Idris frowned. There was indeed something familiar about the chair: a heavy chair with red cushions. One of the legs was new.

It was the chair Ambrose had hurled to save him when he had fallen into the Well.

He remembered the fall through the air, the crash of black water, the boil of monsters, the terror of teeth, the loneliness

346

and the dread. He looked at the faces around him: the faces of his friends, who had saved his life and whose lives he had saved. Dark this world might be, but there was warmth and companionship in it. He saw Ambrose's eye upon him, kind and wise and sad. Idris said, "That was a bad thing, true. We will fight the creatures of the Well and destroy them if we can. Meanwhile we are friends, and at dawn we will march together for what is right." Then he put his head on the table and fell asleep.

There were terrible dreams. Enormous things were under him, pressing upward. He could hear the voice of Fisheagle. *No, she was shrieking, in the extremities of agony. We made a bargain. You were to have the land. And I was to rule below.*

WE LIED, said a monstrous voice, bigger and deeper than any Idris had heard in the Well, and laughed. In his dream Fisheagle screamed again, and he could hear Murther whimpering. And behind it he could feel the deep, deep weariness of the land.

He woke. But the dream still echoed in his mind. He was in bed, in a tent. Sky showed gray beyond the door. From outside came the sound of horses' hooves, the clank of armor, the song of a sword blade on a grindstone. He found he was out of bed, dry-mouthed, dressing, carefully, for what might be his last day on earth. He pulled on the dark blue garments of House Draco, then a hauberk of light mail. Over it he slung the cloak with the Devouring Eel and the Dragon clasps, his hand shaking a little as he engaged the pins. Then came the baldric with Holdwater. His stomach felt hollow. Hollow or not, he found it hard to swallow the spelter cakes and honey on the silver brek-fuss tray. He took a deep breath and stepped out into the cold half-light.

A constellation of cooking fires winked orange on the crests around the camp, where the households of Lyonesse had made temporary homes. The Knights were waiting outside the tent. Tristan was yawning, and Gawaine was polishing a dagger blade, whistling his little war tune. "Anyone frightened?" asked Bors. "Because I am."

Galahd nodded gloomily, not saying anything. Lanz said, "Just keep someone on your right and your left, and fight the man in front. You can't go wrong."

"Quite a good brekfuss, considering," said Merk with his mouth full. And everyone laughed, and the tension broke, and they walked into the tent of the Kings, where Orbach was sitting at a table with a map of dispositions before him and the Kings and the Duke, grave-faced and tense, leaning over his shoulders. They looked up, saw the Knights, and returned their smiles.

"The Overlord is going down to our left," said Orbach. "King Mark and Ar Mor will be on our right. We will be going down the center to take the city. Then the flanks will circle in and mop up."

Idris nodded. His head was buzzing with the dim rumor of thousands of thoughts, all sharpened by the prospect of battle. Not only human thoughts: There were monstervoices down there, too, howling with something like triumph.

Ignore them, as a brave King and good groom should.

He said, firmly, to hide the shake in his voice, "To horse, my Knights."

Trumpets sounded through the throng: not a great throng, but with the people of Lyonesse and Beyondsea, more than five thousand men. There was a great shuffling of feet and hooves. Silence fell, like a mass indrawing of breath. In the silence a single trumpet blast, high and clear: *advance*.

Banners waving, Idris and his Knights and his armies rode out to war.

⇒•⇐

Among the crags they rode, scouting parties out to left and to right, and into the valley running down to the border. The sky was paling as they caught the first jagged glimpse of the Mount, black against the gray land beyond. A window burned poison green in the Kyd Tower. To Idris's left and right, the hills bristled with lances. Behind his armies, the sun was brightening the sky. A first ray shot through a notch in the Kernow hills, lighting a broad swathe of his Kingdom water-silver and grass-green.

Down rode Idris at the head of his army, down toward the border of Lyonesse.

Morning birds shrieked, roused by the army's tramp. As they drew near the white stone, the ground shuddered underfoot like an animal horribly wounded.

"Here come the Mountmen," said Tristan, riding beside Idris with the bringemnear.

Idris put his mind up to Kek. Out of the city gates of the Valley of Apples water was flowing, whether Falwater or Wellwater he could not tell. Wading through the water came regiments, battalions, masses of Mountmen, streaming out to form up on the plain before the city, outnumbering Idris's armies six to one, but not believing in the cause for which they might die.

Another shudder of the ground, rattling even the hard bones of Kernow.

The Mountmen were all out now. They marched into their places on the plain until they made a deep black barrier of steel between Idris and the city. As Kek swooped over horsemen and foot soldiers, Idris saw grim faces turned upward, reinforcements moving up behind, reserves waiting in the rear. In the gull's eye, the Mount army stretched twice as wide as his own force and three times as deep.

Idris knew that he was looking at his doom.

Then the shivering of the ground became a bucking, and he took in his breath and forgot to breathe out.

Something dreadful was happening on the plain.

The ground was shaking the Armies of the Mount from their feet. The towers of the Valley of Apples reeled in the morning light. The shaking went on and on, harder and harder. Mountmen Ordinants yelled. But horses and men began to panic and break.

Idris stayed in Kek, watching.

The Welltowers were falling. Great masses of stone broke away. The palaces broke first, their intricate fretwork crumbling and plunging into the streets. The towers were more massively built, and they held out longer. As Kek glided in front of the Great Ambrose, Idris saw the wall of the Goldfinch Chambers shear off, caught a split-second glimpse of the golden mosaic of corsair ships and birds on thistle heads. Then the little tiles burst outward in a shower of golden motes and rained down on the street far below. The Welltower itself was lurching and waving. Jets of dark water were fountaining up from ground level. The tower rocked left, then right. A crack shot from its bottom to its top, and widened.

Idris felt cool air in his mouth.

The Great Ambrose crumbled and fell.

Black water welled out of the ruins, pushing up in huge boils the color of squidink. The other Wells were down, too. The Old Well was the last to go, stocky and brutal in the ruins; but go it did, spewing black liquid and crumbling into the ruins of the Hall of Meters and the Old Well Square. Filthy water poured up from the Wellworld, displacing air that buffeted and hammered at Kek's wings. The Mount army on the plain threw away its weapons and ran for higher ground.

Roars of triumph blasted Idris's mind. Something the size of a mountain writhed through the ruins of the Ambrose into the lake and vanished. Idris came away from Kek's mind. He sat white and shaking on his horse.

A voice said, "It is over." Ambrose.

"No."

"They have won," said Ambrose. "They told Fisheagle that

if she gave them Lyonesse, she would rule in the Wellworld. She was vain enough to believe them. Now they will take her down, and she will perish."

"What can we do?"

"Destroy them."

"How?"

"There is only one way."

The stamp of nervous horses, the clatter of armor. Idris thought of the Lowland. He knew what was expected of him. "The land is weary," he said. "It told me."

"Then it is for you to act. You must go to the Westgate, to the place where this all began, and do what must be done."

Idris said, "No," his heart pounding with grief and fury.

But into his mind there came a picture of the lands where the salt fires of the Lower Sea had once burned. He saw the tongues of Wellwater consume them, just as the poison water was consuming the last green remnants of Lyonesse. He knew that the time for half measures was gone, and that Ambrose was right.

A scum-tipped ram of black water blasted out of the Wellvale gate and tumbled the ranks of Mountmen. *Treachery!* shrieked the voice of Fisheagle. *This was not the agreement! I am to rule!*

Something the size of a mountain laughed, deep and cruel, and Idris knew it was one of the gigantic things he had seen spiraling under the Wells when he and Morgan and Digby had returned from Aegypt: a Helper. And the Helpers helped only themselves. *WE HAVE CHANGED OUR MINDS*, it said. *YOU ARE TO SERVE.*

A long, fading, unearthly scream, as of a creature plunging down a Well.

"Very well," said Idris, skin crawling with horror. "I shall do what must be done."

SEVENTEEN

I dris and the Knights rode back to the Ar Mor ships in their anchorage by the cliff on the Fal. He had told Galahd what he needed, and Galahd had conferred with the High Margrave of the Flashers, and the Margrave had nodded his whitish-green head, and all was now in hand.

Idris stepped onto the deck of the *Fly*, the smallest and fastest of the Ar Mor ships, followed by Morgan and the Knights. The Kings of Beyondsea remained with the Army of Lyonesse under Orbach, to assist the displaced people of Lyonesse and round up any rags of the Mount army seeking the high ground. Idris had agreed to all this with a strong sense of unreality. For his mind was elsewhere, on the terrible thing he must do.

The moon rose. The night was clear, and the year's first frost brought a tinkling fringe of ice crystals to the river's margins. Galahd called something in the Flasher language. The sailors let go the shore lines and the ship slid into the stream. Idris knew that this was the end of everything he had hoped for, and that there was no going back.

"It's the right thing," said a voice at his side. "Begging your pardon, sire."

Idris turned and saw Ector. He found he was smiling, warmed by his foster father's arrival. Beside him were Ed and Cadmon, the Boys, his foster brothers, grinning shyly under their helms. Idris was delighted. He said, "What are you doing here?"

"Came with King Mark," said Ector. "Thought it best to keep out of the way, you being busy and all. But Master Ambrose told me where you're going, and I thought, Well, I'd better come along."

Idris hugged him.

The ship was moving downstream now. Eight sailors had oars over the side, and the helmsman's shoulders were tense over the tiller. They moved down the river until the water-road stopped at a line of what looked like rubbish. "First dam," said Galahd. "Watch."

As the ship's nose approached the dam, Idris saw hundreds of little shapes scuttling across it. Just as it seemed that the ship must certainly crash into the wall of trees and boulders, the middle section of the dam crumbled. A smooth tongue of water poured through the gap. A lurch and a roar, and the ship slid down it. The banks moved swiftly by. Another dam, another tilt of the ship's deck, another flume roar. And another, and another.

"We're back down the Falls," said Galahd. "On, now."

Someone passed out iron-tipped spears. Idris could hear no monsters in the river, but from beyond the embankments he could hear the sounds of sloshing and howling, and the stink of Wellwater was enough to sting his eyes.

On they went, on and on. Next evening the ship passed the earthen tomb of Cayo in the south of the Shipwright's Garden. Soon afterward, the towers of the Southgate bristled beyond the embankment. Kek's eyes showed Idris ruined streets running with Wellwater, and hideous creatures carousing in a flotsam of house wreckage.

The chain on the Southgate was down. The *Fly* hoisted a cloud of white sail, heeled, glided between the gate towers, and sped into the clean blue sea.

The sky was clear, the breeze keen and from the west, with big clouds massed along the horizon. But in Idris's mind there was a bigger cloud, dark and terrible, that fogged his thoughts and made everything hazy and unreal.

Someone was speaking to him. He looked up. It was the Ar Mor Captain. "Yes?" he said.

"We don' know the water," said the Captain. "No sea maps. It's all silty up 'round here. Many sandbanks."

"I'll pilot you," said Idris.

The Captain's eyebrows lifted a fraction. What would a King know about the sandbanks of a remote part of his Kingdom?

"Trust me," said Idris and put out his mind to the man. It was almost impossible now, for he was full of hard resolutions and ideas, far stronger than when he had been a mere monster-groom, but nowhere near as flexible, so it was difficult to slide into heads merely to listen or persuade. But the Captain saw what Idris showed him, and blinked, and shrugged, in the way of the men of Ar Mor. He gave orders. The *Fly*'s side dug into the cold blue sea, and her wake curved away south, a white road of foam matching the curve of the walls of Lyonesse.

All that day Idris sat with Morgan as the wall of his country slid by at the speed of a cantering horse. The country itself he could not see, as it was below the level of the walls.

Night fell: still clear and cold, the wind light, the moon an icy lantern hanging over the metal sea. From inland came the howl of monstervoices and once a great flare, madness-pink and poison-green, as some manufactory was invaded by Wellwater.

Idris slept for a few hours with his head in Morgan's lap. At dawn he was awake and in the ship's maintop, straining his eyes at the horizon. At last he saw it: a little nick on the smooth curve of the world's edge. He pointed. The wake curved again, and the boat's nose sought the land.

In Idris's mind, he was at school again. A fly was droning in the drowsy warmth of the classroom. Mother Arthrax was in front of the class, old and shriveled and dry. *Name me the marks of the Approach from the Sea.*

That was the last lesson he had ever had, on the day he had stopped being Idris Limpet, schoolboy, and become Idris House Draco of the Vanished Children, King. The last lesson, but perhaps the most useful.

He hailed the deck, pointing. "The Outer Banks buoy," he said. A glass later the *Fly* was tearing past the ancient buoy, copper-green, crested white with gull-muck, beginning the Approach.

The channel was a canal in the seabed, hemmed in by sandbanks that lurked a couple of handspans below the surface. The marks rolled past: Outer Banks, Outer Inner Gobbard, the Gobbard, Harbor View. By the time they were at Harbor View, the Wall stood high, and behind it in a jagged frieze the tallest spires of the Westgate.

Idris's eyes ran along the Wall and found the turret of the Fort. "There," he said, dry-mouthed.

It would end where it had begun.

The Captain was watching the quays with his bringem-near. "Nobody there," he said. "We'll take her in and wait alongside."

"No," said Idris.

The Captain opened his mouth to argue, then saw something in Idris's face that caused him to stop, and bow, and say, "Your Majesty?"

Idris told him what he wanted. The *Fly* hove-to and lowered her longboat. Into the boat stepped Idris, Morgan, Ector, and the Knights. They set the oars and started to row. Idris looked back once at the white sails of the *Fly*. Then the longboat was passing between the gate towers and into the great stone ship basin. There were no ships alongside. They would be at sea, carrying refugees to safe havens. Idris wished them a fair wind.

The longboat came alongside a set of weedy stone steps. Galahd and Bors made fast to a pair of bronze rings, and Tristan cloaked himself and ran up to the quay. Idris listened with his mind. Monsters, yelling and howling. No humans. Tristan beckoned. His freckled face was pale. He said to Idris, "It's not very g-good, I'm afraid."

Idris felt Morgan's hand in his. He went up the steps on heavy feet. When they reached the top he stopped, gasping as if someone had smacked him in the belly.

It was not good at all.

It had been bad watching the Welltowers of the Valley of Apples crumble into ruin. But this was the Westgate, where he had turned from a baby into a little boy who had played with toy ships in the streets, and from a little boy into a bigger boy who had played War in the courts and towers. The lovely crumbling Westgate, with its brilliant light and the glitter of mica in the air, and the salt-smell off the sea...

This Westgate was different. Wet Street was a street no longer, but a black river of Wellwater. A dead sheep floated down it. Something came up like a giant trout, clashed fangs, and the sheep's belly was gone. The world was full of the triumphant screams of monsters.

Idris turned away. "I'm sorry," said Morgan.

Idris said, "Don't be." This chaos and ruin only made it easier to do what he had to do.

He turned to the Knights. "Go back to the ship," he said. "I do not need you."

Nobody moved.

"Go!" said Idris.

"I was born to work on the walls of Lyonesse," said Ector.

"You never know who you might m-meet on the way home," said Tristan.

"So we're staying," said Bors.

Idris looked at their faces and saw there would be no shifting them. He bowed. "Thank you," he said. "To the Fort, then."

To the Fort, where it had all begun. Last time Idris had been here he had been a little boy running to after-school games with his friends. Now he walked, fast and grim and sad, with his friends, Morgan and Ector and the Knights, in a newer, grimmer world, up the sea-pink-tufted spiral steps that had that same old smell of rotting seaweed, and into the tower like a great stone lantern, its all-round windows giving a view of the sea and the town.

The Wellwater was up to the castle hill, lapping higher even as he looked. Beyond, the road through the round-topped Downs was already a dirty river, and threads of water crept along the bottom of the valleys.

Morgan said, "Is there nothing you can do?"

"One thing," said Idris.

He reached into his cloak and took out a lead-headed mallet.

He took a last slow look at his kingdom, for which he had fought, but that he had never ruled and now never would. He would have liked to make straight what was crooked, and make right what was wrong, and care for the weak, and make the strong work for the good of the land as well as their own. Lyonesse was a perfect place to do this: rich enough to feed its people, brave and ancient, fair of land and full of creatures.

And now it was ruined. For a moment, Idris and Morgan, Ector and the Knights gazed over the stinking black waters swirling far below.

"My Knights," said Idris, "this would have been our land."

Morgan said, "Lyonesse is not the only place. You can use what you have learned in a wider world."

Idris nodded. He could not see very well, for his eyes were blurred with tears. He knelt and used the lead-headed mallet to knock bits of fallen stone away from the center of the lantern's floor. The copper boss was in the middle of the floor, exactly where Ambrose had said it would be, green and ancient. Somewhere far away, monsters howled. But Idris made himself think of daisies on a green hillside, and put his mind to the boss.

It began to turn.

It turned thirteen times, lifted itself up, and laid itself aside. Under it, a bronze rod went down into the tower's stone. The rod's top was broad and flat, like the head of a nail.

Idris grasped the handle of the leaden maul in both hands and lifted it high above his head. Tears flew from his face as he slammed it down on the head of the bronze nail.

The nail head went down a finger's length. There was a small *crunch*, felt rather than heard, as if a chisel had broken a crystal rod far, far below.

"Come," said Idris. "Hurry."

There had indeed been a crystal rod. It had braced a small stone deep below the surface on the sea side of the Wall. Unbraced, the stone had fallen. A thin stream of seawater would be jetting into the wall, melting the salt that cemented a series of blocks.

"Out," said Idris, taking Morgan's hand. They ran down the stairs from the Fort. When he came to the top of the Wall he called, "Run!" and turned northward, away from the harbor, the only sound the breath in his ears, the pounding of his companions' feet, the crunch of the swell on the Wallfoot.

The water was in the heart of the Wall now, eating its way through. There was a shine in the mortar around a couple of stones on the land side. The shine became a trickle. The trickle became a stream.

"Faster," urged Idris, but his companions needed no encouragement. They ran, breath harsh in their chests, hearts banging like war drums. The Wall was humming underfoot now, a humming with a quick, hard vibration, not the sickly shuddering of Welltremors, but the power of the clean, bright sea.

With a sudden roar, a jet of water leaped from the Wall below the Fort. A block shot out like a rock from a stonehurler. Idris heard a dim crash over the general roar as the block went through a roof. Then more blocks flew out, and there were more crashes, until the crashes merged into one great roar, and a breach appeared in the Wall of Lyonesse, and the clean salt sea thundered through, tearing the hole bigger as it flowed.

Now they were running for their lives, the Wall crumbling behind them as the water tore it down. A cloud of spray rose from the cauldron that had been the Westgate. Idris had Ector by one hand and Morgan by the other. The breath was fiery in his chest. The crumbling Wall was a bowshot behind them and gaining.

A shout from Galahd, pointing.

And there was the *Fly*, all sail set, rail awash, bearing down on the Wall half a bowshot ahead. They ran, feet hammering, lungs red hot. The *Fly* looked as if she must drive into the Wall. At the final moment the helmsman leaned on his oar, and the hands let go the sheets, and the ship came alongside the Wall, sails roaring, mainyard level with the parapet. "Jump!" cried Idris. Morgan jumped, caught the yard, swung in. Then the Knights went, and Tristan looked back from the yardarm and put out a hand to swing Ector aboard. And last of all came Idris, leaping from the Wall, Kek, his gull, overhead, hands out to catch the yardarm, suspended in the blue air between sky and sea, kingdom and exile. Then his fingers caught the yard, and his feet were on the footrope, and he slid along the spar and down the mast to his friends and his Knights, who were all that remained of his kingdom now.

He felt the wooden deck under his feet. He felt the ship swept back by the rush of water toward the broken Wall. Then the wind caught the sail, and the keel bit, and the *Fly* was sailing again, clawing away from the suck of the breach, far to seaward and into the channel between the outer banks. Astern, the Wall of Lyonesse became a low line of charcoal along the horizon: a line that rubbed itself out from its southern end, until at last there was no line at all, only a great tower of spray reaching into the sky.

Idris would not move. He sat weeping in the angle of the bulwark. Eventually he slept. When he woke, he found that the ship was among islands. Looking around, he saw that these islands had once been the Sundeeps.

He went ashore like a boy in a daze. They took him up a hill to a house of logs. In the house's single room Ambrose was sitting, looking out of a window. The sun was westering and the air was very clear.

Far away to the east, beyond an enormous expanse of blue sea, lay a long, low line of land.

"Your enemies are defeated," said Ambrose. He gestured at the empty sea. "Behold your kingdom. Your palace is above water, should you wish to take up residence."

Idris put his mind out to Kek; he could hardly do it now. He saw the sea lapping an island crowned with towers, sitting in the curve of a deep bay, and realized he was looking at the Mount. On the shores of the bay he saw the Armies of Beyondsea and the encampments of his people. Beyond them lay the wild lands of Kernow. The land of Lyonesse was gone forever, and the tides would clean away the filth Fisheagle had brought into it.

Idris let his eyes rest on the empty sea where once Lyonesse had lain. He said, "That is not my kingdom. My kingdom is among my people. So we will find a new place for them to live. Knights?"

"We are with you, and you with us," said the Knights as one.

And Idris, with Morgan and Ector and the Knights of the Table Round, raised his eyes toward the land of High Kernow, Albion, and a new age of the world.

THE LINE OF THE KINGS OF
LYONESSE

(These words in the Old Tongue were reported to have been found engraved on a stone, now lost, brought up in a fishing net from the sea west of Kernow, modern Cornwall; the stone is also said to have borne the device of a limpet.)

The Tangled Years, otherwise the Time Before Rule, ended with

Great Brutus, known as the Old King, Builder of the Sea Walls, Stopper of the Old Well, Bringer of the Years of Plenty

who begat, by a miracle, Kyd Goch, who married Belwnd of the Knights

and begat Kyd Aengus, who married Camwll of the Knights

and begat Kyd Wilson, who married Storpan of the Knights

and begat the line of Kyd Ploc Ard, who married first Fionnula of the Knights,
then Slabada of the Captains, Digger of New Wells, Ender of the Years of Plenty

who bore him

Kyd Lumsden, who married Drwsla of the Captains

who begat Kyd Draco, who married first Angharad of the Knights, and when she died giving birth to the second of the Vanished Children,
married his mistress, Fisheagle of the Captains

Kyd Draco died suddenly

but had begotten with Fisheagle

Kyd Murther, who reigns over Lyonesse with Fisheagle as his Regent, and will destroy the Vanished Children when they return

unless, as is our hearts' hope, they destroy him first.

AUTHOR'S NOTE

To the reader:

I was born into the watery world of the Isles of Scilly — a few paradisiacal crumbs of granite scattered over the turquoise sea thirty miles west of Land's End, Britain's most southwestern point. The islands are dotted with prehistoric tombs. At low water, the remnants of cyclopean walls can be seen snaking from island to island along the bottom of the sea. My mother's family has lived there for six generations. My childhood was full of tales about a sinking of the land that transformed Scilly from a range of mountains into an archipelago.

In the tales, it was not only Scilly that had sunk. In the mid-eighteenth century, fishermen in the Atlantic trawled up window frames that they assumed came from a drowned village. A petrified forest lurks deep under the sands of Mount's Bay, and the ancient Cornish name for the modern island of St. Michael's Mount is "the great rock in the wood." Just as it was common knowledge on Scilly that Lyonesse had sunk, it was also common knowledge that Lyonesse had been the home of King Arthur, or Idris, as he was called. I was born in a room overlooking the body of water from which the sword Excalibur came, and into which it was flung. We believed in dragons, monsters, star and stone, and that all actions had consequences.

I grew up with the certainty that Arthur and Tristan and Morgan and the rest of them originated here and in the related French Atlantis of Ys. While Lyonesse has featured as a springboard for a wilder type of fantasy, it has had no real chronicler. I decided that this was something I needed to put right.

In a properly constituted legendary universe, Lyonesse cannot sink as a matter of mere geology. It is human wickedness that must cause the inundation, and human virtue that must strive to keep it above water. Idris, I was assured since earliest years, was a good person because he saw that his actions had consequences for others; Fisheagle, Murther, and their monstrous gang were evil because they were interested in the hoggish pursuit of power for its own sake, whatever the consequences for other people, and nobody who deliberately made contact with wickedness could remain unmarked by it. Certainly some readers may find in the story of Lyonesse parallels with the world we live in now.

The battle between the dark and the light lives strongly in my heart. So do the stones and islands of Scilly that are all that remain of the mountains of Lyonesse, and the sun that still shines over Lyonesse, and the gales that still blow there. I visit them often. I am glad that I once again have a chance to take you with me.

A note on language and sources: Notable research sites have of course been Scilly; the library of Trelowarren, home of the greatest of the antediluvian manuscripts; and the stone fields of Carnac in modern Brittany.

Unhappily, the Old Tongue, in which most of these stories were originally told, is now extinct. For certain words I have had to use modern equivalents, which are not always precise. For instance, the ancient *hvaachn* has become *monster*, losing in the process its original sub-meanings of death-beast, enemy, firewood, and helper; and *puttaiyur* has become *corsair*, which is as close as a modern mind can come to this particular form of seagoing slaver and plunderer originating in what is now North Africa.

Sam Llewellyn

Sam Llewellyn
The Tower
Tresco
New Deer Moon, 2010

ABOUT THE AUTHOR

Sam Llewellyn was born in the Isles of Scilly, where as a child he was told the stories on which the Lyonesse books are based. Now he lives with his wife and family in an ancient house in the remote Welsh Marches of Britain. He owns an electric bike, a fifty-year-old guitar, and several boats, in which he spends months every year sailing in the North Atlantic. He believes that telling stories is the summit of human achievement, and that the existence of humanity on earth is a story, and that the story deserves a happy ending.

Sam's children's books, including *The Well Between the Worlds*, Book I of the chronicles of Lyonesse, as well as the Little Darlings series, have been widely praised, and he has written many novels for adults and contributes to several newspapers and magazines.